I0586012

Dream State

By

SJ Banham

This novel is entirely a work of fiction. Any names, character and incidents portrayed are the work of the author's imagination.

Copyright ©2022 SJ Banham

Published by For The Love of Books www.loveofbooks.co.uk

Cover by JessicaBellDesign.com

Edited by HelenBaggott.co.uk

Acknowledgements

Thanks go to my family for helping me make another novel happen.

To Robert and Chloe for allowing me the time and space to write, and for answering ridiculous questions when they arise.

To Bryan Lightbody for answering police-related questions, to Philippa Hawley for answering medicine-related questions, and to Jo and Stan Stuart for answering coma-related questions. I have, clearly used extensive creative licence with all three areas, but that's fiction for you.

A big thank you to fellow author Sarah Dodd on Twitter (@SarahDodd) who held me accountable to finish this novel. Her kind words helped a great deal when she wrote: 'the hardest-working author I've ever known' on social media.

Thank you to my team of beta readers in the UK and the United States: Lynda Taylor, Sue Long, Jo Stuart, Brenda Cox, Chloe Banham, Candance Bise, and Lyn Shahan. And to Sarah Werner and Jimmie Bise. Also Monti Cline, Sarah Lauzon and Cher Worth and all involved with Arcane Quill.

To my editor Helen Baggott helenbaggott.co.uk

To my cover designer Jessica Bell jessicabelldesign.com

To ALLi for their constant support to independently published authors, and to Society of Authors.

Finally, to Samwise, my writing buddy, who was there through most of the novel's creation but had to leave for purring duties elsewhere in the universe.

Author's Note

This novel began nearly a decade ago but after 30,000 words stopped because the story became too complex. Upon reading it after I graduated from Open University, and as Covid-19 took place, I decided the story 'had legs' and I got my teeth into it. I took it to 105,000 words then pared it down to 95k.

I generally form a crush on one or two characters as I write since I spend all waking hours for months (sometimes years) creating them. In Dream State, however, that crush moved to a whole new level.

I hope you feel the same way too.

Sjb ☺

www.loveofbooks.co.uk

PS Authors rely on reviews to get their books noticed. Please take the time to write a (hopefully good) review. If you'd like to connect with me on social media, my details are below:

Facebook: Sarah Banham

Twitter: @sjbwrites

Instagram: @s.j.banham

Linked In: Sarah Banham BA(Hons)

Chapter One

"An extension?" Ruth Trent's husky voice roared down the telephone. "You have got to be kidding me, Lilah! That's completely out of the question."

"Please. I just want to give them a good ending, a fair ending. It'll be worth it in the end. It's just taking a little bit of time." She didn't want to let on that a major plot change was intended, nor did she intend to sound so submissive, but Ruth's dominance was too much to handle some days.

"Time is the one thing you don't have, darling."

Writing all day, every day, for months without even a weekend as a break had taken its toll on Delilah McCallister. Exhaustion had become the norm. She inhaled deeply letting it out slowly, meditation style. She had glossed over an article on how to deal with difficult people with one of her characters in mind and the advice fit perfectly for Ruth. Breathing was the top tip. Ruth's abrupt responses, and expletives, had reached a point where Lilah could feel the irritation on her skin and anxiety in her stomach at the mere thought of the woman. She took another deep breath to calm herself, hoping it wouldn't be heard over the phone.

"I just need a short break. Just so I can think clearly and…"

"A break?" Ruth let out a sound that might have been a laugh, or it might have been her forty-a-day cough. "Listen to me. For three bloody years I've stood by you. By now I'd have hoped you'd learn that when I say jump, you jump. You can take a break when it's complete."

"That's a little unfair." As soon as she'd said the words, she wanted to take them back. Lilah knew other authors didn't live with whips cracking against their keyboards like they did with the Ruth Trent Literary Agency. Working with her had taken all the fun out of the job.

"How dare you? I have never been unfair in my life! Aren't I always there when you've messaged me at two in the morning?"

Two in the morning because I've been working that late, she wanted to say but thought better of it. "I thought you said it was okay to do that. You actually said you liked it because it showed…"

"I don't care what I said. I was lying. Listen, I want Catie and Jack to get it together and I'm utterly past caring how you do that. I gave you a deadline. Meet it."

"Can't you be a bit flexible?" She almost dropped the phone with nerves. A soft ping came from the phone as she grabbed it, steadying it in her hand. If it sounded like she'd hung up on Ruth, that would create the next world war.

"It's forty-eight hours away and the clock's ticking."

"But there's still so much to write."

"Like what? I've read two thirds of it already. It doesn't need any changes."

"There's some chapters that - I thought your deadline was just a guideline."

"Then you thought wrong."

"But, Ruth, nobody can write a decent story in just a few months. It needs time."

"No."

"It's not finished though." It was starting to sound like Ruth didn't want her on board with the sabotage and bullying tactics going on. If it wasn't unreasonable deadlines, it was the rude phone calls, or unprofessional emails. Anything to undermine Lilah's confidence. She wondered if the other, more established writers under the RTLA's banner received the same treatment or if she'd been singled out. Three months to complete a novel was ridiculous; even the 'Big Boys' Ruth competed with didn't churn out decent stories in that time. It needed time to brew, for characters to blossom, for a plot to feel realistic. "Or edited," Lilah blurted out. "Gordon will need time to…," she trailed off, fearing even that might been seen as putting her nose where it wasn't welcomed.

She wanted to add that, aside from rushing everyone, it was a pointless use of Ruth's time. It might make her look like she ran her agency brilliantly and with efficiency, but that was only to the untrained eye. In reality, running people ragged highlighted a disorganised leader. Although Ruth thrived on the idea that she was considered top in her game, rushing towards an unachievable goal was foolhardy. It would all come crashing down upon her. But Lilah held her tongue.

"I do hope you're not presuming to tell me my job. You've been an author all of two minutes. I've been doing this long before you were even born. I know how it works and I know how to run my agency which is why I gave you a deadline. If you don't reach it – and please don't tell me you haven't – it'll be your arse on the line, darling, not mine. I'll still be employed. I've got other authors. Reliable ones."

Lilah had crossed a line and couldn't even appease her with an apology because, according to Ruth, apologising showed weakness. She heard the threat loud and clear. It wasn't the first and probably wouldn't be the last. Even though she knew she was a good writer, Lilah had no choice but to take Ruth's wrath. Again.

"I'm not unreliable, Ruth. I just meant that Gordon'll need time to edit. Everything takes time."

"Well, then it's just as well my assistant is looking for a decent Copy Editor, isn't it?"

"Looking for one? What's wrong with Gordon?"

"He's gone."

Lilah's shock was impossible to hide. "Why?"

"A difference of opinion. I've got no time for unreasonable people."

Lilah gasped at the irony. She guessed 'unreasonable' meant he wouldn't run himself ragged over Ruth's ridiculous deadlines anymore. It was a shame, she liked him. He reminded Lilah of her late father. Gordon was an older man with years of publishing and editing experience. Heaven only knew why he agreed to freelance with Ruth in the first place. The two had never seen eye to eye from day one; it had been a love-hate relationship, but without the love.

"Emma's filling the role. Temporarily."

Lilah stopped dead in her tracks. "Emma? Not wishing to be rude but she's eighteen. She only left school a couple of months ago." Her words came out both insulting and cautious, yet neither were intended but two questions dominated her mind: would Emma even know what to look for within a manuscript, and was Ruth exploiting the teen? Emma hadn't so much as stepped foot outside the country yet. Would she be relying completely on the Internet and TV to get it right? The news made Lilah anxious and she felt a pang of guilt having engineered Emma's role.

Lilah's love of Americana, the US landscape, the differing accents from state to state, it all found its way into her stories. Finding an English agent who could sell her books to an American publisher was a complex process for which she could only thank Ruth. Gordon had been an important cog in that huge wheel and was perfect in his role. American-born but with thirty years in the UK, he knew the differences in constructing a sentence. He could not have been a more perfect fit for Lilah's writing style or novel settings. Stories based wholly in the USA by a debut English author was what won Lilah the daytime TV competition in the first place. 'A New Voice - A Niche Writer' she had been described at the televised ceremony.

"She's learning as we speak. Sometimes you have to learn quickly in life, or the opportunity is gone. Clearly Emma's not the only one learning that life lesson."

And then the words came out that she wasn't expecting to leave her lips. "Does she actually *want* to be a Copy Editor though?"

"I didn't ask her, I *told* her. Just like I'm telling you," Ruth said. "She'll thank me for it one day. Anyway, I'm not paying for this call just to get your opinion over my staffing decisions. That's got absolutely nothing to do with you." There was a pause, Lilah imagined it was for Ruth to inhale her cigarette, and she dared not fill it. "Your deadline was for Friday. The mere fact we're having this conversation suggests that I'm going to be disappointed."

"Ruth, there's something about Jack. He's not right for Catie. He's bringing out the worst in her and she deserves better. She's coming across as a total ...," she didn't finish the sentence. She wasn't exactly sure how to since Catie's behaviour was utterly down to Lilah's imagination and was probably a by-product of fatigue dealing with and influenced by Ruth's attitude. She wanted to call Catie a 'diva', or 'unlikeable', or something in between, but that wouldn't have helped. "She's going through something. I just need to understand why she's behaving like she is so I can put her back on the right track." It was as if Lilah had knitted a scarf with holes in. She just needed to unpick where the holes had begun and re-knit the pattern from there.

"Don't get too involved. It's bloody fiction for Christ's sake! They're not real people. Anyway, Jack's perfect for her. He's strong, he's got a good job. What else is there for a woman like her? She's just a waitress. She's no right to ask for more than that."

"Ruth!"

"If they're not right, you should have realised when you first started."

"But they've evolved, and in ways I couldn't have predicted." Whatever she said, Ruth would have a comeback. It was like climbing a mountain knowing that at the top there would be more mountain. The incentive to finish this book wasn't nearly as sweet as she originally hoped.

"Get it together, Lilah. This readership likes strong men and weak women."

"They're not weak. They're relatable."

"I said weak and I'm not wrong."

"Maybe it's a matter of opinion, or perception. Or maybe…"

"I'm not debating this. We agreed to a three-book deal so get this third one finished. It would be sad to lose you over this but you're not so well-known that we'll all just move our deadlines for you. This is a business, not a bloody creative writing class for wannabees. I've got exactly no time for amateurs. Give me the manuscript by the date we agreed because, I'm telling you now, if you make me look bad, I will crush you." Ruth's words ripped through her like a machete. "Are we on the same page yet? Our combined arses are depending on it. So, finish it. Tonight. No excuses."

Lilah gave one last attempt at reasoning. "I'd really want to stick by Catie. Jack's nothing like the hero we believed he was. The readers will see that too."

"The readers will see whatever we tell them to see. They'll love him and they'll be thrilled he got together with a waitress. People love a Cinderella story, an underdog, and Catie's the perfect sob story. Readers love a loser. It'll make them feel better about their own pathetic lives."

That touched a nerve. "She's not a loser. She's confused."

"She's a blank canvas, a nobody, a nothing," Ruth's shrug was clear in her voice, then she altered her tone from sinister to manipulative. "And she's a nothing with a body-clock that's ticking loud too. Give her the man who'll give her the babies. You tell me, darling, what woman wants to keep working in a seedy diner when she's on the other end of a rich banker? And do remind me, Lilah, has anyone else proposed marriage?"

"It's not a seedy diner and there's more to life than marrying the first man who asks. I think we're in danger of making Catie unlikeable."

Ruth blew the smoke out forcefully. It sounded like she was blowing out birthday candles. "Then make her likable and relatable and do it *tonight*."

"I can't do that in one sitting. It's tough, I can barely think straight. I'm really tired. I just need a night off. I'm too close to it. Please, Ruth."

"Stop being lazy and get on with it."

"I'm not la…"

"Darling, know now that I'm just not listening to you anymore. You're saying nothing that interests me. This is me not listening to you. Can you hear that? Hmm, can you? Good. Now pour yourself a glass of wine. Right now. Go on," she demanded. "I want to hear it wetting the glass."

Being patronised was creating a specific kind of feeling in Lilah, one that wasn't conducive to writing a romantic story with dreamy characters or a happy-ever-after. This one was likely best used on a horror story with gnashing teeth, blood, and gore starring Ruth Trent as prey. She felt trapped with Ruth and after this book was over, she would put out feelers; this wasn't a marriage made in heaven anymore.

Reluctantly she went to the mahogany dresser, one of the pieces of furniture passed down in the family. It accommodated the only bottle of wine in the house; Riesling, leftover from last Christmas Day when Becca visited for dinner. It had almost a year's worth of dust covering its gently sloping emerald shoulders, as if it, too, had been lonely, depressed, and exhausted. Next to it was the empty crystal decanter, another heirloom, and beside that stood two small wine glasses.

A momentary thought of both parents flew through her mind. Dad would deal with Ruth in his own silent way while her mother would've had an out and out argument with the woman. Nobody spoke to her girls like this without answering for it. Lilah gave the smallest smile at the thought. Feeling as dejected as the bottle, she dusted off its shoulders and unscrewed the top. Then she put the phone onto speaker and held it up to the glass so Ruth could hear the wine being poured. She filled it to three-quarters full.

Ruth continued. "And to be frank with you...". It was as if she had opened her own verbal lid and was unable to stop.

Lilah held her breath. She hated Ruth being frank. It was so final. So hurtful.

"You're getting a really good deal for someone like you."

Someone like me? What does that even mean? "I'm not lazy or stroppy. I just have an opinion."

"I don't care about your opinion. Or you for that matter."

She downed half of what she'd poured. *An afternoon tipple*, she told herself to justify it. *If nothing else, it'll keep out the nasties*. Ruth currently topping the list of all known nasties.

"Then get straight back to it. Catie and Jack are going to get it together whether you like it or not. Do you hear me? If I don't hear the patter of tiny Jacks and Caties at the launch, there will be some serious arse-kicking going on because there won't be a launch. No book, no money. So you can say goodbye to your cottage in the woods and that lovely little Beemer sitting in your drive. You'll be relying on the Tube and living in a grubby little flat."

"Ruth, let me speak. Shouldn't I be doing what is best for the characters rather than wrapping it up to meet a deadline? I mean, Jack's not been entirely truthful, has he?"

"Catie doesn't care about any of that. She just wants to settle down and marry her man. So make it happen."

"But..."

"Lilah! Why are we still discussing this?"

"I just don't think Jack *is* her man. Maybe there's someone else?"

"There's no other men of interest in the story and we don't have time to create a new character or a new storyline. This is the one we sold to the publisher."

"It's evolved though. It could be a twist."

"Jesus, Lilah! It really would be a twist, wouldn't it? Listen, there's no money in a failed deadline. You saw how quickly you were taken up after your début novel, just bear in mind how easily the situation could be reversed. Drink some more wine. Drain the whole bloody bottle. Get yourself stoned if that's what it takes but reach that bloody deadline!"

"So, you're not going to listen to me?" Lilah asked, a stifled laugh came through as a mixture of sarcasm and hesitancy.

"I've never bothered so far. Though I should tell you, you're the only author whose career is starting to lose my interest."

"So, to hell with what is best for the character? Forget that the story might not work? Just reach the deadline?"

"Finally. When will I hear from you?"

"I'll e-mail you." The sadness in Lilah's voice was hard to hide.

"Good." Without saying goodbye or altering her tone, Ruth finished the call.

Lilah felt like she'd been reprimanded to within an inch of her life. Listening to the tirade made her long for balance or at least to tip the scales back up in her favour. Nature would do it. Leaving the phone and the glass on the dresser, she wandered into the garden trying to breathe out the negativity in the cold air. She replayed the comments, repeating them to build up her resilience each time they pierced her heart. She took a deep breath and let it out, adding a growl that progressed into a scream.

The bottle-green ivy that had weaved its way around the frame of the garden mirror and up the red brick shed wall shivered as if Lilah's voice had scared it. She approached the mirror imagining it as a gateway to Catie. The face reflected wore dark rings around her eyes and made her face look even paler. If it wasn't for her red hair, she would look quite insipid. The scent of the earlier rain made her feel alive and away from claustrophobic prison in which Ruth enveloped her. The woman was poison personified and Lilah needed to escape.

She imagined Ruth dressed in a military uniform, a stick under her arm, and yelling into a row of authors' faces; saliva flying from her mouth like it was effervescent bubbles leaping from a glass of champagne.

Over the years, bigger names than Delilah McCallister - the thirty-something-year-old who was only in this position because she pitched her novel to the right people on the right TV show at the right time - must have gone through the same treatment.

Being represented was a dream come true but with Ruth's dirty tricks and bullying tactics, life had gone from dreamy to dreary in just three short years. Lilah needed to clear her head, to breathe.

"Catie, show me what you're made of. Show Ruth you deserve someone better than Jack. I'll make your life perfect, just tell me who you want. I'm not giving up your future for the sake of a stupid deadline. I need to think. I need to breathe." She raked her hands through her hair and let out a deep sigh before running back inside and putting on her shoes. Thoughtlessly, she grabbed the keys to her BMW Roadster and left hardly registering the pebbles beneath her soles, and slammed the car door shut. "Damn you, Ruth. How dare you do that to Catie? She deserves better."

Pulling out of the drive of her cottage, Lilah pushed hard on the accelerator pedal and the engine roared as if to add its own anger. The sound of both windows descending into the doors and the roof disappearing into the back could just be made out over the engine. She sped out onto the country lane opposite as tiny pebbles and dust flew up behind the wheels. She followed the tight bends with increasing speed. The air, damp with rain, coated her skin and sent her hair flying in all directions. Increasing the speed, she inhaled hard. This was what she needed; something to expel the frustration.

"Let me breathe!" The adrenalin was exhilarating. She'd never felt so alive. Swooping from corner to corner, around the bends and through a darkened tunnel fashioned from branches. She threw out a rebellious laugh as she took in a sharp bend that felt like the car was on two wheels. G-force kept her in her seat. The blind bend, with a slippery carpet of orange and crimson leaves, facilitated the car to cross the white lines like it had a mind of its own. An oncoming car, dimly lit in the dreariness the over-hanging trees created, approached at such speed that the two instantly joined. Between adrenalin and distraction, Lilah didn't have time to do anything.

Her smile lost, the last thing she registered was the face of the man driving the other car. He was young with shaggy chestnut hair that framed his face. His mouth fell open in shock and in that split second, he looked as scared as she felt. Lilah's blood-red sports car and the sky-blue Astra formed a vehicular ballet, spinning together in a beautifully artistic, yet horrifyingly mangled wreck. The vicious sound of twisting metal and smashing glass formed an almighty cacophony in both drivers' ears.

Finally, the cars stopped, and a cloud of steam plumed between them with a soft hiss. Then bird song ruled the country lane once more.

Chapter Two

Ben Christopher stared at the statue and the angel stared back. The morning rain had facilitated an atmospheric darkness within the studio giving way to shafts of sunlight through occasional breaks in the cloud.

The statue stood on a plinth next to his work bench. At this height, its head stood at a level equal to Ben's and seemed to look him in the eye. It appeared satisfied with its appearance, smiling and not smiling all at once. Androgenous features presented as attractive. It looked as if its heart might beat, or its lips might part for just the right conversation. Neither would surprise or shock Ben. In fact, he'd welcome it now it had become the friend, confidant, and even guardian he yearned for. It had been some time since a real-life companion had provided a distraction. The dreamer within chose to believe the stars had aligned beautifully enabling him to craft realistic eyes, cheek bones, and lips.

He studied every inch of it, partly to ensure it fit the brief and partly to say goodbye. He couldn't remember the last time a piece of art had held such a place in his heart. A mixture of feelings ran through him: relief because it had taken so much out of him, and a sense of bereavement because he knew this was goodbye. A firm farewell floated in the air between them. Ben would miss their one-way chats as they shared the studio every day. It enhanced the feeling of working with someone rather than some*thing*, an inanimate lump of clay.

The client in St. Weatherly had commissioned it. Their office was half an hour from Ben's studio, just outside London. It was an unusual brief, especially from a solicitor. It stood tall with hands clasped together holding an olive branch, symbolic of peace. It was an odd feature to request, Ben thought. Wasn't conflict their hope? It brought business their way, after all. Or maybe it was representative of a peaceful resolution that the angel was intended to inspire.

There was to be no inference of faith or religion, the brief requested, and Ben was to channel vibes of an independent guardian watching over the legal team ensuring the sculpture represented peace. It wasn't the oddest brief he had ever received, but it was the most interesting and challenging. With finely crafted slender fingers and nail detailing, Ben was particularly happy with its finish.

Unclothed and genderless - its nakedness evidenced a smooth area between the legs, not unlike a child's doll - it gave nothing away. Its set of intricately carved wings, that would have filled over two metres of space if outstretched, were folded. They gave the figure a more practical means for display at its destination and certainly less chance of being knocked off during transport. If it was a person, its age would have been somewhere between twenty and forty, Ben decided. Twenty suggested youth and forty implied wisdom; two attributes that perfectly described the client.

He had enjoyed creating it, his hands and brain in unison. It was as if its soul had connected with Ben's. This piece of clay that had been shoved and prodded, moulded and shaped into an angel, had a presence unlike anything he had ever known.

Photographs of its creation were on his mobile phone, one of the only two pieces of modern technology he used at work. That and his laptop, the lid of which was covered in multi-coloured fingerprints of paint and clay. He'd get around to cleaning it one day. That day wasn't today, and certainly not while he was admiring the celestial being or considering the logistics of its destination.

"Yeah, I'm happy with you," he said, smiling. "What do you reckon? It feels like a wish-making moment to me." He sighed, listening to the echo of his own words. "Okay, let's do it. I wish you would stay with me forever. There I said it. Don't look at me like that."

The thought caressed a guilty nerve for charging the client what he did even though he knew he had earned every penny. He gave it a farewell nod as a pang of sadness lay in his heart, glad of the photos to reminisce. He knew there were new commissions to focus on after the Christmas break, and that every piece would be original. The irony wasn't lost on him that he'd created an angel at Christmas time, even when religion didn't play a part in Ben's life or the brief.

"Now," he said, thoughtfully, looking around the studio. "Let's think about…" He trailed off, raking his hand through his shaggy brown hair. Fragile or awkwardly shaped art pieces always required that extra bit of help to remain in one piece. He considered bubble wrapping it and using the accumulation of old blankets, sheets, and curtains he had collected over the years.

Waste not, want not had become his motto, mostly when being resourceful was the only way forwards. It was a tough mindset to stop but being in business meant that every penny was spoken for, often before it was earned. Every time a household item or product had finished its primary purpose, Ben considered what else it could be used for: food tins became paint brush holders, washed, sanded, and painted to ensure the job was done properly for longevity. Broken coat-hanger hooks became companions for bull-dog clips which suspended freshly painted pictures below a two-foot square window on its once-white painted sill. Old or torn linen could be repurposed into padding.

After a time, he realised this philosophy could turn him into a hoarder. A brutal clear-out using his logical mind, meant only items he absolutely knew would be reused left his creative mind to consider new lives for the remaining items. Anything else had been sentenced to a rubbish tip death and recycled.

He knew if prospective art buyers visited the studio, what looked like rubbish to the lay person could scupper future commissions. Being artistic meant he wasn't always neat and tidy: a washcloth or two here, a lump of clay there. It could be seen as messy, disorganised, and even eccentric, all traits that described Ben perfectly. They filled him with a sense of pride but could also reflect his business practices negatively.

Cafes, book shops, libraries and other community outlets were the obvious choices for Ben to leave his flyers. The coffee shop, not five miles from where Ben stood in his studio and which the solicitor had visited, had a manager whose wife was also interested in several pieces in the new year.

Being a freelance artist hadn't always been as lucrative, but the funds from the angel enabled Ben to invest in tools as well as promote his services further afield. Interviews on community and regional radio stations raised his profile and garnered attention from groups and clubs wanting talks. It all meant the opportunity to show off his skills. Colleges approached him to share his thoughts on the importance of art within the community, society in general, and in business. Fitting it all in was challenging, yet exciting. What he couldn't physically do, he posted to social media for more exposure. Business was looking unusually healthy. It was as if the angel had smiled upon him and encouraged the art gods to do the same.

He rolled out a length of bubble wrap and rolled the artwork in it before taping it in three places: the head, the waist and wings, and the legs. Afterwards, he rolled it in a length of repurposed curtain before carrying it outside to his geriatric estate car, affectionately considered a work-horse.

The rain's fragrance filled the air. It was a refreshing change from breathing in paint, clay, and charcoal dust, and the heavy, warm odour of a paraffin heater. The rain had left watery souvenirs in the parking bay and he felt the drag of water as his canvas high tops waded through puddle after puddle. The December chill reminded him to bring a hoodie for the journey; the unreliable heater promised a miserable time otherwise and his wiry frame would welcome its warmth.

The back seats, that had been laid down longer than they had ever been upright, were to be the angel's new home for the journey. He pushed and pulled it from side to side, up and down ensuring it wouldn't move or roll during the drive. Inevitable potholes and winding lanes were expected and, from the driver's seat, opportunities for over-the-shoulder glances would be limited.

Once secured, Ben ran back to the studio to grab his hoodie and turned off the lights locking the door behind him. He wouldn't be long, maybe a couple of hours at most. He put his phone into his shirt pocket, set his hoodie on the passenger seat, and pulled on his seatbelt. He backed out of the bay, not resisting the temptation to look over his shoulder at the cargo.

Ten minutes of wet country lanes, he looked over his shoulder again half expecting to see the angel leaning on its arms asking, 'are we nearly there yet?'. Then the car hit a pothole and Ben's heart skipped a beat jarring him back to concentrating on the road. There was still a few miles until his exit.

Until now, he hadn't thought about the client's reaction, but anxiety crept into his mind. He hoped excitement and happiness would greet him, but what if they were disappointed? What if he had misinterpreted the brief? Thoughts of a legal battle crossed his mind, and the reluctance to pay the remainder of the fee.

"Stop it," he said aloud. "Don't think like that." He looked in the rear-view mirror imagining the angel looking back at him. "You're an original. There's not a thing wrong with you. You are utter perfection and exactly what they asked for. They'll love you. And why shouldn't they? I made you and I'm brilliant at what I do. I am. I *mean* it." He almost convinced himself.

Still entertaining the image of a less-than-happy solicitor, the scene in front sobered his thoughts. In a split second, a red car appeared from around the blind corner in front of him, on his side of the road. He couldn't process the shock quickly enough as the two cars joined. For the briefest of moments, he fixed his eyes on the other driver's face. In less than a second, he absorbed an image that lasted all of eternity. The driver was a young woman with long, red hair. She stared at him, haunting and terrified in equal measure. An intimate connection, as though they had known each other forever or were about to, was formed. For the millisecond they locked eyes, they both understood how bad this accident was going to be and neither of them could do anything to stop it. The two cars locked in a union that took no time and an eternity to end.

Ben's leg space drastically changed from spacious and boxy to abrupt incarceration. A cacophony filled Ben's ears combining his own screaming, the two cars' screeching tyres, and smashing glass.

Finally, both cars came to a standstill. Dazed and with glass in his mouth, he moved his head as cubes fell from his hair onto his lap. A sorry excuse for an air bag suddenly inflated too late to be of any use then settled, deflated, in his lap. He tried to look at the other driver and saw the windscreen was missing with just a partial frame of jagged glass remaining. The soft rain outside touched his skin, reminding him of the winter temperature.

The seatbelt had held him securely but an eerie silence surrounded him. Somewhere glass fell onto the tarmac as if someone had dropped marbles from their hand, and hissing, like a steam train, was near.

His mind spun, trying to find some semblance to what had just happened. He inhaled to gauge if a stench of fuel laced the air but his chest hurt so he stopped trying. Taking smaller breaths was less painful. He thought about why he was in his car in the first place. The angel. He tried to look over his shoulder to see if his cargo was still in one piece, but everything hurt too much to move. He hoped it was still in one piece but after the severity of the collision, it could be nothing more than a memory.

He looked through the space the window once took. The woman wasn't moving. Air bags had deployed leaving hair partially covering her face. Her eyes were closed and her lips were parted as if she were listening to a conversation and waiting for her moment to respond. She looked like a porcelain doll, as though Ben himself had sculpted her. Was she dead? Unconscious? Not knowing sickened him and the realisation that he was powerless to help her.

He wondered if the car had lost control and that's why she crashed into him. He knew that much; that she crashed into him. Sure, he wasn't paying the attention he should, with crazy thoughts flying through his mind, but she had veered out of her lane into his car. Of that, he had no doubt. He wasn't oblivious to the power of sporty vehicles. It was partially the reason why he kept his old work-horse around. He didn't need power as much as he needed a working vehicle. Its attraction was its ability to keep him in business. He didn't even care about its colour which, currently, looked better off than racy little number entwined within it.

It looked like he was close enough to touch the woman, but that would mean having to open the window. He could barely move to breathe, let alone move his arms. His instinct was that he'd broken a rib. It was a first for him, having never experienced breaking a bone in his life. The pain was incredible, as though he might pass out.

"Hey!" He hoped if they could communicate, they could work together until the emergency services arrived. But for assistance to come, someone would need to alert them. "Hey!" His voice was little more than a whisper.

He thought again about reaching for his phone in his chest pocket. The one time a modern car with a voice activating phone would have been useful was now, or having it fixed to the car dashboard. He had never got around to it.

"I'm gonna try to call the…". He couldn't even make it through the sentence. He concentrated on taking his phone from his shirt pocket. Moving slowly, with fast rhythmic breaths, he touched it with his index finger and thumb but couldn't get a grip before it landed on the carpet. Fighting for breath and trying hard not to panic, logic was lost as a mixture of defeat and terror enveloped him.

And then he heard a voice. Was it her? Was she awake? She hadn't moved an inch but a robotic voice that came from nowhere asked if he was involved in an accident.

"Yes! Help!"

Panicked thoughts filled his mind when his eyes settled on the angle of his leg. The view below his knee turned his stomach as intense white pain crept through to every part of his being. Then his body could endure no more.

A moment later Ben Christopher was unconscious.

Chapter Three

In a dark place without a beginning, middle, or end, the woman who had been Delilah McCallister was now...nothing. Though she still existed as a presence, she couldn't process where she existed because there was no knowledge from which to draw.

Then, slowly, knowledge returned.

She sensed something terrifying was happening or *had* happened, yet she was unaware what it was and had no words to describe it anyway. There was nothing to see, nothing to touch, nothing to gauge what was around her. There was nothing from which to bounce her breath to measure distance, and no sound to help her work it out.

Yet she existed.

Her consciousness told her that just a moment ago Delilah McCallister had been laughing and shouting while driving a car. It was red. It was fast. It was loud. Sound had surrounded her. It came from her throat, from her car, from above her head. Wind blew in her face. Rain fell on her head. G-force thrust her into the door. Then an abrupt explosion of sound filled her being.

But now there was nothing at all but darkness and silence. Some part of Delilah McCallister was still alive; whether it was her brain or her soul, no answer was forthcoming. She was wrong, there *was* a sound. It was a sound she could feel, a rhythmic pulsing somewhere in her chest and inside her ears. An internal sound.

She wanted to move the hair from her face, even though she had no idea if there was any hair against her face. It was just muscle memory, a habit. She couldn't sense or feel her face, or her skin, or anything that was usually familiar, nothing except the rhythmic pulsing. She could feel it all over her body now, the body she was used to living inside but that had now become just packaging.

Knowledge told her this was serious. Knowledge began a diagnostic. She couldn't physically respond to the commands and movements her brain wanted from her hands. She tried to open her eyes, but they weren't responding to the muscles that demanded movement.

Aside from the internal pulsating, competing for attention was another sound. Hissing. It sounded like a snake. She tried to conjure the image of a snake, but nothing came not even to frighten or thrill. It was just the idea of the word 'snake' that remained.

Then there was a third sound. A voice. It wasn't deep nor was it high, but it belonged to a man. Its tone was rich and warm. A voice she was drawn to. Yet he was scared, his voice trying and failing to conceal terror.

"Hey."

She didn't know from which direction in the darkness it came. A moment later a second voice joined in. It was higher, maybe female but robotic. The man's voice sounded frantic, as though trapped between panic and pain until…until he fell silent.

And then there was nothing again. Nothing but pain.

It was a gentle pain at first, a slow, nagging, headache that threatened to get tougher. It was introducing itself, then it befriended her before setting out to assault her like an evil stranger. She pondered it for a few moments, attempting to register the sensation. Then she tried to remember what to do when pain increased as it leapt from gentle to excruciating. There was no in-between, like it had grown bored of vying for her attention.

Well, it was getting her attention now.

It was in her head, in her brain, in her neck, in her face. It produced a thunderstorm of agony sending out lightning bolts which illuminated several areas within her skull. Then she saw colours. No. She could *feel* the colours it produced. White. Blue. Purple. Red. The brighter the colour, the more serious the situation. Now she understood.

Lilah tried again to open her eyes or move her hands, something, anything, but the pain would not allow it. An intense prison trapped her within. No part of her would move except the flashing colours inside her brain, which wouldn't stop moving. The lightning strikes became more frequent, and louder before merging with broader ones until her head was one massive, intense, repeated lightning strike.

Then she could bear it no longer.

She wanted, needed, to find safety, to stop this terrifying experience. If she could run and hide, she would. But nothing would move, no arms, no legs. There was nothing attached except her presence and her brain. Was it only her soul that remained?

Somehow in the dark, desperation forced her to search for light. Imagined hands and greedy fingers lunged out seeking the safety they needed. Finally in the darkness she felt a door handle. It was round and cold and fit into her imagined hand easily. Then, the agonising pain in her head lessened. She turned the door handle and pushed it as a blindingly white light filled her up. It closed behind her and an enormous crash filled her ears.

Without understanding how, she felt her body land on a cold, solid surface. With real eyes that she could view the world though, images and colour filled her field of vision. She looked at the floor beneath. It was black and white tiles in a chess board design. Near her stood a tall metal trolly. Her eyes travelled up to its apex and back down to the lower shelves upon which were plates and dishes with remnants of finished food. She put her hand out to steady herself but instead of achieving her goal, they wobbled. Like a rocky avalanche, unstable crockery fell from the trolly and smashed on the tiles like ceramic confetti. They broke in slow motion, pieces kissing the tiles then bouncing back up to slice her flesh.

Then missiles of silverware fell from the sky and sliced her skin filling her ears with a sound not unlike the percussion section of an orchestra. Tightly closing her eyes to prevent the debris and shield her head from the noise, she tensed up until it had all completely stopped.

And when the silence returned, she opened her eyes to see a brightly lit kitchen. The aroma of freshly baked meatloaf took her straight to a happy childhood memory. As it filled the air, somewhere nearby an audience offered an applause.

Chapter Four

Blue flashes. Red flashes. Blue flashes. Red flashes.

Ben opened his eyes. Everything was blurred. Something green was swaying in the distance, something yellow was closer. He couldn't focus. He heard voices but couldn't speak. The voices and the yellow things were joined, and he registered they were people wearing high-visibility vests.

Blue covered hands that smelled of rubber pulled and pushed his head. One set of hands gently gripped either side of his face and held him still. There was noise, but he didn't know where it was from, and there was colour – flashing - but he couldn't identify it.

"Can you hear me?" The voice was close and clear.

Yes, I can hear you. Ben said calmly, but the words remained in his head.

"Can you hear me?" they repeated.

In his mind Ben confirmed he could.

"No, still nothing," the voice called to someone else.

He felt something around his neck that restricted movement. And lots of hands moving over his body. They were invasive. Nothing hurt and everything hurt simultaneously. He tried to move but nothing worked, arms and hands lead weights. His legs were…agonising. Instantly he stopped trying to move.

Trees swayed in a chilly breeze and cold rain fell onto his face. He felt it trickle down his temple and drips landing like pinpricks on his cheeks. Now aware he was outside but with no memory of where or why, and he understood people were tending him. He trusted their touch, their voices completely and without hesitation. He was in good hands but didn't know how he knew that. Instinct? Intuition? He didn't investigate.

Then, abruptly, he was lifted into an ambulance, the cool air caressed his face reminding him what temperature was. A patter of raindrops fell on to the waterproof sheet covering his body. It sounded like classical music. At the melody, his mind moved instantly to his studio, a room of artwork, the scent of paint and clay and paraffin, the feeling of clay on his fingers.

A feeling of serenity filled him as he recalled an angel once emerging from the clay between his fingers. Instead of in his studio, it – she - was now in human form and lying beside him. She had black skin and a warm, reassuring smile that felt every bit as real as Ben, except somewhere in his mind, he knew he must be hallucinating. He didn't care if he was. He smiled just knowing she was with him.

Nudged back from a surreal reality, he saw a blue car across the road. It was framed by the ambulance doors. *Blue like a summer sky.* It no longer had a roof. A mangled mess of metal lay on the roadside next to it. The green in constant motion was trees, he now realised.

In front of the blue car was a bright red one. Where it ended and the blue car began was a mystery. A team of people dressed in yellow worked on a red-headed woman in the red car. The view was a mixture of primary colours. He studied the scene trying to understand it. His pupils darted from the blue car to the red car and back again. The blue one was his, *had* been his. He recalled wrapping the angel in fabric to protect it. Then he remembered the crash. The red car hit him. *Red hair, red car.* He remembered her face, her eyes, her expression. She'd been terrified and he hadn't been able to help her.

He watched as someone put a collar around her neck and three people lifted her out of the car and placed her on a stretcher. She hadn't moved. His eyes followed them towards an ambulance opposite. Red flashes. Blue flashes. Both flickering on the roof of the ambulance and police cars in the rain.

"He's conscious," someone called out breaking his thoughts. "Sir, if you can you hear me. please move your fingers."

He tried but couldn't so instead managed a sound, a murmur.

"Don't try to speak." It seemed perfectly good, sensible advice, so he complied. "You've been in a car accident. You're safe now. We're taking you to hospital." She pulled the doors closed enveloping them both in the same small area.

He lost sight of the woman with the red hair and, giving in to his injuries, was out cold.

Chapter Five

Ceramic dishes and metal cutlery smashed. The ear-splitting din echoed throughout the diner. Applause overtook it. Catie Cambridge landed unceremoniously on her backside. It didn't feel like a performance worthy of applause, if anything she wanted to scream first and cry later.

"Jesus Christ!" Drew Denby cursed from the front of the diner. He'd jumped at the noise catching the oven-fresh meatloaf by luck. Careful not to burn himself, he put it on the counter. Dropping it would have just about made his day with ingredients and whatever happened in the back lost all at once.

"Jesus, Catie!" Sheryl Laurence shrieked. She'd walked through the swing door in time to see the whole performance. "You okay?" Seeing she was, she peeped back around the door to Drew. "She's okay, but there's a whole lotta mess to clean up."

The laughter and clapping, courtesy of construction workers eating dinner before their shift, had stopped. Now they seemed concerned by Sheryl's remark.

"Clean up on aisle three, huh, Drew?" one called out, winking in Sheryl's direction. "Oughta take it outta their paycheck if you ask me."

"That's if they don't sue me first."

"Don't you got a job to go to?" Sheryl came back quickly, then waved as they left.

Drew followed her into the back room as she went about starting that clean up. She used her apron as a hammock for the larger pieces throwing them into the garbage. Drew's view centred on the casualty sitting on the floor. Catie's forehead dripped blood. The fresh, scarlet stream followed the natural curve around her nose down to her lip.

"What the hell happened? You okay?" He knelt next to her, using his apron to mop it from her face.

Catie stared, confused. She felt his breath on her skin, saw the blue-gray hue that made up his eye color, and the tiny hairs on his jaw that would become a new beard in a few more hours. For an instant, she didn't quite recognise him, like she was looking through someone else's eyes at a man she wanted to know but didn't. Her head throbbed as if an ice pick was working overtime. "Where am I?"

"Sheryl, call an ambulance."

"On it."

"It's gonna be okay. We're gonna get you to a hospital."

Drew? Sheryl? These were Catie's eyes she was looking through and the faces staring at her were friendly, concerned. "Hospital? No. Don't call an ambulance. I'm fine."

Sheryl came back, phone in hand. "Call 'em? Don't call 'em? What's it gonna be?"

"Call 'em. Her head is cut." He shot her a 'why *wouldn't you call 'em'?* look. "She could have a concussion."

"Please don't." Catie shook her head. The blood was clotting, leaving angry wounds. "I'm serious. I'm totally okay."

"I'll need the first aid kit then. Sheryl, can you…"

"Sheryl, do this, Sheryl, do that? C'mon, do I look like a nurse?"

Drew gave her a '*get over it*' look as he took the kit. He grabbed a small bottle of iodine, a roll of gauze, and some sticking plaster. "What the hell happened anyway?"

"She was on the phone." Sheryl gestured to the remains of the cell phone on the tiles. "Came off worse than her by the looks of it. From what I heard you got some bad news. Turned white as a ghost and took half the kitchen with you." She looked at the trolley and sighed. "Kinda sorry the top shelf was already washed."

"Who was on the phone?" Drew asked.

Catie waved her hand dismissing the question, but Drew pressed. "Jack. Dumped me."

"His loss," he fired back quick as a flash. He stuck a small band aid on each of the three wounds. "I still think you need to go to the hospital. Dishes and silver wear are heavy from any height. It'd be sensible to get checked out."

"Sensible?" Sheryl scoffed, now standing behind him. "You ain't gonna find sensible in here today."

Catie looked at the mess not cleared yet. Slivers of ceramics and spaghetti sauce slapped across the floor like they were a modern art installation. The whole room would need bleaching. The floor grew cold against her backside and she tried to move. "I'm so sorry about the mess."

"You saved me a job," he winked. "And because of that, you've put yourself forward for employee of the month."

"Ha!" Sheryl said. "If only we had a system in place."

Drew shrugged. "Maybe we'll start one."

For two years Sheryl had watched Drew's eyes dart when Catie moved, his ears prick up every time she spoke. It was cute at first but now it like watching a soap and waiting for something spicy to happen. It never did and it was getting tired. "Let me guess who's gonna be awarded every damn week."

"What are you trying to say, Sheryl?"

"Thought it was abundantly clear, buddy. Really don't wanna think what the prize is gonna be."

Catie interrupted. "I'll stay late to pay for the damages."

"That's the most ridiculous thing I ever heard," he said. "You'll get someone to look at your head is what you'll do."

She couldn't deny it. That sounded like a really good idea, Catie thought. Someone ought to look at her head and while they were at it they could explain to her exactly why it seemed like a good idea to date Jack Sullivan. Sure, he was charming and way too easy on the eyes but, according to the phone call, she had been dating a married man.

She had ignored her gut believing instead that she was the luckiest woman alive, that Jack was The One. Why shouldn't Catie Cambridge have her Prince Charming? Other women had theirs. His words were so cold and ripped out her heart. 'I'm married. We've got to stop seeing each other'. The shock gave way to gravity and she was on the floor.

"Like a therapist?"

"I guess. If you need one. I was thinking the ER, but..." Drew supported Catie to a chair as Sheryl returned the kit to the box on the wall. Something was missing behind Catie's eyes, those green eyes he frequently fantasized about in his quieter moments. He held up his hand extending three fingers in front of her them. "How many?"

"How many what?"

"Come on now, you can do better than that."

"One."

"One?" he wanted to laugh, but concern got the better of him.

"One hand."

He smiled. "Okay, let's try that again. How many fingers am I holding up?"

"Three."

"Atta girl," he stroked her shoulder. "Okay, last call for the ER. I'll even spring for a cab."

"Hey buddy," Sheryl said, dejected. "You never treat me to a cab."

"Fall on your ass and take half my kitchen with you and I might."

"I dunno. Seems like a lot of work."

"That's what I thought." He glanced through the swing door window to check for customers.

Sheryl noticed his eye line. "If you've got it covered in here, I'll go out front."

"Thanks," he said, relieved for a moment alone with Catie. "You okay?"

"Feels like someone else is inside my head." She touched the injuries one by one. "I'm so embarrassed."

"Don't be. People do all kinds of things when they're in shock." His voice was deep, level, and reassuring. "Listen, I get that the ER is a pain in the ass, but your head is important. It's not now, but later you could collapse or pass out or something. Promise you'll think about it?"

Catie smiled weakly. "And I will pay for the breakages. It's only fair."

He dismissed the comment with a wave of his hand. "Fair would be not getting dumped, wouldn't you say? The guy's an idiot, dumping you of all people."

"He was married." She watched his smile disappear. "I'll bet you're wondering what I was doing. Did I know? Wasn't it obvious? Didn't I see the signs?"

"Did you?"

"No. Yeah. Maybe? Doesn't matter now. It's over anyway."

"It's not your fault, y'know. Cheating's never a great idea but if you didn't know…," he trailed off. "And I'm guessing you're not the first he's done this to."

Catie sighed. She didn't want to think of Jack with anyone else. Even his wife. He had been so passionate, so romantic. "I really thought he was the one."

"Break ups are tough. I mean, it's been a while since I went through one myself, but they don't change. You're stuck with a whole bunch of feelings that can go nowhere. It hurts. It really hurts."

"You know, if I'd have known from day one that he was married, I wouldn't have gotten together with him. I'm not like that."

"I know the kind of woman you are," he gave a subtle smile. "I've known since the first moment you walked into this place. Seems like a lifetime ago, doesn't it? And two minutes ago all at the same time. Goes fast."

She thought about the first time she saw Jack Sullivan. He was attractive, knew it and used it. His confidence pulled her in. She always tried to wait his table not just for the tips, but to be closer. She wasn't lying to herself that money was a big draw, what waitress wouldn't like that, and Drew's Diner was situated in Boston's banking district where patrons threw it around like water. Ten dollar, twenty dollar, even fifty dollar tips were the norm when Jack was around. But now his love was now just a memory.

Drew broke her thoughts. "The main thing is you're okay."

"Thank you," she smiled. She liked Drew's attentive nature and she enjoyed his wit, but he was no Jack. Nobody was Jack.

He craned his head to look through the swing door window, then pushed it open to see Sheryl clearing up. She had set the meatloaf aside to cool for tomorrow's lunchtime rush. "Hey,

Sheryl, I think I'm gonna lock up early. You can head on home. I'll finish here."

She glanced at the clock above the booth seating. "There's still an hour. Are you sure?"

"Yeah. Get on home and give those kids a big hug."

"Thanks, buddy. I appreciate it. How's the patient?"

"She'll live. Hopefully, she won't sue."

"What would I sue for anyway?" Catie stood next to him. "I broke *your* dishes."

"I don't know, I guess a lot of people might use something like this to their advantage. Maybe if my dishes weren't there, you wouldn't have fallen into them," he said, his eyes rolling as he thought of a thousand more scenarios.

Catie held her jacket around her as she headed for the front door. "Thanks for what you did, both of you."

"You'd do the same for us," Sheryl showed no emotion, as if she was just voicing facts. "Anyway, you feel better. You got that?" It was more of an order than a suggestion.

"I'll call that cab. Are you going to the ER?"

She shook her head, then winced at the ache. "I plan to get some rest. I need to figure out what I'm going to do."

He flew out to the sidewalk and threw his hand in the air. A taxi stopped instantly, and Catie got inside. Drew draped himself over the door. "I'll call you later, okay?"

"Thanks for this," she said. "I really do appreciate it."

"You're welcome. After all, what are friends for?" Drew smiled in a way she had never noticed before.

Chapter Six

As she watched the students step away from their desks, Becca McCallister sat back in her chair and gave a long, deep sigh. It had been a trying day with some having difficulties in both their studies and relationships. Cliques were always tough to fathom; she remembered as much when she was at school. Getting them to focus on reason over emotion was tough.

Teaching English Literature and Language to thirteen-year-olds was a challenge. Most were not interested in reading, writing, or learning about the classics, and who could blame them. Hormones aside, dusty, over-thumbed books were not to everyone's taste. Add a few century-old synopses and you found an instant insomnia cure. But she was determined to watch them blossom. If they developed a love of reading, just as she had done through her fellow red-haired kindred spirit, Anne Shirley in Anne of Green Gables courtesy of LM Montgomery, she believed their respective worlds would be richer for it.

They walked, pushed, and shoved their way out. Some deliberately kicked table legs, others did it unconsciously, and a few even knew how to leave a room without issue. She had an inkling on how each of them would fare as adults. Age was one thing; maturity was an entirely different beast.

"Watch where you walk, please. The tables have done nothing but support your learning. Literally." Her subtle humour was too hidden for most of them.

A couple of months into the winter term, she had planned to get Lilah in for a talk. She did it every year once the term had settled. Lilah would impart just how exciting creative writing could be. By planting the seeds in their minds now, Becca could show them a plethora of word-based jobs that could be both fun and lucrative. Even writing to prospective employers required skills that could make or break chances of an interview. Based on the outskirts of London, most students lived nearby so the city was the obvious choice for employment.

She intended to invite other representatives from the Arts too as well as other trades. She knew creativity wasn't for everyone, appreciating students didn't have to be wholly imaginative to get work. There would be opportunities behind the scenes too. Some within theatres, radio studios, and advertising. Voluntary roles and work placements would be considered too.

Having Lilah on speed dial was a fantastic educational resource. Asking wasn't the problem, organising it with the poisonous dragon of an agent was. Ruth and Becca had endured two rounds of disputes in the time Lilah had been a client. The first, at the competition prizegiving Lilah won. Ruth snatched the trophy from Lilah during her acceptance speech. Proud little sister, Becca, was careful and diplomatic in her comments of Ruth's behaviour. Ruth was not. The two spat nails within minutes.

The second dispute, at the launch of Lilah's first book Hobby Husband, Becca had just walked in when Ruth barked, 'Come to have another go at me, have you?' It was not the welcome she expected, and their relationship had been cast in stone.

Since then, Becca couldn't find a reason to be nice to the woman until a strange situation presented itself. Becca's ex-student, Emma, was jobless. With talent being wasted and a young mind being overlooked, Becca phoned Lilah. 'She needs a job. I'm willing to move heaven and hell for this kid. She's bright, hard-working, and easy to get along with. She just needs a break.' A phone call later and Ruth agreed to interview her. The role was for an office junior and Emma was coached and armed with ways to deal with her new boss.

So far as Becca knew, it was going well.

As the last of the students left, the receptionist shuffled her way through. A short, middle-aged, woman with a permanent smile on most days today wore it sympathetically.

"I've got a note," she said as if she had drawn the short straw to deliver it. "I took the call. The Head said to bring it straight away."

Becca read it. 'McCallister. Sister. Accident. Hospital'. Below it was: 'Your sister has been in a car accident. She is in Holcroft A&E. Please call the hospital.' A number was underneath.

A frozen sensation rested in Becca's gut similar to when she was informed of her parents' death. Shock. She needed answers to unasked questions. Instinct forced her heart to skip a few beats while she processed the information.

She recalled sitting in Lilah's garden in August with lush foliage surrounding them. They had enjoyed a barbeque, Pimm's and way too much ice cream, then giggled so much that Becca accidently snorted. That alone induced hilarity and neither of them spoke a sensible word for the rest of the evening. It was one of the best days ever.

A subtle clearing of the throat from the receptionist brought Becca back.

"Paul said go. Don't worry about clearing up. He said to keep him updated. You've got his number."

Becca nodded but it all felt so disconnected, as though the note referred to a student instead. Everything was in slow motion. She grabbed her coat from the rack next to her desk and plunged her hand into the pocket for her car keys. She pulled out the metal initial 'B' dangling on its chain. It was a stocking filler from Lilah years ago. Becca had got one for Lilah too; an 'L' initial. It had been a long running joke between the sisters that, despite being given long, three-syllable names, the pair went with the easier two-syllable ones and, on occasion, even single syllables. Li and Bex were simpler to yell when bickering than Delilah and Rebecca, much to their mother's disappointment.

"Are you going to be okay?" the receptionist asked, her tone soft. She put out her hand to take Becca's but it culminated in an awkward hug. "If you need me," she reassured. "I'm here." It was a bizarre thing to say as the two women barely knew each other. Becca didn't even know her first name.

"It'll will be fine." Becca's voice was robotic, automatic. "Us McCallister's are made of strong stuff." She pulled her coat on and took her oversized satchel from the desk. She marched down the corridor towards the car park feeling emotional. No, that wouldn't do. Then, more practical thoughts entered: the route to the hospital, money for the car park, how long she would need to park, she should take flowers, where she would buy them, was Lilah going to be okay?

First things first, she told herself, get to the car, find the route, then once she was at the hospital – and only then – would she allow herself to think about her sister's condition.

Except that plan did not happen.

The instant she sat inside her car the tears began. It wasn't like her to be so emotionally open. She could usually block them with barrier after barrier. Emotions were Lilah's thing, not hers. This was shock. It had to be. In emergency situations, the first person she would turn to was Lilah. But this was about Lilah.

Becca combed her wavy red hair with her fingers allowing herself a few minutes to sob as the engine ran. The rain had poured intermittently throughout the day but now the clouds mirrored her mood. December rain brought an even earlier dark end to an already trying day. It pattered on the roof, comforting her with memories of caravanning holidays years ago.

'Phone the hospital' was the message. She'd forgotten that part. What would be the point? Knowing Lilah's condition before she got there wouldn't make the journey any easier. She would find out when she got there. It was the safest option. And, if the worst had already happened, there was nothing she could do anyway.

Aside from fall apart.

Trying hard not to be upset – because more tears meant poor vision for driving – she filled her mind with everything non-Lilah-related. She thought about the assignments she had been about to mark when whatever-her-name-is came in. She thought about how old the school was and the friend groups the students were forming. And then her mind forced her to recall the holidays she and Lilah enjoyed. They had gone to America with some of the inheritance; Massachusetts the first year and Maine the second taking in a little of Vermont before coming home.

Both holidays were research trips for Lilah's novels. She had always wanted to visit the States, but local holidays seemed to win every time. Now they had the money there was nothing to stop them. After the trips, Lilah intended to submit to a literary agent first, but the competition arose instead.

During their flight, for entertainment Becca quizzed her sister on US history, its connection with the UK, its accents, culture, and landscapes. In Lilah's excitement, American and Canadian celebrities were highlighted as potential starting blocks for her romantic heroes. It was an interesting way to fill seven hours. Landing in the late afternoon, they headed for the hire car company and Becca drove while Lilah navigated. Lilah made notes and took photos and, for research purposes, drove twice: once to a drive-thru Starbucks and once to dinner just to experience driving on 'the wrong side of the road' with all the controls 'on the wrong side' of the car.

They walked the Paul Revere Trail in the blazing heat, sat in bookshops drinking iced tea and people watched, then visited Quincy Market. Becca learned more about the Pilgrims, Columbus and how the America known today was founded, intending to disseminate the information with her class. On their third day they ate dinner at 'Andrew's' on Franklin Street. It was to provide the foundation for 'Drew's Diner', an eatery in the financial district Lilah planned to use in a future novel.

America provided all that was needed for Lilah to come alive. She would overhear a partial conversation in the street and jot it down knowing it would find a home in a story.

"I've got another crush!" Lilah randomly messaged her sister. "A big one. I'm going to use him for my man's eyes," she'd say. There were other odd, unexpected messages over time, that were similar in theme. "Found a new one! Watch this movie, he's in it. I'm going to use his hair, lips, accent, the way he walks, the way he smiles for my man." Knowing the hap-hazard way Lilah's mind worked, she encouraged her behaviour because she produced great stories. Seeing Lilah's excitement was endearing and a big part of her eccentricity. Although an aspect Becca didn't share, it fascinated her nonetheless.

The two couldn't have been more different yet so similar. They also shared the lack of a boyfriend, though neither was actively seeking one, and Lilah was often too consumed with 'crushes' to find one anyway. Lilah created fictional boyfriends while Becca read hers. Becca still felt it would have been nice to receive some male attention. After all, there had to be something else in life apart from work.

Despite being younger, Becca was the more mature sibling. She was working at her chosen career quicker, had bought a house sooner. Lilah was in no rush to experience the serious side of life, being happy enough renting a flat near her then job. But the role didn't drive her; writing was where she flourished. Winning the competition had quite literally changed her life. The trade-off was force of nature, Ruth Trent.

Happier memories filling her mind, Becca was at the hospital. She parked, paid, and headed to the hospital entrance.

"My sister's been admitted." The words fell out of her mouth as though she had been rehearsing them. "Delilah McCallister."

"She was taken straight to ICU," the young man said, with a sympathetic smile. "The doctor will want to talk to you first. You can find it on the second floor. Take the lift at the end of the corridor."

"ICU?"

"Intensive Care Unit."

The accident was major. Really major. Becca processed the words and nodded politely. She fumbled in her bag for a tissue but couldn't find one. She was guided to a box of them on top of the desk. The smell of the hospital, the staff uniforms, it felt like her parents' accident, like she was reliving it all over again.

"Thank you." She wiped her eyes. "I have a feeling I'm going to need a few of these."

Chapter Seven

Drew finished deep cleaning. He prepared ingredients for the morning, running his eyes over everything that required his attention then closed the door, locking it behind him. He headed home to shower before grabbing something quick to eat before calling Catie, like he promised.

She was embarrassed over the accident but her reaction to its catalyst, the infamous Jack Sullivan, was shock. Drew saw how women reacted around the guy. He had that square jaw thing going on women swooned over, the confident smiles, and he knew how to use those good looks. Ego was a clear driver. He didn't know much more about the man aside from showing up at the diner a couple times a week but only when Catie was on shift. That much he noticed.

Jack was popular and always brought a bunch of hangers-on to the diner. It was great for Drew's bank balance, lousy for his romantic life. Jack was a sleaze ball, but only Drew saw it and it puzzled him. Women were smart about everything else, but rarely spotted the sleaze ball. It came as no surprise the man was a cheat. Catie was worth more than that.

Over the years friends whose break-ups from, in his opinion, unsuitable guys had created a living hell for everyone around them. Drew's twenties were spent being the best friend and brother figure, rarely the boyfriend and he'd taken a swing at more guys than he cared to remember. Some women took break ups well and others got over them by spending every last cent they had on clothes and jewelry. Then there were the ones who'd get themselves drunk and attract some other lowlife. Whichever Catie was, she would need rebuilding first.

From the moment she walked in, he'd fallen in love with her. For him, she was perfection: smart, beautiful, funny all rolled up into Catie Cambridge, the woman of his dreams. He'd intended to keep his hand close to his chest hoping nobody would figure it out until he found the right words. Knowing might have made her run. But one person knew. Sheryl Laurence: the impatient New Yorker whose in-built Drew-radar was switched on to maximum. At every opportunity she gave him the *why haven't you done anything about it yet* look. He could never give her a straight answer. He had hoped Catie would come to see him as a potential boyfriend, but it hadn't happened. Even if she did only have eyes for Jack, Drew silently accepted it on one condition, that the guy treated her well.

Now he knew otherwise and all he wanted to do was throw his arms around the woman, love her, and protect her from everything bad in the world, including Jack Sullivan. Because Jack was bad. Rotten to the core. The man was a roach, and a married roach at that.

Home, he kicked the door shut throwing his keys into a glass bowl on the hallway shelf. He mindlessly peeled off clothing on the way to his bedroom: his jacket fell onto the back of a chair in the living room, his sneakers in the bedroom at right angles just like he'd left them as a teenager. He pulled off his socks then his t-shirt, grabbing it from the back of his neck over his head casting it aside to land on the cover. He turned on the shower and stepped inside welcoming the water over his skin. It flowed in streams, running through his hair and down his chest and back. Afterwards, with just a towel around his waist, he bare-footed his way back to the kitchen. The other half of last night's pizza, diner leftovers. More substantial items were offered to Sheryl or Catie and everything else unused that wouldn't keep was distributed to those sleeping rough on his way home. Nothing was wasted.

He nuked the pizza to return it into something more appetizing. The sooner he ate, the sooner he could check on Catie. He washed it down with half a bottle of alcohol-free beer. A decade ago, the beer might have been a different story.

Alcohol played a major role becoming his only source of fun when rare relationships went sour. You could rely on a cold beer to see you through, he told himself justifying the routine, with a couple at lunch, after work, at dinner, before bed. Now in his mid-thirties, he channelled all energies that weren't focused on Catie on the business and keeping himself fit and healthy. Without a healthy body and mind, he couldn't run his business. Recreational drinking was limited to either low-alcohol or alcohol-free. He only had eyes for one woman so why spend an evening drinking with another he wasn't even into?

After devouring dinner, he dialed Catie's number. There was no answer. He tried again. A third time lit up warning signs inside his mind. What if she went to the emergency room after all? Maybe she had concussion and was confused and all alone. He stopped himself from worrying. She was a grown woman who didn't need a rescuer. Then he imagined worse scenarios. She left the diner covered in cuts and bruises. She looked vulnerable, maybe the driver... He stopped, telling himself she didn't need a knight in shining armor. If Catie was anything, she wasn't a damsel in distress, no matter how much he wanted to show his protective side. She was probably asleep. He tried her cell phone once more but endless ringing filled him with trepidation.

"Answer the damn phone, would you?" he barked. "Just answer it and let me know you're okay."

He sighed hard as he got dressed, wearing a sweater with a hoodie over the top. A scarf and a leather jacket would keep him warm and he grabbed his keys before slamming the door. It took him thirty minutes to walk to her apartment block. The cold air was a stark contrast to the hot shower he'd enjoyed an hour ago.

As someone left Catie's apartment block, Drew kept the exterior door open and walked inside up two flights of stairs. He rapped his knuckles against the door and waited. Beneath it he saw a light was on. At least she was home.

Whether that was safely or not was a whole other thought process.

Chapter Eight

Ben opened his eyes. Everything hurt. What didn't hurt throbbed. He lifted his head, gently moving it from side to side to ease the pain in his neck. He blinked to clear his vision, but everything was still blurred. He was in bed, but it wasn't his bedroom. He rested his head before mustering the energy to repeat the process. He gave himself a diagnostic check from the tip of his toes right up to the uppermost brown curl on top of his head.

Slowly...slowly, he told himself. *Take it down to basics.* Starting at his feet, he tried to move his toes to gauge if he could feel them. He couldn't, nor could he feel his legs. Indeed, nothing from the hips down would move. *Don't panic. It'll be perfectly reasonable why I can't feel them. Just keep your cool and be logical.* He would revisit this after he finished the body check.

His mind imagined his chest as he took in a deep breath. *Stop – that hurts!* Bright red lightning bolts of pain shot through his rib cage the longer his mind remained there. He quickly moved to his mouth, his tongue cautiously probed, seeking injuries. His teeth were fine but several cuts the size of sesame seeds got his attention, as if he had been munching on glass. His cheek bones throbbed, and his forehead was sore as though he had abruptly stopped on a roller coaster.

A flash of memory shot through his mind of smashing glass and deploying air bags. *Boof!* Whiplash. Then the sensation of cold air on his face.

He focused on the crown of his head. It seemed okay so he moved to his hands. He gave a thankful sigh of relieve when he moved his fingers. With all the commissions he had lined up, he needed those hands more than any other part of his body. A distant memory came to mind of him joking that even if the rest of him didn't work, so long as he had his brain, his eyes and his hands, he could still remain an artist. He hadn't given merit to the realisation of such things.

He lifted his head again and looked back down to his legs, noticing the end of the bed was like those they have in hospitals. A white cover took the shape of his legs, the right one being wider like it was in plaster. Then another flashback came. His blue car entwined with a racy little red number. Eyes closed upon a perfect face. Red hair. The crash. It was no dream or nightmare, it was real. He was in hospital.

He tried to lift his arms intending to settle them on his elbows for support before lifting his body up to look around. He got as far as lifting his arms an inch or two before screwing up his eyes and crying out in pain. The noise he heard sounded like a wounded animal.

"My lovely! You've slept for hours. I'll be looking after you while you're visiting. I'm Margaret."

He hadn't heard her approach, but the first thing he noticed was a welcoming smile as if she imparted all the emotions in the world through it. It was warm, reassuring, and calming. Then he looked upwards and saw big brown eyes and short afro hair. Her uniform only just covered her buxom figure, with buttons doing their utmost not to pop apart at the chest area while her breasts fought to be released. "I'm in hospital?"

"Yes, you are, Mister Christopher. But I'm going to make sure you're out of here as soon as possible."

"It was….a car accident?" Recurring images flashed through his mind. Crimson and azure…red and blue…scarlet and sky, all shades from his paint tray.

Her smile fell but her eyebrows rose at the arches, knitting together in the middle. "A very nasty one."

"What's wrong with my legs?"

"One's in plaster. The other…is in sympathy," she said. "I think you had someone watching over you. But the most important thing is that you're safe. We'll work on the rest together."

"My chest hurts. My throat…"

She nodded sympathetically. "Broken rib. Broken leg. Broken glass from the windscreen caused the abrasions in your mouth. Cuts and bruises and a spell of concussion. You'll be here for a little while and you'll ache and feel lousy. They've got you on some good stuff though. You'll heal. Just give it time."

He absorbed all she said. Broken rib, yes, that made sense. Broken leg, that too. "But I can't feel my legs."

"That'll be the medication. It's powerful. But you're a strong and healthy young man by the looks of you. You'll be up and about in no time. When it wears off you'll know about it, so don't be shy asking for a top up."

Everything hurt now *with* medication, what was it going to be like when it wore off? Oh yes, she'd know about it. Heck, the whole hospital would know about it. "How long will it all take to heal? How long until I can go home?"

"It'll take as long as it takes." She checked the notes at the end of his bed, giving a smile, a frown, a nod, and a shake of the head with each line she read. She came to his side giving him the kind of smile you got when things were bad. She took his right hand and held it in hers against her chest. His long, slender white hand interlaced with her chubby black one evoked a sensation, as though love had manifested from her permeating his skin from his fingertips, then cascading through his body. "It's all going to be fine, my lovely."

He smiled, grateful for her empathy and unusual bedside manner.

Margaret returned the smile. "The painkillers are working. Do you have anyone you'd like me to contact? Wife? Girlfriend? Boyfriend?"

There wasn't anyone. He had long given up on having such a person in his life. His artwork had become his 'significant other'. He shook his head. "The woman in the other car," he said softly. "Did she…did she make it?" he stumbled over his words to get them out. He heard the worry in his voice. He couldn't hide it, and the trauma trickled in. Warm tears edged down the sides of his temples. "She looked…dead. Please tell me she made it."

"She made it."

"She did?" Something about the way she answered made him cautious of hope.

"Sleep now, my lovely. It's a wonderful healer."

He closed his eyes to rid them of tears and when he opened them again, she was gone. In a ward of four beds, he was the only one awake. He lifted his hand to see a white clip over his index finger. Its cable fed a machine monitoring his pulse and a drip attached to the back of his hand was attached to a rubberised pocket that stood above his bed on a metal stand. In his other hand was a button that he could press should he need assistance.

He took Margaret's advice and close his eyes. The next time he woke, he focused easily. A white clock with black Roman numerals above the nurses' station reported it was nearly midnight – or nearly midday - he didn't know. He needed the bathroom. A feeble attempt to try to lift himself out of the bed proved pointless, so he pressed the buzzer. Was life going to be this awkward for the foreseeable future? Bleak didn't cover it.

A tall, thin nurse with a pursed mouth and lank grey hair approached, armed with a bedpan intuiting his needs. Dark rings around her eyes evidenced her fatigue. She looked like a real life black and white picture. "You've been asleep a while, Mister Christopher. I was wondering if you'd grace us with your presence," her tone prickly. She made a movement with her lips that might have been a smile, but it held no emotion. "Right, let's get you toileted."

"And some water too please, if you don't mind." He rested on his elbows to raise himself out of bed, but she firmly urged him back.

"You're not strong enough for that yet." As if she had hidden it behind her back, she produced a urinal bottle. "We'll be using one of these for the time being." She surrounded his bed with the curtain dramatically as if awaking it from its own slumber and created a private space for them both. She lifted the covers and thrust it towards its destination. He hoped she would leave allowing him privacy to complete the task. When she left, she threw the curtain aside as though for dramatic effect.

It was the first time he had ever used a urinal bottle but the relief it brought was exceptional. It didn't matter how embarrassing the scenario might be, he was too injured and reliant on medical staff to care about any awkwardness. Only after he had finished, he considered how undignified the whole experience had been. She returned after a few minutes to exchange it for a small plastic cup filled with water from the covered jug at the side of his bed. After he had finished with it, she updated his notes. She had barely spoken sharing none of the friendliness Margaret oozed. She pulled the curtains back and lifted the bed head to help him raise his head and chest.

"The other nurse told me what happened," Ben said, wishing he didn't feel obliged to make conversation, wishing she was Margaret. This one behaved like she ate maggots for lunch and was forced to eat seconds. "My leg and rib." He didn't get a reaction, so tried again. "Do you know anything about the woman in the crash?"

"What other nurse?" She looked puzzled. The dark rings around her gaunt face made her appear ghostlike.

"Margaret, I think she said."

"There's nobody named Margaret in the team. And we don't give out first names to patients anyway. It's a security risk."

Ben was perplexed. With a broken leg and soreness everywhere else, what threat could he possibly be to her?

"As for this other patient," she went on. "It's confidential so you'll have to just focus on yourself, Mister Christopher."

"You can call me Ben."

"Do you need a medication top up yet, Mister Christopher?"

He nodded, feeling like he'd been told off. Fine, if she didn't want to be friendly, that was good with him. He'd save his pleasantries for Margaret.

"Right, I'll go and find you something to eat as well," she said as though he was taking up her time. "Anything you don't like?"

He wanted to say, 'Yes, you,', but shook his head.

"Keep sipping the water. We can't help you if you don't help yourself." Then she marched away.

Being able to converse made him feel brighter, that and being able to go to the toilet, even if it was in an unorthodox way. He looked at the other patients. One next to him, another opposite and a fourth man diagonal to him. From this angle, he couldn't tell ages or medical conditions, and nobody was awake anyhow. Two were snoring. After a few minutes, he heard a familiar voice.

"My lovely!" Margaret appeared at the end of his bed genuinely happy to see him, and Ben was relieved to see her. "I haven't forgotten your request. As soon as I know something, you will too."

"The other nurse said you can't tell me about other patients," he said, crestfallen.

She dismissed it with a wave of her hand. "How are you feeling?"

He swayed his head from side to side indicating he didn't feel so great. "She's getting me something to eat. And more painkillers."

"Good. It'll help you heal." When she spoke, it felt like she was an offering a personal service, not like the other nurse who was the officious epitome of emotionless efficiency. "I'll pop back later."

Ben watched her walk around the corner of the ward out of sight as the other nurse returned with a tray. Upon it was a plastic film-wrapped cheese sandwich on brown bread, a carton of orange juice, and a plastic pot of strawberry jelly. None of it looked particularly appetising, but he hadn't eaten for almost twenty-four hours so was eager to work his way through it. Gingerly, he opened the sandwich and nibbled the corner of the triangle-shape in which it was cut. The cheese was bland and rubbery and the bread tasteless, but he ate half a sandwich, sipped the juice, and ate the jelly and it was done with the speed and agility of a ninety-year-old man with his arms tied behind his back. He had never felt so dependent, not since childhood. He had also never in his life endured agony from so many parts of his body in one go.

The entire performance of eating, drinking, thinking, and conversing had exhausted him like he had never experienced. He rested into his pillow and stared at the ceiling for a few minutes thinking about the impact, the woman, and the intensity of the experience. The slow-motion speed encouraged an analytical replay in his mind, repeatedly, as if his mind was deliberately torturing him.

The nurse reappeared with a small pot. Inside were two white tablets which he swallowed with water and was relieved when she left him alone and, just as he grew drowsy, Margaret returned. She was sideways to his head. Her presence became a mixture of shapes and noise that he couldn't properly focus upon.

"Sleep, my lovely. You're going to need the rest. Everything's happening as planned."

He wasn't sure he understood and, as she left the ward, he drifted off.

Chapter Nine

Catie opened her purse to pay as the cab stopped outside her apartment building.

"It's covered." The driver's brown eyes bore holes into hers from the rear-view mirror. He had hardly taken his eyes from her the entire journey. "The guy paid. Thought you knew."

Now the car was stationary, he seemed to be exploiting the opportunity and it unnerved her. It wouldn't be the first time she'd been the focus of unwanted attention. If she could just get into her apartment where she could start licking her wounds.

The wrinkled skin surrounding his eyes stretched as he smiled. "Looked like he cared though. He your boyfriend? Husband?"

"Boss."

His eyebrows rose in surprise as though the idea of a caring boss was strange. "You're pretty. You sure you don't want me to take you to the ER?"

She dismissed his question. The last thing she needed was a stranger showing any kind of interest. She gathered her purse and edged nearer the door. "I'm fine. I'm sure it looks worse than it is."

"You look like a truck rolled over you a couple times. So, what the hell happened?" As he rested his arm on the back of his seat turning to face her, his expression was suddenly void of any pleasant emotion. Easily in his fifties, he had an unusual paternal look about him. "Tell me that guy didn't do it."

"What?" The comment threw her completely. He wasn't coming on to her at all. He was genuinely concerned and trying to protect her.

"'Cause if he did, I'm telling you now, I'm going back over there and we're gonna have a conversation, me and him. And I can promise you this, he ain't gonna do it again, that's for damn sure."

"Drew? No, of course not." His concern was a shock, and it was a further shock that he thought Drew of all people - probably the sweetest man on the planet - was capable of such a thing. That he could be responsible for her injuries was incomprehensible. She gently touched the dressings. "Nobody did anything to me. It was just an accident."

"So long as you're okay." His concern remained but his vigilance diminished. "Just checking is all."

Embarrassed they were even having this conversation, that a cab driver could be more concerned over her welfare than Jack was when he ended things, she opened the door. "Thanks for the ride." She shouldered through the exterior door and gently made her way up the stairs trying not to let the headache progress, but by the time she reached the top it was throbbing harder.

Inside, she headed straight for a pack of pain killers swallowing two with a glass of cold water. She allowed herself a moment to calm down and untense. There was a lot to process: the cab driver, Jack, her head, her future – if any. She wanted to cry - scream - at Jack's idiotic decision to end things. They were good together. So what if there was a wife in tow? She couldn't have been that important if Catie had been on his radar, could she? "You lied, Jack." She pictured him in her head, reminding herself how charming he could be. A charming liar. A million emotions took hold from sadness to shame to grief to rage. She sipped at the water as the first tears welled in her eyes.

Dating had been a distant memory when she started at the diner. She hadn't sought a boyfriend, Jack just… happened. He was everything she ever hoped for: smart, attractive, charming, employed, a great body in and out of clothes. Plus, he told her he loved her. And that was the clincher. He was too perfect, she now realised. And too married. The writing was on the wall from day one if she had bothered to listen to her gut. She had been too gullible, too trusting, too eager to believe everything he told her.

Why couldn't she have her fairy tale? She was ready to settle down, ready for the next step. She even had a bunch of baby names milling around in her head, fantasies of pushing a stroller through the park, and holding that perfect new-born in her arms. Time was getting on; she wasn't going to be young forever. Now in her thirties, would she ever marry? Have kids? Would she ever have any type of family life?

She missed being part of a family from the age of twelve. After her mom left, her father became a single parent raising a pre-pubescent girl with more unreasonable moods than were necessary. It was a perfect storm, tough with tantrums and frequent fights. She ran away for a day, spending it wandering around Quincy Market. Her dad hadn't been aware or else he would have had the entire police department out looking for her. She left in the morning like normal but, instead of arriving at school, she just didn't go. Guilt fuelled her journey home arriving just before him. Dinner was on the table as he walked through the door. She watched him eat it, realising he was doing his absolute best for her, so she had to do her best for him. That meant cooking, cleaning, and doing her best at school. His old-before-his-years face and sad-filled eyes killed her every time she looked at them.

An absent mother had created baggage. The only kid in her class without a mom when puberty hit, when boys showed an interest, when exams were taken, when advice was needed. The events parents attended together her dad attended alone. She saw what he went through with the other parents: the gossip, the humiliation, the hidden tears, the polite smiles when one was expected and got but not meant. They adapted. It brought them closer together.

Now she was almost the same age as her mom was when she left and vowed if she ever had kids, she would never do that to them. She would never abandon them. Then it struck her. She wasn't completely sure Jack didn't have children. He never even mentioned it, just like he'd never mentioned he was married. If he did, and Catie had gotten her way, she would have been the same person as her mother was all those years ago. The thought killed her inside.

The painkillers were taking their sweet time to work so she took her thumping head and moved to the sofa. It was soft and embraced her with an excess of scatter cushions, one of which she hugged to herself, holding it like it was a baby. Still dressed in her work uniform and jacket, she had no intention of changing. What was the point? She didn't have plans, nor did she feel particularly sociable anyway. She wouldn't bother with dinner. She could thank the charming Jack Sullivan for removing her appetite for the second time in six months. Falling in love was great for the figure but so was breaking up. Though, right now, she didn't care if she lost a few pounds, gain a hundred, or dropped dead completely. Numbness set in and the tears fell freely.

She may spend the night alone, but she would do it with a bottle of wine and an impressive crying session that would make any recently dumped woman proud. A wave of rebellious abandon filled her as she downed the first glass in one go. The second glass went the same way, but she sipped at the third. Who cared if she got drunk? It didn't matter now anyway. It was a small comfort after an incredibly painful day, both emotionally and physically.

A vision of her father in his chair at the care home filled her head and she sighed hard again, this time with guilt. What would he say if he saw her downing a bottle of wine like that? It wasn't classy and it wasn't who he raised. Not his Catie-girl.

The feeling the wooziness enveloped her as she remembered the last proper date she and Jack shared. The last time they spent more than an hour together, was a walk through the park. Boston's autumnal leaves were gone and winter had arrived. They'd wrapped up warm for dinner, then it was back to her place. He kept checking his watch, she remembered. Why hadn't she noticed that at the time? It was another clue her gut chose to ignore.

As always, he left her to sleep. Jack never stayed over. Foolishly she believed him when he said a gentleman would never free load the use of a lady's apartment overnight. When they did spend an entire night together, he would pay for the most exquisite hotel room for their decadent and erotic pleasures. She believed he was the perfect man – more than that, that he had been the perfect man *for her*. She felt like a princess being lavished with gifts and had fallen for the lifestyle he provided, and the rhetoric he used. He had, quite literally, charmed his way into her pants. Blinded by love, and money, how stupid she now felt, how ridiculously foolish. And ashamed. And violated.

Falling into slumber, a thudding noise filled the room bringing her abruptly back to the waking world. Her headache had progressed to vertigo, and the mixture of tablets and alcohol made her nauseous as she came to her senses.

"Catie, are you okay?"

It was a familiar voice. Her first thought was that it belonged to Jack, that he had come to tell her it was a huge mistake, some kind of schoolboy prank that had gone disastrously wrong and he was here to say things were back to normal. Or, better yet, it was a bad dream brought on by the bang to her head. The streak of hope was replaced too quickly by a cynical thought. Why the hell would he come to the apartment in person, he couldn't break up in person. Wasn't it easier to phone instead and let the silence surrounding the unreasonably cold words do the talking for you? It was the coward's way out.

"Catie? It's Drew. Are you in there?"

Drew? Why was he here? She tried to pull herself to her feet, but it was an enormous task that took more effort than she could muster. She felt as if her head weighed five hundred pounds. Her head and tummy swam in a rhythm that wasn't joined. She stood, dazed, and held her head.

"Catie? Are you in there?"

"Yeah."

"Are you okay? Can I come in?"

She moved gingerly along the living room with the cushion still held to her chest as though it was the baby Jack hadn't given her. She opened the door and saw Drew standing there. "Hey," he smiled instantly. He looked warm and strong and inviting. "You okay?"

Trying to focus into his twinkling eyes and inhaling his freshness, she nodded slowly wincing. Her eyes were dark with tears and intoxication.

"How's your head? Did you go to the ER? What did they say?"

That was a lot of questions. "I didn't go. I took a couple painkillers." She saw him look over her shoulder.

"You been drinking?"

"I guess," she shrugged, turning back to the sofa, leaving the door open for him to enter. He walked in closing it quietly.

"Are you sure that's a good idea? I mean, your head was hit pretty hard."

"I thought it would numb the pain."

"Did it?"

"Hurts like hell, so I guess not."

"Was that wise?"

"Didn't you hear?" She shot him a glare. "I don't do wise things."

"How many?"

"One. Maybe?"

"One glass or one bottle?" He lifted the bottle looking at the level remaining. "Did you drink all this tonight? By yourself?"

She raised her eyebrows. "Are you judging me now?"

"What? No. I'd never do that."

"I think I can handle one glass."

"This is more than one glass. And with pills, after a head injury? Even one glass isn't a good idea. Good thing I came along when I did." He asked again, "Catie, did you open this tonight?"

"Mixing pills and drink? Is that what you think I've done."

"You just said that's what you've done."

She sighed, caught out. "Well, in case you think I was about end it all over the likes of Jack Sullivan, you'd be wrong," she slurred, covering her eyes with her hands. "I'm miserable and a little drunk but I'm not completely stupid."

"I happen to think you can do a whole lot better than him anyway." He took the seat next to her, perching on the edge.

"You do? I'm pretty sick of liars so if you can find me a guy who doesn't lie, that'd be a start."

"I get it, you're mad and you're hurting. Why don't you stop wasting your time thinking about him? There are other guys out there. Good guys. The kind who'll take care of you and give you the world if you'd just let them."

"It's you who's wasting your time. That guy doesn't exist." She reached for the bottle.

"I'm serious, Catie. Please don't." He paused and softly sighed. "Y'know what? I think I'm gonna take you to the hospital."

"What?" Frustration didn't cover it. "Why?"

"Just to be on the safe side."

"I've already had one guy overrule my feelings today, please don't be the second," she growled. "I mean it when I say I'm okay."

"Alright. But I'd feel a whole lot better if I knew you were going to leave that stuff alone. How many pain killers did you take anyway?"

"I dunno," she shrugged. "One or two."

"Was it one or two?"

She tried to hold back her growing frustration. "One. I think. Is that okay with you?"

He raised his palms to her in surrender. "Relax, would you? I'm trying to help you. Since you won't let me take you to the hospital, I'm gonna put on some coffee. Is that allowed?" He waited for an answer but didn't get one. "And I'm not leaving here until we get you sober."

"I *am* sober."

"Then *more* sober." He opened every cupboard door until he found two mugs and switched on the filter machine. "Anyway, how can you be sober? You just told me you got through a bottle of wine by yourself. What are you? A hundred and thirty pounds? Believe me, you're not sober."

"Why do you care anyway? Worried I'll sue your ass for the accident at work?" She had a smart mouth when she was drunk. She had never been any different.

"I should have taken you to the hospital when it happened. I don't know what I was thinking sending you home with a head injury. I must be nuts."

"You're a guy," she said. "You're nuts by nature."

"I'm not denying it, but it's you who makes me nuts."

Her eyebrows knitted together as suspicion filled her mind. Her intention was to head towards him, but she wobbled on her feet, so it took more than just a little concentration. She held the furniture for support walking like she was negotiating a rope bridge. "Wait - what does that mean?"

He didn't answer. He'd brewed enough coffee to half fill two mugs and poured them both, handing one to her. "Here, drink this."

"Trying to help me huh? Do you know how bossy you are?" She noticed how close he was to her, like he was when the accident happened. It felt nice. She looked into his eyes as he studied the dressings on her forehead.

"Assertive, I think it's called. And, I dunno, maybe you need someone to take care of you. You certainly look like you do."

She couldn't deny it. She felt awful. "So, how's my head, Doctor Denby? You're good at this. You should've been a doctor." She gave him the smallest of smiles. "You'd look great in a white coat." Liquor always bought out the flirt in her. She couldn't stop herself and with Drew standing so close, she didn't want to stop herself either. What was the worst that could happen, he'd be embarrassed? So what. Maybe Drew ought to feel a little embarrassment. Catie had been through enough emotion for one day, let someone else get theirs for a change.

"I think you can take the dressings off in the morning and let the air get to them." He didn't stop staring at them and remained close. "Man, you smell good."

"I'm not sure Jack would've been like this," she said, comparing the two men. "Wait, what did you say?" Did she hear right or was it the drink toying with her imagination. Or maybe the head trauma? Or confusion. He was so close, she wanted to touch him, hold him, just to see what he felt like. His heat radiated out as if inviting her in. She was tempted.

"Not that I want hear about him but, sure, I'll play along. Like what?"

"Hmm? What's that?"

"You said Jack wouldn't have been like this."

"Considerate. Caring. Compassionate. We'd have been in there by now," she gestured to the bedroom. "Probably inside thirty seconds of him setting foot in the place."

"Well, I'm not him. I actually *care* about you."

She sipped her coffee, never taking her eyes from his. "You do?"

"Why d'you think I made a house call?"

"'Cause you thought you might be minutes away from a lawsuit?"

"Am I?" He paused for an answer but didn't look worried when he didn't get it. "I guessed not. You're not the type. For what it's worth though, there's not too many people I'd go the extra mile for."

She lifted her index finger and stuck it squarely on his chest. It was solid and sexy. For some reason everything about him tonight was. "I'll bet Sheryl's one, for sure."

"Aside from Sheryl. And that's only 'cause if I didn't, she'd find me and kill me. And she's the kind of woman who'd bury the body so well, nobody'd ever find it." He laughed. "I'd do anything for her, but I still wouldn't want to be on her wrong side."

"You do know she's crazy about you, right?"

"She's sees me as one of her kids, I think. Keeps me on the straight and narrow. She's been like that from day one."

"If you were one of her kids, she'd kick your ass."

"She already does!"

"She's tough."

"She's had to be too." He drained his mug. "Raising a couple kids alone isn't easy."

"If anyone can do it, it's her."

"Yeah, but she shouldn't have to. I don't know what it is with some guys. Wow, what the heck is in this coffee? It's good." It took him a couple of minutes to get a new filter dripping into the jug.

The fresh aroma was welcome and filled the kitchen quickly. Catie watched him work his way around it. He was naturally suited to them no matter where it was. "I guess I should've put some coffee on earlier instead of heading straight for the wine."

"Sobering up now, huh?" He winked and gave her a friendly grin. "Starting to see sense?"

"I guess I chose wrong. It's not the only wrong decision I ever made." A lifetime of bad ideas culminated as a tsunami of memories. If Drew only knew the half of it. She closed her eyes tightly trying to remove them all. Now was not the time.

"Don't beat yourself up. Things happen. It's how we deal with them that makes it right."

"Stuff like this makes you question yourself, doesn't it?" *Damn Jack Sullivan!* "I honestly believed he was…"

He interrupted her train of thought. "I know you did. I wasn't lying when I said he was an idiot."

"Can I tell you something?"

Drew inhaled slowly, hesitantly, as if he was wondering where it was going. "Sure. You can tell me anything."

"I've been thinking of baby names."

Drew instantly looked at her tummy, his eyes widening with the shock. "You're…?"

"No. I mean I thought we were going to settle down, have a couple kids together. I was serious about him. Then, completely out of the blue, he phones to say his wife's found out about us. His *wife*, I mean…" She sighed. "How the hell did that happen?"

"Gotta say though, six months in and his wife didn't know? It's a long time to keep something like that a secret." He poured fresh coffee into the mugs again. "I'm just saying, things couldn't have been that great with them."

Catie sighed. "I don't know. I don't wanna know either. I don't wanna know anything about her, or their life together. He'll be home with her right now making babies. *My* babies."

"What?" He blinked slowly, trying to fathom her thoughts. "What are you talking about?"

"I don't have much time left, Drew. My body clock is ticking."

"Don't have much time left, my ass! You've got plenty of time. What are you? Twenty-eight? Twenty-nine?"

"Thirty-one and running out of time."

"You've got at least another ten years to make those babies of yours, I wouldn't worry just yet."

"You don't understand. I want to be in love. I want the husband and the family. I want the whole nine yards. When I was a little girl, I thought I would meet someone, get married and have a family and live happily ever after but I'm in my thirties, and I've been dumped yet again. I didn't think it would be this hard. I mean, what the hell's wrong with me?"

And then the tears came again, this time they were full on.

"Hey, come on." He took her mug and put it on the counter then pulled her to him, holding her in his arms. "Any man would be lucky to have you in his life. Don't waste it on a guy like him when he doesn't deserve you anyhow. Sometimes you've got to go through the bad stuff to see the good stuff that's been there the whole time, right under your nose if only you thought about looking for him - it."

She looked up, sobbing. "Real life doesn't work like that though, does it?"

"Sure, it does." He stroked her hair, careful of the pain. "It happens all the time, Catie. You mustn't give up on any of it."

"I just want my fairy tale."

"And you'll get it. You'll get your husband and your babies. The man of your dreams might be closer than you think."

"You really think so?"

"Sure, I do."

"What if you're wrong?"

"Come on, have you ever known me to be wrong before?"

It made her laugh which made him laugh. He pulled back to see her smile, but she went straight back to the safe place of his chest. It was like home.

Chapter Ten

Being taken to private room after private room, Becca was
told even more detailed information each time. She was losing
patience and energy. Fear and anxiety had used up both.

Finally, she found herself in the smallest room yet. It was big
enough to house the burgundy two-seater sofa and share the
intimate space with a wooden chair and the smallest of side
tables. She sat on one side of the sofa leaving the two cushions,
that had, originally, had a seat each, on the other half. An ivy in
a white pot stood upon the table. It looked real from three feet
away but as Becca began to focus on it while she waited for the
doctor, the plant was no more real than she was a plant. Its
plastic stem wound around a thicker plastic trunk, the size of her
thumb. In some unknown world it was dreaming its best life.

She wondered how many other people had waited inside the
room; how many others had been given the worst news of their
lives. It had a certain smell about it, like disinfectant mixed with
air freshener. She supposed the air freshener was intended to
mask the cleaner, but it wasn't working. It made her want to
choke but she held it back. Without warning, the door handle
turned and the shock of it brought her to her senses. A man
wearing a white coat and steel-framed glasses walked in. The
room suddenly felt so much smaller than it already was. He
looked like he was in his late fifties, or he might have just
worked more hours than he ought. It was hard to tell but his
unshaven jaw gave away some clues. As he extended his hand to
her, Becca shot to her feet.

"I'm Doctor Griffin. First of all, Miss McCallister, I'm sorry
to meet you under these circumstances. My notes say you're
Delilah McCallister's sister and next of kin. Is that right?"

"Yes, that's right."

"Good. Right, well let's bring you up to speed." He gestured for her to retake her seat on the sofa while he sat on the wooden chair. His knees almost touched hers within the small space. It must have been a frequent issue as he deliberately moved them diagonally to avoid her. "Delilah…"

"Lilah. We…I call her Lilah." She smiled politely. "I'm just saying…it's just easier. Sorry, carry on." She wasn't sure where the voice or words had come from, she just said them. She took a subtle deep breath to compose herself, expecting him to tell her the worst.

"Lilah," he said, "was involved in a pretty horrific traffic accident with another vehicle. I suspect you know that much."

"Yes."

"Okay, well there's two things I need to let you know. Firstly, and most importantly, she's alive." He paused, as if awaiting her response but she said nothing opting instead for more information. "But she's also in a coma."

"A coma? Right."

"It was self-induced. Occasionally, it's necessary for medical teams to induce a coma but this one has happened naturally. Interestingly, there is very little else wrong with her considering the severity of the crash. She has suffered a few cuts and bruises but nothing more serious than that, which is," he nodded as if surprised, "nothing short of miraculous. I know you'll have lots of questions for me but before you do, please know that comas are the body's way of switching everything off to repair themselves. You could think of it as when you have a problem with your computer, you switch it off and on again, don't you?" he said.

Becca nodded, it was something she dealt with both at school and at home.

"Well, your sister's body has switched itself off because of the shock of the accident. It's protecting itself and once it's sure there's nothing sinister going on, which I'm almost certain there isn't, it's possible she'll start everything up again, all the parts of her brain that have been put on standby, until she's back to where she was."

"That sounds simple," she said, wincing at her own words knowing it must be anything but simple. "You said, 'it's possible' though, does that mean it might not happen?"

He inhaled tipping his head from side to side. "Comas are tricky things. The brain is a very powerful organ and there is still so much about it we just don't know. What I do know though, is that I've been doing this for a long time and every single coma is completely different. Sometimes the switching off and on again is instant and sometimes it can take longer."

"How much longer? Are we talking hours?" She stared at every nuanced gesture his face gave in case she could read between the lines. "Days? Longer?"

He paused sympathetically. "It could be hours, yes. Or it could be longer. Occasionally it doesn't switch back on again for some considerable time. It would be sensible to prepare yourself in case…"

"…in case she never recovers?" Her voice came out hoarse, as if all the moisture in her mouth had vanished. "Is that what you're saying?"

"You see, that's one of the problems with comas. We cannot say for sure because the body is very much in control of itself.

We can help it, heal it, even guide it, but if it doesn't respond to our poking and prodding…" As his voice trailed off, he shifted in his seat as though he was trying to find the right words but couldn't, even though he must have done this a hundred times over. "At the moment it's protecting her. But we're not helpless while it does," he said reassuringly. "We can give her time, the time she needs. It might help to think of it as a dream state. She's a writer, is that correct?"

His voice was lighter now, casual. It had altered so quickly. Becca didn't try to analyse why. She just dived straight in to answer the question.

"Yes. A novelist." She said it with pride, then realised how pointless it might all have been hoping and praying she got into the big leagues.

As if sensing her rapid steps towards despair, Dr Griffin reassuringly touched her sleeve at the shoulder. "Who knows, perhaps she's dreaming of her next book?"

Becca's eyes widened at the thought. Yes, that could be it. Lilah always did have the most amazingly vivid dreams.

"Clearly comas can be tough on the patient's family." Of the paperwork he had brought in, a small, white notebook was one part. He fanned the pages outwards and the air it produced gently lifted her hair. "One thing I'd like to recommend is that, while your sister is sleeping, you could write a journal."

"I don't understand," she said, perplexed. "Surely we ought to be focussing on Lilah?"

He nodded. "Yes, but if you add entries each day it can help you process the situation. Often, when the patient wakes up, they read what happened while they were away. Keeping this diary can help them to fit things into spaces they hadn't realised existed. It can be a major therapeutic resource for everyone involved."

Becca saw the logic. It made sense and sounded like a good idea. She took the booklet, holding it against her chest as thought it was a piece of her sister that she didn't want to let go.

"When they wake up, they don't know how long they've been away, or indeed what their families have been through during that time. Your sister's last memory may have been getting into her car or even the day before, so waking up in a different location can be unsettling. It can provide answers to otherwise painful questions."

"You said there was a second thing," she reminded him. "What was that?"

"One of the tests we carried out showed that there was alcohol in her blood. She wasn't over the limit, but it is possible that alcohol played a part in the accident."

"Jesus Christ!" It wasn't like Lilah to drink and drive. In fact, it was the last thing she would do. "Surely that's a mistake?"

He shook his head. "We tested it twice. I'm only telling you because, at some point, the police will want to talk to you." Having the police involved made the whole situation feel even more real than it already did. It brought back memories from the crash her parents died in just a few years before. Whatever energy she had left tonight, she needed more, for without it she questioned how long she could keep up her emotional barriers.

Keep practical. Stay logical.

"Do you have anyone who can support you through this? Any friends you can stay with?"

"It's literally just the two of us. We lost out parents in a car crash."

"I'm sorry to hear that." He looked genuinely sorry. "Neighbours?"

She shook her head. They were fine for a quick polite smile but nothing for this level of support.

"I'd suggest keeping yourself occupied if you can. These situations have a nasty habit of eating away at us."

"I'm a teacher, I've got papers to mark, students to teach. Plus it's nearly Christmas so…" She heard her words, wondering what Christmas would look like now. What if Lilah didn't come out of the coma? Or worse, if she… She stopped herself. "I'll need to check Lilah's house too, pick up post."

"That's good in the short term, but just in case it becomes longer term, we can discuss ways forward. In the meantime, you can phone in each morning for updates and the nurses will let you know when you can visit. As you might imagine, ICU visiting is extremely limited."

He gave her another piece of paper. This one had doctor's names, the ward name and a telephone number as well as the hospital website. She took it and placed it inside the booklet, as a bookmark.

"I can let you see her for a couple of minutes now, then the best advice I can give you is to go home, eat and sleep. She's in the best place for her condition and we'll do everything in our power to ensure she's as comfortable as possible. Are there any questions?"

"I can't think of anything. It's quite to a lot to absorb to be honest. A couple of hours ago I was sitting in my classroom."

Finally, he stood, put out his hand again to shake hers and then left her with a nurse who guided her to Lilah's bed. Becca bundled her coat, bag, and the paperwork together as she sat down. The machines that monitored her progress beeped, buzzed, and whirred. The doctor was right, aside from the machines, tubes, and bags coming out of all areas of her sister's body, there was barely a scratch on her. Lilah's red hair was pulled to one side. She looked just like she was sleeping.

Becca tried to keep her tears locked up inside as she took Lilah's pale, limp hand and held it. She was cool, not cold, and her skin felt soft and silky. Everything she wanted to say, she said inside her head. *What on earth happened? Were you drinking? Are you alive inside there?* "I wish you'd come back," she said aloud.

"I can see she's related to you. You're both such beauties." A different nurse approached to the one who had brought her there. "I'll be taking great care of her so don't worry about a thing," she beamed. "It's time now for you to go home. You must take care of yourself though. Get some food inside you, okay? And get some rest. Phone us in the morning."

Becca nodded, forced a polite smile, and thanked her. She left ICU walking dazed through a maze of corridors to the carpark. Once she found her car and sat inside, she realised she hadn't recalled getting there.

Night had settled in and the rain had begun again. She wasn't hungry, that'd be the shock, but her stomach rumbled. She thought about all the things she'd been asked to do: keep Paul updated, keep in mind the police would be in touch, write in the journal, look after herself, eat, sleep. It was a lot.

At ten, she found herself parked in her bay outside her house. The parking area housed six bays, one for each of the two-bedroomed houses. She barely knew her neighbours aside from a daily wave to and from work. It suited her. She wasn't overtly social, focusing primarily on work and her sister afterwards. She rarely went out, which had put a block on dating. That also had come to suit her. Dating was the one thing she was the least equipped to do. She wasn't chatty and being friendly was an effort. She was just practical and logical enough to be good at her job and keep being an adult. How people found that special someone was beyond her. Most of her brain space was filled with marking papers and class preparation, finding someone to settle down with was both terrifying and required skills she didn't have.

That was where she admired her sister the most. Lilah could fall in love with the people she wrote about, even if they were fictional. Sometimes, fictional was the best choice. There was no back chat, no jealousy, nothing that couldn't be written into or out of a story. Life in novels seemed fantastic. If only all of life could be scripted. For a start there would be no horrific accidents to deal with, and heroes came along just at the right time.

So many things were going through her mind, so much to deal with, and so many memories vying for her energy. She got out of the car and went into the house. Switching on her interior lights, she was in her own space. She could now be herself and nobody would see the wreck she really was. She wiped away a tear, knowing more were coming.

She listened as rain pelted against the window as she switched on the kettle. She took out the milk and closed the fridge when a photo of her with Lilah, in front of the USS

Constitution in Boston, stared back at her. Once her drink was made, she sat on the sofa and went through her phone. Since leaving school she hadn't looked at it even once. Aside from social media posts, there were several texts from Paul, the Head, each enquiring how things were and to message him at any time no matter if it was day or night.

'Thanks for your messages. Lilah's in a coma. Nothing more I can do tonight. Going to bed shortly. See you in the morning,' she wrote. Instantly a message was being typed back.

'I'm so sorry to hear that. Please don't worry about coming into school. Take a few days off. Family comes first.'

'Thank you. I will be in though. I need to keep my mind occupied. See you tomorrow.'

It was good of Paul to say as much, she thought. He was a good Head Teacher, caring about his staff that way.

As she lay in bed, Becca thought about the accident site. Then it flew through her mind. There had been another vehicle involved. What of the other person? Not once had she thought about them. The implication was that Lilah crashed into someone, what was their condition? The doctor hadn't indicated fatalities, so they must be alive, and the police would be crawling all over her if there was. Maybe they were in the same hospital?

She imagined if Lilah had killed someone. The idea that anyone she knew could do such a thing, however accidentally, was abhorrent. She sat up in bed, ready to rush to the bathroom, but after a few moments, she calmed herself.

So, who was the other person, or people? Had they been drinking too? Was it one person, a couple, a family? Were children involved? She made a mental note to ask when she visited tomorrow. Maybe it wasn't all down to Lilah, perhaps it was a mistake both drivers had made? Or maybe it was wholly the other driver's fault.

Then Ruth Trent came into her mind. She needed to know the situation. Thoughts of Ruth's face, her black bobbed hairstyle, scarlet lips, and those ridiculously red-rimmed oversized glasses filled Becca's mind. The woman oozed darkness, bad vibes and nastiness. Maybe this would soften her?

She sighed, closed her eyes, and rested. She would wake up with a different perspective, one with logic and practical mindedness. After the emotions she'd experienced tonight, it was the version of herself she preferred the most.

Chapter Eleven

Catie forced open the door a little after ten the next morning then kicked it behind her. She headed for the staff room as diners watched on. Sheryl glanced over her shoulder at the dramatic entrance while taking an order from a couple in the booth and Drew focused on serving a customer, though didn't ignore the interruption. A metal tong filled with slices of pork between its long silver fingers was in one hand while the sub he intended to fill was in the other. He packaged up the meal in a paper bag adding two paper napkins and handed it over with a smile.

Inside the staff room, Catie unwrapped her scarf and coat launching them onto the rack not caring whether they made it or not. She grabbed a pencil and notepad from the counter and dropped them into her apron pocket before heading back outside.

"Morning," Drew smiled. He noticed all her Band Aids were gone and each cut had begun to heal. To the untrained eye, she looked like she was recovering from chicken pox, with a handful of scabbed-over cuts. Considering the amount of blood that had dripped down her face after the accident, the wounds were exceptionally minimal. Bruising covered her forehead and temples but she wore her hair in a loose pony tail leaving bangs to cover them.

But it was her mood, not her hair, that everyone noticed.

"Feeling better today?" Sheryl said, quicker than anyone could humanly process.

"Yes," she said abruptly.

Drew wiped his hands down his apron. "Something going on I oughtta know about?"

"What are you talking about?"

"Call me sensitive but you don't seem your usual self." Dark rings around her eyes said she hadn't slept a wink, but Drew spent most of the night on the couch with her draped over him sleeping. Neither had intended to fall asleep in that position, it had just happened. He committed to memory the look on her face while she slept, and how he felt every time her breathing changed. He was still prepared to take her to the ER at two in the morning had it been necessary but by three, she was safely asleep so he reluctantly carried her to her bedroom before leaving. If anyone could use some more sleep, it was him. "Is something wrong?"

Catie gave a subtle shake of her head as if thinking about his question. "I said I'm good."

He overlooked the attitude. She wasn't the Catie he'd spent hours with on the couch. He gestured on his own face. "All okay today? You look better."

She shrugged.

"You should still probably see a doctor. Check everything out. Make sure you're okay."

"I said I'm fine." She stared him in the eye from two meters away. "What do you want from me?"

He didn't overlook it this time. "What the hell's gotten into you? You're two hours late. You're slamming doors, and you're cranky. How about you go back inside there and take a breather?" He kept his voice low to prevent causing more of a scene. It frustrated him that he'd had to take it down to basics. "Come back out here when you're ready to serve. We're customer-facing, for Christ's sake. You want everyone to up and leave?"

Shocked, she let out a huge sigh, ripped off her apron and threw it on the floor before heading back to the staff room.

Sheryl handed him the order slip. "What the hell was that? What did I miss?"

"I'd love to know. I don't care who you are, but take that tone with me, and I'm gonna have something to say about it." He glanced at the customers Sheryl had just served: a couple in their seventies, holding hands across the table who looked like they might be reliving their youth, or sharing an illicit moment. He threw a smile their way after he looked at the slip. "Brunch huh? I'll get right on it."

"Did you go to her place last night?" She realised how it sounded as she picked up Catie's apron. "You said you were gonna check on her. Did you?"

"I called a couple times, but she didn't answer. We talked for a while and had coffee."

"That was it?"

"Pretty much."

"Pretty much?" She knew those words covered something else. "What does that mean?"

He lowered his voice even more. "She'd mixed pills and booze." His eyes darted to her face. "Yeah, that's what I thought."

"You sayin' she was gonna…".

"She said not."

"You asked her though? Like, outright?"

"Kinda. I don't know, maybe I got there in time? I mean, would you do that over a guy like him?"

Sheryl leaned against the counter, throwing Catie's apron over her shoulder. "To be honest, I wouldn't do it period. But then I ain't wired that way, and I'm completely over the guy thing. Suckers are all idiots as far as I'm concerned. They show up, make a couple kids, and walk away. I got no time for 'em, and even that's too much. Present company excluded."

"Thank you."

"Don't thank me. It ain't a high bar."

"She was a completely different person last night. Sure, she was cranky. She had every right to be, getting dumped like that. But after, she softened. She opened up and we talked. It was good."

"So, what was this deep and meaningful about?"

"Marriage. Babies."

She smirked. "Gotta hand it to you, buddy…"

"You don't understand. It wasn't like that."

"Then what was it like?"

"You know."

"No, I don't. That's why I'm asking."

"Sheryl!" The more she pressed, the shyer he became. "Look, I'm just saying I stayed over…no, I mean I was there half the night." He watched Sheryl's expression and quickly added, "on the couch. We were both on the couch. Nothing happened," he said as though confessing his sins. "There was nothing *like that* going on."

"Like what?" Her face was a mixture of hope and mischief. She knew he was terrible at hiding his feelings towards Catie. Playing with him filled her days with joy. "Relax, just tell me one thing."

"What?"

"She knows, right?" She waited for an answer but didn't get one. "Seriously? I know everything inside your head. Even the stuff you don't know about yet. Does she know you're in love with her?"

"I don't know," he shrugged. "I mean it's not like it's common knowledge."

"Gimme a break!"

"Just go to work, will you? I'm not paying you to interrogate me." He sighed, handing her the two plates. "Here, take these. I'm gonna check on her."

"Remember how that turned out last time. Marriage. Babies. No need to rush in all guns blazing."

"For the record, it wasn't me who brought it up."

"No, but I'd bet serious money you thought about it all the way home."

"Shut up." He couldn't deny it. Sheryl was too quick for him.

Through the swing doors, he craned his head to see Catie in the staff room. She stood in the doorway. "Wanna talk?"

"Not if you're gonna yell again."

"I didn't yell."

"I just wanna stop feeling like this. And I wanna stop crying too but I can't."

"Come on, was he really that great?" He threw his palms up at her glare. "Okay, I'm sorry."

"You just don't get it. You're a guy. You're all the same."

"I understand enough to be here, don't I? I gotta ask though, if we're all the same, why are you so broken up over him. I've never seen you so bitter. Listen, if you want to talk, I'm here. Let me help."

Without a thought, she fell into his chest and sobbed. He felt the heat from her face through his T-shirt as he stroked her hair and breathed her in. He wanted the hug to mean as much to her as it did to him.

"It's gonna be okay. I promise. It's just a break-up. It's not the end of the world."

"Then why does it feel like it?"

"I know it does right now. But believe me when I say that there's someone out there for you so much better than that guy. Remember what I said last night? I said you'd get your husband and your babies. It'll happen, just not with him. He wasn't right for you."

"I really thought he was the one. If I can make a mistake like that with someone I thought was perfect for me, what does the future even look like?"

"Listen, if it helps, there's a guy out there right now who already loves you."

"What?"

"I mean there's someone for everyone. I truly believe that."

"So where is he then? This guy you keep talking about. Why haven't I met him? Does he even live in the US? He could be the other side of the world for all I know."

Drew stood back, wanting so much to say what was in his head. And then, without realising it, the words left his lips. "He's standing right in front of you." Silence filled the small space between them. He stared trying to gauge her response, confused, wondering what on earth he had just confessed.

"What? Did something happen last night when you came over? Did we…"

"No, of course not."

"I woke up in bed this morning with no memory of getting there."

"I'd never take advantage...Wait, did you hear what I just said?"

"Yeah. What does that even mean? There's nothing between us."

Drew's throat was suddenly too dry. It was now or never. "Isn't there? I dunno, maybe there is. Would it be so bad if there was?"

"You're my boss," she said as though it made a difference. "Did I say something last night that made you think...?"

"No. Nothing. Look, let's just lay it out there. I have feelings for you, Catie. Strong feelings. I have ever since that day you walked into the diner." His heart pounded with hope and terror as he watched her process his words. "I tried to keep it in check, but I got the feeling it was obvious. You mean you didn't know?"

"Why would I? I've been pre-occupied with my boyfriend."

"Your *ex*-boyfriend."

She sighed, seemingly not to have heard him. "Then I guess it's kind of sad." She leaned into her jacket and took out an envelope. "Because I have to give you this. It's why I was late this morning. I was going to leave it on the counter when I left tonight."

He sliced the top of the envelope with his finger and took out the hand-written note inside. His heart sank as he read each word.

"I think this is the best way. You know, for everyone. And especially now since you lay this on me."

"But…"

"I can't stay, Drew. Not after Jack. I can't be here when he shows up. I can't do that again. Staying's just too hard." She took a breath as if rearranging her mind's contents. "I guess I finally made a decent decision in life. I'm gonna leave town."

The news punched him in the gut. He watched her reach for her coat, wanting to take her in his arms and hold her there. "So you're gonna leave right now? Where are you gonna go? Do you have somewhere to stay? You don't have another job to go to. I've got to say it's a pretty big decision to just up and leave like this."

"I have to." She wrapped her scarf around her neck and threw her coat over her arm.

"Of course you don't. Catie, stop. Just wait a minute. Just listen to me. There's nothing that says you have to leave right away. This is a big decision. You've got commitments here. You've got to think about this." He was floundering, trying to find things that would ensure she remained. "What about your father? What are you going to do about him? If you leave, you won't see him. All this just to avoid an idiot who broke up with you?"

She threw up her hands. "I don't know. Just…stop asking me so many questions, I can't think. Look, I haven't thought that far ahead yet. I just know I have to leave." She covered her face breathing into her palms, trying to hold onto any dignity she had left.

She was panicking right in front of him and he was panicking right back. "Just take some time to think about it, that's all I'm saying. Take a couple days off. I'll forget I saw this," he gestured to the letter. "Please don't do anything rash. Just…"

"What is there to think about? You?"

"No, forget all about me. I shouldn't have said anything. I admit my timing was off but I'm not a rebound guy."

"Here then? The diner?" She stared, angry at what he might say yet needing his advice at the same time. "You're only mad 'cause I came in late and now I'm leaving town."

"I mean sure, I'm a little mad that you're leaving me one waitress short right on top of Christmas, but I'll deal with it." He took a breath, lowered his voice and tried to be calm even when the woman he loved was about to make the worst decision of her life. "Just put things into perspective, won't you? You're falling apart, Catie, all over some guy who doesn't even care about you."

"But you do?"

"Yeah. I do." He sighed. The whole thing was a less-than-subtle kick in the gut. "Take a few days. We'll cover."

"No, I'm not coming back." She somehow cut him in half with her eyes. She flung open the staff room door and made her way through the kitchen to the diner and into the street. The couple in the booth watched the commotion as though it was part of their brunch; entertainment thrown in.

Sheryl spun around seeing Drew standing at the swing door, dejected. "What the hell did you say to her?"

He stood at the swing door, dejected. "She's leaving."

"I can see that."

"Boston," he said, choking on his words. "She's leaving town."

Chapter Twelve

Harsh, clinical lighting woke Ben and the first thing he saw was Margaret standing at the end of his bed. She was reading the notes.

"Margaret?"

"It is, my lovely. You slept very well. How are you feeling today? Do you need more painkillers yet? Are you hungry?"

He blinked, confused which question he should answer first. "Leg," he winced. His hand moved to his ribs and his wince turned into a soft yelp. "Yeah, painkillers, please."

She returned with the medication. "I'll bet you're thirsty too." She poured water into a fresh cup and handed it to him. He drained it, swallowing the pills, then gestured for more water. "This is good sign," she said. "You're a very good patient."

"How come you told me your name? The other nurse said staff aren't supposed to give out their names."

She shrugged. "What harm can it do? Let's sit you up. It's better for your ribs. I can plump your pillows, so you feel more comfortable. It won't help your body if you're straining to see people."

"Thank you. It's not like I'm inundated with visitors though. You've been my only one so far." He tried to make it sound like a joke, but it just came out flat, as though he was complaining. "Oh, and that other nurse. And the doctor, of course." He thought how sad it sounded to have only medical staff as visitors, but he wasn't likely to get anyone else as nobody knew he was there.

He worked with her to lift his upper half and struggled until she told him to relax. She was firm, confident but gentle. The metal rack beneath the pile of pillows was folded into a high angle. While adjusting it, her enormous breasts hovered over his face. Built as she was, it would take a blind man not to notice her curves. He closed his eyes, hoping not to catch sight of them quite so near, until she finished and stepped away. It didn't seem to bother her. Occupational hazard, he guessed. Unlike the other nurse, nothing was too much trouble with Margaret. She treated him as if he was her only patient.

"That's much better. Thank you." He breathed in the ward's air more easily at this more upright position. It seemed to make a difference even if the air was mostly filled with the scent of cleaning fluid.

"You're very welcome, Mister Christopher."

"Since I'm calling you Margaret, you should call me Ben."

"Then I will, Ben."

"The other nurse either ignored me or didn't hear me when I said the same to her. Based on the rest of her attitude, I'm going with the former."

"Unfriendly?"

"Just rude, to be honest. I got the feeling she doesn't like me."

"I cannot imagine that for one second."

"Maybe I was rude when I was asleep or something."

"You don't have a rude bone in your body, Ben," she smiled. "You're a darling!"

Her words reached his ears in a maternal way, as though she was a lioness protecting her cub. It had been a while since he felt that. Her presence made him feel warm and cosy.

"Thank you. The other nurses don't seem to talk to you much, do they?"

She tapped her mountain of a chest. "Different team," as if that should answer all his questions. It didn't. She continued around his bed smoothing the covers and checking the notes.

"How long have you been with..." He didn't get a chance to finish his question before she predicted his question.

"I've been doing this for as long as I remember. They're not all friendly. It all balances out. We go wherever we're sent. Anyway, guess what?"

He tipped his head with a mixture of curiosity and concern, but the curiosity was winning and took his mind away from her cryptic comment.

She lowered her voice and looked around, panto-style. "The police were in here earlier. I think they want to talk to you."

"Me?" Suddenly, the atmosphere felt very serious and he stopped trying to analyse her words. "Why?"

"Because of the accident."

"The other driver...She didn't ...die, did she?"

She answered with another question. "Are you up to talking to them?"

Margaret was too economical with the truth. He had forgotten the police would be involved. Talking to them seemed like such a formal thing to do, like everything was set in stone. What if he didn't remember everything correctly? He hadn't a clue how he was going to handle the situation.

"Did you find out about her? The other driver?"

"Before we get to that, are you up to seeing them? I *can* delay them," she said it like she was suggesting it.

"I suppose so. I can't tell them much. It all happened so quickly." The more he thought about their questions, the more Margaret's delaying tactic sounded appealing.

"It'll all work out alright, my lovely," she reassured him. Then, as if she had received an invisible shock of adrenalin, she suddenly got over-excited and giddy as if she was bursting to tell him a secret. "Guess what? She looked around for over-interested ears, then leaned into his face. Six inches from his ears, she said, "Just between us though. Okay?"

He nodded, feeling her cool breath on his skin. He wondered what he was agreeing to but she easily pulled him into her excitement.

"She's in the ICU. Your lady. I saw her."

"Intensive Care?" Ben's thick brown eyebrows knitted together. He hoped things weren't that bleak and made a horrid situation feel worse. "She's that bad?"

"Coma," she parted with the word so simply.

He recalled the look on the driver's face at the crash site. She looked peaceful. Had the coma begun then? "I got away with broken bones but she could die. Why are you smiling? It's terrible news."

"It's not terrible, it's great news. It means she's still alive."

"Well, yes."

"It means she's still with us. And that's a start." Her optimism was incredible. She was right. It was a start. A tough start, but a start all the same."

"I don't know much about comas, but doesn't that mean she's, I don't know, dying?"

Margaret shook her head. "There's something else. "She's *someone*. Someone famous."

Ben didn't recognise her when they locked eyes, but terror had taken over. She just looked like a scared young woman who he could no more rescue, as stop the accident from happening in the first place. He remembered feeling so helpless, so powerless at not being able to leave his car or keep her awake with his voice. He could barely breathe. He wanted to have been that person who carried her to safety, or at very least kept her awake and talking until help came.

He knew he was not made of the stuff of heroes, but as he sat in the car helpless, in his mind, he felt like the worst kind of man; a useless one. He wasn't raised like that. He felt as if he had let her down.

"Who?"

"A writer. Exciting, isn't it?"

Ben couldn't quite get his head around this unusual nurse. Telling him her first name, carrying out requests that were prohibited, giving him the heads up about the police. It was strange. Helpful, friendly, and appreciated. But strange.

"You said she's in a coma. She might not come out of it to write any more books."

"Shh!" she hushed his voice lower and tucked in his lower sheet again as if finding jobs just to keep talking. "Comas are a body's way of shutting down to repair itself. I love a good read, don't you?"

He was perplexed at how easily Margaret's mind could move from 'she's in a coma' to 'loving a good read'. While she exuded care and compassion, she overrode all of that with the excitement of celebrity. Resigned to Margaret's odd view on life, he nodded. "I haven't for a while though. I've been busy."

"Making art," she said. She had such an intense way of diverting his attention. "Those hands," she studied them. "I knew from the first moment I set eyes on them. And your eyes. You have such soulful eyes. Only someone with soulful eyes and slender fingers like yours could create art," she told him emphatically. "A creator. A sculptor," she said, adding, "An artist."

Her words spoke straight to his heart, filling him with excitement so instantly it felt like a lightning bolt had left her body and shot through his soul. An instant connection was created. Ben grinned wildly, his passion igniting.

"Yes! That's right. How could you know?"

"I know a thing or two," she giggled. "I do my research. Anyway, while you're in here, you'll have plenty of time to read, won't you?" her voice changed from nurturing to implying a challenge. "I've got one of her books. I'll bring it in for you. It'll give you something to focus on while your body is healing. Maybe you can spend some time inside her head and get to know her for a while?"

The idea filled him with the motivation he usually got from forming a new piece of art. Excitement and energy joined together and formed a line from his brain through to his lips. A broad smile covered his mouth and being in pain was nothing but a memory, and all because of the woman named Margaret.

"What kind of books does she write?"

"Romance. Are you up for a romantic romp between the covers?" she chuckled.

Ben stared blankly. "It's not my go-to. Is it raunchy?" he grinned.

"I meant your covers, on the bed, Ben." Then she winked and gave him a flirty smile. "Whatever were you thinking?" She threw back her head in laughter, but no sound escaped her throat. "I'm teasing. I'll bring it next time. It's called Hobby Husband. It'll do you the world of good. When was the last time you had a little bit of romance in your life?"

The fact she was so forward was no longer shocking and that she conversed and made him smile was worth all the jewels in the world. "It's been a while. Too long, actually."

"Thought so. A young man needs excitement in his life and I have a feeling things are going to get quite exciting while you're visiting."

"Has anyone ever told you how cryptic you are?"

"They have now. Ready for breakfast?" She giggled. "On my way, my lovely."

Chapter Thirteen

Drew was the last to leave as he held the door for Sheryl. The forecasters predicted snowfall before the night was out and the cold air hit them both like a brick wall. It had been a long, busy day, and with just the two of them. By five, he called it quits for the day. Whatever else needed cleaning, he would do it in the morning. If he saw another plate, bowl, or cup tonight, he would launch it into the garbage disposal and let that deal with it instead.

He turned off the lights and locked up behind them. Despite Sheryl's upbeat teasing, it had been miserable without Catie's smile. And now it was a miserable night because she had left in a bad way. He fully intended to check on her again knowing that whatever condition he found her in, it was likely to be colder than the weather. Despite wanting desperately to help her mindset and situation, he also knew he needed to stay away.

Being close was messing with his emotions. Laying on the sofa with her soft, warm body draped over his was idyllic but after their fight that morning, it was unlikely to happen again. Still, he needed to know she was okay. Even if he could be the brother figure, he would take it if it meant he could spend time with her.

"Night, buddy," Sheryl called out as she headed to the subway. The grocery bag she carried was full of leftovers for the kids. A 'thank you' for staying longer and ensured she didn't need to cook when she got home. It was a perk of the job and though it wasn't every day, it helped her out when it happened. "And thanks again for this."

"Welcome. Give those kids a big hug from me."

Sheryl turned, hunched over trying to keep the warmth inside her coat. "Tell you what, I'll bring 'em in tomorrow? You can have 'em for Christmas. My gift to you. Show you how much I care."

"Aww, man," Drew called. "Come on!" He watched as she laughed, waved, and turned back towards the subway.

He held a smaller white bag in his gloved hands. Winter in Boston was extraordinarily beautiful as Christmas lights punctuated the street. Yet it was terrifyingly bleak too. The homeless community on his way home were always the worst hit. He distributed several filled and wrapped subs and each man or woman who took it, went back under their sleeping bag as though hibernating. Plumes of warm breath filled the air in front of his face as he tried to stay warm. Walking usually did it, even jogging helped, but tonight's air chilled his bones, disturbed from Catie's intentions.

Somewhere in the distance, he could hear Christmas carols, or was it a radio from someone's car. The stark contrast between the haves and have-nots at this time of year was daunting. The irony of carols about giving and being kind didn't go unnoticed when most of the listeners couldn't give and rarely received. Workers simply walked past them without thinking twice. For Drew, giving was the very least he could do. Once empty-handed, he headed home in the quickest time yet, motivated to get out of the chill.

Nights like this were best spent keeping warm by fantasizing about walking home with Catie's hand in his under the decorated trees. He hoped one day it would be a reality but after today it was looking less and less likely. He knew he was in a precarious position. If he gave her the emotional space she needed she could up and leave, but if he didn't at least attempt to guide her melt down to a reasonable level, he might lose her forever. He recalled her saying she wanted to leave town and that created a bad taste in his mouth. Life without Catie was a life unworthy of contemplation.

Being a friend to others was one thing but right now he could use a friend himself. They were a rare commodity, becoming rarer by the day. His drinking days were filled with them, all leaning up against the bar downing beer after beer and putting right a wrong world. Mostly from the hospitality industry, they would each go home and forget everything they had argued over, satisfied they had at least gotten themselves wasted before sleep.

That life was a distant memory along with the friends. Now his only confidant was Sheryl: the New Yorker single mother with two kids. He imagined a night out on the town drinking was a long-distant memory for her too. He wanted to count Catie as a friend, but she was so wrapped up in that piece of crap banker that she hadn't seen Drew as anything but a boss. Confident in every part of life except the Catie part. She was his Achilles heel. He longed to sit and chat with her, hold her tight, protect her from the world, and give her the best life he could. But she was oblivious to his feelings.

Why was life so frustrating at times?

The sound of the exterior door banged echoing all the way upstairs. Inside his apartment, it was warmer – or less cold – than outside. His usual routine of throwing down his keys created an echo that felt like the apartment's sarcastic way of reminding him he lived alone, like its sick sense of humour was watching him suck at romance.

Throwing on the light switch, he headed straight for the shower to rid himself of work thoughts and heat up his body from the chill. It was his way of drawing a line between work and home life, of which there was little. With large flat hands against the tiled wall, Drew let the water rush between his shoulder blades to warm him from the outside in. He breathed in the fresh scent of soap bubbles as they slid down his muscular physique.

Dry and dressed in jeans, a T shirt and a hoodie, he made fresh coffee enjoying the aroma permeating around the room. It was pointless making food; he'd lost his appetite when Catie announced she was leaving town. He threw himself onto the sofa and stared up at the ceiling while he gathered his thoughts.

"What the hell are you doing?" he said aloud, hoping he would listen to his own words. "If she goes, you've lost her forever. She's not gonna come back once she's gone. What's she got to come back for? You? Are you serious? Listen to yourself. She doesn't even know you exist." A voice inside his head answered, countering the argument. 'But I could convince her to stay. I could talk to her, let her know how I feel. It could work.' He conjured several scenarios that might keep her in town but each ended with a plausible reason why it wouldn't work:

She wasn't in love with him.

She wasn't even interested in him.

She didn't care for her job anymore.

She didn't even care for Boston.

He wanted her to stay there because *she* wanted to, not because he did, otherwise six months from now she would find another reason to jump ship and he didn't want to be the reason she would try leaving for the second time. That would be too much.

He had to find something to keep her interested in remaining, something that would take her mind away from the idiot who dumped her, Jack Sullivan-Breaker of Hearts, and fill her with a new sense of love, a new hope for excitement, and a new future. Her intentions ripped out his heart. Having one waitress down was going to be tough, but worse still was the feeling of emptiness, the incredible void Catie's absence would create.

He grabbed his cell phone but something told him she wouldn't answer it, and he was right.

"C'mon Catie, just answer." He pressed 'end call' and got to his feet. The coffee's aroma had filled the room with roasted beans, nuts, and chocolate. It was like a dinner and dessert all in one but he switched it off. Just the scent of it was sufficient and sometimes cold coffee was just as good.

Dressing for the weather this time, he left his building rehearsing the words he wanted to say. Walking meant thinking time, and he needed to come up with an airtight plan. Pre-occupied in the darkness, he walked to Catie's apartment building as a light flurry fell silently.

Chapter Fourteen

After storming out of Drew's diner minutes after showing up, Catie's head was all over the place. Her instincts said she needed to get on a bus and go talk to her dad. She needed his take on her situation.

Jack Sullivan and his break-up call had brought her to her knees so it was natural to want to protect herself, and leaving town seemed the best way. Realistically, right on top of Christmas wasn't the best idea and now Drew had opened up to her. Why hadn't he asked her out all this time? Why hadn't she noticed? He was in a league all of his own, more covert than Jack but maybe he didn't need to be as showy because Drew had depth. He was sweet, kind, considerate, and he certainly had his head screwed on.

Before seeing her dad, she needed to gather her thoughts. The diner opposite was the perfect location to release some of her anxiety and ease her mind. Inside, it was a similar staff setup to Drew's: one manager, two waitresses, except this one didn't have even half the soul or character. Two other differences caught her eye too: the chef was hidden behind a wall of white ceramic tiles with only a three by six feet hole that gave access to the waiting staff. It also gave customers a minimal view of the kitchen that would have driven Drew crazy. He liked to engage directly with customers and staff alike.

The second difference was the lack of banter. While functional, it lacked soul and chatter. Catie watched the waitresses pass orders to the chef, before bringing drinks over to the table. She couldn't imagine this chef offering a piece of whatever he had just cooked so it could translate in their descriptions to customers.

It was then that she realised how good she had it, and that was all down to Drew. He understood how to get the best out of everyone, how to excite them, motivate them, and how to give them exactly what they needed whether that was food, humour, or help. She knew she had fallen on her feet. Instantly she saw how capable - and attractive - the owner was, then learned first-hand how straight-forward Sheryl was. She recalled the first time she saw them both. Sheryl's hair was longer back then and in cornrows. The forty-something mother of two had a way about her that captured even the most unsuspecting heart. Shorter than the owner by at least a foot, she packed a fierce bark through instant wit and rhetoric, yet still had the utmost respect for him. Sheryl kept him in line, like he was one of her kids. She used initiative when it was needed and carried out orders efficiently when it wasn't.

Catie hadn't even intended to eat or drink anything, she was only there to find a job but somehow had her mind changed through a two-pronged attack from them both. Between laughter, food, and a rundown of the role, she had been interviewed and the atmosphere hadn't changed from that moment.

This one had vending machines with toys and candy stood at the front near the door hoping to catch eager young eyes with their multi-colored temptations. They would interest the children who visited their grandparents next door. Easy money. Boston's banking district didn't call for quarter-dollar candy or plastic toys at their diners because customers were more interested in financial meetings and adult conversations. Buying home-cooked wholesome food and seeing the chef/owner carving up meatloaf and roast beef, chicken, and pork in front of them was part of the draw.

Between the vending machines was a Christmas tree that had probably been displayed more times than it ought to have with its dusty plastic pine needles that might have passed for Halloween webbing a couple months before.

Ninety minutes outside of downtown Boston the air felt cleaner, even if it wasn't. It was psychological but it allowed Catie to think with ease. The booth's picture window said the sky was about to drop its snow, if not today then tonight. The day was gray and cheerless but out here it felt less frantic and frenetic and certainly less dramatic.

Comfort food was the answer to Catie's prayers. She stayed for an hour, enjoying coffee afterwards then heading across the street. Surrounding the care home were blossom trees that gave way to green leaves in the summer. Now their outstretched arms were bare as if offering a hug that might break them. Soon, nature's rhythm would see buds re-appear and birds singing a rainbow of colourful songs.

David Cambridge had chosen the care home alone. The speed of city life had gotten too much. Being a pragmatic man, he had already done his research. He didn't want one too expensive, nor too cheap. Cheap meant he could be overlooked and expensive meant he could be made a fool of every time rent was due. He narrowed his choices and discussed both with Catie, reminding her the final choice was his to make and, no matter what, she wasn't to be upset. But, of course, she was. While he expected her to live her life as she saw fit, he stipulated that she visited once a month and if she couldn't, he wanted a phone call instead. It didn't sound like much to ask. Enjoying his right to live out his winter years how he saw fit, David took up residence in the farthest room from the entrance.

Catie rapped her knuckles against the wooden door, recalling the last time she visited. It was over a month ago. She'd made an excuse, opting to see Jack instead. As she waited for her dad to answer, an abundance of thoughts clouded her mind. What if visiting was the wrong decision? What if he judged her for being with Jack? What if Drew really was the right one for her? If she did leave Boston, what if her dad got ill? What if Jack wanted her back?

"Come in," his familiar voice called back breaking her thoughts.

He sounded shaky, fragile, and weak. She didn't like the idea of him getting older. He had always been a quiet man, and proud. Getting older meant he might fade away too quickly. She wasn't ready for him to go anywhere yet. She pushed open the door and saw him gather himself and stand to his feet, catching hold of the chair arm to steady his frame.

The room was tastefully decorated with a bed, a side table, two arm-chairs and a table large enough for a tray. A narrow desk at the wall doubled as a writing place so he could correspond with his daughter between visits. The buttermilk and china blue floral wallpaper gave a homely feel but, in winter months, yielded coolness. Orange and yellow autumnal-themed silk flowers tried hard to bring warmth into the room, but it was a big job for such a small arrangement.

"Catie-girl, is that you?" He smiled which lit up his face and, somehow, illuminated the room. No matter what happened in life, so long as she had her father around, life would be good. He flung out his arms and ushered her to him enveloping her inside his protective hug. "Ah, my best girl. I wasn't expecting to see you today. Did I get the date wrong? Did I lose track?"

"No, Daddy, I didn't know I was coming. It was a last-minute thing. I should have called." She breathed him in noticing the after shave he wore when she was young. Old Spice reminded her of the cinnamon rolls she made when he came home from work. It was a fragrance that screamed nostalgia, sentiment, and home. Safety. Protection. All the things he meant to her.

"Aren't you working today? Come here, sit down. Tell me what's been going on in your world. Are you crying? Oh Catie, what's happened?" He wrapped his arms around her again, holding her to his thin, bony chest. There used to be more muscle and now there was a lot less to hug. "My little girl, what's going on? This ain't like you." He pulled her away to study her face then pulled her back to his chest again. "If someone's made you cry, they're gonna have to deal with me, y'know. I'll take 'em to one side and beat 'em to a pulp if I catch 'em." Feeling bones beneath his clothes made fighting seem both foolhardy and redundant.

"There's a lot going on," she said. "I don't even know where to start."

He let her go, sat her down on the chair opposite his, and gave her a tissue. "You wipe those silly tears away and start from the beginning. We'll get some hot chocolate just like we used to after school, remember?"

She nodded and, taking a deep breath, tried to compose herself. "I should have brought you a gift."

"You're the gift!" he said emphatically. "Just look at you." He buzzed the intercom and asked for two mugs of hot chocolate. "Do you want some candy? Cookies?"

"I'm not hungry Dad. I came here because I just don't know which way is up anymore."

Moments later, the nurse brought in a tray with two mugs on top. She put down the tray on the table between them and left with a smile.

"See?" he said, pushing one mug nearer Catie. "Anything I want."

"I'm glad you like it here. It suits you."

"Oh, I don't need much. But what I do need, I've got. So," he patted her arm then replaced his hands over his leg, its thinness evident under his baggy gray trousers. "Tell me what's happened to make my little girl need her Daddy so much?"

"I broke up with my boyfriend, Jack." As she said the words, she realised how easily they fell from her lips. It felt like history now, and not current news. "He was married," she nodded, "I didn't know."

David looked at her eye-to-eye. "You didn't know? Or you didn't *want* to know?"

"I'm not *her*, Dad. I've never been her."

"You're still carrying that, huh? She did what she needed to do for herself. We all have to. But we'll come back to that. Tell me about this break-up."

"He said his wife found out and we had to finish. He called me at work. I collapsed and took a whole load of dishes with me." She gestured to her forehead and the scratches.

"You oughtta get your head looked at, Catie-girl."

"Because he was married?"

"Because it was a bang to your head." He laughed. "That's guilt talking, I'm telling you. But you're right, you should see a shrink. They'll take care of you."

"My boss said I should've gone to the ER too."

"And did you?" He watched her shake her head. "Catie-girl, you gotta take better care of yourself. I'm not gonna be around forever."

"Yes, you are. Don't talk like that. Anyway, I'm fine. It's just a few scratches."

"So, you broke up?" He shrugged, paused, imagining her next step. "You gotta get back on the saddle. Find a good man who'll take care of you."

"It's not that easy. I loved him."

"It sounds like it wasn't meant to be. Not if he already had someone. Sounds like he was only sticking around for one thing."

"But I was picking out kids' names."

"You can pick out names all you like but a man like that won't stick around long enough to help you raise 'em."

"I'm not gonna be young forever, Dad. Time's running out."

"Ah," he dismissed her comments. "You've got years yet. So, you're set on little kids running about, are you?"

"Yeah. I want a whole bunch. That's what it's all about. Family time. Play dates."

"You're still searching for that, are ya?" He shrugged. "It ain't like that for everyone. It wasn't like that for us. Sometimes you've gotta take what life dishes out and be happy with it." He fell silent as his mind took him back to the days of raising a little girl alone. A smile drifted across his lips and a murmur escaped his throat as though he laughed but not quite. "We made it work though, didn't we? We had some great times. Anyway, I don't imagine this man you broke up with was the right fit. And if I know you, Catie-girl, the right one is probably right under your nose and you're not even seeing it. That's what I think."

She gasped. "That's incredible you should say that."

He gave her a knowing smile. "There, you see? Got someone else lined up already, have you? Wouldn't surprise me, pretty thing like you."

"Maybe? I'm not sure exactly. It's a long story."

"Talk to me, Catie-girl. I've got no plans today as you can plainly see. But I do have two arms to hold you and two ears to hear you. Speak to me, girl."

"Well," she began.

"He ain't married," he interrupted instantly. "Is he?"

She shook her head. As she thought of Drew, she remembered that cute smile he gave her just before she got into the cab after the incident in the kitchen. When she considered Jack against Drew, there was no comparison in the way each man treated her.

"Handsome? Strong?" he asked.

She nodded. "He knows what he wants in life. He's the kind of guy a girl could take home to meet mom and dad."

"Reliable?"

"Yes."

"Won't mess you around?"

"No. And he always has time for me. He's got a great smile. Mischievous." It was the kind of smile that reminded her of schooldays when innocent crushes meant everything and nothing. That was Drew Denby. Perfect husband material. Perfect father material too, she thought. Why hadn't she seen it before? Had circumstances been entirely different, Catie could imagine herself with a man like him.

After the accident, the way he tended to her injuries and cared for her opened her eyes. He joked all the time with both her and Sheryl at work. They were always laughing. It was a big part of the job. That was how she took the sudden attention, not because he was in love with her or because he cared, but because Drew was always bright and upbeat. She'd been caught unawares when he expressed his true feelings. Maybe this new information had come at the right time?

"Got a job? David asked.

"He's my boss. He owns the diner."

"Sounds like he likes you."

"He already told me he does," she nodded confidently.

"Well, that's a big step in the right direction. So what exactly are you waiting for? A neon sign? Why are you lacking the smarts to see this man as a boyfriend? It sounds like it's being laid out on the ground for you but you just ain't looking. Wake up, Catie-girl."

"Can it be just that easy though?" She had never dated a guy like Drew before. Every boy she'd been with had made something difficult for her, whether it was their thoughts on what they wanted her to look like, how she dressed, decisions on sex, her lifestyle, everything. It was like she'd been a magnet for difficult men. Maybe that's why she had become a people-pleaser? It had happened so often that she didn't know anything else. Love was difficult. It just was. Wasn't that why her mom left?

"Why not?" David said with a shrug. "I don't reckon most folks wait around for a sign or permission or approval. Most folks realise life'll pass 'em by if they don't act on it. If this man is making it so easy to like him because he likes you, you gotta act on it."

"But it's so soon after my break-up."

"Okay, listen to me. Tell me how you feel about this man."

"He's real nice, Daddy."

"And how would you feel if some other woman walked in and they stepped out together. How would you feel then? Fine? A little jealous? Mad, even? What if you saw 'em kissing?"

Catie's stomach wrenched, and she winced. "Yeah, that'd be tough."

"Well, don't let that happen. Tell him how you feel."

"What if people talk about me? I've literally just broken up with Jack."

"The married one? Well, this might smart a little but dating a married man will've got lips flapping already. At least this one is single. No-one can say anything about that."

Her father made a good point. For the first time in a long time, Catie felt the corners of her mouth turn up and her skin stretch across her cheeks. She'd almost forgotten what smiling felt like.

"And it's just that easy?" she laughed. "I didn't know it could be."

"Love is incredibly easy when it's meant to be."

"I'm so glad I came to see you today. I couldn't see straight and now I feel so much better."

"What are Daddies for if not to make their little girls smile?"

She leaned in and kissed his cheek. "I love you, Dad."

"And I love you too, Catie-girl, ever since the first moment I set eyes on you."

"There's something else though."

"Go on."

"With the break-up, I couldn't think straight. I resigned. I told Drew I was leaving."

"Well, that's easy. You go right back there and tell him you made a mistake and you want your job back. Sounds like he wouldn't want you to go anyways." He paused and looked her in the eyes. "Unless you wanna leave town of course."

"I thought I did. I thought it would help me think clearly."

"Ain't we just done that?"

"But if I stay, what if I run into Jack?"

"Then he'll see what a jerk he was messing around behind his wife's back. But running away won't help you anyway. Setting up, finding a place to live, a new job, it'll all take a while, Catie. Doing that 'cause you wanna relocate is one thing, but doing it 'cause you're running away from some guy who already has his life sorted out is another. But," he added, trying his hardest to give her a balanced view. "You gotta do what's right for you. I can give you all kinds of advice 'cause it ain't me doing it. It's you. It's your life Catie-girl. I will say one thing though. If you do leave Boston, you ain't gonna get back easy to visit. That's plain as day. But I don't want you to ever worry about me. I've had my life. It's time for you to focus on yourself."

"You spent all those years doing right by me." The practicalities of leaving her dad in his final years made her realise even more how important he was. "What was I thinking? There I was considering leaving you. *Abandoning* you," she emphasised. "Like *she* did to us."

He smiled sympathetically. "You mustn't think of it like that. It's a completely different situation."

"How else can I think of it? It's already bad enough it takes me hours to get here. If I left Boston, who knows when I'd get a chance to come back?"

"Well, it wouldn't hurt you to pick up a telephone once in a while. I hear they have 'em in the city. Or you could write me a letter. You remember how to put pen to paper, don't ya?" he winked, but she could sense there was something serious about his question. "And anyway, I don't think you give me half the credit I deserve. I've been alone for a long time and it doesn't frighten me anymore. I have all I need in this room. I've got the paintings you did for me when you were in school. And I've got the letters you sent. I've got this beautiful view outside my window. I don't need much. I know you love me. We've had a wonderful life together. That's enough for me."

His words broke her heart. She watched his lips move and could barely allow the sound to reach her ears. If they did, she would have to register them and that was too hard.

"But it's not enough, Dad. It's not enough! It's never going to be enough."

"Listen, my girl. I might look like a helpless old man from where you're sitting, but I've achieved a lot in my life and most of that was before I met your mother. She was just part of my life, she wasn't all of it. You are. You and I did the best we could and I know you look at me and see a sorry old man, but you need to give me more credit than that. I raised you, I worked hard, I put food on the table and a roof over our heads. I wasn't fragile then and I'm not fragile now. It's not up to you to save me. I'm still your Daddy. It's up to me to save you. And I'm telling you if you need to move away, then you do it."

"What if it's a mistake?"

"You'll work it out. And while you're at it, you also need to forgive her. If you don't, it'll eat away at you inside. It ain't healthy, certainly not for someone your age. I forgave her," he shrugged. "I didn't do it gracefully, I grant you. I barely think about the bad times, I haven't for a long time. And hell, I chose this place, didn't I? I'm doing what I need to do for me, ain't I? I'm living my life by doing exactly what I want. It's beautiful here. In the summertime the fields are covered with flowers and in the winter, well, you look out there. Tell me what you see?"

"It's cold. It's bleak. The leaves have gone. The birds have flown away. It's not great, Dad."

He laughed. "You're not in a great head space right now, Catie-girl. That man Jack took away your love of life. What I see out there is nature. I breathe in the air and I look up to the sky. I think you need to remember what that feels like. I think you've forgotten how to smell the roses."

It felt like some time since she'd been close to nature. Her whole focus had been on watching her body-clock tick away, grabbing the first man who had shown any interest and gone full force into a crazily intense relationship filled with lies and lust. But not love. It had been spontaneous and sexy but, now she thought about it, exactly how healthy had it been?

"You forgave Mom?" her small voice was almost lost in her throat.

"Not long afterwards to be truthful. I saw how it affected you and knew that my own anger wasn't good for a little girl to live with, so I moved on."

"But you never dated anyone else."

"I never felt the urge. What would dating have given me? Someone else to think about? I had you to think about, I didn't need someone else. She was great before she got itchy feet. A completely different woman. Then she hit a tricky age that didn't sit well with her at all. Vanity was probably some of the problem, a wrinkle here, an ache there. But what you've got to do is embrace all that, not fight it. She couldn't handle getting older. Being with a younger man made her feel youthful, I guess."

Catie wondered if that's what she was feeling. Thirty-one and counting. "But you were so broken when she left."

"'Course I was. She was my wife and your mother. But she was like a butterfly, and you can't trap a butterfly. It's gotta fly free. They don't get a lotta time, so they gotta live their lives their way."

"How can you be so forgiving? She ruined our lives."

"Don't be so dramatic," he said, firmly. "She did nothing of the sort. Believing that makes us victims and we ain't victims at all. We never were. Think of it as a puzzle. We were all puzzle pieces fitting together. All she did was leave a void, an empty space. We filled it with bits of ourselves. Whatever space she created, we filled. I became your mother and father and, looking at you now, girl, I think I did a damn good job too. If she hadn't left us, we might never have become so close. When you think about it, she actually did us a favor. 'Sides, I heard on the grapevine the young man she left us for left her. They never stayed together longer than a couple years."

Catie was stunned. That piece of information was the last thing she ever imagined she'd hear.

"When did you hear that?"

"Over the years you hear stuff. Thought you knew. Anyways, I'm sorry you've been carrying the weight of it with you all this time. That's completely unnecessary. It's taught us both lessons though, and that's the part you gotta be proud about. Learning from those lessons."

His words hit her several times over. *It taught us both lessons*. Yes, it had.

Before she left, she told him she'd see him at Christmas as planned and they would open their presents together, just like they always did. The hug they shared stayed with her for the journey home. His words too. She repeated them until they repeated themselves. She felt the clearest she had in days.

She decided she would talk to Drew first thing. She wasn't going to leave Boston, in fact, she wasn't going to leave the diner. Her dad was right, she couldn't just up and walk out of her job, aside from anything else she still needed an income. She would sleep on it all, but as things stood right now, Catie could see a brighter future. The idea of it even sparked the tiniest bit of excitement in her tummy.

Finally, back inside her apartment, she barely took off her coat when there was a knock at the door. As she opened it, Jack Sullivan stared back.

Chapter Fifteen

Ben had expected to return to his studio within a few hours when he left to deliver the artwork. Now it looked like it would be days - or longer - until he could get back there. Had he turned off his lights? Had he locked his doors? There was no good time of year to be in hospital and the approach to Christmas was probably one of the worst. With commissions needing attention, quotes to go out, and still the angel to deliver, his mind was filled with worry.

Breaking him from his thoughts, two police officers approached the nurse's station. He saw them in his peripheral vision: a shorter woman and a taller man. They both pointed at him adding a blatant over-the-shoulder look. The grouchy nurse pointed towards Ben, confirming to him they were there for the interview. They approached in a kind of slow motion, neither one of them taking their eyes from him. The female officer took out her notebook and pen while the man spoke.

"Good morning, Mister Christopher," he said. "This is PC Kent and I'm PC Wilson.

"Morning." He smiled, smoothing down the pyjama shirt the nurses provided.

"How are you feeling?"

"Very well, thank you." He wondered if it was a trick question. Having never been interviewed by the police before, he worried his memory would be unreliable for their records. His nightmares hadn't helped, and it all seemed like a blur. Each time he tried to wake himself to avoid reliving the trauma and if that didn't work, he was trapped with the terror.

"Really? You don't look it." She followed the shape his body made under the white sheets, down to his toes and back up to his face. "You've really been through it, haven't you?"

"It was quite a surprise when I woke up here."

"A surprise?" she said. "A shock would be a better word, wouldn't it?"

He agreed as if being reprimanded for his choice of words. Seeing PC Kent already making notes gave it all a feeling of permanence. Knowing they were focusing on every single thing he said and did was killing him inside. "Sorry, I'm a bit nervous. I'm not used to this sort of thing." He tried to stop talking but his lips wouldn't comply. "I suppose I just feel naturally guilty."

"Interesting," PC Kent said. "Why's that then?"

His eyes widened as all attention was on him. "No, I mean...I'm not saying I'm guilty of anything. I just mean..."

"I would have thought being nervous was the least of your problems by the look of your injuries," PC Wilson cut in. His voice was deep and reassuring, but his presence cast doubt. "We just have a few questions. It's just a formality. Do you feel up to talking, Mr Christopher?"

He nodded with a mixture of wanting to be helpful and a sense of reluctance.

"What were you were doing on the day of the accident?" PC Wilson asked, then immediately clarified. "Beforehand. Set the scene for us."

"I was wrapping up a commission for a client. I'm an artist."

"What was it?"

"A sculpture. An angel. Almost four feet tall. It was a hefty piece. I was covering it in wrap and fabric and was packing it in the back of my car. I was about to deliver it."

"Who was it for?"

"Bridgit Blake, a solicitor in Saint Weatherby. She doesn't know about the accident. I think my phone is still in the car and there's no way I can tell her what happened." He had a memory of the roof being peeled off but couldn't instantly recall if that was just a dream. "Is there any way I can get hold of it? The artwork and the phone. Can someone do that?"

"Let's focus on one thing at a time." PC Kent said. "The car is being investigated in our pound. I'll find out about the phone though."

"And the artwork?" His question went unanswered.

"What was the weather like?"

"Wet. Dull. It'd been raining all morning."

"Was it raining when you left?"

"Drips here and there," he shrugged then winced. He recalled walking through a puddle and soaking his high tops. "It was wet though, definitely wet. There were puddles outside my studio."

"How long were you driving before the accident happened?"

"I don't really remember. Maybe ten, fifteen minutes? There was a lot to focus on. Potholes, winding lanes, you can imagine.

One bump and three months of work could be right down the drain."

"So, you were concerned with the artwork?"

"Yes, of course. I had to be careful."

"Was it standing up or lying down?"

"Lying down and lodged in place. But that doesn't mean it wouldn't have moved. These things have a habit of shifting once you get on the road. It was a worry." He thought about how he had set it in place. He remembered he'd been thinking about the solicitor's reaction if she would be happy or disappointed with the piece. Between that, the sculpture itself, and the weather, maybe his mind had been elsewhere. Maybe it had made a difference to his driving? "As it turns out I must've hit just about every single pothole anyway. They startled me. I was just worried about damaging the sculpture."

"How would you describe being startled?"

"I kept looking at it."

"In the mirror or over your shoulder?"

"Both, actually," he nodded.

"Would you say your concentration was elsewhere?"

He had volunteered the information. He couldn't take it back. He nodded, embarrassed. "A few times, I suppose. Yes."

"What was your recollection of the incident?" Wilson asked.

Ben inhaled and allowed the exhale to come while he took his mind back. He didn't want to relive the incident, nor did he want to say anything that could make things worse for the woman or himself. Knowing PC Kent was about to write everything he said like it was being set in stone worried him more.

"Take your time," PC Kent said. "We appreciate you've had a traumatic experience."

"It just appeared. Then it hit me. It happened so quickly."

"It hit you? Are you sure of that?"

He nodded. "Yes. It was a blind bend and there it was, a bright red sports car. A BMW, I think. It was on my side."

"You *think* it was over the lines? Or are you sure?"

"I'm sure…no, um, I think…umm…"

"Had you been drinking?"

"No, of course not."

"How about the night before?"

He shook his head. "I'd been working all through the night and finished about two in the morning. I went to bed, I got up and went straight into the studio to pack up. I hadn't even eaten breakfast."

"Could you have been tired?"

He shook his head. "I'd slept okay. I was fine. A bit nervous of handing it over. You never know for sure how they're going to react. If it's how they wanted it, if your interpretation is spot on. That kind of thing."

"So, nervous then?" Wilson repeated.

"A bit, yeah."

"When did you first see the other car?" PC Kent asked.

"Like I said, as I turned into the bend it was already there."

"Was it a left-hand bend or a right-hand bend?"

"Left."

"Do you recall how it was being driven?"

"I didn't see it do much driving. I mean, it was moving. It wasn't parked or anything. I went into the bend and it was there," he said, unsure how else he could say the same thing. "Right there in front of me. One second I was driving and the next a great force hit me. There was no time to react. There was glass all over me and I couldn't move my legs. I could hardly breathe. I had glass in my hair and in my mouth. I remember feeling the air on my face and it was then that I realised the windscreen had gone." He closed his eyes trying to recall but feeling his heartbeat quicken. Having to relive on his own terms was one thing but this felt forced, for their benefit. With closed eyes, he saw the woman's face. Terror filled her eyes, and it tore his heart to shreds. If only he could have helped her, called the ambulance sooner, it might have stopped the coma she'd entered. "It might've gone out of control."

"Did it seem out of control?"

"I don't think it was the driver's fault."

"That's not what I asked," PC Wilson said.

PC Kent looked quizzical. "That's an interesting turn of phrase, Mr Christopher. Why would you say that?"

Ben felt like a deer in headlights. What had he said? He recalled his words and tried to act relaxed. "I just mean that she looked like the kind of person who would be in control if she was driving."

"She *was* driving. And she drove into you."

Stress filled him with what felt like a relentless cross-examination. Questions came thick and fast.

"But my car is old. It's a work horse. A wreck really. It's slow. And maybe my reflexes weren't as quick as they could've been. I was probably more focused on keeping the sculpture in one piece and avoiding the potholes. And I had an appointment to keep. And it was raining."

"It was raining then?"

"Um…yes. Actually, maybe it was." He was landing himself deeper and deeper into trouble, he knew it. It wouldn't surprise him if they slapped cuffs on him there and then. Careless driving? Reckless driving? Driving without due care and attention? Any one of those would fit. Had he caused the accident by not paying attention? If so, he had put her into a coma. No, he reminded himself. She was on his side. She was in front of him. She had definitely crossed the lines. If only he hadn't left the studio when he did. If only he'd left an hour earlier or an hour later, or another day altogether. Not at all.

"You just said that *she* looked like the kind of person who would be in control. Did you see the other driver's face?"

"Yes," he said, emphatically. "I did." Of this he had no doubt. He had been having constant flashbacks to her face every time he closed his eyes. "I'll never forget it. She was perfect, like a doll. She was about my age with long, red hair. We stared at each other for a split second, but it felt like forever. I could see the fear in her eyes, like she knew what was about to happen and there was nothing either of us could do to stop it. It scared her as much as it scared me. And a moment later, she looked…dead. I tried to call out to her, but I couldn't catch my breath." There was a crack in his voice, his cheeks reddened, and his eyes became glassy. "I've been trying to find out what happened to her but nobody will tell me. It's a horrible feeling not knowing, do you realise that? It's torture. I tried to call out to her. I did, I really tried. I'll never forget her face. It'll stay with me for the rest of my life." He tried to hold on to his tears for as long as possible, but he had no choice to let them fall.

PC Kent leaned forwards with a tissue. "Mr Christopher, if there had been any fatalities, this investigation would have taken a very different tack. Nobody died. We suspect alcohol was involved thought."

"Alcohol?" He stared the officers one by one. "She was drunk?" He hadn't considered that. She looked terrified, not drunk. "No, she was alert." Now he was conflicted. Could her drinking have caused his injuries? But the poor woman was in a coma. *She came out of it much worse than me. Surely that's punishment enough?* The idea that she was drinking and driving made him feel like every word he had told the police could land her in even more trouble. His internal conflict tortured him. *Was she over the limit? Was it a bottle or a sip? Was it a low reading?* There were a ton of variables to consider. According to Margaret, the woman was a famous author. Whether the drinking was deliberate or not, that could be the end of her career if the press found out. No, he told himself, she didn't do it deliberately.

"Not drunk, sir. Been drinking." Kent said. "There's a difference."

If looks were anything to go by, in that split second they locked eyes, he saw a frightened woman and nothing else. And worse still he couldn't protect her.

"You said you called to her. Did she speak to you?"

He shook his head. "I said I tried to call out. I couldn't." He palmed his chest. "My voice wouldn't carry. I was in so much pain, I didn't dare breathe harder to shout. I wanted to let her know I was trying to get help but I couldn't breathe." He wiped his eyes with the back of his hands and sniffed. "She didn't even move and then I blacked out. I wish I could have done more to help her. What's going to happen now?"

"Providing she recovers, she'll probably be prosecuted. Considering what you've been through, you'll probably want a slice of that. Right now, we're just gathering all the facts and appealing for witnesses."

A slice of that... That seemed sly. Sure, he was in a hospital bed recovering from injuries she caused, but he wasn't vindictive. He didn't want revenge. He only wanted to know she was going to come out of her coma. That was more important to him than anything, even the artwork. "It was an accident. She didn't set out to hurt me. She doesn't even know me." He didn't expect to sound angry. "And there was nobody else around. It was just the two of us."

"You said you blacked out, Mister Christopher," Wilson said. "Anyone might have seen you."

"She was drinking, and she was driving," Kent reminded him. "It's a very serious aspect of this case. You could have been killed."

"So could she."

PC Wilson nodded. "Yes, that's right. Okay, it's possible we may have a few more questions in the next couple of days, so we may see you again."

"I don't think I'll be going anywhere." Frustrated as they left, he couldn't help feeling he had made matters much worse. He let out a deep sigh trying to remove the interview from his mind. Exhausted, he finally fell asleep.

He was at the movies, at a cinema he didn't recognise but whose seats were swathed in red velvet. A crimson curtain, as tall as it was wide, covered the gigantic screen in front of him…them. Ben was sitting next to a woman. The pair of them were the only people in the whole room seated in the centre of the row and in the centre of the auditorium. He sensed she was beautiful both inside and out, but he couldn't turn to see. He looked down noticing he was strapped into the seat as though secured in a car.

The curtains glided open, slowly but deliberately, until they gathered in neat pleats framing the screen. Music played. It was classical, the kind that played in high-end hotel foyers where someone would be on hand to take your luggage to your room.

As the curtains collected at the sides, Ben focused on the screen. It was as if the experience was all about the screen and him rather than him and the woman. Upon the screen came a woman's face and the music stopped. Her head and shoulders filled the screen. She was in a deep sleep with no REM movements beneath her eyelids. The lack of sound emphasised her slumber as though the film makers wanted Ben to feel the full depth of the sleep. Aside from the red of her hair, darker shadows appeared upon her skin as if the movie was in black and white. Then, raindrops began to fall in slow motion upon her face. But the droplets didn't burst into smaller ones when they landed, instead they remained solid like diamonds scratching and slicing her flesh, tearing her beautifully peaceful face to shreds. Skin that was so white was now shades of scarlet, crimson, ruby, and what was once a perfectly peaceful image was now horrific. Fleshy red muscle emerged until, finally, her eyes shot open and…

Ben screamed himself awake. Automatically he pushed away whatever secured him to the cinema chair but he felt nothing in waking life. He tried to sit up in his hospital bed but his chest reminded him why he was there. His eyes darted around taking in the clinical white and grey ward he'd been in for the past few days, realising that the noise filling his ears was from his own throat. He stopped as it echoed around the ward. Disapproving groans from his ward-mates added to the chorus.

Breathing heavily, in quick gasps, he attracted the attention of the tall, thin nurse. Her elongated neck gave an alien quality to her presence. Large pale blue eyes made her white-grey hair look even more insipid. Even her lips didn't add colour to her complexion. She looked like a black and white sketch personified. There was something sinister about her colourless face, as if she had been dug up from a fresh grave.

"Finally awake then?" she sounded inconvenienced. Her voice was hoarse like she had swallowed gravel or smoked her whole life.

Ben composed himself. Carefully, so as not to upset his bruised chest and throat even more, he wiped away a covering of sweat from his forehead, pushing his dark curls from his face.

"It was a really horrible dream." He remembered it vividly. It was mostly about colour. And horror. And it was the woman from the crash, he knew that now. He knew brains had a strange way of distorting and intensifying memories, but this dream had been so realistic. It made him wonder if he ever wanted to go back to sleep again if that was going to be waiting there for him.

The nurse had brought a tray. He guessed it was lunch.

"What time is it?"

"Keeping you, are we? Got to be somewhere else, have you?" she barked, laying the tray by his side on the table. "No, because you're in here. You should be more grateful."

It sounded like she was taking joy in his dependency. He wanted to ask why she was so rude but didn't have the energy to receive the answer. He was all for politeness, even when pushed, but this nurse seemed like she was goading him. The longer he was there, the ruder she was. Nurses were meant to be caring but this one must have missed that class. He hadn't seen her tend to other patients so didn't know if it was just her way or if she had a problem with him.

"Seven-thirty!" She barked.

"It's dinner then? Not lunch."

"You slept all day."

"I did?" He was surprised. It had felt like minutes, not hours. He looked at the food realising he was, indeed, hungry. He needed the toilet too, but he didn't want her to help so he kept quiet. He could hold it a bit longer. "Thank you. By the way, is Margaret on duty at all today?"

She stood still at the end of his bed. She looked as if she was going to answer him but picked up his chart instead. She studied it and put it back down. "You asked me about a Margaret before? We have no Margaret on staff. I put it down to the condition you were in when you came in."

"I believe she's an agency nurse," he said, slightly nervous that she was going to bite his head off again.

"I said there's no Margaret. This could be down to the medication. Hallucinations. I'll talk to the doctor if you carry on like that. She'll reduce your meds and your pain will increase. See how you like that. Eat your dinner."

Talking to the doctor sounded like a threat rather than a recommendation, he thought. Hallucinations? There was no way Margaret was a hallucination. She was as real as anyone he had seen, nurses, doctors, police officers. He kept quiet and worked his way through dinner. There was nothing to be thrilled about on that tray but he was thankful for it all the same.

He longed to get out of hospital so at least he could prepare himself a decent meal. Once he finished, he settled back down staring up at the ceiling. Ten-inch square tiles with a design of wriggling tiny black worms. The curtain wasn't much better.

"Morning, lovely!" a beaming smiled appeared above his face.

"Margaret!" his whole spirit lifted as he focused directly on her. She looked at the notes hanging there. "Thank goodness you're here. I'm so pleased to see you. Listen, I asked the other nurse about you and they don't even know you exist. They think I'm hallucinating."

She dismissed his question with a wave of her hand. It reminded him of how a mother responds to a child's mention of bullies at school and to just 'ignore then'. "They sometimes send someone from the other team to balance things out," she said, too cryptically for Ben.

"What other team?"

"Agency," she said again as if that was the answer to all his curious questions. "And you're not hallucinating. I'm definitely here." She crossed something out on the notes and added something else. It looked like she was annotating it.

"How do you know?"

"Do I look like an hallucination to you?" she asked, wide eyed, and slightly confrontational. She didn't wait for a response. "Your meds are fine too. Everything's just as it should be. I'm making sure of that." She put down the notes and focused on Ben. "Anyway, it's gift time!" She delved into her tight uniform pocket placed something small on his bed covers.

"My phone!" he cried. "You got my phone back. Margaret, you're an absolute angel! Where was it, the police said they'd try to find it, but…"

"I just picked it up from the nurse's station when I came on shift."

He switched it on hoping for a multitude of notifications, but the screen didn't illuminate. "Unbelievable. He giveth and he taketh away," he said to himself.

Margaret laughed. "Oh, my lovely, you have no idea!"

"You wouldn't happen to know if there's a charger knocking around somewhere, would you? It's out of juice."

"I'll do my best to find out for you." She took his tray as she hurried off. Ten minutes passed and the grouchy nurse returned. Ben hid his phone under the cover.

"Finished then? I suppose you're ready for the painkillers now?"

"I'm managing it a bit more. Comes and goes."

"Doctor now, are you?"

"No," he sighed. "I just meant…" She thrust them in his face and left before he swallowed them.

Before he realised it, he had drifted off. The same pale-faced, red-haired woman in the nightmare was back. Rain droplets manifested into diamonds and landed hard onto her flesh, ripping it apart, all in slow motion so he could see – analyse – every rip and tear close up. He forced his eyes open and saw Margaret staring at him. This time the familiar smile that usually covered her lips was nowhere to be seen. Instead compassion oozed from her every pore.

"My lovely, take a breath. It was just a dream. It's common after accidents like yours. You'll be fine. Give it time."

That was the kind of bed side manner skill set the other nurse could have learned from, he thought. Reassured by Margaret, he took a moment to settle his breathing.

"At least you've had another hour. I'm still looking for a charger, but this will keep you out of harm's way." From behind her back, she revealed a paperback book as she smiled mischievously. "And I've got an idea you're going to love. I'll tell you tomorrow."

Before Ben could respond, she was gone. But the book remained in his lap.

Chapter Sixteen

Becca floated far out at sea. The tiny rowing boat, big enough for just two people, was painted scarlet and bobbed upon the waves. The empty seat beside her overwhelmingly illustrated how alone she felt.

The ocean seemed to go on forever into the horizon, so much so she could barely comprehend its vastness. Then, without warning, or logic, night arrived far too quickly and stars overtook. Any sunshine that had existed was now lost and the boat bobbed without direction in darkness. It reminded her of when she was a child and she looked up into space. On a clear night the stars were endless. Now, the horizon was nothing more than a vague line between the dark blue of the water and the sky's indigo hues.

She was drifting, rudderless and oarless, for forevermore it seemed, floating whichever way the almost-breeze took her. Was someone or something with a more powerful sense of direction than her guiding the vessel? She hugged herself to keep out the chill, yet there was none but the expectation of it since the sunlight had vanished. The self-hug brought comfort and that was welcome. The moonlight cast a cool shaft of light onto the inside of the boat like it was caught in a stage spotlight.

The loneliness was overpowering. There was no warmth of an equal, no contemporary, no company to impart love or companionship. Company: the word drifted through Becca's mind. Another person's interpretation of it influenced her. Her mother. She used the word often. 'We're having company,' she'd say. 'Company's arrived.' Company brought with it warmth and laughter, a social event. Within this vessel, company was lacking just as it was missing within her life. She was as lonely as a boat on the sea.

Within the rowboat Becca noticed she was dressed as she would be for her job, but with the addition of a navy blue chiffon scarf around her neck. This wasn't her usual school attire, it was more like the one her mother wore. It felt tighter than it ought to be and its tightness increased. She sought the knot but found a double one where a single should have been. As the breeze took the boat further into a watery nowhere, her throat constricted as if the scarf itself was intent on strangling her to death. Choking, panic was close. A blast from a ship's horn broke her concentration. She jumped at the noise but as loud as it was, there was no ship.

She opened her eyes and saw her bedroom. Unusually grateful for its intrusion, it was the alarm clock that woke her. Any other day and she would have been spitting nails in its direction but today she felt relief. Unconsciously she felt the skin at her neck, ensuring nothing was twisted around it.

Seconds later, the previous day's events rushed back along with remnants of the dream, filling her mind to capacity. Thoughts of missing someone, her parents – although quite separately from the someone – her mother's scarf and her father's logical mind being sabotaged by panic. And then the intense feeling of loneliness swept through her entire being. Lilah. Becca wanted to sob, but she would not afford herself any more tears. Crying was not permitted. Yesterday she had outdone herself. Instead, she took a deep breath and let it out slowly, meditatively, trying not to allow sad thoughts to flood her mind any more than was absolutely necessary. She would deal with each priority at a time, logically. If her father was here, he would agree it was the most practical path to take. She remembered him saying emotions and tears were an inefficient use of time.

Skills like thinking logically and behaving practically were learned rather than Becca being born with them. Lilah had missed that memo. Emotions had become her bread and butter since her mind was constantly thinking up new stories, plots, and characters. Becca's career, like their father's, was guided away from emotion and planted directly into logic.

He had been a tutor, not for schools but universities, and had implanted that fondness to teach young minds in Becca's own head. Her mother, classically stylish with that infamous navy-blue chiffon scarf swathed around her neck, was his doting and supportive wife. When, later in life, she was asked why she always wore it to university functions and shopping trips alike, she said, 'to give people something else to look at - an older woman's craggy neck is not for anyone's eyes'. Their societal and fashion attitudes respectively were born from the late fifties and, while not always aligning with their daughters', were respected, nonetheless.

It took Becca a while to rid her mind of absent relatives. Instead she focused on the day ahead. First things first, she would go into school. Aside from wanting, needing, to show she was still capable even while enduring a cruel personal situation, she needed to focus on something other than her big sister.

After showering and having breakfast, Becca knew phoning Ruth Trent could not be avoided any longer. Then she would prepare class notes before driving to work. She craned her head to look outside at the December dreariness. She continued with her list as she sipped coffee: During lunch she would phone the ward for updates, after school she would spend some time with her sister. This was going to be her routine for the foreseeable future. Routine came into its own when life was upside down, so making plans was the best way to deal with it.

"Hurrah for Dad's practical-mindedness," she said dryly. "You can deal with this. Lilah's condition is out of your control. Lilah's condition is out of your control," then changing the mantra to one more personal, "Lilah's condition is out of *my* control." She repeated the affirmation aloud countless times until it was lodged inside her mind without the need for her voice to reinforce it.

Then, reluctantly, the moment came. She picked up her mobile phone and scrolled through until she found the number for the Ruth Trent Literary Agency. She tapped 'call' and waited, reminding herself that chances were Ruth wouldn't be in the office yet anyway. Becca could simply leave a message and move on with that list. That was until someone answered. The voice was familiar, but it wasn't Ruth.

"Good morning, Ruth Trent Literary Agency. Emma speaking. How may I help you?"

"Oh, Emma! I'd forgotten you worked there."

"Um, who's calling please?" Emma giggled.

"It's me. Becca McCallister."

"Miss McCallister!" Emma's sing-song voice filled the phone line with butterflies and unicorns, the anti-venom to Ruth's poison. "It's great to hear you. How are you?"

"Actually, I've got some really horrible news."

"Oh no, are you okay?"

"Yeah, it's not me. Is Ruth in?"

"She's just on her way. I can hear her walking up the stairs right now. Hold on a mo."

As Emma finished her sentence, Becca could hear Ruth walking into the office.

"Who is it?" Ruth barked.

"Becca McCallister. Lilah's sister."

"What does *she* want?" Ruth snatched the phone from Emma and Becca could feel the scowl coming down the phone at her. "Good morning, Miss McCallister. And what can I do for you?"

Becca swallowed hard. *Please don't make this a tough conversation. Please make Ruth be nice for once. Please.* "Hi Ruth. How are you?"

"I've just walked up two flights of stairs because the lift isn't working and I'm dying for a cigarette, but the law says I can't smoke in my own office which is utterly ridiculous. So that's how I am. How are you?"

"I'm fine thank you," she said as a throwaway comment. It was the kind of response that people said without thinking about how they really were, the kind of comment that gave the questioner what they wanted to hear rather than the truth. She paused, then said, "Actually, I'm not fine at all. I've got some horrid news."

"Oh," Ruth sounded concerned. The tone in her voice dropped in mood and pace. "What's that?"

"My sister." She didn't get much further before she felt something wet on her cheek. She wiped it away then more joined it. Realising what it was, she sniffed taking a tissue from her handbag and giving in to the tears. It was a detached, surreal feeling as though she was dabbing the tears from a student's face. She mopped them up before they became unmanageable.

"Go on," Ruth prompted.

"She's had an accident." She tried to hide further emotion. That wouldn't do, certainly in front of Ruth Trent. "It happened yesterday. A car accident. She's in the ICU in Holcroft. Ruth. She's in a coma." Becca could hear Ruth breathing, the loud, rattling sound of her smoker's lungs, but no words. "Are you there?"

"I am." Ruth sounded like she had been physically hurt. "I'm...so sorry. Is there anything I can do?"

Of course it took a near-death situation to make it happen, but it seemed absolutely possible that the woman was capable of being nice. That threw Becca.

"Um...I'm not exactly sure at the moment. As you might imagine, I'm still processing it all. It's not been twenty-four hours yet. I suppose I'm just telling you because, well, she won't be working today." She didn't know why she said those words, they just came out. It was as though she was ringing in for an absent student. "I'm sorry, Ruth. I suppose that was obvious. I'm a bit of a mess at the moment. I'm sure you understand."

"Completely. This is dreadful news, Rebecca. Delilah's a wonderful young woman. May I visit her?"

"Of course. The ICU have quite strict visiting hours so you should phone them first."

"Thank you. If you need anything, Rebecca, anything at all, please don't hesitate to get in touch. Your sister is very dear to us all in the business. Thank you for letting me know."

It wasn't until she thought about it, she realised she could have declined any visits from Ruth. Becca was Lilah's next of kin after all. Whatever she said, went. She could hardly take it back now by saying, 'No, Ruth, you're a horrible piece of work and I don't want you anywhere near my sister, thank you very much'. In a moment of vulnerable confusion, being polite and helpful had taken over. As the line fell silent, Becca recalled the conversation. Considering she cried, it had gone extremely well.

She cried again on the way to school, and in the car park but as soon as she was through the school doors, she decided she would be 'stoic and professional' personified. The short time she spent in the staff room to make a drink she was uninterrupted. Whether others knew about her situation or not, she didn't know and she didn't intend to volunteer the information anyway. She wasn't big on discussing her private life, that usually led to colleagues trying to set her up on romantic dates, something that hadn't happened, thankfully, in over a year. It was also not what she considered a teacher to be. Becca was there to teach students and guide them in their thinking, not to be a weepy wreck useful to nobody.

She found herself in her classroom, hung her coat on the rack, and set her bag down on the desk. She took a welcome sip from her coffee just as the rain pelted against the classroom window. As the rain's volume increased on the glass, she took out her paperwork and began looking through the day's lesson plan as the clock ticked nearer nine. Student by student began to appear through the doorway, each taking their seats. Some were constant chatter machines while others were utterly silent. Within a few minutes, the entire class was seated and ready for the morning register.

Becca called them in alphabetical order, awaiting each student to confirm their attendance. As she reached the end, a mobile phone sang out the electronic version of a pop song everyone in the class recognised. Thirty sets of eyes were wide with excitement and apprehension. The melody was thick in the air and gaining volume as it continued. Their collective gasp was audible as the pupils stared at their classmate not knowing whether to giggle, knowing that person was in trouble, or pretend it wasn't happening.

"All phones should be switched off during school time," Becca reprimanded. "Or left at home, which is what I'd prefer from my class," she added with an air of frustration. "You all know this. Whoever has that phone, switch it off, please. You know better than that."

"Sorry, Miss. I thought it was off." The guilty teen, rarely on teachers' radars for bad manners or poor behaviour, looked up with a mixture of shock and confusion planted across her young face. As she reached in her bag to turn it off, she briefly looked at the screen.

"It's a message."

"Turn it off. Now!"

"But Miss," she said, determined. "Oh my god, Miss? I've got to…"

"Hurry up, please," Becca said. "We're all waiting for you so we can begin. You're holding everyone up."

She held up her phone as if Becca could see the message from the back of the classroom. "I've got a message."

"And you can look at it at break time. Put the phone away now." The emphasis on the final word came out angrier than she had intended. "I'm very disappointed in you."

"It's about your sister," she announced outright, then read from the screen. "Your teacher's famous sister is in hospital. It's on the news." Her classmates collectively gasped again as though they were auditioning for the school's Christmas panto.

Becca's heart stopped and shock filled her stomach. It churned as though she would vomit. "What?"

The girl's expression grew from shock and confusion to sadness and horror. "She's in hospital. It's on the news. Did you know?"

Another pupil asked, "Is it true, Miss? She's a writer, isn't she?"

"She's famous," another said. "It might be true. Was she in an accident, Miss?"

And from another, "What happened? Is she going to die?"

Within seconds, the concern, the juvenile banter, the giggles, the shock, and the cacophony of noise filled the classroom to its brim. And once more within the space of a few hours, Becca McCallister was unable to stop the tears from falling. She covered her face while the cacophony surrounded her. Each child stared having never seen a teacher cry before, and certainly not Miss McCallister. Slowly the noise ceased.

Confusion and compassion filled the classroom until one student left the class to inform the school office and another teacher took over the class. It was almost lunch time when she left Paul's office. Her eyes were almost as red as her hair while her face was as pale as a sheet of paper. The box of tissues on his desk were now empty.

"I'm so embarrassed," she said as she stood at the door.

"You needn't be. It's a shocking situation," he said. "I wish you'd listened to me yesterday when I told you to stay off. You should take all the time you need. And if I see you on school premises, I'll just send you back home again," he told her gently but meaning every word. "This isn't something you can put to one side, Becca. It's close to home and needs processing properly. You're just going to have to do that. You wouldn't expect one of your kids to come back in straight away with something like this going on, would you? So why's it okay for you to do?"

She shook her head. Paul sounded like her dad. Their ages were a decade apart, but their attitudes came from the same place.

"Come on, Becca, you know better than that. Give yourself time. You're allowed to be emotional with this one," he said. "Sit in front of the TV with a bucket of chicken or a box of chocolates. I don't know, neck a bottle of wine. Just give yourself time."

"I just feel so useless at home. At least at work I've got something to focus on."

"Come in next week. The Christmas concert will be on by then. It'll be a social event, everyone will be in high spirits. It'll be better than focussing on work, okay?"

"A week? It seems like such a long time to be away from the kids. It's an important time of year, Paul."

"If I'm really not getting through to you, look at it this way. Christmas is about family, isn't it? Isn't that what we teach the kids? Focus on your family. We've got everything covered here. Get some rest."

"I'm sorry the kids know," Becca sighed. "It'll feed the gossips at the school gate."

The receptionist smiled. "It's a plus point really. Since it's on the news, everyone will already know. You know, so you don't have people gossiping about why you're off."

"I cannot imagine how the news got hold of it," Becca shrugged. "Maybe the hospital? Maybe they talk to the press when someone's a bit famous?"

"I wouldn't worry about them or the school gate brigade, Becca. Just get yourself home or to the hospital and be with your sister. Everything will fall into place. You'll see."

Becca left afterwards. She drove back home feeling empty and emotionally lost. She changed her clothes and stepped into her jeans and a fluffy pink jumper. Getting out of work gear gave her a sense of time-off. She took the opportunity to phone the hospital to get an update on her Lilah's condition. So far there was no change, but they were hopeful, the nurse told her. It made her feel a little brighter, as though there was some light at the end of this unexpectedly dark tunnel.

She forced herself to eat some lunch and was surprised that she ate every bit. While she did, she checked her phone for the latest local news. Sure enough, the news item the student had mentioned was there in black and white. Delilah McCallister's name was the headline. So much for keeping things low-key, she thought. She glossed over the words 'an unknown source' and finished reading.

It wasn't the first time she had seen her sister's name in the tabloids, but it was the first time she read about her like this.

Chapter Seventeen

"Catie," Jack grinned.

His five feet ten frame filled her view. In heels, her height matched his which made kissing on the dance floor perfect and snuggling in the street adorable. When dressed up and out they resembled a couple of A listers.

Jack had everything, great job, popularity, was polished with perfect white teeth, a strong jawbone, and a smile that could have been his ticket to a modelling career. He even had great style with clothes. He knew how to wear a winter coat and scarf as well as a shirt and tie.

The only thing he lacked, Catie had recently discovered, was morals.

"Jack." Her heart pounded at the sight of him. His brown eyes seemed huge and those long eyelashes – unusual on a man, but notable – framed them perfectly. The whole package had bewitched her from day one.

"Wow, you look incredible. Can I come in?" Without waiting for an answer, he strode across the hardwood flooring and stopped at the sofa, whereupon he threw his jacket over the back. He looked like he intended to stay for a while as he loosened his tie. "It's been a heck of a week so far, hasn't it?" His smile was still fixed as though it was drawn there. "You're such a sight for sore eyes. No matter what's going on or what time of the week it is, honey you always look fantastic." He threw himself onto the sofa and leaned right back, extending his arms either side. He took a long blink as though he was fighting sleep. "How about some coffee? I need something, that's for sure. Have you got any on? Or a glass of wine? That would be great right now. Or something stronger?"

Had he been drinking? Was he on something else? Unsure if this was a dream state or if Jack really was there unannounced and sitting comfortably on her sofa, dishing out orders as though he owned the place, she pushed the door closed, stunned at his presence.

Ordinarily, running around after his every whim was fine with her, sort of, to a point, but right now it seemed like he was taking it a bit far. She only waited on people at the diner. And, for that, she got paid. She sought out a half bottle of wine that had taken up residence in the refrigerator. Since she had nothing else stronger, he would have to make do. She took two glasses from the cupboard and set about pouring one and handing it to him.

"How are you?" he gulped it, almost finishing it in one go. "You look amazing."

It seemed pointless pouring the remains for herself if he was getting through it that quickly. "I'm confused. I'm sorry, Jack, and please remind me if I got this wrong, but didn't we break up?" Her words came out sarcastically where there had been no intention of sarcasm. She wondered how he might take it. She needn't have worried as Jack's permanent grin broke into a laugh, as though he couldn't hold it back from a joke they'd been sharing, except she hadn't been a part of it. She sat on the arm of the chair opposite seeing the lust in his eyes and, while it was nice to be lusted over, something was off.

"Yeah, about that. Like I said, what a week." His eyes followed her figure from her mouth down to her legs then back up again. "Wow. Just perfect."

"What the hell's going on?"

"Okay, I get it. I completely understand. It's probably about time I said something, so let's get things out in the open. So, here it is. It's possible I might have forgotten to tell you I was married." He giggled, as though it was the biggest and best joke he had ever heard. "I mean, sure, it *sounds* like it was a pretty big deal forgetting something like that but, technically…technically, you see I'm not *really* married."

"You're not?" It all sounded a little strange to her, like his incessant smiling was a mask, a façade to whatever he was hiding.

She didn't like viewing him with suspicion, because it was Jack, the man she had loved right up until his words crushed her life's dreams. But suspicion remained. Maybe Jack was hurting too. Maybe this was his way of dealing with whatever *this* was. Could he be embarrassed, his pride hurt?

Compassion had been her downfall when it came to romance. It enabled dates to walk all over her. Giving them what they wanted could mean them giving her what she needed. In this case, with Jack, it was a life of love and a family. But some men had seen her as a target, an easy lay. Jack would never do such a sinister thing, would he? They were in love, weren't they?

"What does that mean? What does 'not really married' look like to you?"

He shrugged, extending both palms outwards. "What can I say? I'm not. I'm just trying to be honest with you."

The word hit hard. She would have done anything for him a week ago, but now? Now he was married. She wasn't sure if this new information marred everything or if her gut was trying to communicate with her heart for a change. Warning bells were ringing but it was a new sound to her body. It didn't know how to listen.

"You're not married as in you didn't exchange vows or you're not married," she used air quotes, "because you don't love her?"

"I mean, sweetheart, that there is nothing that you might call a marriage going on in our lives. Nothing at all." His eyes grew larger as his eyebrows rose with innocence. If he could have found a halo, he would have set it neatly atop his head.

"Do you share a house?"

"Well, yeah, but...but she works away most of the week. I hardly see her. Basically, I live alone. I'm practically a bachelor."

"When she's home, do you share a bed?"

"I mean...yeah, but..."

"Do you share children?"

"No, absolutely not. I never wanted kids anyway. Can't deal with 'em. But it turns out, it was a good thing 'cause neither of us have any time anyway. I mean, look at me, do I look like I'm the kind of guy that wants a couple kids pulling on my suit, taking my money, and crying all the time? We should never have gotten together in the first place really. It was a rookie move. Just something I did to get her father off my back."

She parked the idea of him not wanting children while she focused on the rest. "To get her father off your back? What the hell are you talking about, Jack? You're either married or you're not married."

"Okay, the thing is. We're married in law only." He looked her right in the eyes. "*Only,*" he repeated.

"But marriage is *based* on law. It's a legal contract."

"Okay, yeah," he said, caught out. "I'll accept that. But in all other aspects of the relationship, we just happen to share an apartment, like roommates. Honey, that's it," he lifted his glass as if to propose a toast to the idea. "We are, essentially, just roommates." Still that smile remained.

It was tough to sit opposite him and not have his arms draped over her shoulders or even look at him without wrapping herself around him. But the words his lips delivered were not the words Jack Sullivan would usually use. This Jack Sullivan sounded flippant, like he was filled with bravado just to get her on his side and see things his way. Usually he was suave, elegant, and sophisticated. Today he was floundering.

"How come you never said anything?"

He sat forward, as though he now realised this was a serious conversation and not just about venting about his day. "Honestly? I didn't think it was important."

There was that word again. "What?"

"I mean I could never foresee a time that it would need to be dealt with."

"You're married, and you couldn't see that it was going to be a problem dating me? Just explain that to me because you're losing me here."

Suddenly his smile dropped, and his expression seemed more sinister as though she had touched a nerve.

"Lighten up, Catie. Like you've never made a mistake before? What about all those guys you told me you slept with in high school?" He said it like he was trying to bring her down to his level or beneath.

Sleeping around in school had been an error in judgement, but she had told him that in confidence because she thought she was going to spend her life with him. She didn't understand why he brought it up other than to get him off the hook.

"Like I said, she means nothing to me. She hasn't for a long time. You and I were getting pretty serious, and I thought I'd just sign a piece of paper to annul the marriage and then propose to you."

She wanted to say she didn't think annulling a marriage and remarrying would all take place in the matter of days he seemed to think, but then her brain heard the word 'propose' and she lost track of the rest.

"You were going to propose?"

"Sure, for the holidays."

"To me?"

He nodded, and the grin returned even bigger than before. "I had this idea of the tree, and it'd be classy, you know, with the lights, the festivities. I mean everyone's in high spirits already, it'd be a ready-made party. Sure, the surprise is out now, but it can still happen. Just you and me around a perfect Christmas tree, imagine the photos." His eyes twinkled at the idea. "Honey, I even have a ring picked out and it's packing some major ice. All I gotta do is buy it. You want a ring on your finger, don't you?"

Parked alongside the idea of not having a family, and being married, it irked her that she wouldn't have been involved in choosing her own ring, but Jack's intentions were aligning with what she had always wanted. Could she organise a wedding in just a couple of weeks? Who would she invite? Where would she hold the ceremony? A million unanswered questions powered their way through her head like a tsunami. Everything she decided an hour ago was bordering on nothing more than a memory. Not now Jack was back.

And then she took a breath and ran her hands through her hair front to back. As soon as she touched the skin on her forehead, the bruises ached and brought her straight back to reality.

"Yeah, I do. But, Jack, can you hear yourself? Do you have any idea how I've been since you broke up with me?"

"Sad, I hope. We were in love. We *are* in love. You can't stop something that strong overnight."

She nodded, confused and angry. "Sad doesn't even begin to cover it. You told me by phone."

"She was standing right next to me issuing demands that I call you to end it. That's why I had to do it like I did. We were fighting. It was a mess."

There was still no apology, she noticed. "It was a mess? *I* was a mess! I collapsed with shock. At work, Jack. Can you imagine how humiliating that is? I brought down a huge stack of shelves with a million dishes on it that fell on me. Did you even notice these?" She pointed to her forehead just as she saw his lips curl upwards.

"I didn't, no." He did nothing to prevent the laughter. "That sounds so comical. Are you okay?"

She paused, frowned, and reconsidered. She wasn't expecting that kind of response. She was hoping for some genuine concern and sympathy like Drew had given. But Jack was laughing. Maybe she was making a big deal out of the collapse. It had hurt and she had been dizzy, then and now, but if Jack found it funny, perhaps it wasn't that serious.

"I am now, but I wasn't at the time. I think I was concussed. I've been making all kinds of ridiculous decisions and my mood's been all over the place."

"Now that's a lawsuit, right there." He downed the remainder of his wine, lifting the glass in the air awaiting her to retrieve it. "Great wine this, any more of it?"

"I'm not suing anyone." She reached for the bottle and gave it to him to refill his own glass. "Until a couple of hours ago, I couldn't even think clearly. I haven't stopped crying. I've not been myself at all. I was going to leave town."

He ushered her to sit next to him as he drained the last of his glass. "And all this was over me? I'm impressed. The infamous Jack Sullivan gift still works."

Reluctantly, she snuggled up, inhaling his scent and the slight odor of perspiration from hours in the office.

"This is more like it," he said, kissing her head. "I missed you, baby. Have you missed me?"

"I was utterly lost without you. I didn't know which way was up. And you just show up here, completely out of the blue." She stared up at him, allowing his kisses, and giving him some too. "It was pure luck I was home."

"I'm so glad you were." He caressed her neck, pulling her hair to one side and kissing her skin from her ear lobe to her shoulder and back up to her forehead, taking in each of her wounds. "Hey, you wanna go in there?" he gestured to her bedroom.

"Yeah."

As they both stood, Jack ripped off his tie and left it on the sofa along with his jacket and seconds later they were tearing off each other's clothes. It felt like a surreal dream making love with Jack Sullivan again.

And then it was all over.

"Wow, make up sex is the best, isn't it?" he moved to his side of the bed, picked up, his cell phone, and began scrolling.

She lay next to him, trying to process the last twenty minutes. "So, what happens now?"

"Hmm? What was that?"

"I said what happens now?"

"I've got an hour. We can talk. Drink. Whatever you want."

"An hour?"

"Yeah. I mean, you know the truth now." He scrolled some more but nothing caught his eye, so he put it back down. "It can't be a surprise to you that I've got to get back."

"You're still together?"

He shrugged. "Yeah, kinda."

"But she doesn't know you're here? Right?"

"Why would she?" He pulled her onto his bare chest. "Anyway, let's not talk about that. Our time is limited and precious, let's just focus on us. I've been thinking about you all day. All I wanted to do was see you naked. That image alone is what got me through the day."

She wished he would stop making it sleezy. "We probably can't go on seeing each other, Jack. Not if she knows."

"What? Why not? We managed it before, didn't we?" He winked.

Ordinarily that made her melt but this time, it felt wrong and bloody-minded. He stroked her shoulder blades and her spine until she purred. There was something so magnetising about Jack Sullivan, she was putty in his hands. When he spoke, the world disappeared. All that mattered was that they were together.

"So," he went on. "As far as I'm concerned, nothing's changed. In fact, it kinda feels better because she knows."

She sighed. This wasn't the kind of relationship she wanted. She didn't want to be 'the other woman'. For all her sins, she knew she was worth more than that.

"I don't know. I think we should give this some more thought."

"Give what more thought?"

"Us. Being together. I'm just saying maybe we shouldn't see each other anymore. Shouldn't you at least be thinking about a divorce?"

He smirked. "What are you talking about? Come on, you said so yourself. You were lost without me. I had a problem. I'll fix it. Where's the issue?"

"What's her name?"

"What? Who?"

She sat up, supporting herself by her elbow. "Your wife, Jack. What's her name?"

"Are you serious right now? It doesn't matter what her name is. When I'm with you, all I want to think about is you. Us, our future."

"How do we have a future if you're not getting a divorce."

"Catie, come on."

"What's her name?"

"Catie!" he barked.

"I need to know. Please."

He supported himself with both arms, bent at the elbow and reached forwards to kiss her nose. He left a wet mark on it which made him smile.

"Carla. Her name is Carla."

"How did she find out about us?"

"Apparently through a dinner receipt in my wallet. Maybe I got a little careless, I don't know."

"Was she looking for it? Did she suspect something?"

"I've no idea. I didn't ask. I try not talk to her much."

"You said she works away. It sounds like an important job. What does she do?"

"Catie! Come on, are you crazy? What's with you tonight? I don't wanna be lying in bed with you and talking about her. You've gotta be able to see that. Now, I've had a tough day at work, the last thing I wanna do is argue with you. I don't come here to do that with you. I came here to see this," he peered down at her chest and lower down. "Okay?"

"I'm sorry. I didn't mean…" She nodded, compliant. She had never noticed how controlling he was before. Was this new? But she still had questions. She wanted to ask how long they'd been married, what Carla's job was, why he hadn't gotten a divorce yet if he wasn't happy, and a thousand others. But she didn't. She just wanted to please him like he was pleasing her. For a fleeting moment, she believed she could overlook the lies and his indifference in wanting a family.

Just for a fleeting moment.

"I'm still gonna need that coffee though," he said, breaking the silence and slapping her backside. "How about it?"

"Then I guess I'd better go put some on." She dressed herself, putting on the white T shirt and jeans he'd ripped off, but not bothering to wear her bra. She bare-footed her way to the kitchen while Jack got dressed. "So," she called from the kitchen. "After your surprise entrance tonight, when am I gonna see you again."

He put on his pants and buttoned his shirt. "I guess I'll let you know when I'm free."

"What if I want to see you?"

"It might not be convenient, honey." He walked into the living room and dropped himself back onto the sofa, waiting for the coffee.

She turned to see him sitting exactly where he usually sat and, simultaneously, it warmed her heart and felt illicit. Having an inkling the guy you were dating was married was one thing but knowing it, that was another. Was there really enough of Jack to go around? And it seemed like it was all on his terms. What if he decided to leave her, just like he wanted to do with Carla? Just like her mom had done with Catie. Being abandoned once had left life-long scars. Being abandoned twice would be devastating.

"You're looking at me strange," he said. "Something you wanna share?"

"I just can't believe you're sitting on my sofa again." There was no need to go into the dark shadows of her childhood trauma.

"Lucky girl, huh?" He grinned, lapping up the positive attention. He stared at his watch, watching the minutes tick down until he had to leave. "How long until the coffee…"

"Just another minute," she smiled. "And then you can have your caffeine fix."

"You're my fix."

"You'd better believe it."

Three knocks interrupted their flirting. Three knocks that forced Catie back into reality. She grabbed the door handle and opened it just a few inches. Drew Denby stared at her from the other side.

"Boy, am I pleased you're still here. I thought you might've left town already."

"Drew?"

"You look like an angel."

She gasped, running a hand over her face and through her hair knowing what she had just being doing and with whom. "I'm no angel."

"Look, I just wanted to check you were okay. This morning was...well, it was pretty intense. And after you left, I had this crazy idea you just took off without so much as a goodbye." He looked relieved, excited, and thrilled all at once just to share the same space as her.

"Yeah...I went...um...I'm still here." She could see he was elated that she hadn't left and that made her even sorrier.

"And I can't tell you how happy that makes me." Drew's eyes sparkled. "Can I come in? Maybe we can talk?"

She swallowed back the awkwardness, closed her eyes, then let the door swing open wide enough so Drew could see behind her. She opened her eyes, both curious and apologetic at his expression. His face had completely fallen. The mischievous smile he had worn was replaced with shock, as though he'd been punched in the gut with Catie's own fist.

"I understand. I'm sorry I bothered you."

"Wait," she called after him as he made his way back down the stairs.

Jack flew to his feet and was suddenly behind her. "Who was that?" He pulled her shoulders into his chest as if to claim her as his own. "So, who's interested in my Catie then?"

Chapter Eighteen

It felt like it had taken the rest of the day to find a parking space. Parking on the hospital roof was the only choice and, as the rain fell and Becca battled with her umbrella, she walked to the ticket machine. Other visitors in the queue were going through their own personal hell. It seemed like fate was playing a cruel game and winning. Between the incident at school and finding a space, she was mentally and emotionally exhausted. Being bombarded with emotion at every step, the last twenty-four hours had taken their toll. There was only so much she could block out.

Emotions, she thought, were strange things, grabbing you when you least expected them and remaining at bay when exhibiting them would be beneficial. The last few hours had been testament to that. Somewhere inside her was a box whose lid was kept tightly closed. Lilah's accident had nudged it free, and emotions were beginning to creep out one by one. Some she recognised, while others were new. It was as unsettling as it was uncontrollable.

Role-reversal was in progress. Lilah's stories had taught Becca that emotions could empower you, give you strength, and allow you the confidence to take over the world. Too much of it could bring about euphoria, and enduring heartache could engender suffering so bad, it had the potential to remove all compassion forever. Those emotions, and every one in between, could make you vulnerable to the exploitation of others, and it was there that Becca felt the most uncomfortable.

In the right person, vulnerability was incredible. But not for her. Allowing it meant she might experience further grief like when she lost her parents. It meant being out of control and showing her students a side that wasn't acceptable. She was the adult; she couldn't be seen having a mini breakdown in front of them. What message would that give them for the future? That it was okay to become hysterical and shut off when you heard something sad or shocking? That might be okay for others, but not for Becca McCallister. She had to be the grown up because her big sister wasn't, and they were the only two left so she had to take care of Lilah.

A tidal wave of emotion had struck every part of her body when she was informed of their parents' passing. It paralysed her for what felt like a lifetime while she processed the news. Theirs was a motorway pile up; something you only saw in Hollywood block buster movies. From the pictures on the news, it was a spectacular pile up involving ten vehicles. Drone photography showed cars, vans, and lorries became a once-writhing now-stationary snake of metal and plastic along the motorway. The McCallister's car was somewhere in the middle.

They had been on their way home from the airport having just flown in from Bali, another post-retirement holidays. It had been a long-haul flight, and Becca always wondered if fatigue had played a part. Her father's body had been recovered from behind the wheel; he was well-known to be incapable of sleeping on flights. She only hoped that her mother had been out cold when it happened.

What was it with her family and car accidents? It made her question ever stepping inside a vehicle again.

"Stop it," she whispered aloud, finally at the ticket machine. She inserted the money and took the paper ticket. After locking her car she bundled up her scarf around her neck. The car park was as bleak as the weather.

She made her way down to the entrance that she guessed would become so familiar that she might walk it on autopilot. As she approached the entrance, there was a gathering ahead. Her first thought was, because the hospital entrance was opposite shops, that people were Christmas shopping. With festive decorations in the widows and fairy lights framing shop fronts, it made sense. Then she wondered if they were even protesting about something, considering how tightly packed they stood. But when she grew closer, she saw instead around a dozen men stood hunched over to keep out the cold. They ranged in age, some wearing baseball caps, others in flat caps, and almost all wore jeans. It reminded her of the older boys at school who gathered in crowds like wild animals when a fight broke out.

The tension concerned her. In the pit of her stomach, she was alert because to get past them she needed to either walk in the road or right through the middle. As she grew closer, she noticed that each one held a camera or voice recorder. They were not protesters or even festive shoppers, far from it, and the only thing they were shopping for were updates on her sister's situation. It was the paparazzi.

"Here we go," one of them called. "It's the sister."

Instantly the gathering broke apart and each man shot in a different direction like a flock of feeding birds. Instead of flying away, their vulture-like poses circled her as if about to feed, pecking off her flesh leaving only a carcass. Each took an angle different to the next man, thrusting voice recorders and cameras into her face. Surrounded, she hunched over, closing her eyes tightly and standing frozen to the pavement. They closed in, enveloping her into a darkness that seemed to remove all air from her lungs. Then the darkness let in intermittent bursts of light that stabbed her body and face until she inhaled like she was taking her first breath. Her eyes flew open as she faced this new monster head on.

Flash!

"Miss McCallister, what's your sister's condition?

Flash!

"Was the accident drug-related, Becca?"

Flash!

"Rebecca, was your sister drunk?"

Flash!

"Have the police spoken to you yet?"

Flash!

"If she lives, will she be arrested?"

Flash!

"How are you coping with this so soon after losing your parents?

Flash!

"If Lilah lives, do you think she'll use this story in her next novel?"

Flash!

"Is there any news on her condition?"

Flash!

"Will you be off school for long?"

Flash!

"Do you think your students' education will be compromised because of your absence?"

Flash!

With her heart pounding, Becca pushed through them, elbows out and head down and ran as fast as she could inside the hospital entrance. They didn't follow her but the cameras flashing continued. She could see it bounce off the hospital's faux marble walls. It was like rushing to safety through a terrible lightning storm; the protective arms of the hospital wrapped around her as she willed the doors shut.

She reached the lift as fast as she could. Two other people were already waiting when the light illuminated and, one by one, they all entered. The doors closed and the lift moved. It was then that Becca realised she was shaking.

She replayed their heartless questions in her head.

"...If she lives..."

"...drunk...drug related..."

"...will she be arrested..."

"...students' education be compromised..."

"...so soon after losing your parents..."

The soft ring filled her ears as the doors opened. She took a step to leave, trying hard to stop trembling but her body shook involuntarily from her thighs up to her face. The loud-speaker called out for a doctor to go immediately to the cardiac ward, while several more equipped with stethoscopes and white coats all but ran past her.

The extraordinarily long corridor towards the Intensive Care Unit reminded her of a tunnel punctuated by lights just beneath the ceiling. The odd colourful, often thought-provoking, framed print on the walls broke up the off-white monotony. Echoes of feet marching, walking slowly, scuffling, and bed and trolly wheels provided the only noises throughout the walkway. It was a sorry metaphor for the journey of life and the proverbial light at the end of this tunnel, it seemed, was nowhere in sight.

Two nurses pushed an occupied bed past her. The occupant, an old man easily in his nineties, looked like he didn't have long left. He was deathly grey. Tubes and bags joined to his bed jostled as they rolled him past. The nurses gave polite, thin smiles to onlookers. It felt like he was being exhibited en route to his final destination, like a depressing ritual to highlight that life was over in two minutes. Becca locked eyes with the man as an unknown and silent conversation took place between them. A chill ran through her body resulting in an all-over body shake that made her realise she had stopped trembling from the paparazzi just minutes ago. Seconds later, the patient had been pushed out of view.

The ICU door was locked and a notice on the wall beside it asked visitors to buzz for attention. A row of six seats were opposite. She pressed the button and pulled the sanitizer tab to release a blob of gel into her hands rubbing it in as she sat down. A minute later, a nurse came to the door.

"Hello. I'm here to see my sister, Delilah McCallister." Using Lilah's full name always sounded so formal to Becca, like she was telling on her to the Head.

The nurse let her in. "How are you holding up?"

Becca took a deep breath and followed her. "I don't know, to be honest," she added a small laugh, as if that was expected. Make light of any situation, she thought. In fact, there was no right way to behave when intense stress surrounded you. "I think I'm still processing it all."

She extended her arm to the bed nearest them both. "Her condition hasn't changed. She's stable though, and as comfortable as we can make her."

"Thank you."

"While I'm here, do you have any questions? I know it's only when you go home you think of everything and say to yourself, 'why didn't I ask this or that'. It's only natural."

"I can't think of anything."

She pulled a seat up and parked it next to the side of the bed. "Well, I'll be over there. If anything comes to mind. Just let me know and I'll do my best to answer them for you."

"I'm back," Becca whispered, as she sat down. Lilah had a multitude of tubes, bags, and very serious looking machines surrounding her. She reached for Lilah's hand and held it, stroking her fingers. "I hope you're okay. They say you're dreaming, that you're in a dream state. Although that's not the technical term. You're in a coma, Lilah. Yep, I know what you're thinking. How crazy is this? I know, believe me," she sighed hard. "I know."

She considered what Lilah might be working on inside her mind. "I'll bet there's a hero roaming around in your head, isn't there? Is he nice? After our last trip, I'm going to bet it's based in Boston. You loved Massachusetts, didn't you? Wasn't that your favourite state for your next novel? Your dream choice. If it isn't, we're going to have some serious words as soon as you wake up, Miss. You have us go all that way and then don't use your research," she tried to smile but tears fell as she spoke. She sniffed and laughed at the same time. "I hope you're happy, you're making me cry. I don't do emotion, that's your job. Just wake up, Lilah, there's work to do."

Another nurse approached, a black lady with a huge smile and a tissue box in her hand. "I thought you might need this."

Becca took it. "Thanks. I just can't seem to stop today. It's not like me."

"And this isn't like her," she said, looking at Lilah's lifeless body. "But we'll get there."

"She's always so much inside her own head that she forgets there's a world out there. A real one." She paused and then added, "but, to be honest, maybe her fictional world is better." She looked at the nurse. "If that's what she's dreaming about, it can't be any worse than this one, can it?"

She didn't understand why she was rambling about nothing and certainly not something the nurse would have any idea about. She didn't know the sisters, or what they talked about together. Nobody did. Nobody but them.

"She's a writer," Becca explained with unexpected pride. "That's what I mean when I say she's inside her own head."

"I know," she nodded. "A good one too. I read her first novel, the book she won the competition with. It's very good. I love a romance."

Becca was caught off-guard but her smile lit her whole face. "You've read her work? That's incredible. You know about her? That's lovely! I hope she knows she's got a fan here. I'm just sorry you had to meet her like this."

"She's got a lot of support. We're all pulling her way."

Becca wanted to believe it but guessed it was a standard comment. "The other nurse said if I had any questions I could ask."

"Of course, fire away."

"Apparently the police will interview me. The doctor told me she had alcohol in her blood. Was it a lot? I mean, could it have made a difference to the outcome?"

"I don't believe it wasn't a significant amount. It's just that in situations like this, anything can be a factor."

"I just wanted to say that it's not like her. She's not an irresponsible person. "I just wanted you to know that. We weren't raised to break the law. I'm sure that wasn't your first thought, but…". The nurse gently touched her shoulder in reassurance. "Do you know what happened to the other driver? Was it a man? A woman? Are they okay?"

"Just between us," she brought her head closer as if to share a secret. "He's a young man. I have a feeling he's going to be fine."

Becca let out a sob and a sigh. "Thank heavens for that."

"Indeed."

"I'm not judging him or anything, I just want to have the facts straight in my head but could he have been drinking?"

The nurse shook her head. "I'm pretty sure he wasn't."

Resigned, she said, "So it was Lilah's fault then?" That was hard to bear. Her father would have gone crazy over that knowledge. "Maybe her car was out of control? It's a sporty one. I wanted her to have something sensible but she never listens to me." The nurse exuded a type of comfort that warmed Becca's whole body and, after dealing with the paparazzi outside, she needed all the support she could get. The longer the two women were close, the more comforted Becca felt. Unable to stop speaking, she said, "You say he's a '*young*' man this other driver. How young is young?"

"About your age. We're not meant to share information, but I appreciate some people need to know. It helps to process things. I bend the rules when it's necessary."

"Thank you. I won't say anything." She stared at the machines surrounding the bed. "I can't understand how you can do this day in day out. It would just about finish me off. Too much emotion for me."

"I've been doing it a long time. I go where I'm needed."

"Sorry about the tears. I suppose you get that all the time?"

"Never apologise for showing your emotions," she told her. "They'll help you get through this."

"I'm not great with emotions. That's her job," she gestured to Lilah.

"Well, you have to allow your body to care for you sometimes. Crying is like a soggy hug," she winked. It made Becca laugh a little. "While we take care of her, do you have someone at home who's looking after you?"

Becca shook her head.

"A husband? Boyfriend?"

Again, she shook her head.

"And so pretty too. Well, we'll keep an eye on that," she said. "Who knows what's around the corner?"

"Thanks, but I'm not looking at the moment. I've got enough on my plate."

"Understandable."

"Thank you for caring for Lilah, though. I really do appreciate it. You're an absolute angel."

She giggled. "I've heard that before. Right, I'll leave you to sit with her. If you need me, I'll be close," she said. "My name is Margaret."

Chapter Nineteen

As she walked into the diner at six the next morning, Catie kept her head low; partly due to the temperature, and because she was embarrassed about the night before. She had been full of exciting plans when she returned from visiting her dad only to see Jack at her door. Learning what she believed was love was just lust left her with an emptiness that might never be filled.

A moment of clarity with her dad had brought Jack's character to light and that was further evidenced with his behaviour. But strong feelings remained, although he had seemed hell bent on fulfilling his own needs and wants first. An honest conversation was all Catie needed, but maybe honesty wasn't his strong suit. Covering up his marriage and views on children was such a shock. How many times had he lied to her? Had she been so bewitched that his flaws were not only hidden, but invisible? Or, like her dad said, had she chosen to overlook them?

When Drew showed up, it was a shock and surprise all at once. If ever there was a right time, that was not it. Though, given the choice of either man, she was drawn to Drew. He would have listened and cared, and she would have discussed her new plans. Except it hadn't gone that way. It ought to have been so easy: Jack had dumped her, and Drew showed interest. Her father saw it all so clearly. If she could just remove the fear of being abandoned yet again, then falling for Drew might just happen. On paper, it worked. In real life, there was a lot to consider. Add a bump on the head to the mix, and Catie was more bewildered than ever.

It was still dark outside. Sunrise was trying its best to show up for work but the snow clouds, while not currently yielding snow, countered its efforts. The overnight snowstorm, which had covered the street with a thin layer, told a different story.

There was still more to come. It was enough to make everything look like a wedding cake, but it was best left to Christmas cards designs. The freezing temperatures were exacerbated by loneliness and, during a holiday dedicated to togetherness, who wanted to be alone?

Someone, probably Drew, had spread salt on the sidewalk directly outside and ten feet either side of the doorway. Getting customers in was hard enough, adding another challenge was not smart where competition was fierce. Without the salt, it was a personal injury case waiting to happen.

The Christmas lights wrapped around trees along the street shone as though imitating sunlight in its absence. They gave a white-yellow glow, never being extinguished until well into January. It was a welcoming sight, friendly to both residents and tourists. The world could use some more friendly, Catie thought, but then saw Sheryl's unwelcoming expression through the window. Friendly would have to wait until the apologies were dished out.

"Hey." Catie offered a small, polite smile, hoping it would be an easy, amicable way back into Sheryl's good books. Storming out was nobody's fault but hers. She knew that and was willing to take as much on the chin.

"Hey yourself. Thought you'd left town. Heard Boston wasn't good enough for you."

So that was it. Sheryl's disappointment was showing in snarky comments. That was fine, she could handle it. She probably deserved it anyway. She hadn't treated either of them particularly well.

"I made a couple snap decisions I had no business making. I'm sorry, Sheryl. I hope I didn't …"

"You're sticking around then?" She didn't allow the apology to linger.

"I think so."

"You know, it ain't a bother to me. I don't care who I work with, but for that guy back there," she gestured over her shoulder like she was thumbing a lift. "He deserves a little respect, don't you think? It's the holidays for Christ's sake, Catie. He needs all the help he can get and you just up and leave. What the hell were you thinking? He can't run it alone, he has enough on his plate. He always pulls in our direction, always paying us hours we don't work just so we don't lose out. But what about him? Didn't you think about that when you pulled your little stunt?"

"To be honest, I wasn't really thinking anything. I've been…"

"We've been covering for you and it ain't fair. There's a job to do and you're not doing it."

She took a breath to apologise once again but Sheryl was set on continuing.

"I don't think you appreciate how good you got it here. He's a good man and doesn't deserve to be dismissed like that. He lets so much slide. It's not only the hours he pays, he gives you time off to go see your dad. Not many bosses would do that. Everything he's ever worked for has gone into this place and if it doesn't work out, what then? That's his livelihood and his future down the toilet." As if she heard her own words, she added, "In fact it's everyone's job down the toilet. I don't know if you've got it easy at home or something, but I got kids that need feeding, and child care that needs paying on top of rent and everything else."

"I get it."

"You can't treat him that way. It's totally disrespectful." She finally stopped to take a breath. "There. I said it."

"I get it, Sheryl. I know things haven't been great. I said I'm sorry and I meant it."

Catie had barely unfastened her coat when Drew emerged from the back room. He nodded but said nothing. His apron bore wet handprints as though he'd used that instead of a towel. He seemed both preoccupied and crestfallen, and he looked tired. Catie hoped she wasn't to blame for his silence but after Sheryl's tirade, she felt guilty.

"Morning. Are there dishes to wash back there? I can start on that first, you know, if you like."

"Already in the dishwasher," he said. "I oughta've cleaned up before I left last night but I couldn't wait to get outta here." His gaze darted to her for the briefest of moments. "Real stupid too. Should've just stayed. It only creates more work the next day."

Catie analyzed his words. Did she detect a dig in there?

"On account there wasn't the staff?" Sheryl's point was liberally covered with a huge dollop of passive aggression.

"On account I hadn't thought it through," he countered. "Nobody's fault but mine, Sheryl. Oh, and we just got a bread delivery."

"I can put it away," Catie offered.

"I've already done it."

"You could've left it," Catie said, eager to please them both, and keen to smooth over the obvious rough edges.

"He said it's done," Sheryl repeated, her tone bordering on 'angry mom'.

"I got that." Catie glared. "Loud and clear. I'm just saying I'm happy to help with whatever needs doing."

"Then you can carry on with the floor if you actually *want* to do some work around here."

"Hey!" That got their attention. It was uncharacteristic of Drew to show any kind of temper.

"Right." Catie sighed. "I can see there's a lot that needs to be said. Let's get it out in the open 'cause it seems you're both mad at me for different reasons."

"No shit!" Sheryl slammed the mop against the metal bucket and water splashed back onto the floor. "What more have you got to say, sweetheart, 'cause I'm all ears."

Catie saw the raised eyebrow Drew shot Sheryl. It was a rare sight indeed. He was grouchy, Sheryl was mad, what had she walked into? "I'm sorry I walked out on you both and for speaking to you the way I did. It wasn't fair."

"You got that right." Sheryl mumbled like a sulky teenager.

"Knock it off, Sheryl," Drew growled. With dark circles around his eyes, he looked like he wanted to climb back in bed and sleep for days. "Can't you just let her speak?"

Catie thanked him with a small smile. "I don't know where my head's been lately, but I just want to say that, Drew, you were right. I just needed time to think, and I did that. You've both worked with me a while now. Have I ever been that way before?" She waited for them to respond, but neither did. "Right. So, please know that when I say I'm sorry, I actually am. If I hadn't just gone through hell and back, things would've been different. I'm sorry I took it out on you both, I guess a bang on the head will do that." She hoped to get a 'thank you' in response, but they both sent a silent nod her way. "Right, so are we all okay?" She got another nod. She took off her coat and scarf and rested them over her arm as she edged towards the swing door. "Okay, so now that's over, I'll get to it. Seems I've got some making up to do."

"Sure seems that way," Sheryl mopped up the spillage draining the mop of its moisture. "And just so we're clear, *I* don't forgive that easy, lady."

Catie wasn't going to let that go. "I can take the snippy comments when I deserve them, Sheryl, but I've apologized. I'm not one of your kids, so please don't speak to me like I am. I've said I'm sorry. I am. It's over. Okay?" She waited, hoping Sheryl didn't add to it. She didn't, but it was clear she was silently spitting nails. "Good."

"Take your time," Drew called out. "It's not like anybody's kicking down the door for breakfast yet anyway."

Catie stood at the swing door out of sight but listening. She had never seen them like this before. They fought all the time, but it was masked with humour. This went deeper.

"Jeez, what's with the look, Sheryl? What now?"

"I just think you oughta be straight with her. I wouldn't let her get away with it."

"Get away with what? She said sorry."

"So that's okay, is it?"

"Well, yeah. What else can she do?"

"We ain't here just to keep her happy, buddy. We're both pulling our weight. She's hardly been a princess, has she?"

"So, now you're mad at her for having a private life?"

"No, I don't give a flying whatever about her private life. I don't care about any of it. I care about you, and this place. We all bring our private lives in. It can't be avoided. But she took it to the extreme, don't you think?"

Catie listened with guilt. It was a horrible feeling being the instigator of their fight.

"I dunno. Like she said, she's been through hell. It can't have been easy. And she's right, she's never been like this before in all the time she's worked here. I'm just saying I think you could cut her a little slack."

"Of course you'd say that!"

"What?"

"If you weren't so puppy-eyed over her, we wouldn't even be having this conversation. She'd be out of here and don't tell me she wouldn't. Nobody else would get away with it."

"So, you're jealous?"

"No, you idiot! I'm not jealous. I'm mad. I watch you work your ass off and she waltzes around here like, 'I'm working, I'm not working'. I just think-"

"It's clear what you think," he said abruptly, bordering on anger. "Anyway. I'm handling it."

"I'm just saying, I'd have handled it differently."

"But you don't need to, do you? It's my place, Sheryl. I don't need you to hold my hand. In fact, I've never needed it. I'm not a kid."

Sheryl backed off. "Buddy, I'm just looking out for you. The way she's treated you, I just can't let it go. She disrespected you. I mean, what would you have said if it was me and I spoke to you like that? What if I talked trash to you? Huh?"

Drew laughed, letting the anger go and diffusing the situation. "What? Are you crazy? You do, all the time. And, for what it's worth, I don't take any notice of you either."

"If one of my kids did that, I'd make 'em see sense real quick."

"Of that I have no doubt, but she's an adult and she just going through some stuff. What? You never went through anything before? Where's your compassion?"

Catie quietly pushed open the door and watched them both.

"I guess I don't got a lot left. And what little I do have I save for people who I think deserve it. Right now, you're probably the only one."

"You don't think she deserves a little compassion? After what she's been through? You're one tough lady."

"Amen to that. 'Sides, I gotta be, the hand I been dealt."

"I know, but you've got me," he said. "You just gotta ask. And I've got some plans in here," he tapped his head. "I just need to think 'em through and put 'em in place. But know this, we're all in for an interesting ride pretty soon." He tried to sound optimistic, and after a decent night's sleep he would be.

"Define interesting." Sheryl waited but Drew yielded nothing but a curious smile laced with hope and anticipation. She took the mop and bucket past Catie and through the swing door. As she returned, Drew was standing in front of the window. He switched on the fairy lights that framed the door and the two floor-to-ceiling windows that book-ended it. In the fallen snow, they brought as much festive feel as they could gather, but it wasn't much. The rest was down to staff, and good cheer was tough to come by lately. It was tough being cheery on a cold, wintry morning when everyone was miserable.

It was still dark outside and bus drivers, bankers, and other shop owners would be demanding their first coffee and breakfast sub of the day in a matter of minutes, providing the frozen conditions hadn't made a difference to their journey to work.

"Goddamned weather!" Drew said.

"It's winter," Sheryl barked. "What the hell were you expecting? Forty degrees?" She stood next to him as the pair watched the world come alive at the start of the day. The difference in their height was reflected in the glass; he, the gentle giant and she, the feisty fighter.

It was good seeing them make up, Catie thought as she wiped down the counter. She remained silent, allowing them time to adjust to her.

"For what it's worth, whatever these new plans are," Sheryl said. "I ain't going nowhere. You got that?" It sounded like a threat, but it came from a good place. Sheryl had a knack of making good stuff sound sinister. Her kids would vouch for that.

"I do. 'Sides, this place would fall to its knees without you by my side. You're the glue that holds it all together."

"Damn straight. And just so as you know, I ain't gonna be this nice to you all day." She shot him a smile, a mixture of mischief and sincerity, love and respect, the kind of mixture that only she could brew. She went about cleaning the booths. "You gonna put on the carols or do I gotta do that too?"

"Relax, would you? Anyone would think I worked for you." Drew said, flipping the CD player switch.

"It's a surprise to me every damn day."

"What were you saying before about talking trash?" He gazed at Catie as he said it and they shared a smile. "You see what I have to put up with?"

"Buddy, I only kick your ass 'cause no-one else will. And 'cause I love ya."

"You know that feeling's mutual, don't you?"

"It damn well better be." She swiped her dish cloth across his arm. "'Cause I ain't busting my ass here for nothing."

***

As the day woke up and customers came and went, brunch and lunch time diners slowed. The five booths had been constantly filled and take-outs had queued over the two-hour lunch period. Snow threatened but didn't fall, leaving customers with easy access inside. Two intense hours serving, cooking, and clearing and the three were able to stagger thirty-minute breaks.

When it was Drew's turn, he walked several blocks hoping to feel awake again in the cold air. He downed an energy drink while he walked and gave thought to his plans. When he returned, there were no customers; the lull between lunch and dinner service. The place was so quiet without the constant chatter of lunch-time diners that had been there all morning. The carols emanating from the CD player were ingrained in his mind. He swore if he turned it off, he'd still hear them.

"Ladies," he clapped his hands, grabbing their attention. "I gotta talk to you both."

"What's going on?" Sheryl stared blankly.

"I've been thinking about a shake up for a while, but, y'know, the holidays. So I think it'd be good to make some changes for the new year."

"Changes?" Sheryl asked. "Staff or diner?"

"All of it. It needs brightening up, the diner, the menu. She's looking a little tired, and hell I know I am so she must be too. I think we're working way harder than we need to and I wanna look at ways to lighten the load while still bringing us all in a decent wage. I'd like your thoughts on how to do that. Both of you, give it some thought please? I've got my own ideas, but I'd like to hear yours. I'm open to anything and everything."

"I've heard that about you," Sheryl smirked. "Sure, buddy, whatever you want."

"And, while it's quiet, Catie, can I talk to you out back?"

The way he asked sent her defences up as they went behind the swing door. "Hey, if you're gonna fire me, can I at least work out the rest of the day?"

"Didn't you hear what I just said? I need you both. And anyway, that's the farthest thing from my mind."

"The firing or the paying?"

He waved away the question. "Listen, I can't run this place on my own or with just one of you, especially this time of year. To be honest, I need more staff but that's another conversation. Right now I just need to know if you're leaving town or not 'cause if you're staying, I could really use the help. But if you're not," he didn't want her to answer if it was. "Then I'm gonna need to find cover and that won't be easy this time of year."

She nodded. "Yeah, I understand. All I can say is that it's on the back-burner for now."

"That's seriously good news," he grinned like it meant more to him than staff cover. "I've asked Sheryl to work late tomorrow night, Saturday, can you do the same? Come in at lunch time if you need to or you can work a double, it's your choice. I just need to know. We've got a few reservations lined up, dinner before the theatre or clubs. Tips will be good. Christmas dinner with a side of high spirits and laughter. I guess we could all use some of that. I just can't turn away business right now. We'll finish around ten and I'll make it worth your while."

"Sure. I can work a double. Like I said, I've got some making up to do so I guess I'll start now. And I *am* sorry about before."

"Don't beat yourself up over it. I get it."

"I wish Sheryl did."

"Don't take it personally. We've been together a while now and she's as loyal as they come. She's just a little protective over me and I can't see it changing anytime soon."

"My dad made me see sense. About staying, I mean. I visited him yesterday and we talked a lot of it through. I wasn't messing with you when I said I'm going through something. I told him everything that's happened, the accident, Jack. And then when I got back Jack showed up out of the blue and then you knocked -"

"I'm sorry about that," he interrupted. "I had no idea you and he were...I just wanted to make sure you were okay."

"I don't know what you saw but,"

"Enough." He sighed, crestfallen. "I guess it means you're back together now?"

"Actually, there's something you ought to know."

He ran through a million scenarios in his head, wondering which it would be and how each one was connected to Jack Sullivan because wasn't that what life was about now?

"What's that?"

"Jack proposed."

Chapter Twenty

Becca turned off the engine and sat in the driveway. It had been a while since she had visited Lilah's cottage. She never could have expected the next time she did Lilah would be lying in a hospital bed fighting for her life.

'A pretty little cottage', her mother would have called it. 'The sort you'd find on a chocolate box or a tin of posh biscuits.' She wasn't wrong. It was nicer looking than her own two-bedroomed terraced house. Lilah's idea of perfection was exactly this. Becca remembered accompanying Lilah to view it.

"Looks like the kind of thing an old lady would live in," she said as the two stood in the driveway staring up at the ivy covering the front of it.

"Except for the fact I'm young," Lilah smiled, taking the passive aggressive comment on the chin.

"Older than me though."

"But young for my age. Childlike."

"Child*ish*," Becca smirked.

"You'd know," Lilah came back quickly. "I'm older than you, but not old. There's a difference."

"Says the woman who's probably going to live in an 'old lady' house," Becca teased, satisfied she could hear the irritation in her sister's voice. Pressing her buttons was the name of the sibling game and she was doing it perfectly.

"I think I've got a few years left in me, Bec."

"You'd better have if you're buying it. That's a life-time's mortgage. It's just as well it's an old lady house 'cause you'll still be paying off for it when you're an old lady."

"Like you are with yours, you mean?" she said, getting her own back. She heard Becca's reluctant sigh and smiled.

"Touché."

"It'll suit me now and it'll suit me then. I'll never have to move again and go through this whole stupid process."

Becca was jealous about that part. Hers wasn't big enough for a growing family should she ever have one. It would be passable for a couple, but only temporarily. It didn't have a large garden, just a small area of decking for two seats and a modest table. Nor did it have a second bedroom that could take a bed. In fact, why even call it a bedroom? Yep, Lilah was right, Becca would have to go through the process again if someone else came on the scene. Not that it was a problem, it had been ages since she'd had a date. "Do you think it's got ghosts?" There was a touch of cynicism lacing Becca's tone. "I mean, it is really old, like by a century at least. It looks like it should be completely filled with them."

"Probably. Hopefully friendly ones. I'm surprised you even thought about them. Doesn't your brain expel anything that's not factual?"

Becca ignored the comment. "I'm not sure I could live in something this old."

"Nobody's asking you to." Lilah looked again at the paperwork in her hands. "It says it's ninety-nine years old."

"Oh, so it is nearly as old as you then?" Becca smirked at her own jibe, then paused to think about the span of time. Who else would have lived in it? It looked like a great prompt for a class writing project. "That's quite exact. I mean, wouldn't it be better saying something like, 'a century old?"

"I don't know," Lilah shrugged. "It's old. That's all I need to know really. And it's perfect for writing in." Lilah tipped her head and lifted her eyebrows. "So long as they let me write, there can be as many ghosts as they like. It's such a romantic looking place, if ghosts do live here, who'd blame them?"

"Ugh! I hate it when you make a valid argument. Come on then. Let's look inside, but if we see any, you can deal with them. I'll be-"

"Cowering in the corner? Running back to the car?"

Becca recalled the conversation to the letter and their banter made her sigh, then and now. Lilah was more open-minded than she would ever be. She was right, she had a factual brain. Entertaining anything outside of that was scary territory, the kind of thing that never had a definitive answer made her shudder.

It was a two-bedroomed brick-built cottage covered in whitewash which made the ivy 'pop' as Lilah's beloved Americans would say. A pebbled drive turned out onto a narrow, winding road one side and on the other side of the cottage was the edge of woodland. The nearest neighbour was half a mile away which suited Lilah perfectly; no obvious distractions from writing, plus a plethora of wildlife at night that was sure to enthral her imagination.

The little red Beemer that was usually parked outside was the only thing that didn't really fit into the chocolate box style. It was far too modern for the style of the house. It wasn't even her sister's first choice; she got talked into it by the salesman. Becca expected Lilah to plump for something a bit more sensible than a flighty sports car, but between her half of the inheritance and winning the writing competition, Lilah McCallister let herself grow. She was the proud owner of a stunning little sporty number and an ancient cottage. The two could not have been more juxtaposed, just like Lilah's imagination and Becca's practicality.

She put the key into the hole knowing that the last time the door was touched was with her sister's fingers. She turned it, hearing the clarity of the click as the lock pulled from the doorway. She hoped Lilah would pull it from the other side with a giggle, but nothing nearly as wonderful happened.

Once inside, she'd forgotten how dark it was with its low ceilings, uneven floors, and thick wooden doors. The dreariness outside made everything look depressingly dark. Grey clouds threatened as if they understood and empathised with Becca's situation. She flipped the hallway light switch instantly illuminating it before closing the front door behind her. On the floor was post, junk mail mostly. She would need to check the post often ensuring bills got paid promptly. Running two households, she thought, that'd be a stretch.

"So, what were you doing before you left?" She felt awkward being there without her sister and going through her things without permission. It felt like a violation of privacy. The first door on the right was the kitchen. Inside, there was nothing out of the ordinary. No food uncovered, no coffee or tea mugs that needed washing. Maybe Lilah hadn't been in there before she left or maybe she had washed up already.

In the living room, Becca was quick to notice Lilah's laptop. It was always plugged in. A low battery was one of Lilah's pet peeves.

"If it's always charged up, I can write any time I like. I don't have to wait for it, it can wait for me," she'd say. The same with her phone, she always kept it charged. The laptop was on power save mode and as soon as she moved the mouse, it instantly woke up displaying a screen of words. It was half-way through something. Had Lilah left unexpectedly? What had prompted her to go?

Becca noticed the phone was on the dresser next to a bottle of wine and a small wine glass. "Ah, the infamous alcohol. *Were* you drinking? That's so not like you, and how come you didn't take your mobile with you when you left? This is all so weird."

She picked up the phone and saw its battery was on just two per cent so she charged it next to the laptop. Instantly it came into life. Aside from a dozen emails and a multitude of social media notifications, one other thing caught her eye. Something had been recorded. Becca left it to charge a bit more before listening to it.

She saw her sister's bag next to her desk. Lilah's purse was still inside. It was strange not taking anything when she left. "You weren't intending to be out for long, were you? Did you just nip out for five minutes or something? Where were you going if you didn't need them? Why didn't you take it all with you? Not even ID. What if you'd needed your drivers' licence, Lilah?"

Next to the laptop was a pen and a spiral bound pad. It was open and folded back on itself with copious handwritten notes and reminders. Becca read the bits she could understand, the rest – in Lilah's semi-aware scrawl that she used when she needed to remind herself of something during a scene but didn't want to stop typing – was unintelligible. '*Catie's attitude sucks! Fix it!*' was underlined three times. '*Jack to dump her. Off the rails. Drew is THE ONE!!!*' The three exclamation marks both riled and amused Becca. Then '*REWRITE! Talk to R asap – d/line approaching!* "I'll bet that went well," she said, ruefully. "And my gut's telling me that she had something to do with this whole situation too."

She scrolled up a few screens. Lilah was well into the story, over a hundred thousand words according to the document's wordcount, which would need to be pared down to ninety. Eventually, that would be Gordon's job.

"What did you need to talk to Ruth about, I wonder. And did you?" She clicked onto her sister's e-mail, the last one was from Ruth. It felt invasive and, once she'd read a few lines and realised it wasn't pleasant, further compounded the fact she was prying into her sister's private business.

Ruth's e-mails were similar in tone to her behaviour. Thinly veiled threats laced most of the content. It didn't seem like the best working relationship and, knowing her sister's sensitivities, she guessed those threats had been taken to heart.

"I'm no detective, but I'll put serious money on you as the catalyst, Ruth Trent."

In the quiet space between her and her sister's writing, Becca's mobile trilled like a terrified bird calling for help.

"Hello?"

"Is this Rebecca McCallister?" It was an unfamiliar male voice.

"Who's calling please?"

"This is PC Hutton from Holcroft Police Station. I'd like to ask a few questions regarding your sister's accident. Would it be okay if I came to your house about three this afternoon? It shouldn't take too long."

It was the police interview that she had been expecting. "That's fine. Do you have the address?" He reeled off the one he had, and she confirmed it with a suitable time. Once the call was over, her heart pounded at the anticipation. The last 'few questions' the police had with her were over her parent's accident. This was becoming a habit she didn't want to continue.

She checked upstairs ensuring everything was fine in both the bedrooms and the bathroom before taking a brief look in the garden through the upstairs window. On her way down she listened to the recording on Lilah's mobile phone. She imagined it would be verbal notes for the novel. Instead, an eye-opening conversation played out:

"It's forty-eight hours away. The clock's ticking…it's just as well my assistant is looking for a decent Copy Editor, isn't it? …I've got no time for unreasonable people. Surely you've learned that by now? Emma's filling the role temporarily."

She listened further.

"Not wishing to be rude, Ruth, but she's eighteen… Does she actually want to be a Copy Editor though?"

"I didn't ask her. I told her, just like I'm telling you… Don't get too involved, Lilah. It's a bloody book for Christ's sake! … What else is there for a woman like her? She's just a waitress for God's sake, she's no right to ask for more than that…We agreed to a three-book deal so get this third one complete. … you're not so well-known …You're not that big; carry on like this you'll never be either."

Becca's blood boiled as she listened to Ruth's threats.

"...if you make me look bad, I will crush you. Catie's a perfect sob story. Readers love a loser. It'll make them feel better about their own pathetic little lives."

"I can barely think straight. I'm really tired, Ruth..."

"... Now pour yourself a glass of wine. You're getting a really good deal for someone like you ... you can say goodbye to your cottage in the woods and that lovely little Beemer sitting in your drive...You saw how quickly you were taken up... just bear in mind how easily the situation could be reversed..."

Becca sat down, shocked at the way Lilah had been threatened, coerced, and blackmailed. What she held in her hand was evidence. Had Lilah been so on top of it that she deliberately recorded the conversation? She grabbed the charger from the wall and put it, with the phone, inside her bag. The police officer would have some interest in it, surely. Once she arrived home, the policeman was already in the parking bay. As he left the vehicle, she saw he was a balding fifty-year-old with a slight paunch who stood at least six feet tall.

"I'm PC Hutton. Sorry I was early. Thanks for seeing me," he said following her inside.

"That's fine. Can I get you a coffee? Tea?" The officer shook his head and the two sat in the living room. "I was just at my sister's house. Checking everything's fine."

"And was it?"

She nodded. "It always feels weird going through someone else's place though, doesn't it? Especially when they're not there."

He smiled sympathetically. "Let's hope she's back soon."

"If she isn't, I'm going to have to go through it all over again." She spoke as if he knew what she meant. When he looked confused, she added, "That big pile up on the motorway a couple of years ago. Our parents were in it. We had to clear out their place. It's becoming a bit of a habit."

He smiled reassuringly and took out his pen and pad. He reeled off his questions: When was the last time she'd seen her sister? What kind of person is she? Does she make rash decisions? Was she on any medication? Does she drink? Smoke? Take drugs? What kind of driver is she? Sensible, wild? Is she married? Was she dating? Was she under stress?

By the time he finished, Becca's head was revolving. "Thinking about it, yes, she was under a lot of stress actually." She took out the phone from her bag and held it in her hand. "You might be interested in this. When I was over there earlier, I happened to notice she hadn't taken her bag, her ID, her purse, or her phone. Nothing at all. Lilah's not the kind of person to leave the house without at least one of those things. I charged her phone and found a recording on it. I think you should listen to it."

"What's it a recording of?"

"It's a conversation between Ruth Trent, my sister's agent, and Lilah. They had a massive argument and Ruth made all kinds of threats. I'm pretty sure some of it is blackmail. The doctor told me Lilah had alcohol in her blood. I think she coerced my sister into drinking it." She played the whole recording.

PC Hutton made notes as he listened. Finally, it ended. "That's interesting. Coercion is a big accusation though. So is blackmail. May I take it with me? I'll get it back to you as soon as possible."

Becca nodded. "There's plenty of emails from Ruth on Lilah's laptop that back up the recording. I can get it if you want that too. What's going to happen to my sister, you know, if she wakes up?" The choice of words she used and the calm in which she delivered them made her sound cold.

"Undoubtedly, she would get points on her licence and, chances are, she would have it revoked for some time. But let's take it one step at a time. We'll be looking into this recording though."

After he left, Becca phoned the hospital but she was not prepared for the answer. The nurse on duty reported that a donor had sourced a private room in the hospital for Delilah McCallister and she had already been taken down there.

"If you come to ICU as usual, we'll walk you there."

"Sorry, what? A donor? What does that mean?"

"It means someone has paid for your sister to have her own private Intensive Care room. It won't make a lot of difference to her condition, she will still receive the care she is getting now, but it means you'll have some space to be with her privately."

"Is this normal? I've never heard of this sort of thing before. Who was it?"

"Ruth Trent."

Chapter Twenty-One

Drew had felt a physical punch right in his gut the day before when Catie told him Jack had proposed.

"Wow! That's some news, right there," he had feigned excitement. "Congratulations. So, the wife – ex-wife – she's out of the picture now?"

They were definitely over and when Catie left the room Drew stayed back. He was left with too many emotions to just walk back out to the diner and face people. He took a few deep breaths and buried whatever he was feeling as deep as it could possibly go. The sensation remained for hours. His appetite was lost, and he could barely switch off to sleep despite how much he needed it. Somehow, being a nice guy was never going to win him any medals, or girls. The Jack Sullivans of the world would always win.

But that was yesterday. Today it was just him and Catie, Sheryl would be in for the evening shift, and it had been busy enough for him to keep his mind focused on the job at hand. He had been civil, but the hurt just wouldn't go. Between fatigue and frustration, there was just no extra energy left for 'Drew jokes'. Over lunch, while she was out, he downed a few espressos. They would keep him going to the end of the night. It promised to be a rough one, requiring much more than he was able to give.

Sheryl showed up for her shift, pushing the door harder than needed. It slammed against the counter and the fairy lights jiggled around like they were all laughing at him.

Drew tutted. "Great start, Sheryl."

"And hey to you too. What the hell's up with you? You look like someone took a dollar and left a penny". He shook his head and raised his hand, making it explicitly clear he wasn't in the mood to talk about it. "Okay, so how's the morning been?"

"Busy."

"Usually busy makes you happy."

"Usually, I don't get told the woman I love is marrying another guy," he said flatly.

"Wh-what?"

"You heard."

"When did this revelation happen?"

"Yesterday."

"And you waited 'til today to tell me?"

"It wasn't on my priority list. What was I gonna say? Oh, hey Sheryl, I've been dumped again?"

"Technically, buddy, you weren't dating so you couldn't have been dumped." She caught his glare and shrugged it off. "I'm just saying."

"Never been given the chance."

"Seriously? You're gonna go there, are you? You've had a couple years. You just need to stop avoiding it and get your ass in gear."

"I told you. She's getting married."

Sheryl dismissed the idea. "She's only marrying him if another guy doesn't give her a better reason first. Be the other guy. The worst she can do is say no. And no never killed anyone before."

"What? I can't do that. I barely told her I liked her the other day. I can't jump in with a proposal."

"Says who?"

He thought about it, how it would go. Then shook his head. "No. I should leave it all alone, not get involved."

"I ain't buying this reserved crap. I've been riding this Catie merry-go-round with you forever. It's getting tired. I wanna see some action before I'm too old to know what's happening." She saw his face and backed off. "Okay, okay. I get it. On the plus side, you've admitted out loud you're in love with her. A step in the right direction, huh?"

"Where the hell's it gonna get me though, huh? The whole thing is pointless if she marries that guy. I just need to do myself a favor and forget she even exists."

"Oh, that's new, sulking? I've got a couple kids you'd be in good company with. Well, you have fun with that. I'm gonna get ready for my shift. One of us still needs to be an adult." She took off her coat and pushed the swing doors open heading to the staff room.

"Sympathetic as always, I see?" he called out. "Oh, and before you shout your mouth off, it's not common knowledge, okay, none of it is. So, I'd appreciate a little discretion this time. Can you manage that?"

A second later Sheryl returned wrapping her apron around her waist and tying it in a bow. "Whatever. Not down to me to cast judgement on anyone."

"Never stopped you before."

"Lighten up, will ya? You know what? I'm not crazy about you when you're like this. You're cranky as hell. You need to get some sleep."

"No shit."

"Grouch on your own time, will ya? We've got work to do. There's a lot to get through tonight." She headed back through the swing doors to ready the crockery for the evening's reservations.

When Catie returned from her lunch break, she was bright and cheery and wore a smile. As much as Drew wanted to punch Jack in the face for proposing and shake Catie until she understood what Jack's motives were, she still made his heart flutter and he still wanted her. Frustrated, he sighed hard.

"Wow. That sounded like a big deal. Everything alright?"

"Everything's just peachy," he said sarcastically. "Good lunch?"

"Yeah, I actually feel good, like I'm finally clear-headed. I feel like a weight's been lifted. Like I can actually breath now. I don't remember the last time I felt that way. Crazy, isn't it?"

"Perfect."

She detected something off with his answer. "Did something happen while I was out?"

"Nope. Everything is just fine."

"Sheryl in yet?"

Drew tipped his head in the direction of the kitchen and Catie went in. He could hear them both talking, a raised tone here and a whisper there, but he couldn't make out words. Then Sheryl stepped out.

"This is one for you," she took over the counter and ushered him out.

"What's going on?"

"Like I said. She wants to talk to you."

"Why? What about? I don't need any drama today."

"Who said anything about drama? She sounded pretty level-headed actually."

"I'm tired, Sheryl. Can we just get through the day please?"

"I'm tired too, so get your ass in there. Go talk to her."

"I really don't need this." Reluctantly, he headed to Catie. Inside, she was leaning against the counter waiting for him. "What's going on? What's this about?"

"I just asked Sheryl that exact same thing. Seems you're upset with me."

"I am? What am I upset about?"

"You've got something to say apparently. Something to ask me?"

"Jesus Christ! I asked her to be discreet."

Catie looked confused. "Discreet? About what?"

"Wait, what did she say?"

"She said you were tired and a pain in the ass, that you had a lot on your mind and you just wanted the day over with," Catie said. "But what you were really talking about with her was more involved than that, wasn't it?" She waited for him to speak but he didn't. "I know you two talk. So, what's going on? I got the impression when I got back from lunch that you were upset with me. I don't know why because I've apologised for my behaviour like a million times already. So, if there's something you need to say, just say it. I'm a big girl."

"Because, apparently, you're so clear-headed now."

"What?"

"You said as much not five minutes ago."

"Right. So why do I feel like you're saying that's wrong?"

And then he blew.

"Clear-headed enough to accept the thoughtless knee jerk proposal from a liar and a cheat?" he said, unaware the voice he just heard was his. "I mean, the guy is not even divorced yet and you're planning the color scheme of your god damn wedding? What is wrong with you? Think about what you are doing. He already broke your heart at least once that I know about and you're giving him free rein to do it all over again. He's shown you time and again that he's unreliable and unworthy, but you can't stop yourself, can you?"

"Wow!" she said. "Don't hold back. Where the hell has all this come from? And I suppose you are perfect, are you?"

"Compared to this guy, I'm a god damned saint! And I don't know why you can't see that. You know me, Catie. I wouldn't mess you around, I'm reliable and better yet, I even love you, damn it. What more do you need? Oh wait, you need a guy whose idea of love is lust. You don't want someone to care about your every waking moment or your future, you just want a booty call and a ring on your finger."

"How dare you!"

"How dare I? You gotta be kidding me. Tell me one thing the incredible Jack Sullivan has done that didn't result in you crying or climbing inside a bottle? Just one. I'll wait."

She took a deep breath and let it out slowly, attempting to keep hold of what little of her temper and composure she had left. "He is the only man ever to think enough of me to propose marriage. A guy like him could have any woman but he asked me. Catie Cambridge. You claim to have feelings for me but I don't remember you ever asking me out. What was I supposed to do? Hold off on a proposal just in case you might?"

Drew's heart pumped so hard he could feel it in his throat. "Well, if it is just about a proposal, the words, then I guess you're doing the right thing."

"What?"

"If that's all you need to hear," he said, his words edged in ice. "Then go for it. Get married, have babies. Have a thousand and have a great time making them. In fact, have a great life."

"Stop it!"

"I care about you, your future, about what you think and feel. I care about you so damned much it hurts. But you're intent on throwing your life away with him. Have you ever asked yourself if he thinks about you when he *doesn't* want sex or are you just his go-to on speed dial?"

"That's enough," she sobbed.

"You're the first thing I think of when I wake up in the morning and the last thing I think about before I go to sleep – when I get sleep - but if all you need is a guy to propose when there's absolutely nothing to back it up with, then who am I to question his motives."

"What are you talking about?"

"Don't you get it, Catie? He proposed *after* he saw me at your door. He was threatened, and I'm not even being conceited. It was obvious. I saw the look on his face. If I hadn't shown up, he'd still be stringing you along. And worse yet, you'd still be hanging there like a fish on a hook. Wake up, Catie Cambridge. You're smarter than that. Where the hell is your self-respect?"

"He said he had plans to marry me anyway. He said he was going to leave his wife and marry me just as soon as he annulled their marriage." As she recalled Jack's words, she also remembered that he referred to Carla as a roommate, that he only married her to get her father off his back. That he hadn't considered marriage a reason to stop seeing Catie and he didn't want children. And now Drew was querying her self-respect. The man had a point.

"Out with the old and in with the new? Marriage means that much to him, does it? If he dropped her that quickly to marry you, how easy is it gonna be to drop you for the next pretty thing he sees, and the one after that? The guy's a jerk, why the hell can't you see that?"

She was beginning to, but pride was getting in the way.

"Don't you remember he dumped you just a few days ago?"

"Because she found out," she cried. "Jack told me she forced him to call."

"So if she hadn't found out, he'd still be lying to you. He dishes it out and you believe it. Every single word. He throws you a line and you don't question a thing."

It hurt that Drew was right. Jack had sold her the idea of a great life, all on his terms, and she went for it. No questions asked.

"What else am I supposed to do? I'm not getting any younger."

"You're supposed to love the person who proposes because you want to be with them for the rest of your life, not because you think time is running out. This ridiculous deadline you've given yourself is the root of it all." He sighed, trying to calm himself down but it wasn't working. "I take it he wants kids?"

She shook her head then covered her face.

"You've got to be kidding me. After all this, he doesn't even want any?"

"I just wanted to be married. And I wanted you to be happy for me."

"What did you expect?" He pushed the door about to leave. "A god damned parade?"

She wiped her tears with her apron and gaze at him. "So, shall I leave?"

"Right on top of this evening's plans, that's what you come up with? You know what? Do whatever the hell you want. I'm done talking. I can't help you anymore."

Catie grabbed his hand, keeping him from leaving. "You can't do this to me, Drew. I *wanted* your blessing."

He laughed hard. "If you can't see what a massive mistake you're making, I seriously wonder how you made it this far in life. He's the guy you're gonna run to if you have a problem? He's the guy whose shoulder you'll cry on when you have a bad day? Jack Sullivan will be there, will he? Or will he be with some other woman while you're at home wishing you'd seen sense? Catie, you don't need my blessing and you sure as hell won't get it." He pushed her hand away. "You know what? You should've gone to the ER when you collapsed 'cause if you need anything, it's a shrink." He stormed through the swing door rushing past Sheryl.

She heard every word. If passers-by in the street hadn't heard, it would have been a Christmas miracle.

"So much for not being dramatic," she said.

He pushed the front door so hard the panes shook. "Go to hell!"

Chapter Twenty-Two

After a busy day at her sister's cottage, talking to the police, and eating, Becca headed out to the hospital. As before, the paparazzi were there. This time, at least fifteen of them waited, but she was prepared. Becca pulled her scarf up to her face, taking comfort in the warm folds and hiding there. An onslaught of camera flashes and questions launched into her face.

She made a mental note to show up at different times thus making their wait as long, unpleasant, and unfruitful as possible. She hoped it might deter them. She elbowed and pushed her way through.

The Christmas tree in the entrance was lit up beautifully, but the breeze and temperature from the constantly opening electric doors had buckled and dirtied the lower branches. They looked wretched and ragged. She could relate. At the lift, her phone vibrated and trilled from inside her bag. Emma's name was on the screen.

"Miss McCallister, thank god I caught you." There was anxiety in her voice.

"What's wrong?"

"I've got to be quick because Ruth will be back. I've just found out something you ought to know."

"Go on."

"Ruth emailed the press. She's using your sister's accident as a publicity stunt for the next book. I'm so sorry."

"I've been battling with the paparazzi for the last two days. Thank you for letting me know. At least I know it's down to her. She's such a nightmare, isn't she?"

"We sent flowers and signed a card," Emma added quickly. "I'm sorry but I've got to go."

Becca put away her phone, angry that the teen was frightened in her job and angrier that she helped put her there. At the ICU, she pressed the buzzer and took a blob of sanitizer before sitting down on the chair opposite. A young boy and a man sat in two seats and Becca took the one next to the boy. He was draped over the arm of his chair and leaning against his father's arm. The pair of them looked exhausted.

"Tough times, huh?" the man said. Becca nodded back, not expecting to converse. "It's not the kind of thing you expect to happen, is it? Sitting outside ICU right on top of Christmas."

"No," unsure what to say and how appropriate it was to say anything, she said, "Are you visiting someone special?"

"My wife. The boy's mother. She came off her horse this morning. It's taken a few hours to get her a bed in here. We did a bit of hoping and praying and somehow one became free. I just hope the person whose bed it was recovered and they're not..." He looked at the boy. "You know. It'd ease my worrying if I knew that. How about you?"

She had some idea what they were going through. In some ways it was better and in others it was worse. They had each other at least, but then having to console a child in a situation like this was unbearable.

"My sister. Car accident." Then it occurred to her that if Lilah was in a different room, that may have made the space. "It might have been my sister. She's been moved. Maybe she freed up the bed? I'm sure it'll be okay." He seemed to visibly brighten knowing that and stroked the boy's head. It made her feel less cross over Lilah being moved without her consent. It wasn't something she had even considered but at least it helped another family. "I hope it all works out for you."

"And you."

"Miss McCallister?" A nurse called from the door. "If you'd like to come this way."

As she stood, the man said something else. She wasn't sure if it was to her or the boy, so she turned back. He was smiling sympathetically as if he knew who she was.

"Good luck with your sister. My wife loves her books."

Becca returned the smile. She had forgotten about the local news reports. She wondered how many people other knew about her situation. There weren't that many McCallisters in Holcroft hospital's ICU.

"Thank you."

Thirty seconds later, they stood outside the private room. "We've set her up in here. I'm sure she'll be comfortable." She opened the door and saw Lilah's bed surrounded by all the machines she had before. It was a brighter room, with beige walls, and prints in frames of flowers and abstract art. They tried hard to add some home comfort, but there was only so much a picture could do. The room's size seemed compact in comparison to the ICU ward, but it was big enough for Lilah's needs. Two comfy-looking chairs were angled at the base of the bed with a table in between.

The walls were pale, along with slightly darker tan coloured curtains in front of a Venetian blind. It was pulled half-way down and Becca looked down to see the roofs of vehicles and the lights in the shop windows opposite. In the darkness of winter, multi-coloured Christmas lights were the only welcome piece of colour to be found.

"While you make yourself comfortable, can I get you some coffee or tea?"

Lilah smiled. "Actually, that would be lovely. Coffee please." Having a little time alone with Lilah in a private space was surprisingly pleasant.

On the table were two vases and inside both were generous bouquets of flowers: one in shades of white while the other a selection of rich festive tones. Both brightened the room and were as welcome as they were festive. Next to the white bouquet was a card which Becca eyed thoughtfully. It was from Paul and the staff at school. She wasn't surprised. Paul was a caring man, considerate with his staff, and promoted family life. He had been supportive during her parents' funeral and his wife had assisted with the food at the wake.

She sniffed the orange tiger lilies and roses as she picked up the card. It was from Ruth Trent Literary Agency and signed by Ruth and Emma. Seeing Emma's handwriting took her back to the days when Becca marked her work. It was a momentary flash of nostalgia when everything was right with the world and Lilah was well, even her parents were still living and breathing.

"Look at this, Lilah. Ruth's dug deep and found a heart. She's sent you a card. Emma's signed it too. They've sent flowers. Nice ones. It's about time that woman did something nice for you."

The door opened, interrupting Becca's thoughts, and a nurse brought in a tray with a mug of coffee and a plate of biscuits upon it. She placed it on the table next to the flowers. A big beaming smile covered her lips.

"Hello, my lovely. It's good to see you again."

"Margaret, isn't it?" Becca said. "It's good to see you too."

"How are you?"

"It's been quite a day to be honest."

"Are you still working?"

"I'm on compassionate leave." Becca volunteered the information without a moment's hesitation. Margaret was the easiest person to speak to. "I did try to work but my boss sent me home. I went to Lilah's house, had a chat with the police. You know," she quipped, "as you do. Then had to deal with the reporters outside."

Margaret absorbed all the information. "I heard about them. Your sister's quite the celebrity."

"It seems my sister's wonderful agent has something to do with them," she said in dark tones. "And this room."

"They must be very fond of her."

"I suppose. I don't want to sound ungrateful, but I know Ruth. She did it because she wants something later down the line. You never get anything for free with her. I'm sorry to say I've been on the other end of her. It's not pretty." She suddenly hated saying anything against Ruth considering the room and the flowers, but she knew the real Ruth. It was just a matter of time to see where the payback would be. "Has anything changed with Lilah?"

Margaret gently plumped the pillows and checked the notes on her clipboard at the end of her bed.

"No, but she's in the best place. We'll monitor her and keep her comfortable while she sleeps. I heard you talking to her when I walked in. That's a good thing, I do it too. You just never know how much she can hear. She might not show it, but there's nothing to say she can't hear what we're talking about, or even recognise familiar voices. Who knows? Maybe it'll be enough to pull her back?"

Becca listened. That made sense. Just because Lilah looked like she was asleep, didn't mean that she wasn't listening. "Let's hope so."

"How did it go with the police?" Margaret queried.

"Interesting. I think they'll be in touch again."

"Did they say what'll happen?"

"She'll probably get a fine and points on her licence. She might be arrested. To be honest, it doesn't matter what they do, does it? So long as she's alive. Maybe the other driver will press charges? Who knows? I'll cross that bridge when I come to it." Becca stopped in her tracks when she saw the beam across Margaret's lips. "What?"

"I'm almost certain he isn't that kind. He's a very gentle soul, a sensitive creature who wouldn't hurt a fly. Even if they hurt him, inadvertently."

"Have you met him?"

"Yes."

"But he's not in ICU?"

"No."

Margaret's economical word choice was bewildering. Becca accepted what she heard. "He's going to be okay though?"

"A few broken bones but he is healing nicely. Actually, I wanted to talk to you about something a little delicate."

"That sounds ominous."

"Far from it. The young man is interested in finding out more about your sister."

"You mean her celebrity status?" Becca's disappointment showed. It was rare for anyone to want to get to know Lilah nowadays without wanting some of the limelight. "He can do that on the Internet."

"I don't think you understand. He's really worried about her. It's the trauma. I think reading her novel will help him get to know her. I gave him my copy earlier."

"It's a romance novel," she said more abruptly than she intended. "Do men read romances?" She hated herself for the assumption, especially when she had a class filled with both boys and girls. Getting them to read any book was a chore.

Margaret smiled knowingly. "I have a feeling he's open to it. I was hoping you'd be open to him reading to her."

Becca's entire body froze at the idea. "Um…" The awkwardness overwhelmed her.

"Just hear me out. I think if she hears a familiar story, it could help her recover. What do you think?"

"I could do that myself," she said. "It'd save him the trouble."

"I don't think it'd be any trouble," Margaret replied. "In fact, it would be therapy for him too. They both shared this trauma," she emphasised. "Maybe they could share the therapy too?" Margaret had provided a good argument; one for which Becca could not form a rebuttal. "There is a problem though. It's against hospital policy. Patients from the same accident are not meant to meet as it's possible it could compromise police cases, though I've never known that to happen." Margaret continued, her tone becoming more serious as she spoke. "But I'm more of the opinion of what's right for the individual, rather than what's right for bureaucracy. Red tape can be an unnecessary and impossible nightmare. I'm sure you can appreciate that with the students at school."

"Well…" she trailed off, unsure what to think. She sighed gently, unable to think of a single counter-argument. "Will someone be here with him?"

"Me."

"It seems a bit…"

"What?"

"I don't know what the word is. It's just that, ordinarily I'm protective of her but having her in a coma, I'm doubly protective."

"Of course. I understand. And that is another reason why it'd be helpful for them both."

"How do you mean?"

"You could think of it as doing a good deed. Letting him see your sister could help him to heal quicker and while he's reading, she could come back. I think it's an experiment worth trying. The pros far outweigh the cons."

She nodded. It was tough to argue such a good case. And she would do anything to help Lilah get well again. "He's a good person, is he? Trustworthy?"

Margaret nodded. "He's a very caring and lovely young man. Very considerate, adorable actually. I think you'd get along with him too. Is it a yes?"

Becca nodded.

"Good. Then just leave everything up to me. I can't wait to tell him the good news. Don't forget to drink your coffee while it's hot," she said, and left the room.

Becca pulled the seat next to her sister's bedside with her coffee in her hand. "I'm not sure what I just agreed to, Lilah, but it looks like you're getting some company."

Chapter Twenty-Three

"What *are* you doing?" Ben said in a stage whisper. He hoped not to catch anyone else's attention as Margaret tiptoed through the ward. He watched her peek around corners with exaggerated movements like she was a spy in a silent movie. "Are you looking for something? Or someone? You look like you're auditioning for a play." He didn't know whether to laughed or be concerned. "Seriously, what are you doing?"

She placed her index finger over her lips as she stared in his direction. She then held it in the air as if to imply 'hold on.' He nodded his acknowledgement and waited but for what, he didn't know. She disappeared around the corner and was out of his sight for a full two minutes, leaving Ben to sit in bed, confused, waiting for the next instalment. Then, when he saw her again, she was pushing a wheelchair so purposefully towards him, he wondered if she would stop in time or just smash into his bed. He tensed waiting for the nudge to the bed's frame. It didn't come.

"Ready?"

"Ready for what? I don't know what's going on." Startled and confused, he waited for an explanation with wide eyes. It was as if she had pre-arranged something with him but overlooked telling him exactly what the thing was. "Are we going somewhere? What's happening?"

She didn't answer but, with an immediacy that shocked him, she pulled back his sheets as if to reveal something he had never seen before. Exposed and surprised, he stared down at his legs clothed in the hospital pyjamas and cast he'd worn since being admitted. It wasn't the grand reveal he was expecting. Though not worried, this was somewhere between assault and assistance, yet he didn't understand why she would do either.

"Margaret, what are you…?"

"Trust me," she whispered. "We don't have a lot of time."

"Why don't we?"

Handling him confidently, she manoeuvred him into the wheelchair highlighting years of experience. Her arms and chest were soft, bouncing under the fabric of her uniform next to Ben's face and body. It was the nearest he'd had to a hug in the longest time. She smelled earthy, as though she had recently doused herself in herbs and grass, like he was being manhandled by the branches of the strongest tree in a forest. He was a wiry man, it was true, but what he lacked in muscle, he made up for in height, hidden strength, and witty conversation. She took the top cover from the bed and threw it over his lap then reached for the book and phone.

"Is this about the charger?" He was amazed at how easily and quickly she moved him. "It's a little elaborate, don't you think?"

"Put them under the blanket," she whispered directly into his ear. "And shh! We've got seconds to pull this off."

"Pull what off?"

She kicked off the brake and pushed him towards the nurse's station then swung him around the corner, through the doors, and into the corridor. He took her lead and remained silent until she gave him the all-clear to speak again.

It was a fresh view for him since waking up in his bed days ago. Seeing other parts of the hospital gave context to his current home. There was more than just the grey box of the ward with fellow patients who never woke or spoke, one nice nurse and one horrid one. Whatever this mysterious escapade was that Margaret had in store, it was a welcome break.

Nobody was in the corridor as they stopped at the lift. Whether it was pure luck, or she had somehow arranged her timing beautifully, he didn't know. She'd done a good job getting him, unchallenged, out of the ward, but it felt like a mystery tour that he hadn't signed up for. Finally, the lift opened, and she bundled him inside. She leaned over him to press the button for the second floor.

"We're alone now," she said.

"Margaret, are you kidnapping me?" his question was part serious, part humour, but all genuine. He felt the vibration of her laughter through her tummy as it pressed against the canvas fabric of the wheelchair. It made him smile. For some reason, he trusted her, whatever she was up to, he somehow knew instinctively that it was for the good of something or someone.

"My lovely, I'm doing a good deed for a host of very special people. If anyone challenges us, close your eyes and then it'll looks like you're resting."

"I *was* resting before you abducted me. And you didn't answer my question. Are you kidnapping me?"

By the time the lift reached the second floor his question still wasn't answered. He feigned sleep as the doors parted and Margaret pushed the wheelchair out. As she wheeled him down the corridor, he opened one eye ever so slightly. It was enough to see they were moving down a long, wide corridor. It was easily long enough to be an airport terminal, with lights high up on the walls, punctuating the greyness, but for this journey, he wasn't aware of the destination. Doctors, nurses, orderlies, janitors, and patients all walked, or were wheeled, past and alongside them.

Abruptly, Margaret stopped next to a door. It felt like they were exactly above his own ward if his sense of direction was working correctly. She opened the door and backed him in, as if keeping an eye out for any onlookers. Ben found himself looking too. Giving time for the chair to be inside the room comfortably, she let the door close with a thumping sound that absorbed into the wall.

"So, where are we?" Then she swung him around to see an occupied bed. Immediately he felt awkward, as if sharing a space with someone equally as unaware of what was happening. He looked at her: a young clear-faced woman with the reddest of hair framing her face. She looked asleep. Tubes fed into her arms, and machines surrounded the bed. And then, instinctively, Ben understood. "It's her, isn't it?"

Chapter Twenty-Four

Plumes of breath left Drew's lips as though he was a dragon breathing fire. He felt like it. He'd lost it, completely lost control. Adrenalin dominated his body and fatigue was a distant memory.

At first his anger and frustration kept the adrenalin pumping so he didn't care about being cold, but after ten minutes of walking around the block, the chill had penetrated the cotton of his T shirt onto his skin and, as the seconds ticked by, his lungs grew raw from inhaling freezing air. Then the temperature won its fight with his temper, shocking him enough to return to his senses and he strode back towards the diner.

He went over it again in his head as he headed back down Franklin Street. Things were voiced that needed to be said but what didn't sit well was how hard he ripped into Catie. She didn't deserve that. Between his fatigue and frustration and her being in the firing line, it was a mess. He felt bad. Worse than that, he told Sheryl – his closest friend and confidant - to go to hell. Not just said it either, he'd roared it so loud his throat was sore. And he had meant it too with every single fiber of his being. They had been bickering all day, but he didn't remember the last time he'd had a bad word to say to her. And she deserved not one iota of it.

It was a first for them both. He hadn't seen her face when he yelled, but he guessed she wouldn't be thrilled. She had a way of dealing with unruly behaviour with two kids at home and used logic, care, and caution knowing there was no point in starting a shouting match. And Sheryl understood the Catie-situation had him running in unnecessary circles, that love made people do crazy things. In the deepest part of his heart, he knew he never meant to shout at either of them.

Fairy lights shone in the darkness like a beacon of peace guiding him back. He looked through the window to see both Catie and Sheryl working as though nothing had happened. The first set of six diners were already seated, drinking, and enjoying festive merriment. His absence enabled Sheryl to deal with them. All the preparation work had been done and every ingredient was ready, thanks to his earlier diligence. He pushed open the door and both waitresses stared, perhaps expecting the second reservation to be standing there. As soon as they registered it was Drew, they continued working.

The heat hit him instantly winding him, but he was thankful for the diner's warm embrace. It would still take a while to warm back up. A cacophony of voices filled the air: waiting staff, diners, and carols playing in the background. Except there was nothing even slightly festive about how he felt: a mixture of sorrow and guilt. He went behind the counter and reached for his sweater that he left on his bar stool.

"You must be freezing, put it on." Sheryl saw it in his hands. She sounded like she was talking to one of her kids, with words measured and careful like she was diffusing a bomb even though the explosion had already happened. "Everything's under control, okay?"

He analysed her words. Was she referring to the diner or his temper? Did she expect another explosion?

"Is your mind here, buddy?" she asked without an ounce of emotion.

"Yes, ma'am."

"Good." She handed him the food order. "Catie's covering drinks. Next one's set to arrive in a couple minutes. "Let's get to work."

"Sheryl, I shouldn't have -"

"We've got a job to do right now. Save it, okay?"

Sometimes, he thought, she really did excel in being the boss. He nodded.

The door almost flew off its hinges with a party of six women, all high-spirited and all laughing at the effect they had opening the door. All office-workers from the same street with nothing on their mind but partying, each one dressed like a Christmas decoration in glitter, sparkles, and sequins. Sheryl sat them down in the second booth as Drew delivered the first table's food and agreeing to take a couple of group photos. When the second group saw him, they wanted photos too which, quickly switching on the smiles and laughter, he obliged before being instantly yet unexpectedly devoured by them. Sheryl rescued him on her way back to the counter.

Minutes later, a party of two stood at the door so Catie readied two menus in preparation.

"Table for two. Name of 'Carla'."

Catie guided them to the last booth then saw their faces. Jack grinned. The woman with him gave her a polite smile. Shock forced Catie motionless, along with her heart. For a few seconds, she felt nothing. Overwhelmed with trying to process what she was seeing, jealousy, anger, loss, betrayal, and sadness filled her entire body rendering her utterly numb. Her mouth was dry and no words would leave it. The woman's lips were moving, but Catie couldn't absorb the words.

"Miss?" the woman prompted. "Are you okay?"

"She's fine. Can we get a couple drinks or are you going to stare at us all night? I mean, I know we're incredible, but..." Jack laughed as he looked right into Catie's eyes, right *through* Catie's eyes. It was as if they had never met before, never shared a kiss, never shared a bed before. He stared as if it was the first time they'd ever met. How could he be so cold, so thoughtless? So cruel and callous? Why would he do this? Why would he bring together his wife and his lover? Was it for sport? Was he drunk? Had he taken something?

Catie studied Carla. She looked like a nice person. Her blonde hair framed a heart-shaped face which was full of concern. She wore an evening dress, a sequin and lace design around the neckline that was both elegant and dignified. The two looked good together. They looked as if they were headed out to the theatre. Then it struck her, they were out on a date. Jack was patching things up with his wife. Catie imagined them at home together, living their life - a life she had no business interfering with. She tried to breathe, but her chest and throat stopped working as panic filled them both. She felt sick.

Drew watched from the counter. He recognised the man in the couple but didn't instantly place him. When he saw Catie's reaction he understood straight away. He moved around the counter with immense speed.

"How's it going, folks?"

"I can't do this," Catie said in a tiny voice, almost unheard beneath the carols. She turned and ran into the back room attracting Sheryl's attention.

"You got some nerve, pal." Sheryl leaned against the booth focussing only on Jack, a sly smile covering her face.

"What I do?"

"I think the question is, what didn't you do? Wouldn't you say?" she said.

Carla lost her smile, and curiosity took over. "What's going on, Jack?"

Rage rose from the pit of Drew's stomach, but one yelling session a day was way more than enough.

"She's had a tough week, guys." He managed a polite, sympathetic smile for Carla's sake. "Boyfriend trouble. They can be jerks. Know what I mean?"

"You know what?" Sheryl said, unable to hold back. "Maybe you should eat somewhere else tonight. I'm pretty sure this diner's full. I hear the food can get stuck in your throat, and you don't want to choke on it, do you, pal?"

Carla sank back into her seat. "I don't understand what's going on. We had a reservation. Jack, didn't you make this reservation?"

"I did, yeah," he grinned. "I thought it'd be good. Guess I got it wrong."

"Let's just say your husband likes the dessert here a little more than he ought," Sheryl said. "Sorry, Ma'am, but I think it's time you both left." She pulled open the front door and held it while the two edged off the booth's seat.

Drew stood between the booth and the door, not taking his eyes from Jack once, but ensuring a smooth departure.

"You know," Jack whispered. "I always knew you had a thing for her. You know what your problem was? You were just too weak to do anything about it. But whatever chance you think you have, it won't last 'cause she knows how good she had it with me."

Drew smirked. "Make this your last visit. Or I'll make next time your *last.* Understand?"

Sheryl slammed the door and they watched Carla's animated response. Jack's smile wasn't going to cut it this time.

"And you wanna know why I've turned my back on men. If I've lost you a couple of customers tonight, I'll hold my hands up, buddy, I'm real sorry. Once I started, I had a hard time stopping. That was something special, wasn't it?"

"Don't be sorry, we don't need his kind. Never did. Never will." He looked at the customers whose attention had been completely focused on the commotion. It looked like it had made their night. "Give them drinks on the house, will ya? The cabaret's over. Heck of a shift this is turning out to be." Drew took off his apron and handed it to her. "Gimme ten minutes. I gotta go talk to Catie."

"Sure. I got it covered."

He strode through the swing doors and into the tiny staff room in the corner as if it was a life and death situation. Without a word, he scooped her up in his arms. His bulging biceps enveloping her, protecting her from everything Jack Sullivan. He filled his face with her hair, inhaling it hard as if she was all the breath he needed to go on living.

"I can't handle it anymore," she sobbed, breaking into a million pieces. "It's relentless. It's like I'm having a breakdown or something. He said they'd finished. He said it was over between them."

"He's a goddamn piece of work. I'll give him that. It's gonna be okay, I promise."

After the tears passed, Catie finally pulled from his grip, her eyes as red as rose petals. "I'm fine now, I am. Honest." She stepped back, seeing his sweater was a mess of tears and mascara. "I'm sorry. I ruined it."

"This isn't ruined. In fact I'm gonna put it in a glass case so it stays like this. I'm gonna treasure it forever."

Chapter Twenty-Five

Ben was motionless, transfixed, as he relived the car crash frame by cinematic frame. He couldn't take his eyes off her face then or now. She was a lifeless woman with an unknown past and an unforeseeable future. The motionless eyelids, the delicately formed lips. She looked like she was made of porcelain. She looked exactly the same as she did in the car. And in the dreams. And in the nightmares.

"She looks so peaceful. She looks so perfect."

"She didn't sustain any injuries aside from a few bruises."

"And a coma," his voice came as crisp as a winter's morning cutting through the air.

"Yes, my lovely. A coma. Talk to her, maybe she'll hear you."

Tears misted his view. He dropped his face into his hands and wept. Margaret comforted him, stroking his crown, circling it with her fingers as though it was a halo.

"She's going to be okay, Ben."

He looked up at her and sniffed, wiping away his tears with the back of his hand. "Can I touch her?"

Margaret nodded.

He stroked Lilah's skin, moving his fingers around her hand it until he was holding it. His heart pounded. For the second time, a connection had been formed. "She's so soft, so real," he sobbed. "I'm sorry this happened to you." He wiped his tears and looked at Margaret. "I'd give anything to go back before it happened and just not leave the studio that day. This is tougher than I thought."

"It's done now. Nobody can go back. I know it's tough, but it was meant to happen."

"This feels intensely personal. I'm not sure I ought to be here, or if I'm the right person to be here."

"You are the only person in the entire universe who should be here. You two went through something hellish together, but you both came out the other side. Trauma takes time to heal. This will start the healing process for you both."

She poured him a plastic cup of water from Lilah's visitor's water jug. He drained it and wiped his mouth.

"Ben, I want you to read to her, from her novel. They're words from deep within her mind. They'll mean something and the characters might jog her memory. She's already lived it. Maybe if you read to her, you'll pull her back this way."

He stared at Margaret intently, as if what she was suggesting was the most natural thing in the world. She might be a scheming manipulator, but she was doing it with the very best of intentions.

"Alright?" she asked.

He lifted the book and looked at Lilah. "However long it takes, one way or another, I'll read you back to life."

He opened the book where he had finished reading and took a breath. With a soft voice, he began reading Lilah's own words back to her.

Chapter Twenty-Six

Unbearably vivid dreams filled her mind until Becca woke to an incoming message on her phone. With only the screen lighting the room, it was unnerving.

Bad news. Just seen another email to the press in the outbox. Sorry. Emma x

Becca shook away her drowsiness as her heartbeat rose. What had Ruth been up to this time? She hadn't realised she had fallen asleep on the sofa. The day had somehow run away with her and after lunch the police called asking for access to Lilah's laptop. Perhaps Becca's comment about Ruth's attitude had planted a seed in their minds? If there was information to be found, they would find it organically, rather than accept hearsay from an angry sister looking for revenge. She wasn't opposed to launching a hate campaign on Ruth, but it wouldn't help Lilah if Becca was charged.

"She's quite a confrontational person," Becca had told PC Hutton. "My sister's particularly sensitive and I think Ruth saw that as weakness so bullied her. Maybe that's why she left in a hurry. She probably needed to clear her head after being threatened. And she wouldn't have taken anything with her because she wasn't going to be five minutes."

"After a glass of wine?" he queried.

"Well, yeah, I understand it's not ideal, but you heard the recording," Becca said. "She was coerced, threatened. It's as clear as day. And it was a small glass. And even then, I don't think it was a whole small glass." She stopped herself before she said anything else.

She wiped her sleepy eyes and switched on a lamp bringing light into the darkness of the lounge. If only she could do that with Ruth, she thought. Grabbing a bite to eat, she looked at Emma's message again. Ruth was so confusing. In one breath she was rude as hell and in the next she pays for Lilah's private hospital room. It was helpful to have Emma 'on the inside', but knowing she partly engineered the teenager's job, made her feel guilty to put her through working with Ruth at all.

She left for Lilah's cottage to pick up the laptop - going through the empty house made her shiver – then, after dropping it off at the police station, she parked at the hospital. She was more confident with the reporters this time because she knew Ruth was behind it. She could handle Ruth; she just didn't want to. It took up too much emotional energy. As she pushed through, she gave a disgusted sigh. They would get nothing from her. At least, not willingly.

Their questions had progressed from, 'How long until she dies?' to a blander and less harrowing, 'Have you any comment?' It highlighted that the shine was dimming from this particular story. If Emma's warning was anything to go by, maybe Ruth was upping her game to keep the attention switched on and the story relevant.

As she neared the lift, her phone vibrated. Local news popped up with a publicity picture of Lilah and a candid photograph of Becca. It was from the day before. Becca looked shocked and scared. She scanned down the screen. Ruth had done a good job of smearing her client's name implying Lilah had a scandalous alcoholic lifestyle that landed her in a coma, rather than the rage-induced accident instigated by Ruth herself.

'AUTHOR IN COMA!'. 'COMA AUTHOR ON DEATHBED!'. 'AUTHOR – JUST DAYS LEFT!' were among the related articles. Hashtags on social media dedicated to Lilah's condition included #DelilahMcCallister and

#LetLilahLive. Becca read a few posts, most being supportive from well-wishers. A few were libellous, but it was nothing she hadn't expected after the information Ruth was feeding the press. Becca understood the journalists didn't need facts to create stories - they were as much fiction as her sister's novels. Sensationalising her condition upped ratings, good news didn't. What did it matter if Lilah's reputation was lost in the process? According to the recording, Ruth was intent on cutting ties anyway. Doing that buried within a scandal was all PR for the agency.

Alone, she walked up the corridor and stood silently outside Lilah's room. Before she turned the handle, she mentally prepared herself. There was so much extra to process every day. She closed her eyes and whispered a hope, a wish, and a prayer. If anyone was listening, she hoped they would deliver some positive news soon.

"A-ha, I was hoping to catch you. Have you just arrived?" Margaret appeared.

"Hello. Yes, I have." Becca removed her fingers from the door handle.

"How's everything going?"

"How do I answer that? Well, it's been a really trying day. I've been playing detective and it's wiped me out." She saw Margaret's head tip with curiosity. "It's a long story."

"Try me."

"I saw the police again. It's all getting very involved, and Ruth Trent has outdone herself with nastiness. It's crazy, isn't it? You know, all I really want to do is sit down with my sister and chat over a coffee." She paused, thinking about that very scenario before adding, "And the worst thing is, I don't know if we'll ever even do that again."

"I have a feeling you will."

"I hope so."

"And how are *you*?" she asked in a way that focused attention directly upon Becca and her health.

"I've barely given it any thought. I've no idea which way is up or down to be honest. I'm not sleeping particularly well, though I suppose that's understandable. Christmas is almost here and I'm completely unprepared. Not that I'll have anyone to buy for anyway."

Margaret took her hand in reassurance. "It's going to be alright, my lovely."

Her soft tones hit all the right notes inside Becca's head. It was like an intensive therapy session just listening to her. "Is it?"

She nodded. "Right. Are you ready?"

"For what?"

"The young man I told you about," Margaret beamed as if proud. "He's here."

"What?" She gasped, lowering her voice. "Oh my god, I forgot all about him. He's here? In there? Right now? I can't do this. Not tonight. It's been a bad day and I'm…"

"Why not?" Margaret interrupted.

"Sorry?"

"Why can't you meet him now?"

She tried to find answers. "I just can't. I mean, the crash only happened a few days ago. It all feels so raw. He's probably really angry and I just don't have the energy to…. I wouldn't even know what to say."

"How about 'hello'," Margaret said softly. "Most people respond to friendliness."

"I don't think it's going to be that easy, Margaret. Friendliness can progress into conflict very quickly." Her heart pounded so much she was sure Margaret would hear it. "I'm just not up to it."

"But –" It was rare for Margaret not to be heard.

"Please, Margaret. I'm sorry if it's an inconvenience to him – and you for organising it. I'll wait elsewhere while he leaves. I'm sorry." She started to move away but Margaret took her hand again in hers.

"Believe me, my lovely, when I tell you that this gentle soul wants nothing more than to help your sister recover." Margaret didn't release her hand while she spoke. "Isn't that what you want too?" She watched Becca nod. "Then you've already got one thing in common."

"But I feel a sense of responsibility for what happened to him. When you mentioned him at first, it sounded fine, but I completely forgot all about it and now I'm here… Maybe we can do it another night?"

Margaret pleaded and pushed simultaneously. "It's for the good of all three of you. If it doesn't work out, I promise you I'll take him back to his ward and you'll never have to see him again."

"But what'll I say? What if it's awkward?"

"Just take a deep breath and compose yourself. We're going to walk in there now. Together. Okay?"

It was clear there was no way she was letting up. Becca inhaled deeply and let it out slowly. As Margaret opened the door, she followed her in as clueless and bewildered as one of her students. As the door automatically closed behind them, Becca forgot to even look at her sister, focussing instead on the man in the wheelchair at Lilah's bedside. He sat with his back to her but she could see he was slim and wiry with a head of curly, chestnut hair that almost reached his shoulders. From this angle that was his most interesting feature. As she moved nearer, she saw he was dressed in pyjamas and wore a blanket over his lap.

Margaret broke the silence. "Ben, I've got someone I'd like you to meet."

Becca tensed everything within her body. This was it. There was no going back now. He looked over his shoulder and she saw his face. Margaret was right, he was around Becca's age. He offered her a polite smile as he pulled the wheelchair around to face them both. His jaw was unshaven after days on a hospital ward and soft beard growth had made its way through. Under thick brown eyebrows, Becca saw his most appealing feature, his eyes. They were large, khaki, and intense. The skin around them was red and his eyes were glassy as if he'd recently cried. They came alive as he focused on her. Not usually one for over-dramatics, she was astounded at how easily they left her breathless.

Margaret was right again. There was nothing threatening about him in the least. In fact, he drew Becca in rather than push her away. He set the book down in his lap and smiled. What began as a polite smile had grown into a bigger, friendlier one. Extending his arm, he put out his hand.

"Hello. I'm Ben Christopher." His rich yet light voice was laced with a slight rasp that enriched its sound. "I'm really sorry to meet you under such horrid circumstances, but I'm still glad to meet you."

Becca received his hand which, she noticed, was warm in hers. The handshake was nothing like the men she worked with. This man's handshake wasn't about evidencing power, it was about making a connection and he was doing it in a unique and inexplicable way. One that unexpectedly increased her heartbeat.

"I'm Rebecca McCallister. I'm Lilah's sister. It's good to meet you too."

"I'd get up but…" His joke fell awkwardly on deaf ears. He added a soft laugh at the end. "I will soon, though. A couple of weeks and I'll be running marathons. Not that I've ever run one before, so that'll be new."

Margaret chuckled and then Becca broke a smile. "I'm…um…so sorry about your…" she looked down at his legs, unsure how an apology could make even the slightest difference to his situation. "I mean…I just…"

He waved his hand dismissing her words. "Don't give it a second thought. I quite like being waited on to be honest."

"Would you both like something to drink?" Margaret interrupted, breaking the awkwardness. "Tea, coffee? I might even be able to rustle up a hot chocolate or two?"

"Gosh, Margaret, that's an exciting idea," Ben said, over-egging it. "Hospital coffee is just *the* best. These coffee shops on every street corner can't hold a candle to the stuff you get here." He looked at Becca, "Have you tried it? You'll be spoiled for coffee anywhere else. Put me down for one, please, Margaret."

After such an introduction, she didn't dare decline the offer. "And for me too, please. White, no sugar."

"Black for me, please. Also, no sugar." He winked at Becca, adding. "Sweet enough, me."

Armed with the order, Margaret left the pair alone.

Becca nodded to the dog-eared book in his lap. "I think it's a lovely gesture you wanting to read to her. Thank you." She looked at Lilah, realising she hadn't even said hello yet.

"Thank you for allowing it, Rebecca."

She laughed awkwardly. "Oh, um, you can call me Becca. Rebecca sounds so formal, and I can't imagine formality is even needed in a situation like this. Although I've no idea what situation 'this' is."

"Becca it is." He gave a calm and measured nod that was laced with thoughtfulness. "I suppose we're just three people in the universe pulled together by a single event."

"That's profound!" She wanted to ensure those words remained in her mind forever. "And so poetic."

"Really? Good. I probably can't do it twice in a row, so best not expect it again." A noticeable pause ensued until Ben grinned. "Well, it's nice that this isn't awkward, isn't it?"

Becca laughed, instantly connecting with his sense of humour. She tucked her hair behind her ears, suddenly nervous like she was on a first date with a new boyfriend. He was interesting and mischievous, light-hearted, and philosophical all at the same time. She instinctively knew he was the kind of man she was drawn to. It was as if he exuded meaning like no-one she had ever met and was hit with a jolt of energy in his presence. Then she realised she could put a name to the feeling: attraction. It felt good that he seemed awkward around her too. Levelling.

"Margaret's a bit cheeky, organising this, isn't she?" he said. "Though I'm glad she did. I needed to see your sister, just to complete the circle. It's just that I've been lying in a hospital bed not knowing whether your sister was dead or alive and, if it's okay to be utterly honest with you, it was one of the worst feelings I've ever felt. Rather selfishly, the police wouldn't tell me a thing, nor would any of the other nurses and it's been like torture. Margaret's the only one who's been human enough to actually understand how I feel."

"You've been worrying about Lilah? After what you've been through, and you were thinking of her?"

"Of course," he nodded. Seriousness and sincerity covered his face. "Whatever I've been through is nothing to what she's experiencing. But Margaret's been incredible. She's there when I wake up, when I got to sleep, when I need painkillers. I've been having nightmares, really awful ones since the accident, and not knowing if your sister was okay was compounding it all. I couldn't bear it. That woman ought to be up for 'Nurse of The Year' award in my opinion."

"You're in a different ward, aren't you? I thought she only worked in Intensive Care."

"She's always on my ward."

"That's odd." Feeling more comfortable, she finally removed her coat and put her bag down. "It's strange you should mention your dreams. I don't usually remember mine and since all this happened, it's all I can do to stop remembering them. I wouldn't mind if they were something special but they're terrifying."

"The bad ones always hang around, don't they? It something about our minds that keeps hold of the horrid stuff to torment us. Imagine what life would be like if we didn't beat ourselves up with them all day long. That'd be great, wouldn't it? So, tell me about your dreams." He said, quickly adding in a higher voice, 'I want someone tall, dark, and handsome. No, sorry, I'm joking."

Becca watched and listened, finding it all surreal but secretly hilarious.

"I'm a bit nervous," he went on. "This is an unusual situation and I rarely get to meet anyone so…not that I'm usually locked up in some dungeon. I'm quite normal. Well, normal*ish*. No, what I meant was, I'm only asking about your dreams because I've researched them a bit. For work. Interpreting them helps understand where my mind is. Although you're probably wondering where it is right now. I just mean, for me, interpreting dreams helps with my work. Maybe a bit of analysis could do the same with you?"

"What exactly do you do, Mister Christopher?"

"Really? Come on. It's Ben. I'm an artist. You?"

"Teacher."

"Interesting."

She enjoyed his quick rhetoric. "They're vivid. That much I remember. I suppose it's the shock. There's nothing logical about them though."

"There rarely is. It's usually just a chunk of time your brain plays with, add to that colour and images from your day or your memories or something that popped up recently. Analysing them does help, though. I do believe that. I mean, it's just an interpretation, of course, but it can make sense."

"There's one that was…" Her smile fell as she recalled it. "I was on a vast ocean. On a small rowing boat. I had an overwhelming feeling of loneliness. The boat was red yet it was at night. How did I know it was red if it was night? I don't know. There were no sails, no rudder. No direction. I was just drifting. The waves were massive, and I was wearing my mother's scarf which was choking me. My alarm went off and I woke up. It wasn't a particularly positive dream to be honest."

"Water usually signifies emotions. Have you ever heard the expression 'as lonely as a boat'? Emotional and lonely while your sister is here, and maybe the choking is about being unable to breathe while this whole thing's going on. It's understandable. The colour's interesting. Colour is a major part of mine. Red. Red's everywhere. I put it down to your hair."

She instantly took a section of it between her fingers, then raked it away from her face as if she had meant to do that anyway. "My hair?"

"Well, your sister's hair, but yours is very similar. It's beautiful. I don't mean to be forward. I know I've only just met you."

"It's fine. Thank you."

"In the collision, I saw a red car coming at me then I saw her hair. It was so striking, so bold. When I close my eyes, all I can see is the fear in her eyes and her hair moving in all directions before she comes to a standstill. And then there's the blood, of course." He flung out his hand to reassure her. "Not that there was any in the accident, but you can't have a scary dream without blood, can you? My imagination was just trying to have its fifteen minutes of fame. You can't really blame it for trying."

She imagined the two cars joined and the drivers opposite each other. "It must've been terrifying."

He nodded, reluctant to speak, and pursing his lips as if to let out breath slowly. Was he in pain, or recalling the pain? Was it mental pain or physical? Or both, Becca wondered. She watched him shuffle the book between long, slender fingers before settling his gaze on Lilah. Was he trying to not cry?

He sniffed. "As traumatising as it all was, I just wanted to reach outside and keep her awake. I wanted to make sure she was breathing. I wanted to protect her." He closed his eyes and exhaled, then opened them again. "It was one of the worst times I can remember. I felt so powerless to help her."

"You did help though. You saved both of you. They said if it wasn't for you, the emergency services might not have responded. That's incredible. I've a lot to thank you for."

"Anyone would have done the same."

"I don't think so. Not everyone would have had the presence of mind that you did, Ben."

He gazed at Becca and gave a tiny, mischievous smile. "I wouldn't want you to think of me as a superhero, you know, what with this incredibly muscular physique of mine. I didn't need an ambulance as much as her. And, rather selfishly, there's the artwork too. I was on my way to St Weatherby to deliver it to a client. St Weatherby – that's just half an hour from my studio. You'd think I'd be capable of driving there in one piece, wouldn't you? I'm a grown man. It shouldn't be out of the realms of possibility. But leave it up to me to mess things up."

"I think your client will forgive you. Besides, I don't think it was you who messed things up. My sister played a massive role. I'm so sorry."

"There's no need." He waved away her apology. "I'm probably as much to blame. And I still don't know if the artwork is in one piece. The police are very cagey on what they tell you. They love keeping their cards close to their chest. Although, telling me whether or not a sculpture made it through the accident intact is hardly front-page news." He picked up the phone from the pocket at the side of the wheelchair. "I managed to get my phone back but it's out of juice. Margaret was trying to find a charger but I'm sure there was much more pressing jobs to do than that. It'd be nice to let the client know I was on my way to deliver it."

"What was it?"

"An angel. All four feet tall of it. Enormous thing, it was. *Is.* I hope."

"That's a big angel."

"It's an absolutely beauty too. You can imagine what mess I'd have got into if the wings were outstretched," he said. "There's no way that would've survived the accident. Knowing me, it wouldn't have survived getting out of the studio. Far too delicate. I'd have tripped or something. Total write-off, undoubtedly. Thankfully they weren't. But it's a gorgeous piece, best I've ever created. I loved every minute making it too."

"How long did it take?"

"Three months and I never missed a single day working on it. It's probably why we connected so much. Sometimes art becomes part of the artist, like it manifests into a real entity. A person, in this case. I didn't want to say goodbye. I'd talk to it every day, treat it like a co-worker. Does that sound weird?"

Becca smiled. "No. I think anyone creative has a gift and everything they make carries meaning." Without realising it she looked up at her sister. "Lilah talks to her characters all the time. They're totally real to her and if she does the job right, they become totally real to readers too. I tell my class if something they create resonates with them, then they've done a good job."

"Well, this piece certainly did. 'Course, if I can just let them know I didn't just run off with her money, that would be good. It's a team of solicitors too, so it would be helpful not to upset them."

She reached into her bag and took out Lilah's phone charger. "Do you think this would fit?"

Ben's eyes lit up. "Unbelievable!" He inserted the lead, and a connection was made.

"Maybe me showing up was the answer to all your prayers."

"An angel in disguise? Thanks so much."

She plugged it into the wall and left it there. Within a few seconds, his phone began bleeping as messages started coming through. "I'm glad I could help. Sounds like you're popular."

"I expect it'll be spam mostly. It's funny, I usually hate phones. I hate how they encourage people focus on them and not see the world around them. But I've really missed it. Lesson learned, huh? Don't judge."

"For what it's worth, I totally agree with you. I feel like I'm always telling my class to put their phones away." She looked at his fingers as they smoothed over the cover of Lilah's book. "How's the book? Is it tough going?"

He tipped his head. "I like it so far. Why would it be tough going?"

"Romance."

"Who doesn't love a bit of that?" He sounded sincere, without even a note of sarcasm. "Romance is a rare commodity nowadays. Although, if I'm honest, I'd rather not be reading it from a hospital wheelchair. That said, if I wasn't, I wouldn't have met its author. Or her sister." He eyebrows twitched ever so slightly, giving away his feelings. "Not that I usually go to these lengths to meet an author. This is definitely a one-off. Not to mention, it'd be a huge part of the working week hanging around in hospitals just to meet them. Probably a bit creepy too." He looked at his leg. "Not a fan."

Becca attempted to keep her giggles to a minimum, but he kept cracking jokes and she loved it. It had been some time since she felt this at ease in a man's presence, not to mention excited.

"Have they still got you working or are you on compassionate leave?"

"Compassionate leave. My Head Teacher, Paul, he's been really good about it. I made the mistake of thinking I could cope with this and school on top but one of the kids' phones went off in class." Becca nodded an acknowledgement of his earlier point. "It was on the news and she blurted it out in front of everyone."

"In front of the whole class?" his lips took a dramatic 'O' shape.

"I don't know what I was thinking imagining it'd be kept quiet. I hadn't realised the toll it was taking. I broke down in front of them all. Me, their teacher. It wasn't pretty."

"You're human though. You're allowed to have emotions."

"Ooh," she smirked. "Emotions. That's a conversation for another day."

"Tough, are they?"

"We're just not best friends. I prefer to be a little more practical around my class. I leave emotions to Lilah, she's much better at them."

Margaret knocked and opened the door in one swift motion. Becca instantly moved to help her with the tray, moving the flowers a half an inch from where they were, trying to justify the movement.

"Getting along, are we?"

"An understatement, I'd say."

Becca saw the wink he gave Margaret, as if they were sharing a private joke. She watched as Margaret checked Lilah's machines, making notes on the board at the end of the bed. "The flowers look good," she said. "Family friends?"

"Ruth?" Becca smirked and scoffed in one. "God, no. She's the devil's spawn personified."

Ben roared with laughter, catching both women unawares. His entire face lit up, as he held his chest in pain. His grin transferred to a grimace within a split second.

"Well, it's true. She's got a real darkness to her. She's unpleasant, untrustworthy, uncooperative and all the other 'un' words you can think of."

"Wow," Ben said. "Remind me never to upset you."

"I had to phone her about Lilah and she was as nice as pie. The best she has ever been with me. And then I find out the paparazzi that've been hounding the hospital entrance are down to her. They've said some truly awful things to me, things that would make you feel sick. Then there's the articles she sent to the local news, and I discovered she paid for this room. And here's the worst bit, she's using the situation as a PR stunt for the next book. I mean, how low can you go?"

Ben's face dropped. "That's rough."

"You never know where you stand." Becca picked up Ben's coffee and handed it to him. Being closer to that smile and those khaki eyes made her heart pound with excitement. She could barely stop looking.

"If you don't want her to visit," Margaret said. "I can find a reason to stop her."

"I'd give that some thought if I were you," Ben said. "It protects Lilah at least."

"What can you do exactly?"

"I know just how to deal with people with a bit of darkness in them. I've had an eternity's experience. Leave it with me." And with that, she left the room.

"Sounds like she's on the case. So, Becca, what do you think of this book? I take it you've read it?"

"Before it was published, actually. Family perk. I liked it."

"And not just because your sister wrote it?"

"Actually, that'd be a reason not to like it. Don't you have siblings? That's how it works."

"Nope, only child. Probably spoiled rotten as a kid, but relatively balanced as an adult. But that does depend on your interpretation of balanced. Anyway, I read to her earlier and she's been very polite. I've not had a single complaint. Yet."

She liked his humour. "She'd appreciate you reading it. I hope she's listening."

"That's the idea. And I'll do it until they kick me out. Although, if they do, it'll be Christmas dinner for one and a pair of crutches for company. And if they keep me in, it'll be Christmas in hospital. Either way it sounds pret-ty bleak."

"I can't imagine much will change for her, but if you're still here at Christmas, why don't we all spend it in here? The three of us," Becca said, unsure how she'd felt confident enough to voice it.

"You know that makes me want to do everything I can to stay in hospital."

"It's just an idea. I wouldn't want to scupper your recovery."

"Suddenly I'm totally up for a good scuppering," he flashed his eyebrows.

"If there's someone at home you'd rather…"

"There's no-one," he confessed. "No partner, no parents, no siblings. I don't even have neighbours. It was just me and the angel. I take it there's no Mister Becca?" he asked, blatantly digging.

"There's no Mister Becca. Dating's been a pointless endeavour, so I stopped a while back. They're all either married, or gay, or experimenting."

"Well, just to lay my cards on the table, we're not all married or experimenting. And some of us are very happily into women." He gave her a sideways glance and tapped his nose. "Just saying."

"I'll keep that in mind." She couldn't hold back her smile, outrageously flirting with him. She felt like a teenager in his presence. He couldn't be any cuter, she thought. "I'm just curious but, if you don't mind me asking, when did you lose your parents? For us it was just a few years ago."

"Wow, you've had a rough few. About seven years for me. I'm not sure you ever get over it, you just sort of grow with it. Mine had me late. They were quite sweet really. Dad treated mum like they were forever on a first date and she was always trying to make him laugh." He sighed at the memories. "It can all get a bit rubbish, can't it? Christmas is meant to be all about family but when there's no family left, who do you share it with? It's no wonder we throw ourselves into work. It's the only stable thing left."

Becca looked at Lilah, motionless in the hospital bed, wondering if she was following the conversation, or the flirting. It was the most enjoyable use of thirty minutes Becca had had in a long time.

"If you'd like, I can carry on reading…Until the guards take me back, that is."

"I'd really like that."

Ben blinked. "Me too."

Chapter Twenty-Seven

Winter nights on the east coast were expected to be cold, but tonight felt like the coldest yet. Catie stood on the sidewalk holding her scarf up to her face as she hailed a cab. Mischievous breaks in the clouds teased humankind that maybe it would snow, maybe it wouldn't. The weather always had the last laugh.

With the morning to herself, she decided it was time to do something about the mess she was living in. The housekeeping wouldn't do itself, and there was nobody to do it for her. Like her love life, it was time to organise the laundry. She even indulged in putting up a Christmas tree, a small one just three feet high. She picked it up from the market the year before along with the one her father had. Both were artificial with bottle green pine needles. She decorated hers with silver baubles, silver teddy bears, and cherubs. On top was a pre-made silver star covered in glitter.

At the curb side, she watched a group of women roar with laughter as they celebrated their office party night. They staggered past the sparkling displays in shop windows, and the rows of apartment buildings. Dressed in clothes more suited to the summer - the cold didn't seem to be a bother when alcohol and high spirits took over - she wondered what kind of night they'd be enjoying and if romance would play a part.

A cab pulled up and she gave Drew Denby's address and sat back in the darkness, watching the party-goers dancing on the sidewalk. Every one of them wore a grin as if nothing in the world mattered. From the outside looking in, it appeared everyone in the world was having a great time, as if everyone's life was perfect.

Everyone except Catie.

Last night's entertainment, courtesy of Jack's poor acting skills, made her stomach wrench with a mixture of embarrassment and humiliation. What was it about him that he had to be playing people all the time? If not his wife, then his lover, and if not Catie, then bystanders. Drew and Sheryl had instantly and automatically fought her corner. After their earlier fight, it was incredible they had all pull ed the same way, but that said more about their respective characters than giving in to a rough day.

Jack had been an embarrassment and it was unforgiveable. He was usually so charming that acting sadistically felt completely out of character. How hadn't she seen him like that before? How had he hidden that part of him? Perhaps, like her dad said, Catie had decided not to see it. There was so much fake about Jack that she questioned everything he had ever said. The last six months may well have never happened for all the honesty in it.

As she sat in the cab, she relived the moment he said he didn't want children. He was so cold, so emotionless. She realised it was the first time she caught herself thinking negatively about him. It felt as natural as a thunderstorm after a sunny day. Relieved she had rejected his proposal, she now considered the affair nothing more than another oversight of judgement. Sure it was another for Catie's list, but she was learning.

She thought about Drew, how he held her afterwards. How caring, considerate, and loving he was. And then, in that split second, she realised something. Drew was the one she'd turn to after a bad day at work. He was the one whose shoulder she would cry on when things turned bad. Drew was The One.

Ten minutes later, the driver pulled up outside Drew's apartment. She leaned over the buzzers, reading each one to see which was his. She hadn't visited since the summer she started working at the diner. He held a barbeque and now she realised she was invited because he liked her. She wished she had known about it back then. It would have saved them both a lot of heartache. Once she identified which apartment it was, she pressed it and waited.

"Yeah?" Drew sounded curious. "Who is it?"

"It's me, Catie. Catie Cambridge," she added. "Can I come up?"

. The door buzzed open and she headed up to the second floor, trying to remember which door it was. Before, she'd followed Sheryl and her children up the stairs.

As soon as she was outside, the door flung open as if Drew had been waiting. He wore a blue sweater, faded denim jeans, and a curious smile. He hadn't shaved today and the growth looked good on him. Even from a meter away, she could smell his clean, manly scent. It was alluring.

"Catie Cambridge? Because I needed the clarification." He grinned, "What's going on?"

"I was…um…"

"You weren't gonna say you were *just* in the neighborhood, were you? On a Sunday night?"

"Well, it wouldn't be a lie. I mean, it took a cab to get to the neighborhood but," she paused trying to find the right words. She'd had all the journey to find them but now he was standing opposite, somehow her brain had been cleared of logical thought. "I just wanted to …um…"

"Why don't you come on in?"

She hadn't felt this awkward around him since her first day at the diner. She followed him through to the living room, unable to stop staring at his butt as he walked ahead of her. He filled a pair of jeans like no other man she knew. Maybe it was his height that made his long strides look so good, so appealing. *Stop lusting, Catie, that's what got you into trouble before. And that's not why you're here.*

"I'm sorry to just show up like this."

"Something on your mind?"

"Er…yeah, actually. I wanted to talk to you. I probably should've called first."

"It's fine. Take a seat."

She sat down and cast her eye around the room, trying to recall how it looked when she was there before. It was bigger than her living room and with a different layout. Drew had focused his sofa and armchair around the TV, which was off, with an off-white leather chair in the corner of the room. A curved steel stand with a glass globe on its end – a statement reading lamp that said something about its owner – seemed to hover overhead from the carpet to the seat to illuminate his books when reading. It looked as if it had been fashioned from a giant lollypop.

The light shone on the cover of the open book on the seat rendering its identification useless. The chair itself was worn at the corners and matched nothing else in the apartment. Perhaps it was an old favourite that moved from home to home with him. It suited him; it was elegant and dignified. It faced a full-length window whose blinds were not pulled yet. The view was limited by apartment lights punctuating the darkness and, in the distance between the buildings, a plane's lights intermittently flashed. It was either taking off or landing through the winter clouds. Next to the chair was a wooden table that accommodated a pile of books, genres of which she noticed ranged from archaeology to business to cookery.

In the corner, next to a three-quarter wall-wide bookshelf stood a Christmas tree that was easily as tall as Catie. The scent of pine seductively merged with Drew's own. The tree proudly claimed the space and upon each outstretched arm was a scarlet bauble that reflected the lamp's light. At the tree's trunk was berry-red tinsel and, at its apex, was a curious star. Sheriff-style.

"I'd forgotten what a great place you've got."

"Thanks. It's near enough to the diner to walk and far enough away that I don't spend every waking hour there. Although," he smirked, "sometimes it doesn't feel like that."

"Nice tree. I'll bet there's a story behind the star. Childhood toy?"

"Right. That I wanted to be a cop so bad I kept the plastic star I wore when I was eight so I could hang it on my Christmas tree each year?" He laughed.

"I mean…I didn't know you wanted to be a cop, but I can see that could happen."

"I don't. I never did. I was the kid watching my mom's every move in the kitchen. Keeping streets free of crime is not my thing. I found it in the street. Some poor kid must've dropped it. So now it lives here."

"Sheriff Denby. Protector of all," she said. "I kinda like that."

"Not Chef at Drew's Diner, then? Thought it had kind of a ring to it."

"We were here that first summer I worked for you. Sheryl brought her kids. Do you remember that day?"

"Of course, it was a great. You sat right where you are now too. We should do more of those, shouldn't we? Oh, this shows you how often I don't have guests. Can I take your coat?"

She stood, unravelled the scarf from her neck, and unbuttoned the pink and white checked coat then watched him put them both on the chair. "Good book?" she asked, genuinely interested.

"It is, actually." He laughed as if caught out. "You look great, by the way."

"Thank you. So do you." As she said it, she noticed how shy he seemed.

"I should offer you a drink. Wow, I'm bad at this."

"I thought you had a thing about drinking?"

"I have a thing about people drinking *alone*. But I'm not alone and neither are you, so…" he grinned. "I'll be right back. I've got a bottle somewhere, and some glasses," he said, raising his voice from the kitchen. "As you can tell I don't entertain much, so it's a little…ah, here we are. It's red. That okay?"

"Sure."

He returned with the bottle and two glasses, setting one down in front of her. He plunged the corkscrew in and twisted it. As it yielded, the loud pop made them both smile. He filled her glass.

"So, you came all this way to talk to me. Must be pretty important. I hope it's not bad news."

She shook her head. "Not at all. I just wanted to apologize."

"For what exactly?"

"Oh wow, where to begin. For being a pain in the ass lately. I guess sorry for breaking your dishes, sorry for the way I treated you and Sheryl, sorry for getting mad, and for last night's entertainment. It got pretty ugly, didn't it. Yeah," she ran through them all in her head. "I think that about covers it."

"That's a whole lot of sorry."

"There's a whole lot to be sorry for."

"Well, the insurance will cover the dishes. Sheryl's no wallflower and can take care of herself. And whatever happened last night wasn't down to you. Thanks for the apology but, for what it's worth, I think you've been through a lot and to come out the other side and still be smiling, that's something. But while we're handing out apologies, I think you're way overdue one from me. I had no right to talk to you the way I did. Between a few sleepless nights, a couple of personal disappointments, and a bellyful of Jack Sullivan to see me through a lifetime, I guess you were in the firing line. I completely lost it. I came down way too hard. It was unacceptable and I'm real sorry."

"You were only looking out for me. It's not like I have anyone else to do that for me."

"I don't know what I was thinking. I even told Sheryl to go to hell."

"I have a feeling she'd already forgiven you before it even happened. She's crazy about you."

"I swear she thinks I'm one of her kids. It's kinda nice sometimes though. Not that I'm not thrilled to see you, but you didn't need to come all the way over here to apologize."

"Coming here feels more…"

"Personal?" he said, cradling his glass in his hand. "Meaningful?"

"I hope I've not overstepped…"

"Not a bit," he interrupted. "In fact, I'm glad you did. I'm always down for getting things personal. I mean…", he laughed, resigned. "Well, I think you know what I mean."

She sipped her wine. "I had no idea he was gonna be there you know. Jack, I mean."

"He's a piece of work. It was a pretty low. You've gotta wonder what goes through the mind of someone who gets off on seeing others hurting. I've gotta ask, what the hell did you see in him?"

"He used to be sweet and charming. I really didn't know he was married, you know. I mean he had some strange time-keeping going on but I just went with it. You do when it's someone you like. You want to please them and accept their ways. When you came to my apartment the other night, he showed up out of the blue."

"You don't need to explain anything to me."

"I just want you to know. I was as surprised as you."

"Surprise wouldn't have been my choice of words."

"What would?"

"Disappointment. Sadness."

"He hadn't been in touch since we broke up. Then he shows up acting like everything's fine. He said his wife had never meant anything to him, and that he only married her to keep her father off his back. Who says that?"

"The guy's a jerk. It sounds like the actions of a sociopath. He cares about nobody but himself and that was more than evident last night."

She looked him in the eyes as he spoke. "You're right. I hadn't seen it before, but that's exactly it. He didn't even seem to realise how horrible he was being. I just wonder what else I missed in all that time."

"Maybe you were so desperate to be loved, you let it all fly. Love makes us incredibly forgiving."

She listened to his words applying them to her and realised how patient Drew must have been. "That makes a lot of sense if I think about some of the guys I've dated." She raked her fingers through her hair and let it fall back over her ears. "I've dated some losers! What the hell is wrong with me?"

He smiled sympathetically. "Actually, I don't think there's anything wrong with you at all. We all have something from our childhood that plagues us in later life. Maybe that's yours?"

"What's yours?"

"Probably staying *out* of trouble. I remember one time I stole my dad's car and I totally intended to crash it just to get his attention. I was mad about something. I don't even remember what, but I knew that car was his pride and joy and it would hurt him."

"How old were you?"

"Maybe thirteen? I wasn't that tall yet and could barely reach the pedals. I got it out of the garage, put it in reverse, and hit one of the garbage cans at the end of the driveway. My sister came out because she heard the noise. I told her I was doing a job for Dad, and she believed me. I drove it back into the space it was in originally. Nobody ever knew except her." He watched Catie laugh. "My sister still remembers. She'll probably use it against me some day. Smart girl. Insurance."

"She's younger?"

"We're six years apart. She's the baby. I was the proverbial protective big brother from the word go. But if I did anything wrong, she ratted me in every single time. Little brat. She does it every chance she gets. So, yeah, I've always avoided getting into trouble."

"Where do your parents live now?" she asked.

"They moved down to Florida a couple years ago. Jennifer and Tom, her husband, are still in New York. I don't get to see them much, but I think we're all probably due a visit."

"A family like that sounds perfect. And not getting into trouble seems like common sense. A history of dating losers is different."

"It's a skill. You did real good if Jack was anything to go by. So, how about you? What's your story? What were you like as a kid?"

"I was a lot to handle. My poor dad! I mean, without making this a therapy session, I had an unusual upbringing. My dad raised me since I was twelve."

"How come?"

"Mom left us for a younger guy. I guess when you peel away all the layers, that's the essence of it. She just left. Maybe there was a build up from Dad's point of view, but for me, one day she was there and the next she wasn't."

"I'm so sorry."

"It was tough," she nodded. "I mean, it wasn't like she'd died, so we couldn't go to a gravestone and grieve or anything. She was just gone. Puberty's tough enough but going through it without a mom…I gotta hand it to my dad though, he had answers for every single question I threw his way."

"I expect that's why you're so close with him now."

"He's everything," she nodded. "Back then, I was a bratty teenager. I ran away one day, and he didn't even know."

"How could he not know?"

"I left after he went to work and I got back before he did. I spent the day walking through the city and hooked up with a couple boys from school. I stole a lipstick and they thought I was cool so I kept kissing them all day. It was innocent really, 'cause if you think about it, I could've gone a whole lot further. I got a little wayward for a while after that."

She wondered what his response was going to be. Would he judge her for her teenaged rebellion like Jack had? When she saw he was listening, she continued with her story. "I was mad with life, with Mom for leaving, with Dad for letting her go. Just about everything. But then I also didn't want him to be worried that I'd gone. I mean, she'd left him, I didn't want him to think I'd abandoned him too. He didn't deserve that. Can you run away to make a point but not even make that point? It was a crazy time. He still doesn't know even now."

"Did you ever see her again?"

"No."

"Did you try searching for her?"

"I thought about it but the older I got I started thinking if she didn't want me when I was a kid, why would she be interested now? When I saw my dad the other day, we talked about her. I met him once, this other guy. It was at the store. I remember she was real excited but I didn't understand why. Dad said he heard the guy left her for someone else a couple years later."

"What happened to her?"

She shrugged. "I don't know. I don't know if I even want to know. She could be dead. It's been such a long time since she abandoned us, it feels like another life. Dad said something strange, though. He said she didn't abandon us, she left us. If I consider it abandonment, that makes us victims, and we're not. That we adapted to fit the hole she left. Kinda puts things in a different light, doesn't it?"

"Your dad sounds like he's a smart guy."

Catie smiled then drained her glass before Drew refilled it.

"We've worked together a while now and I didn't know any of this. Talking with you is probably one of the most exciting things I've done in a while."

"Maybe you need to get out more."

He laughed. "Have you given any more thought to leaving? I know you said it was on the back burner, but I know how quickly plans change in the world of Catie Cambridge."

"My dad said it's up to me but I could hear it in his voice he doesn't want me to go."

"Understandable. You're his only family."

"He said it would be a lot of upheaval for nothing because I'm not running to a new job, I'm running away from…well…you know all about that."

"I gotta say, I agree with him. Sure, I'm biased because I want you to stay but moving out of state…It's a lot. And running away isn't the way to deal with things anyway. You gotta face the tough stuff head on. Maybe your mom would've stayed if she'd faced her problems?"

Each time Drew spoke it was like he gave her mini life lessons she hadn't realised she needed. She was astounded at how intuitive and perceptive he was. He really did listen to her when she spoke. It was so refreshing.

"What would tip the scales for you?" he asked.

"Maybe the idea of a fresh start, new surroundings. I can't deny it, it sounds pretty good."

"You've got to do what's right for you. But please think about it because leaving would affect a whole lot of people. And I know someone who'd be sad if they didn't see that smile every day. I take it you gave Jack the bad news?"

"I think he already knew. It couldn't have been that surprising, could it? He hardly said a word, like he wasn't even interested. Kinda took the wind outta my sails though. He was always one step ahead of me."

"Not anymore."

"You're right. Not anymore." Saying the words aloud reminded her that Jack was in the past. And perhaps there was someone new on the horizon.

"All you gotta do now is look to the future."

"That sounds like a really good idea. Any suggestions on how?"

"Oh, I thought you'd never ask. I've got a few." He looked into his wine glass and swirled the last few drops around as if he was reading the leaves inside a teacup. "So what does the future hold for Catie Cambridge?" He pointed inside the glass. "Wow. It's pretty good actually. It says here you're going on a date. The guy's a chef; runs a diner right here in town. He's a couple years older than you," his eyes flashed up to meet hers and he winked. "It says his head's screwed on and better than all of that, he's incredibly easy on the eyes."

"He is, is he?" As she laughed, the weight of the world she'd been carrying was gone.

"He sounds like a catch," Drew said. "You should definitely go."

"When is it?"

"Tomorrow evening. A dinner date, a seafood restaurant. It's a great choice. You're gonna love it."

"Can you ask it who this amazing guy is? I just can't imagine who he is."

"Ah, let's take a look." He focused back on the glass. "Oh wow! You are not going to believe this. It's me. I didn't see that coming at all."

She saw his smile was filled with mischief and relief. Finally, he found the courage to ask her out. "Impressive. You're good."

"I've heard it said. I can only agree."

"It sounds romantic." She sipped the last of her wine, enjoying this playful side to him. It felt natural and wherever there was genuine laughter, she wanted some of it. No fixed fake grins, and no demands or orders. Just two people enjoying each other's company.

"That's me. Hell, baby, cut me in half and you'll see it runs all the way through."

She noticed he couldn't take his eyes from her. "How come I didn't see it before?"

"Maybe you were looking in the wrong places? So how about you focus on romance and happiness instead?"

With a flutter in her heart, she giggled. "I can't wait."

Chapter Twenty-Eight

Pulling out of the hospital car park, Becca decided on three things: that Christmas dinner with Lilah and Ben would happen, however it manifested, that she would drive past his studio to check it was secure, and that Ben Christopher was possibly the most enchanting man she had ever met.

In the short time she spent with him, it had felt like a blind date, but good. They had covered more topics of conversation and found out more about each other than she had ever done on any date. She thought about the way he asked and answered questions. He wasn't just being polite, Ben was actively listening, and flirting too. He was a breath of fresh air.

And those eyes.

Margaret had been quite insistent that they meet, and Becca wondered if she had been match-making all along. Now they had met, she wasn't opposed to the idea, indeed she was extremely interested in seeing him again. She just didn't imagine she would meet someone special as the result of Lilah's accident. Nor did she think she would feel something strong for someone after such a short amount of time – minutes!

She headed away from town, towards the accident site and said a silent prayer as she drove past it. The police sign calling for witnesses was still standing but given the circumstances, it was unlikely anyone would have seen anything.

Ten minutes further on, driving through dark windy lanes, she entered a stretch of straight road with potholes punctuating it. She'd been past there before but hadn't given it any thought. On the right of the straight section of road was a small car park, used wisely it would accommodate three cars. Behind the parking bays was a building set back from the road. That, she now realised, was Ben's studio. It was an old warehouse studio on the ground floor with a living area above. It was a regular landmark on trips to meet with Lilah for coffee.

She pulled into one of the bays, being careful to drive around the potholes. Her headlights reflected in the windows and ghostly white shapes of canvasses stared back. She stepped out of the car, leaving the engine running and the lights on. She tried the main studio door, ensuring it was all locked up. Then she pushed her face up against the window, using her hand above her eyes to look inside. Ben was right, there were stacks of artwork everywhere: paintings leaned against the walls, some leaned against the desk, varying shaped pottery stood next to a kiln and, at the back of the studio, she could just about make out another desk and chair.

Pleased everything seemed secure, she got back in her car and headed back the way she'd come to get back home. The whole detour had taken no more than half an hour. Finally home, she got into bed and smiled. Meeting Ben Christopher had been quite the happening. Remembering he still had Lilah's phone charger gave her justified reason for seeing him again and to provide a cover for the excitement she felt.

As she drifted off to sleep, she replayed his profoundly poetic words: *'I suppose we're just three people in the universe pulled together by a single event.'* And, for the first time in days, she slept through the entire night.

***

Margaret wheeled Ben back to his ward as covertly as possible.

"That was quite the event," Ben said. After she helped him back onto his bed, he settled in pulling the covers up to his chin. "Dare I say it, but I think she liked me."

"Of course she likes you. Why wouldn't she?"

"You, my dear Margaret, are a wonderful creature."

She grinned at the compliment. "Do you need some painkillers before you sleep?"

Ben shook his head. "For some reason, nothing hurts at all."

Chapter Twenty-Nine

It was seven when Catie opened the door, grinning at the sight before her. In black jeans, a leather jacket, and a gray and white striped scarf tied in a knot around his neck, Drew held a bouquet of red roses.

"Not too cliché, I hope?" he said as he handed them over. "I haven't bought flowers for a while. Is it still the thing to do?"

"They're beautiful. Thank you, yes, they're perfect. Come on in. Give me a few minutes to put them in water and I'll be ready."

"Take your time. The table's booked for eight."

She unwrapped them and set them on the counter while she sought out a vase. "I'm kinda surprised you booked a restaurant. I thought you'd be tired of food when you work with it all day?"

"Gotta eat, don't we? Besides this restaurant is amazing." He leaned against the counter while she tended to the flowers. He watched her take each stem and arrange it artistically. "You're good at that."

"I like being artistic. I don't get to do it much. So, am I the latest in a long line of dates you've taken to this place?"

Drew mock gasped as though he was insulted. "Seriously, when was the last time you saw me with a date? And I thought you'd have worked out by now that I've only had eyes for one woman in the last couple years."

She lapped up the mention, flashing a smile his way. "Is the chef one of your buddies?"

"Actually no, I don't know who it is. Although you've just highlighted why I ought to network more. I guess I just needed a good reason to go back there, and I'd say you were it."

"Looking to make an impression, huh?"

"Maybe? Kinda? Is it working?"

"I'd say it was." She finished arranging the roses and headed to the closet for her coat.

Set on the edge of the market was a selection of restaurants. Some were more upmarket than others. Drew's choice was one of the much nicer ones. Inside it was easily the classiest restaurant Catie had ever set foot in. Their table ensured they were not overlooked nor overheard by other diners. A tinted window next to them gave them more privacy.

The decor was old English with much of its furniture in rustic wood and beams covering the ceiling. Strings of tiny white-gold lights were wrapped around wooden pillars from the ground to the ceiling, and a large, gold Christmas tree claimed the corner of the room. An open fire, with flames that danced to the soft classical music, warmed the room both in temperature and atmosphere.

She watched people walking past outside, some leaving for the day and others on their way to dinner. One couple caught her eye as they walked hand in hand from the darkness into the soft illumination of the fairy-light lit brick arches. There was no doubt about it, it was Jack. The same fixed grin, the same walk. On his arm was a young woman, clearly not his wife. Her shoulder-length mousy blonde hair, which sat neatly beneath her red, woolly bobble hat proved he had a type. She was laughing, enjoying her time with him. Suddenly, they stopped walking and passionately kissed as though they were the only people there. When they eventually stopped, they turned back on themselves, away from the market as if to head home. Catie could bet what else was on their agenda tonight.

She thought she'd feel shocked, but she didn't. There was nothing but gratitude that he was out of her life. The man was ruthless, a player and a sociopathic player at that. She turned her attention back to Drew who, when she looked in his eyes, she knew she was with the right person.

He sipped from his glass, and she copied. Restaurants were his natural environment, there was no doubt about that. He came alive within them. He looked every bit the experienced man about town, confident and mature. Attractive and sophisticated, he knew how to behave with a woman, with everyone else, how to be respectful yet comical and was confident enough to just enjoy it.

"You okay?"

"I feel like I stand out."

"You do," his lips curved. "And for all the right reasons."

His hand moved across the table and his finger sought hers. When they connected, his fingers flirted with hers, stroking her skin. There was something incredible about him that just seemed to ignite a part of her she hadn't realised existed before. She looked him in the eye while he did it and witnessed his excitement through them. A waiter approached, breaking their moment, to take their order.

"Can you imagine working in a place this size?" she asked. "I wouldn't know where to begin."

"It'd be incredible to own it, wouldn't it? Maybe someday this'll be me. Dream big, huh?"

"Think of all the staff you'd have," she laughed. "The pressure alone would be terrifying."

"But pressure can be a great motivator. I'm an ambitious guy. I love challenges like that. Look at our place. Two of you, one of me. We've made it work over the past couple years and all against the odds. Who'd have thought a place like that would've done so well. Locals love us. Things are looking good."

"I do admire your optimism, and just how much you keep on top of it all. You're organized, you're patient."

"I've built it up from nothing. The diner means a lot. It's my future. The time, effort, and money that goes into it is unreal, but it's so worth it. A few years ago I had different one. It was smaller, still in the city, but off the beaten track so not many people knew it was there. I learned a lot from that. Where we are now makes more sense. You learn so much from mistakes, don't you?"

"Um, you're looking at the poster child for that one."

"I mean, everyone needs to eat. It's just finding that magic formula. If the staff are a good match and the food's great, you can take it to the stars." His mind was working ten steps ahead. "And, do you know what, Catie? I think I've found it, that magic formula. If I hadn't left the other diner when I did, I wouldn't have had this one. And then you wouldn't have walked in that day, and we wouldn't be sitting here now."

"Where did you get your business sense from?"

"I don't know, I think it happened organically. Working for myself seemed to be the most natural thing in the world. I knew I had to work at different restaurants to get as much experience as I could. And there were a lot of chefs I wanted to study with too. The ones I couldn't, I ended up reading their books to learn."

"I saw your interests when I came over. Archaeology if I remember correctly? I share that interest. It's everywhere," she gestured outside, implying all of Boston. "It's fascinating who was here before. It makes you realise it's not just about us. You can get caught up in the 'right nows'. It puts everything into perspective."

"Yeah. I've got a curious mind that needs feeding as frequently as my stomach. I like other things too, sports - keep the body as fit as the mind and all that." As he spoke, their food arrived and glasses were refilled. "I'm in a good position right now. The diner's going from strength to strength and I've got only great things planned. I think I've got to that stage in life where I know what I'm doing. I'm in a good place for...um...I'm ready for the next stage of life and...um..."

She heard his hesitancy. "Are you nervous?"

He tried to hide his laugh. "A little, yeah."

"Why? You seem like the most confident person I've ever met. And comfortable in your skin, in your surroundings, like there's nothing that could stop you."

"Is that what you think? Let me tell you a secret then," he lowered his voice. "I'm nervous as hell because I can't believe I'm sitting here with a smart, amazing, beautiful woman and I'm rambling on about who knows what. I guess I'm a little overwhelmed that you agreed to come out."

That was a leveller. "All you had to do was ask."

"I wanted to so many times. Sheryl gave me such a hard time too. I can't tell you how many times she kicked my ass about it."

"I'm nobody special, Drew."

"But you're everything to me."

She smiled shyly. "Tell me about when you were a teenager? I'll bet you were cute."

"Yeah, I was incredible. No spots, no nerves, just full of confidence," he laughed through his sarcasm. "I mean, puberty's the worst, isn't it?"

"Whoever invented it, needs a slap. Did you have a favorite toy?"

"My bike, probably, then cooking. Mom and I spent a lot of time in the kitchen. Then, when I was old enough, I discovered girls. That was an eye-opener. I'll bet you kept your dad on his toes."

"He built me a doll's house. I loved that thing. Dad built it and I painted it. Each room was a different color. It was great. I'd make up stories that happened in each room. I loved it. Then my mom left. Not a care in the world, then afterwards, not so much." She looked at him, back to reality and breaking the moment of nostalgia. "I kinda miss that, don't you?"

He nodded slowly, thinking. "Yeah, I guess I do. It's interesting you saying you like painting. I have a question I'd like to ask, but I'll leave that until a little later."

"Now I'm worried."

"It's a conversation while walking through the park. With the lights and, who knows, maybe it'll snow too. How does that sound? I thought it might be kinda...I don't know."

"Romantic?"

"Just can't help myself. I'm a sucker for that stuff. Kinda ridiculous, huh."

"Flowers, fancy restaurants, mysterious walks in the park. You're setting a standard here. I could get used to this, Drew."

"I hoped you would."

After dinner, they headed for the park as late-night joggers ran by, some with dogs on leashes, and others without. The snow clouds that had hung around for days were now absent leaving the sky clear and star-filled spotlights punctuated the path. There wouldn't be snow tonight but it was as if Drew had personally ordered the evening to be perfect anyway.

"So what was this mysterious question you wanted to ask?"

Drew's hand found hers and they interlocked fingers. "Is this okay?"

"It couldn't be more okay. That wasn't your question, was it?"

"No. It's a little less gentlemanly than that. I was going to ask that, since you're artistic and enjoy working with colors, I'm planning something big with the diner and wondered if you'd like to help me with it?"

She stopped walking, and faced him with a curiosity-filled expression.

"I want to decorate it, but I haven't a clue what colors would be good. Is that something that would interest you? To design it?"

"Wow. Sure, I'd love to. When?"

"I want to redecorate the old girl and give her a new lease of life. That way we begin the new year properly. Fresh and prepared for the future. A little effort could pay dividends later on down the road. It'd be over the holidays. I understand it's a tricky, but I don't have a lot of time to play with. It'd be great to spend the time with you...of course. I mean, unless you have other plans. It's Christmas after all. I don't wanna get in the way of -."

"I'd love to help," she said, cutting in. "I visit my dad over the holidays, but he's not fixed on dates, just so long as it happens. Aside from that, I've got no plans."

"I can't imagine why but, selfishly, I'm glad you don't. I was playing with the idea that it could be some kind of date. It won't be as fancy as this, but I promise it'll be fun. I'll spring for some pastries and coffee, and we can order lunch in." Then he pointed to his face, "and I'll bring this stupid smile since it just won't go away. How does that sound?"

She laughed. "Yeah. It sounds good."

"So that's a yes?"

"It's a definite yes," she said, as they continued walking. "I'm looking forward to it. What about you? Won't you be visiting your family?"

"Everyone's got their own lives. I'll call them. But when we do all meet up, it can get a pretty intense. Tom and Dad talk,

Mom and I cook, and Jennifer gets away without doing a thing. It's like we're kids all over again. It'd turn you off families for life."

"Your family sound amazing."

"Hey listen, how are you spending Christmas Day?"

She stared at him with large eyes and her palms facing upwards. "Like I said. Nothing's planned."

"You're eating alone?"

"If I even bother cooking at all." She watched his face drop, the smile he'd been wearing for the best part of the date had vanished. "It's okay, Drew. I'm good with it. I'll probably clean the apartment or sleep in late or something. It's not a big deal."

"Ah, Catie, come on! The next thing you'll say is you don't have a tree."

She laughed. "Until a few days ago, I didn't. Who was gonna see it? I live alone."

"So do I, but you should decorate the place anyway."

She shook her head. "Doesn't seem like it's worth it. I'm only going to put it up just so I can take it down again. I mean, what's the point?"

"Oh, Catie, Catie, Catie! Someone's lost their Christmas spirit. "Okay, I have an idea, hear me out. Spend it with me. The whole day."

"What?"

"I volunteer at a shelter each year. We could go together, and after I'll cook us dinner? Just the two of us." His eyes salivated as if he were about to land the biggest prize of his life. "What do you think?"

It was a selfless idea, and one that, guiltily, Catie hadn't ever considered before. "What would I do at the shelter?"

"Literally help out. Whatever needs doing, we do. People are great there. They're friendly, fun, and the whole community gets involved. It's a leveller, you know? We get to make someone's day just that little bit better. I've done it a few times. It keeps me connected with the community. Keeps me grounded. It's a good time, I think you'd enjoy it."

"Okay," she agreed. This was someone who meant every word they said, every gesture they gave, and wasn't just doing it for kicks. "You're quite a guy, aren't you? The surprises never end."

"Too much?" Worry laced his tone. "It's just I've held a lot in for two years. I just wanna share it all with you. I don't wanna scare you off but I don't wanna let you go either."

"You just opened my eyes in ways I never expected. From anyone. You have depth. It's new being with someone who thinks about other people instead of themselves."

Once they'd reached her apartment, Drew stood opposite. He cupped her cheek then leaned in to kiss her. Soft, gentle lips claimed hers and she yielded instantly. She felt valued and protected simultaneously. Feeling his warmth, his body, and his hold on her, it was one of the most sensual experiences she had ever encountered. If there was any lust, it was being controlled. All too soon, it was over.

"I've wanted to do that for the longest time. Before I go, there was one other thing. You said leaving town could be the fresh start you thought you needed." He held their linked hands up to his lips. "Well, could your 'new start' be us and the 'new surroundings' be a redecorated diner?"

She liked the idea. "You've put a lot of thought into that."

"Spoiler alert, I wanna do *everything* I can to stop you thinking about leaving town."

"Really?" Her eyes shone with hope. "Do you mean that?"

"Oh, Catie. You have no idea."

Chapter Thirty

"Philip walked swiftly across the room, slamming the door behind him. He looked through the window, staring to the far end of the garden where the statue stood. Boxes of balloons and bunting were stacked around it. It wouldn't take long before the grounds took shape for the party. Thanks to his staff, the house had already been decorated. The garden hedges wouldn't take five minutes.

He had to talk to Chaz today, but he knew the man would find all kinds of excuses not to show up to Eden's party and Philip knew that would crush her. And all because Chaz shied from conflict. But Eden's feelings didn't matter to Chaz, not so long as he was fine. That kind of cowardice was the one trait Philip just could not stomach in his brother."

Ben had been kidnapped again. He was a willing victim so long as this situation continued. Margaret left him reading to Lilah while she dealt with another patient. She had muttered on her way out something about a horse rider, but Ben had been more interested in Lilah to listen to the details. The clock ticked softly, along with the beeps from Lilah's machinery.

He tried to focus on the novel and not on a certain red-headed teacher he had just met, but his mind kept wandering. He hoped she visited soon. That alone would make his pain less and his hospital stay bearable.

"Frustrated, Philip puffed at his cigarette then flipped it through the window. At two stories up, nobody would know where it came from, but Philip cared not one iota about it or other people."

"Philip's horrible!" He stopped reading to blurt out his thoughts. "You're probably going to make me love him at the end, Lilah, but right now I'm just not a fan. He's arrogant." He looked at Lilah's eyelids, hoping his voice, or the storyline, might trigger movement or memories that would bring her back. "What are you dreaming about?"

He toyed with the idea that if that very miracle happened just as Becca walked in, that she would consider him a hero for saving her sister's life and would fall madly in love with him. The mere fact Lilah McCallister was lying in a coma reminded him that miracles rarely happened, nor did life work that way. He wouldn't be in the hospital with broken bones if it did. He would have delivered the angel as planned, be in his studio working on the next commission on the list and thinking about the coming year.

Knowingly influenced by the tone of the novel, the hope of a happy ever after, he sighed. He gazed at the minute motion of Lilah's long brown-red eyelashes as they danced to a tune only they could hear. Infrequent tiny eyelid muscle movements made it look like she was in REM sleep.

"By the way, you kept that quiet. All that time we spent together, you should've told me, or at least given me the heads up. Your sister's gorgeous, isn't she?" He imagined Becca's face, her smile, and her hair again. Without realising, he smiled. Then, brought back to reality when the novel slipped from his hands onto his lap, he looked at Lilah. "Please wake up." When she didn't, he continued reading.

"Eden stormed into the room two minutes later, the discarded cigarette butt between her fingers.

'I presume this is yours? In fact, it has to be. I don't know anyone else who smokes these things and you're the only person around here ignorant and arrogant enough to expect someone else to clean up after you."

Philip stared blankly.

'Seriously, Philip'. she went on. 'Through a window? That's a new low. People are starting to turn up for the party. There are children playing out there for goodness' sake'. The garden decorations aren't up yet and here you are creating more work.'

'My staff will take care of it.'

'As always, you're completely missing the point.'

'Eden, you're hysterical. Why don't you lie down?'

His audacity generated a feeling in her like no other."

Ben looked back at Lilah. "I'm not surprised either. Eden's lovely. Bright, unwilling to let Philip get away with anything, and very willing to kick his backside. And let's face it, he needs a good kicking. I like her."

Before Ben read any more, the hospital room door flew open dramatically. Becca McCallister, dressed in a beige winter coat with a long burgundy scarf draped around her shoulders, stood there as though she owned the doorway. After the image of Eden bursting in to reprimand Phillip, Ben half expected Becca to do the same with him.

He grinned, slamming the book closed. "And the beautiful Becca McCallister returns." He pushed his wheelchair around to face her, trying to stop his racing heartbeat become obvious. "How are you?"

She smiled cautiously, then stared him straight in the eyes, seemingly unable or unwilling to move them. "I'm fine, thank you. You look great...that is to say, you look well."

"You seem startled. You don't mind me being here, do you? Margaret sort of suggested you'd be expecting me. I didn't think you'd mind."

"It's fine. I hoped you would be…that is, you know, reading to Lilah." She floundered. "That's why you're here. That's quite a smile you've got there. You look happy."

"I can't think of a single reason why I wouldn't be happy." *Not now you're here.* "And the painkillers have been reduced which is always a plus, I reckon."

She nodded to the book on his lap. "How's it going?"

"Oh, she's loving it, she can't get enough. Obviously getting feedback is a bit tricky, but she hasn't said she doesn't like it, so I'm taking from that she does. Why don't you pull up a seat and join us? We've covered a whole chapter so far today and she's not complained once. It's a good story, isn't it? I love Eden, not sure about Chaz, can't stand Philip. Mind you, I expect I'll want to be his best mate at the end."

"You will. She's got this way of making you feel one way about them at the start then completely changing your mind by the end. And then once the book's finished you'll do anything Lilah asks just to spend more time with the characters. The girl's got some serious skills."

She took off her coat and scarf and put them on the hook on the wall then headed for the chair. She began to move it nearer the bed when she noticed another vase of flowers. They stood proudly next to the original ones but were smaller in size.

"These are new. I wonder who sent them?"

"I must admit, I didn't even notice them."

She undid the card and her face turned red with rage. "You have got to be kidding me! Bloody Ruth Trent. Margaret must've banned her already and I'll bet these were sent in retribution."

Ben stared, not knowing what to say. He gave a subtle shrug, and she went back to the card.

"Listen to this," Becca read. "'Darling Lilah, I've got to congratulate you on a job well done. A coma was a bloody good marketing tool, well done you! The press is all over this like a rash. It's fantastic! Unfortunately, your moronic sister has banned me from visiting, so I cannot tell you in person. However, please keep it up. Forever would be good. RT.'"

Ben shivered. "Wow, that was unnecessarily dark."

Becca's hands shook as adrenalin took hold. "It's sinister. I told you, didn't I? I told you what she's like. And people just let her get away with it. She's an appalling excuse for a human being."

"She sounds deranged."

"She's about two minutes away from being sued for harassment. Doesn't she realise the stuff she says is so upsetting? She's saying she wants Lilah to stay in the coma forever. That's what this says. That's horrendous, isn't it? I honestly can't believe how low she's gone."

He could see her eyes were glassy. Was she about to cry with rage? He wanted to comfort her, but he couldn't stand easily. Nor did he know her well enough to know if holding her was okay. Just as he felt with Lilah in the crash, he felt powerless to help Becca. And he hated being that way.

She walked to the window, feigning looking out, but she lifted her hand to her face.

"And libellous too," Ben said. "She knows how to push your buttons; she knew you'd read the card. You should keep it though, should you ever need it. It's evidence of her character and of her intentions."

She turned, nodding at his words. "You're right. I will, thanks."

She sniffed and wiped both cheeks before composing herself again. A moment later, she leaned over Lilah's face and kissed her forehead. She stroked her hair and smoothed her pillow.

"Maybe it is a blessing you can't understand. Although if ever there was another incentive to get you to wake up, this would be it. It's definitely time to rethink your agent."

"Maybe she can hear everything," Ben said, lifting the novel an inch from his lap. "At least, I hope she can."

She walked around the bed and pulled the chair next to Ben's wheelchair. "Sorry about the dramatics."

"Aren't redheads known for their tempers or is that a cliché? It's got to take its toll somewhere though. I wish I could do more to help than just sit here. Anyway, for what it's worth, I'm in total agreement. I've never met the woman, but I hate her already. Mostly for how she made you feel." He didn't care if it gave away his feelings. There were worse things in life than having them known.

Becca smiled. "Thanks. Her behaviour is all just so unnecessary when you take it down to basics."

"Now, I could go on reading, but I have a feeling talking would help more." He faced her, giving her his full attention. "Tell me, how's the dreaming situation? Any lonely boats, or are you sleeping okay?"

"I had a brilliant night's sleep last night. Oh, actually, I've got something to tell you."

He watched her gaze move up to his hair, then to his lips, and finally fixing on his eyes as though she was studying them. Her breathing had changed too. It was faster, like she was excited. Ben prompted, aware of the pause she'd created. "What's that?"

"Um…" Becca was mesmerised.

"Are you okay?"

"Sorry. Slightly off-topic, but has anyone ever told you that you've got the most amazing eyes?"

"I was *not* expecting that." Ben instantly laughed. "No. Nobody's ever said that to me before. It's the eyelashes, isn't it? They're unusually long for a man. Feminine, almost," he said, embarrassed but grateful for the compliment and admiring her spontaneity at the same time. He wiped his hand over his face as if it would remove his features for him to draw them in again. He grinned in a warm, satisfied smile. "I have to admit it's good to know you've been looking."

"It's the colour of them actually," she clarified, unable to stop staring. "They're not just green. They're a very intense shade of khaki. I don't think I've ever seen eye colour that strong before. They're incredible."

She suddenly tore away her gaze and looked vulnerable. Seen. He sensed it wasn't a feeling she enjoyed. She began playing with strands of her hair. It was down today, and straight. The waves and curls she wore before were gone as though she had deliberately removed them. She also wore earrings. He glimpsed at them when she tucked her hair behind her ears. The earrings were studs. Sparkly, matching her eyes and her smile. That smile had a subtle but shiny shade of pink on them today. He hadn't noticed any of this the day before, but as she was seated so close now, he was happy for the opportunity to study her in return.

"I know we only met yesterday," Ben said. "But since we're being open, I should confess that I've become secretly in love with your hair. It's just the most beautiful shade of red. Truly, it's wonderful. And take that compliment with the knowledge it's from a stupidly picky artist. I didn't want to say anything in case it sounded forward, and I realise it's only a day later, but I've thought of nothing else since then." *Or your face. Or you.*

She grinned. "You didn't want to sound forward? I think I might need a lesson in forward myself. I'm so sorry, that was so unlike me. I'm not sure what came over me."

"Embarrassing you wasn't my intention, I'm sorry. But," he laughed, breaking the awkwardness, "you started it. The thing is guys don't usually get compliments, at least I never do. Hearing one just throws you a bit, doesn't it?"

"Red hair isn't usually commented on so favourably. People are generally less than charitable with their opinions, so it's odd hearing a compliment. Thank you for saying it. I quite like my hair though, it's one of my better attributes."

"Are you joking? You're beautiful. I can't imagine how anyone could say anything negative about you. You're absolutely stunning." He shrugged, realising how embarrassed they both seemed. "It's a bit sad, isn't it, both of us feeling awkward over complimenting each other? Someone as beautiful as you ought to be getting them so frequently, you'd be tripping on them." They both laughed. "Okay, I admit it. That one was a bit cheesy, wasn't it?"

"A bit, yeah. Maybe we're both out of practice."

"Well, when I'm out of here, we'll have to get together and practice properly. You wouldn't deny a man with amazing, incredible eyes that much, would you?"

She tried to stop smiling but couldn't. "I'm not going to live that down, am I?"

"Absolutely not. I got a compliment fair and square and I'm going to use it. Trust me."

"Well, as true as it is, that wasn't what I was going to tell you."

"Well, anything else will be a disappointment now. Can you at least try to match it? You could put some effort in. How about my lips?" He pursed them as if offering her a kiss. "Or my hands." He waved them in the air over the novel then up into his hair. "Or even this ridiculous stuff."

"I can try." She laughed. "How about this? On the way home last night, I took a detour."

His face changed, now he was intrigued. "Okay."

"Past the accident site."

The lightness of the mood had dropped a notch or two. It replaced his excitement with a touch of anxiety. Somehow in Becca's presence, he had managed to hide the accident to the back of his mind, but the mention of the crash site reminded him how they met. "Oh?"

"And onto your place. I found your studio."

"Oh." From flirting to trauma to art, his mind rode a roller-coaster to get to its destination.

"I know you said you hadn't expected to leave it for quite so long, so I just parked up and had a look through the window to check everything was secure. It looked fine to me. I just thought you'd be happy knowing everything was okay."

He was touched, like it was a gift she'd given him. "That was really considerate of you. Thank you."

"It's the least I could do."

He reached into the wheelchair's pocket and took out Lilah's phone charger. "I ought to return this. Thanks for coming to my rescue. I finally spoke to my client this morning. Everything's good. Seems like it's all coming together."

"It is. You came to my sister's rescue and you were kind enough to want to read to her. You're a bit of a hero, Ben."

"A hero?" He physically shied away from the word. "No, no. Anyone would have done the same."

"I don't think so."

"I think that's a description best used for very special people."

She nodded in agreement. "Then I'm using it correctly."

"Oh, my lady, you flatter me."

"Then please allow me to flatter you a bit more. When you've recovered, I wonder if you would consider talking to my class about art? I think they'd get a lot out of it. I would too."

His heart beat even faster. "I'd love to." He wanted to look like a serious professional, but with Becca so close it was just a matter of time until his lips stretched into a grin and he resembled a clown. "That's something really exciting to look forward to. Absolutely yes. Ah, but I have a condition."

She smirked. "You're laying down conditions now? Okay. What is it?"

"That you come out for a drink with me sometime."

"A drink?"

"Yep."

"Um…you mean, like, um…"

"A date. Yes. How about it?"

Chapter Thirty-One

After such a busy year and the upcoming holidays, Drew took great pleasure in turning the 'OPEN' sign on the front door to 'CLOSED'. More than symbolic to end a great year, it was about being one day closer to spending time alone with Catie.

Drew stepped into the staff room as Sheryl put on her coat. "Hey, glad I caught you before you took off. Can I talk to you? It won't take long." He pushed the door shut and she looked concerned.

"What's going on?"

"I wanted to run something by you."

"Okay."

"Remember I told you I wanted to make some changes around here?"

"Sure. Decorating. The kids can't wait. You've just about made their Christmas."

"Well, it's not just about decorating. We've had a pretty good couple of years, and I think I've found what I need to make this place work for everyone. How would you feel about coming back in the new year in a different role?"

"You don't want me waiting tables anymore?" She seemed crestfallen and confused. "I don't know what else I can do here, buddy."

"Okay, I have a great idea. Hear me out. I think you're incredible with the diner. You're great with people but you're even better with the business side of it all. How would you feel about coming back and being my business partner?"

"What? Wow." She was taken aback and excited all at once. And then she considered the financial side of such a position and was crestfallen again. "Except I don't have the money."

"You don't understand. That's not what I want from you. I need someone with a good business head on their shoulders. Someone who'll keep me on the straight and narrow with decision making for the good of the diner. Keeping track of the numbers. That kinda thing. We both know you won't hold back if I need my ass kicked. I think you'd be perfect. We can negotiate salary. I'll cover medical and dental for you and the kids. You won't lose out in any way. What do you think?"

"No more waiting tables?"

"Not unless you wanna find time to fit it in, but I'm guessing not. I'm gonna get some new waiting staff, some more tables and chairs to run parallel with the booths. We've easily got the space to increase the seating capacity. It's just gonna take some work and I'd love you on board to do it with me. What do you think?"

Sheryl's concerned morphed into a massive grin. "I think it'd be incredible."

"Your talents are wasted otherwise. I've got some legal papers I need you to sign, but we can do that over the holidays. Are you in?"

She lunged her small frame forwards and pulled him into the biggest, most loving hug she'd ever given. "You'd better believe I'm in, buddy. You just about made my Christmas. You won't regret it."

"I know I won't. It's you, Sheryl."

"If you're getting new staff, what's happening with Catie?"

"Leave that to me. You just get on home and give those kids a big hug from me. I'll see you in a couple days."

She practically skipped through the door on her way out and, before Drew turned off the lights to leave, he gave the place a final look over, and a deep sigh that was edged with relief and happiness.

Things were finally taking shape.

Chapter Thirty-Two

At three on Christmas Day, Catie stood with a gift and a bottle of wine outside Drew's apartment. The earlier visit to the shelter had gone great. She learned a lot about the community she didn't even realise. Drew was opening her eyes in so many ways. She'd returned to her apartment to change for dinner together and he opened the door wearing a Santa hat atop his head, and a mischievous smile on his lips.

"Long time no see," he grinned.

A sprig of mistletoe that hung above the doorway did not go unnoticed. She looked at it, then at Drew. "Seriously?"

"Absolutely, seriously. Being with you is a serious business and I'm not missing a single opportunity." He leaned forwards and kissed her.

Afterwards, she gave him the wine and the gift. It was obviously book-shaped, and she giggled at his expression. "After all you've done, I couldn't show up empty handed. Merry Christmas."

After an exchange of gifts - a cuisine book for him and earrings for her - they ate dinner, laughed, and drank before doing the dishes together. Hours later, snuggled up on the sofa with the tree lights twinkling in the corner, music played softly, and wine flowed freely.

"Today's been amazing," she said. "This morning was spectacular. I've never experienced anything like it."

"I'm glad you enjoyed it," he said, his arm around her shoulders and stroking her skin. The other hand reached out and chinked her glass. "Here's to us."

"You're so classy. Such a gentleman."

"It's easy to be a gentleman around a lady."

"Smooth," she laughed. "Very smooth."

"Smooth is my middle name."

"Do you have one? A middle name, that is."

He traced the shape of the letter 'A' in the space between them. "Why don't you guess?"

She tipped her head in confusion trying to think of men's names starting with A but after several glasses of red wine, she couldn't think of a single one. She shrugged. "I give up."

"You can't give up so soon. We have the whole night ahead of us to play this game and," he winked, "there's a prize for the winner."

"I'm curious at the prize."

"That's good to hear. You don't know what it is yet."

"I'll take my chances. So, are there any clues to the name?"

"Yeah. A big clue. You use it every day."

She lifted her glass, reminding him that she'd been drinking. "I can barely remember my own name."

"You're giving up again?"

She nodded.

"No prize," he warned. "You sure?"

She tried again. "Adam?"

"Nope."

"Aaron?"

He shook his head with disappointment. "No. I thought you'd get it."

"That's too bad. I wanted that prize."

"Me too. Okay, I should apologise, it was kind of a trick answer. It's Andrew. I was named after my father but since we can't both have Alexander as a first name, everyone used my middle name instead and over time it got shortened to Drew."

"Alexander Andrew Denby," she said. "It sounds like a lawyer."

"I don't know about being a lawyer, running the diner's plenty. I'll let my dad know you think he should've been a lawyer the next time I talk to them though. That'll make him laugh. I am more of a Drew. A roll-up-my-sleeves kind of guy. What about you? Do you have a middle name?"

"Mine's very high and mighty. Catherine Eleanor Cambridge," she announced with a one-sided smile. "My parents clearly had high hopes. You can see now why I just use Catie."

"It's elegant."

"And that's kind of where I let it down."

"I think you're incredibly elegant."

"That'll be the wine talking, but I'll take it. I have a feeling you're biased."

"A little, but I'm good with it. And you still get the prize because I tricked you." What began as an affectionate kiss slowly grew deeper and more passionate until they were both outstretched on the sofa. Both wanting more, and not seeing a good enough reason to stop, they continued until finally, reluctantly, Drew lifted his lips from hers. "Can you hear that?"

"I can't hear anything. I was lost somewhere. I don't know where but I wanna go back," she purred. Then she heard it. "What is that? Is that my phone? Who the hell is calling me on Christmas night?"

A quick shot of adrenalin ran through Drew's gut. Things were going so well; now was not the time for another man to be hassling her. If it was Jack Sullivan...

She reluctantly moved away from Drew's grasp fastening the top button on her blouse. More than anything she wanted to be on the sofa again with his hands touching and caressing her body, and his hot lips on and in her mouth. Instead, the phone's incessant beeping made her seek out her purse. She grabbed it and looked at the screen. And then her heart sunk.

"Three missed calls. I didn't hear a thing. It's the home."

"What home?" Drew sat up.

"My dad." The ecstatic expression she wore moments ago and slipped straight into concern.

"We were a little pre-occupied. Maybe they just wanted to wish you happy holidays?"

"They'd never call unless it was an emergency."

She returned the call and waited. Finally, someone answered. "Catie Cambridge here. Someone's been trying to call me." Her mind raced as adrenalin overtook the alcohol. "Oh god, no. I'll be there as soon as I can." She stared at Drew, her eyes glossy with tears.

"What is it?" he asked. It was clear a million things were flying around in her mind, all clambering for her attention. He stood up, taking her hand in his. "Catie, what's going on?"

"My dad. He's not gonna last the night."

Chapter Thirty-Three

Becca's phone rang just as she poured herself a cup of coffee. The caller was unintelligible. For a second, she wondered if the paparazzi had finally caught up with her.

"It's me, Miss McCallister. I didn't know who else to call."

"Emma?" She could hear sobs. "What's the matter?".

"I've walked out. I'm so sorry. I know you got the me the job, but Ruth is horrid!"

"Where are you?"

"In the coffee shop across from the agency."

"Right. Well, stay there and I'll come and get you."

Becca took two bites of her freshly-made sandwich, and cautiously gulped a mouthful of the coffee hoping she didn't burn herself as it moved down her throat. She got into her car, muttering all the way. "Bloody Ruth Trent, you'll be the death of me."

Amid a ridiculous amount of Christmas shoppers – Becca had forgotten everyone else's life continued on as usual - she pushed open the café door. Emma Jones was in a booth wearing a sorry expression and, as soon as she saw Becca, she burst into tears.

"It's going to be fine." Becca hugged her.

Emma brought out a mixture of maternal and mentor feelings in her. Freckles that were scattered over her nose and cheeks when she was in Becca's class, aged eleven, were exactly the same now she was a young woman.

A waitress approached their table. "Is everything okay?"

"It will be. Can we have two cappuccinos, please?" Then, looking at Emma's blotchy face, added, "and two slices of the creamiest, most fattening chocolate cake you've got, please." Both the waitress and Emma chuckled. "So, tell me everything."

"It's like being back at school, Miss, isn't it?" She smoothed her long, brown hair over her ears.

"Except the bullies are generally not in their mid-sixties, and as such ought to know better."

Once the two cappuccinos and cake were delivered and devoured, Emma began. "I hate it there. She started off being nice. She showed me how to do the filing in the cabinets. She said she wanted me to think of ways to make the office more efficient, so I suggested everything ought to be on the computer, but she hated that and I had to put it all back in the cabinets. That was when it all started really. She growls at anything modern. Then she got really cross one day and took it out on Gordon. He's the Copy Editor. He's American and does Lilah's books. Ruth and Gordon had a massive row on the phone and she sacked him. Right there and then. And, because she didn't have anyone to edit, she said I had to learn it. She gave me like forty-eight hours to learn or she'd let me go too, just like she did with Gordon. I tried to learn as much as I could, but I didn't sleep for two nights just so I could give her some results."

"She's got some serious behavioural issues. I don't think anyone's really ever stood up to her."

"I wanted to leave but I knew you'd got me the job. I didn't want to let you down."

"Oh, Emma."

"The other day she was on the phone with Lilah. I heard everything. Ruth was so rude. She was angry because Lilah wanted to change the ending of the book. She wouldn't allow her time off and threatened her. I mean, Lilah was exhausted. You could hear it in her voice. She put up a fight but she was exhausted."

"I have a feeling I know all about that conversation," Becca said.

"If it's not done her way, she makes life unbearable." She took a breath, then added, "And then Lilah had the accident." Her gaze met Becca's. "I think she went out to clear her head and then crashed."

"I do too."

"Doesn't that mean Ruth's responsible?"

"I don't know. I've been talking to the police. They're doing some digging. That's all I know."

"Ruth insisted on paying for that private room," Emma said. "She told me it made good business sense. At first I thought she meant it was a nice thing to do, like stepping up to help. But now I think she felt guilty."

"I'm not sure about that. I don't think sociopaths feel much guilt."

"One minute she's yelling at people and the next she's buying flowers and private rooms. Then I found out she'd sent all these emails to the press and…"

"Go on."

"I don't know if I should tell you."

"You've sort of got to now really, haven't you?" Becca smiled, reassuring her.

"She hired a ghost writer. They've got a fortnight to finish the novel. She gave them what she had of it and said if Lilah dies, the sales will be enormous."

That was a lot to take in. Becca tried hard to fight the tears, but it was no use. Everything seemed to move in slow motion while she processed Emma's words and Ruth's disgusting intentions. Reassuring Emma was one thing but she needed someone to reassure her.

"The woman is devil personified. Just when you think she can't go any lower." Tears trickled in streams down her cheeks. Now it was Becca's turn to notice the waiting staff watching her cry. Becca sought a tissue from her bag and wiped her cheeks.

"Is she going to die, Miss McCallister?"

"No," she said emphatically. "She's got too much to live for. She's young and healthy and I won't let her die. She's all the family I've got. And you're going to have to call me Becca at some point, you know." The two laughed through their tears. "Do you have any proof of all this?"

Emma took out an A4 sheet of paper from her bag. "I printed it all out."

Becca scanned the details and refolded it, placing it inside her bag.

"I do the agency's social media, so I created some hashtags in support of Lilah, just to try and even things out with the press. Lilah's got a supportive following. Ruth doesn't know how to use it, so she won't know it's me. I hope it makes a difference though. I don't know what else I can do. But after everything that's gone on, I'd had enough so I just walked out. She didn't even try to stop me."

"Emma, I need to ask you something, but before I do, you have to be honest with me. Okay? I think I need to give this to the police, and chances are they'll want to talk to you. You've been a witness to Ruth's underhand behaviour, and I think what you've got to say will help Lilah's case. Are you happy to talk to them?"

"Oh gosh, yes. Anything to help you and Lilah."

"Thank you. I can't tell you how much that means. Have you told your parents about any of this?"

"No. They asked because it's been on the news, but I told them I didn't know anything. And, if I hadn't gone snooping, I wouldn't have either."

"I don't care how you found it, but I'm glad you did. Something needs to be done about Ruth and the way she treats people. It isn't right."

"I'm not sure how I'm going to tell my parents about not having a job anymore though. Any ideas?"

"I suggest you tell them the truth, how she's difficult she's been to work with, and you had enough self-respect to walk away and leave her short-handed. That said, it's not going to help your financial situation, especially this time of year." She filled her cheeks with air and let it out. "If you can last for a couple of weeks, I'll talk to Paul, he might be able to sort something out for you at school. I've got to get to the hospital soon. What are you going to do now?"

"Gordon messaged me. He probably wants to know how I'm getting on with copy editing. I'll let you know how it goes."

"Please do." She shuffled her way out of the booth and put her coat and scarf back on, then took out her purse. "I'll get this. Just keep in touch with me, sweetheart, okay?"

"Thank you, Becca," Emma nodded. "I really appreciate it."

"You are so welcome. Any problems, just message me, day or night."

On the way back to her car, thoughts of Ruth's bully tactics filled her with rage. Playground bullies weren't tolerated at school, why did Ruth think it was fine to continue that behaviour in the workplace. Once inside her car, she emailed PC Hutton explaining what Emma had witnessed. With any luck if they contacted her, Emma would mention Gordon's situation too and maybe he would speak up against Ruth as well. She gave PC Hutton Emma's details and hoped he would pass the information along to whoever needed it. With so many people being on the opposite end of Ruth's bullying, there had to be something the police could do about it. It wasn't just bullying any more, not if the police married it together with the recording and the emails. There had to be coercion and blackmail in there along with the threatening behaviour.

The journey to the hospital was becoming so familiar, she wasn't even thinking about it any longer. The paparazzi were half the size they were the first day. Perhaps the shine was wearing off. She walked through them, slower than her usual speed, but with twice the confidence. Even her head was held higher, despite the Ruth-demon on her shoulder tapping away at her imagination.

"Any updates on your sister, Becca?" one asked.

"How long does she have left?" another asked.

"Looking good today, Becca," a third said.

She didn't respond to any of them but having fewer hassles didn't make up for the cutting, hurtful questions. It was just a shame it wasn't pouring down with rain; that would have been a nice touch.

Before she headed up to Lilah's room, she queued at reception. Once it was her turn, she put on her bravest smile, trying to ignore the repetitive voices in her head from the journalists and Ruth's existence. "Can you tell me which ward Ben Christopher is in, please?"

Jacoby Ward was on the ground floor, just a minute's walk from where she currently stood. Once there, she walked past the clusters of four beds each and headed for the nurse's station. Hopefully someone there would be able to highlight Ben's bed without her having to awkwardly look at everyone.

"Hello, my lovely. How are you?" Margaret appeared from around a pillar.

Her welcoming smile put Becca at ease instantly, but seeing Margaret there confused her.

"Hello. I thought you worked upstairs in ICU?"

"I go where I'm needed," she said, then changed the subject. "What you're doing in this ward is more to the point." A mischievous smile said more than Becca wanted to know. "Might you be visiting a certain someone?"

Caught out, Becca suddenly flushed. "I – I…um…thought I'd pay him a visit since he's been good enough to visit Lilah."

"Shh!" Margaret's finger flew to her lips. "It's our secret, remember? I'm glad you two have hit it off though. He's adorable, isn't he? Those curls. Those eyes. Those hands. Such a craftsman."

Becca gave a polite nod, trying to keep her feelings close to her chest. 'Hmm. He's very…friendly."

"Follow me," she walked off, leaving Becca to follow.

The majority of patients were elderly, some with just days remaining. It certainly accounted for the morose feeling within the ward. It reminded her of the feeling she had on the first night when she walked down the corridor and saw the old man in the bed. A multitude of feelings flew through her mind: how long she had left, how long Lilah had. Ben? It was an impossible thought process that led her nowhere but downhill fast. Finally, Margaret slowed as they reached a second nurse's station. She pointed to Ben's bed.

"He's asleep?" Becca whispered. It felt wrong being here when he wasn't aware of it. It felt intrusive. "I'll come back another time."

"No, not at all. He'll be happy to see you, I'm certain."

"But he's sleeping."

"I'm not surprised, he's probably exhausted. He's been having some nasty dreams. It's common in the circumstances. Perhaps physio tired him out? Doctor spoke to him this morning. He's doing well. It's as if he's been injected with something life-giving, something hyper-healing. Maybe it's love?" she giggled

That was a curious thing to say, Becca thought, but she felt nothing but sympathy for his recovery. The trauma was going to hang on long after the initial crash. "I'll come back."

"No, I'd wait." Her tone was insistent, as though urging Becca to stay. "He won't want to miss you, my lovely. In fact, I'll leave you both in peace."

Becca was puzzled after that comment. Cautiously, and with a mixture of curiosity and reluctance, she approached the bed. He looked peaceful. Lilah's book was open but face down, over his chest. It was nice to know he had taken a genuine interest. Long, thick, chestnut curls - his *ridiculous* hair - as he put it, made her want to run her fingers thought it. She smiled at their 'eye' conversation, remembering how embarrassed she was, but how open he was afterwards.

She considered what he might have been like as a child; just as she imagined what the students at school would look like as adults. *Adorable*, was the word Margaret used before. She could see how he'd be described that way. He seemed like the definition of the word. His clowning around was sweet: flirting 101. It had been some time since any man had flirted with her, and she was eager to spend more time with him. He was everything she was attracted to in a man: masculine, considerate, mischievous yet protective. Could he be the Gilbert Blythe to her Anne Shirley? She recalled he'd been raised by older parents and wondered if that had been a contributing factor to his behaviour with Becca.

Just then, Ben's eyes flew open, startling her. His eyebrows shot upwards as though he was in fear of his life and a sob left his throat. He stared straight ahead as if looking at a specific thing, until his eyes filled with tears, magnifying their colour. Whatever he saw in his dream, or nightmare, it was still in his view. She could sense his heart pumping. Then, slowly, he became aware of his surroundings.

"Oh Ben, it's okay. It was a dream." Becca sat at the side of the bed and took his hand, stroking his skin. Without giving it a second thought, she leaned in and hugged him. Feeling his body that close to hers filled her with strength, a strength she could return where he needed it most to repair his emotional scares. She nuzzled her face into his neck noticing how warm his skin was. She breathed him in as his curls caressed her nose. Then, reluctantly, she pulled away. "Are you okay?"

A smile crept onto his lips conflicting with a tear that had fallen down his face. "I am now." Long eyelashes, still moist with tears, both framed his eyes and seemed to beckon her in. He was right, they were longer than usual. He sat up and wiped his face. "What a vision to wake up to."

"You're okay?"

He nodded. "How come you're here? Isn't this role reversal?"

"I wanted to see where you lived," she said, grateful there was no awkwardness this time, especially after hoisting an unexpected hug on him.

"Didn't you do that already? You said it was all securely locked up, remember?"

"I mean your second home."

"Don't say that. I don't want to be here any longer than I have to. Let's just say, not all the nurses around here are as kind and considerate as Margaret."

"She is quite the nurse. ICU and Jacoby Ward. I wonder where else she gets to."

"It's a mystery," Ben said.

"I thought you might like a visitor for a change. You made the effort to see my sister, I thought I should repay the favour."

"I can't think of a nicer visitor, or a nicer way to wake up." He grinned, school-boyishly. "If it means I get hugs, I'll happily have the nightmares first."

She looked embarrassed. "Sorry. I'm usually one for personal space but, for some reason, I didn't even think."

"Don't be sorry, it was wonderful. How are you anyway?"

"Not great," she said, recalling her day. "I discovered Ruth's intentions and learned that, as surprising as it might sound, she's even worse a person than I originally thought. As if she couldn't do more harm. Unfortunately, I think I'm going to have to speak to a lawyer. It's all getting a bit too serious."

"Wow. That's a concern."

"You have no idea."

"My angel client knows all kinds of legal people. I can introduce you."

She nodded, thankful. "I never imagined it might get to this stage, but I can't see another way forwards. The police have got their work cut out, that's for sure. I've got no alternative but to protect Lilah. And Emma. And myself." She let out a small despondent laugh. "I wonder who I've upset. I'm not sure I can take a lot more."

Ben looked sympathetic. "I'm here if you need a shoulder. If I'm nothing else, I'm a good listener." Then his smile was lost, and his eyes seemed sad. "Not that I want to add to it all, but I need to tell you something."

It didn't sound like the kind of tone you would use to deliver something light-hearted. This was heavy. She could feel it. She sought her mind for obvious issues secretly kicking herself for allowing all kinds of emotions to get the better of her. Had she forgotten everything her father had ever taught her about them? Steering clear of them had always been her aim, but this past week had brought an onslaught of emotions she never realised she could feel.

Of course, he was too good to be true, she told herself. Why wouldn't he be? He was everything she wanted in a man. And attractive too. Was he married? She looked at the finger on his left hand. No, Ben didn't seem like a married man. After all, where was his wife while he'd been in hospital. Maybe he had a girlfriend. Again, where was she?

"What is it?"

"I know you said you've had a bad day, and this may well compound it, but I still need to tell you. It's just that the doctor spoke to me this morning."

Becca nodded. Margaret had told her as much.

"She said I'm healing quicker than expected."

"But that's good news, isn't it? Surely that's something you'd want to hear?"

"Except I'm doing very well. And physiotherapy is too."

"Ben, that's all good news."

And then he blurted it out. "She said she wants to discharge me." He said it as though he was being cast out along the side of the road. "And it might be as early as tomorrow morning. They said they need the bed. Funny how one tiny decision like that can make a giant difference in people's lives, isn't it? It's like it doesn't even matter."

She took his words in, placing them somewhere near the new information Emma gave about Ruth. She wondered how much bad news she could take in a single day. Maybe that was the point of life, keep piling it on to see how far she could go before it broke her. It was getting unfathomably close.

"I mean it's a good thing that I'm going home so close to Christmas, but…" he trailed off.

"Honestly, Ben. It's a good thing. You'll be back on your own turf and in your own bed. You'll eat real food. You'll get your life back." It hadn't registered, but she was crying. She only noticed when he wiped the tears from her cheeks.

"But…If they send me home, I won't see you and I really don't want to stop seeing you." He linked fingers with her and held her hand. The connection felt electric, but more than that, it felt right. "I've got to say it out loud. It's been a bit of a whirlwind, but it's as clear as day to me. Becca McCallister, I really like you."

Somewhere within the tears and the high emotion, she found a smile. "Believe me, it's mutual."

Finally, he smiled. "It's so good to have that confirmed. I hoped you did. From the first moment I saw you I knew there was something, but I didn't want to just hope and not know. And then, of course, there's Lilah. I don't want to stop reading to her. I wanted to help her recover, but if I'm out of here, I can't see you or read to her. I hadn't even considered that they might discharge me. It never even crossed my mind. What about our Christmas Day together? I thought we had longer."

Becca leaned in again and this time Ben hugged her. She felt him stroking her hair as he held her close.

"We'll make it work somehow." She pulled away and, with a sparkle in her eye, she said, "Wait, I've got an idea. Why don't we just make the time we have last as long as we can?"

"Okay. How?"

"Let's go to Lilah's room and read to her. Right now. Together. It'll be like old times."

Chapter Thirty-Four

Drew held open the door of the taxi as Catie climbed inside. She gave the address, saw the driver's eyes light up in the rear-view mirror, and then she let out a long exhale. The driver was right to be excited at the long journey ahead, it would be a good fare for him. Rare was the Christmas night he would be paid as well as this one.

"It'll be okay," Drew told her.

"We're visiting family?" the driver asked. "By the look of you both, I'm guessing this ain't gonna be a cheery trip."

"My dad's sick." Catie gave the driver an exhausted, but polite, smile. "I'd appreciate it if you'd get us there quickly."

"It's a long journey. Lucky for me. For you both, not so much."

There was nothing like a cab driver to lay out the obvious. She wanted to say, 'yeah, we get it,' but another polite smile covered her lips instead. She didn't want to speak. In fact, she didn't want anything else in life but to know her dad was going to be okay. But even she wasn't so foolhardy to think everything was going to work out that well.

Not this time.

One parent gone, one about to go. If things ended tonight like she guessed they might, she would be an orphan at thirty-one. She understood the circumstances were completely different this time, but the twelve-year-old Catie inside her was thinking with her childlike brain.

Ridiculous thoughts filled her mind: Should she try to find her mother if her dad died? Was she still alive? Should she see if any other relatives needed to know what was going on? She took a breath and realised that she hadn't seen another living relative since she left home. There was nobody to call. There was nobody to tell. From twelve-years-old, it had always been just the two of them.

And now there was going to be just one.

She wanted to cry away the anguish, but she was too tired to contemplate it. What was it about the holidays that always tinged excitement with melancholy, seduction with sadness? There was always something to balance out the good stuff.

She forced herself to believe everything was going to be okay. Drew said so, and she hadn't known him to lie to her in all the time she worked with him. The man had become a tower of strength, compassion, and…stability. That was what Catie needed in her life. Stability. And Drew brought it in bucket loads. He was the light in all the darkness, the sunshine behind a rain cloud. He was wonder personified. She needed him like she needed breath in her lungs.

Being with Drew for the entire day had looked like it might finish with some amazingly good stuff but ending Christmas this way was heart breaking. She looked at him trying hard to turn up the edges of her lips. Just the sight of his face made her feel lighter inside, like she didn't need to carry the heavy burden of life all alone.

His unshaven jaw looked like the start of a beard in the dim light. She liked the feel of it against her skin when he kissed her. It was scratchy and soft, manly. He looked rugged yet behaved sweetly to her all at the same time. It was an appealing contrast in a man, one that attracted her more and more every day. Being with him was so natural she couldn't imagine not being with him. Ever.

He lifted her hand to his lips. The movement brought her out of her mini fantasy where she was met with a compassionate half-smile. "It's gonna be okay, you know."

"The other day I talked to my dad about this guy I work with. He kept asking me if I liked him."

"And what did you say?"

She nodded adding a lift of her eyebrows.

"You know, this guy had better be me. These shoulders are broad, and I can take a lot if I have to, but I don't wanna be hearing about someone else." His tone was light. "We've been there and got the T-shirt."

"There's only one guy I'm interested in. You've nothing to worry about."

"Well, that's good to hear."

"I hope so. You know, my dad would get a kick out of knowing I was with you tonight."

"He would?"

"Big time."

"You two an item then?" the driver asked, too forwardly for her. "You look like you've been together a while, but it sounds new. Look, we're gonna be best buddies for the next hour at least. What? I can't know?"

"Actually, this was our second date," Drew announced proudly.

"Third, if you count the homeless shelter this morning," Catie said.

"You took her on a date to a homeless shelter on Christmas morning? Buddy, you've got a lot to learn about women."

"Got the girl, didn't I?"

Driver zero, Drew one. Catie chuckled. If he insisted on talking, the least she could do was talk back. It took her mind off her dad.

"It was great actually. I thought it would've been sad, but it wasn't. Not at all. It was all very upbeat. I enjoyed it."

"It's Christmas. Everyone's upbeat," the driver said. "Even my old lady. Probably 'cause she knows I'm out working on Christmas night and she gets the place to herself. It's why we lasted this long. We hardly see each other."

It wasn't meant to be funny, but the driver had an odd take on life that Catie appreciated.

"So whaddya two do for a living then?"

"I run the diner on Franklin Street."

"I work for him."

"Workplace romance, huh? That didn't work out so good for my old lady and me. We both worked at a store. Same shifts for a while. Saw her at home, saw her at work. Couldn't breathe without her knowing about it. Drove me crazy. No time apart, kinda got too much, you know? It was either we split up or I get a different job. Ended up driving this cab instead. Works a whole lot better now. I take the night shift when she's home and she works the day shift when I'm home."

"So when do you see each other?" Catie asked, not sure if she wanted the answer.

"An hour or two here and there. Suits us. Some couples don't need to see each other to be together. I guess that's us."

"But it's Christmas night," she said. "Surely she misses you?"

"If she does, I don't know about it," he laughed. "But, yeah, I figure we're there for each other when we need to be. We ain't the kinda people who walk in the park holding hands. That ain't us. We can go days without saying a word to each other. We'll be together until we die purely 'cause we don't spend time together. And, the best thing is, I never look at another woman because I know I have one there who loves me."

Catie wondered if his wife was actually on the same page as him, and knew it was wise not to raise the question either. After fifteen incessant minutes of mindless chatter, he finally simmered down and focused on the route. If it wasn't for the cab's engine providing a rhythmic tune, the space would have been entirely silent. Drew wrapped his arm around her and was circling an area on her arm with his finger.

"It's gonna be okay," he said again. "It will."

"If it's his time, it's his time," she said. "He's not going to live forever. I can't expect that. I just need to accept that he's gonna go at some point. I just hope I get there in time to say..."

her voice croaked before she finished her sentence. She was wrong, she did have the energy to cry.

"You're gonna ruin me if you do that." Drew kissed her head. "And I've never even met the guy." Streetlights reflected in his eyes, giving away his secrets twinkled with tears.

She snuggled into the gap between his arm and his side, his warmth and heartbeat provided the safety and protection she yearned for. Within a few minutes, she drifted off.

At first, she fell into fractured dreams. Images of her dad sitting at the kitchen table when she was still a child. Then she felt a warm and loving feminine presence, not anything like she had felt from her mother. This was someone else. She was inside a room that was subtly lit and decorated in beige tones. It felt bland, numb, and clinical. The spotlights on the ceiling gave it a modern feel, but the dim illumination they yielded was redundant.

There were two paintings on the wall, prints, unframed, mass produced. She didn't recognise either of them, nor did she care for them. This wasn't a room she knew, and to emphasise that knowledge, somewhere in the distance was a bleeping sound. As she focused on it, she realised it was close, maybe a meter away. She looked in their direction. Even from this angle, sideways on, she knew it was a machine used in hospitals. Then she realised she was in hospital – in a hospital bed to be exact.

Confused, Catie looked around for more clues. Was this a memory? Was it now? The subtle, yet unmistakable scent of cleaning fluid filled her nostrils. She looked down at her hands. Tubes were attached to her skin: a drip in one and a plastic clip over her index finger of the other. It was to monitor her pulse. She was curious why she was there, but not frightened. The maternal presence ensured that. Then she remembered it was a dream, albeit a lucid one. She had Drew's arm around her in a cab, she was safe and protected.

Then she saw a woman next to the bed and she was certain the maternal feeling was from her. She was a nurse. The door to the room was open and she was backlit, almost angelic. She was buxom with a round belly and wide at the hips. Once Catie could see details, the nurse gave a huge, welcoming smile. She lessened the space between her and the bed and picked up Catie's hand, holding it in hers.

You're here, her gentle tones spoke straight into Catie's mind. Her lips remained in that genuine smile. *I'm so pleased you came. I've been taking care of you. I'm Margaret.*

She tried to answer but had a tough time getting her lips to move as she wanted them to.

Don't try to speak. Use your mind. I can still hear you.

Where am I? Catie asked.

In hospital. In London.

England? She smiled inside her mind, confused yet entertained. *I was in the US a moment ago.*

The body you're using was involved in a car accident. But you're safe now. You're almost fixed. There's just a couple more things we have to do.

We?

You've a great deal of support here. A lot of love has settled within this room, it surrounds you, and is waiting for you when you wake up.

Then an odd feeling moved through Catie's mind, as though the nurse believed she was someone else.

I'm Catie Cambridge. The words left her mind and arrived in Margaret's instantly and easily.

And you're also Delilah McCallister.

Without realising it, she lifted her hand with the drip attached to it and touched her forehead. *I hurt my head.*

You did. You're healing though. She saw the look of confusion on Lilah's face, and added, *You've been through something complicated, my lovely, but you're coming back. I cannot explain it right now, but I do need to ask you something. I heard your boyfriend wasn't treating you well and you needed to be with someone else. Did you get him?*

Catie grinned. *I'm with him right now.*

Then I've got something amazing to tell you. This man you're with, he's 'the one'.

Catie's eyes began to fill. Happiness and contentment engulfed her. *You're sure?*

That's what all this has been about. You're going to get your husband and your babies, Margaret told her. *He's besotted with you. I can't wait to find out all about it when you're better. You're going to have such a happy life with him.*

As Catie processed the words, she was distracted by a pull somewhere else. Somewhere not in the hospital room.

Something's happening, she said, disappointed at having to leave this crazy but exciting conversation.

There's no need to fret. Margaret reassured her. *Everything will work out.*

As Margaret held her hand, Catie's mind drifted back into darkness. She could still feel the nurse's fingers wrapped around hers. Warm, comforting, and somehow recognisable. She felt herself smile as she was gone from the hospital bed and back in the taxi cab. Her eyes flew open and Drew's hand was around hers.

"You were out cold," he said. "Good dream?"

"Incredible actually." She looked into his eyes with her newly-acquired knowledge, appreciating how they were twinkling from catching the streetlights. The cab stopped outside the care home. "We're here?"

"You slept the whole journey. You were probably exhausted."

As Drew paid the driver as Catie shot out of the cab like a cannon ball. Inside, harsh lighting and a huge, somewhat tired, Christmas tree greeted her. Wiping her eyes, Catie headed for the receptionist. "I'm David Cambridge's daughter."

"I'll get the doctor, Miss Cambridge."

"It's okay, I know where his room is." Catie dismissed the receptionist and continued down the corridor.

"Miss Cambridge, you really need to see the doctor first," she called out, politely but impatiently. "I can't let you go on your own. Doctor will answer all your questions."

She turned back just as Drew joined her at the desk. A moment later a woman in a white coat approached. She had a soft smile.

"Hello, Miss Cambridge. I'm the duty doctor, please come with me. We can talk more, privately in my office." Once inside the room, she closed the door and gestured for them to sit down. "Your father suffered a heart attack. I'm so sorry. It was quite sudden. He's in his room sleeping at the moment."

"What happened?" Drew asked.

"He was feeling fragile but wanted to join us for Christmas dinner. He even cracked a few jokes. David is one of our brightest, funniest residents. Everyone loves him. One of our nurses took him back to his room and checked on him just thirty minutes later. He was already in cardiac arrest."

Catie took it all in. "I should have visited more. I should've been here."

"There was nothing you could have done to make it any different." She took Catie's hand tenderly. "You should prepare yourself and say your goodbyes, but you don't have to go through this alone, Catie. We're here to support you in whatever way you need."

The sudden familiarity caught her by surprise. She stared into the doctor's eyes. "I feel like we've met. Were you here when I visited the other day?"

"No," she said sympathetically. "We have met. I saw you at the diner. I'm Jack's wife."

Chapter Thirty-Five

Adamant nobody could stop them, Ben watched Margaret unfold the wheelchair she kept against the wall. She shuffled him inside; it was an easier manoeuvre than it had been previously, now his injuries were healing. Becca gave him a cheeky smile as she covered his legs with a blanket and put the novel in her bag.

The three of them bundled out of the ward and towards the lifts. Ben feigned sleep, keeping his eyes open enough to gauge what was going on. Once inside the lift, they each breathed a sigh of relief.

"Well, that was easier than expected," Ben smiled. "You wouldn't believe how cloak and dagger Margaret is. She's been exceptional."

Ben rested on the wheelchair's arm, lifting his fingers as if signalling to Becca to hold his hand. She stroked his hand and tried to look innocent about it.

"You two *do* know I set you up, don't you?" Margaret said, proudly. "I'm an excellent match maker and I don't miss a thing. So, if you're going to hold hands, hold hands because I already know about you both."

The three of them filled the small space with laughter. As the doors opened Ben returned to character, lost his smile, and shut his eyes tightly. Nearer Lilah's room, Becca moved ahead to open the door and sneak them inside. Margaret shuffled the wheelchair in parking it near the bed while Becca quietly closed the door.

"You know," Ben said. "I think that was the best kidnapping yet. Top marks, Margaret."

Becca looked quizzically. "Kidnap?"

"It's a thing. Margaret and I have loads. She secretly loves me."

Margaret didn't deny it. "You've made my job a delight, my lovely. That rarely happens in my line of business."

Becca pulled a chair close to Ben as he opened the book. They exchanged a bittersweet glance, knowing it was the last time they'd be able to do this, and held hands, content in the knowledge they didn't have to hide their feelings.

"Now," Ben said. "This book won't read itself. Let's find out what trouble Philip and Eden are getting into."

"I'll leave you two -." Margaret stopped. Her hand flew up to her chest and she gasped. "No. Not yet. That's not meant to -."

"What?" Ben said. He looked around at her to see she was holding her chest but staring at Lilah's bed. While it looked odd, he sensed the problem wasn't with Margaret, but Lilah. "What's wrong?"

Without warning, the heart monitor beeped loud and fast. All eyes were on Lilah McCallister.

"What's that?" Startled, Becca jumped to her feet. "What's going on? What does that mean?"

"Look!" Ben gasped. "Lilah's moving."

Lilah's fingers lifted. Even though her eyes were still closed, it was as though she noticed she had hands for the first time. She extended them as though she was reaching out for something, or someone.

"You've got to do something, Margaret," Becca cried. "Get a doctor!"

"It's not meant to go like this," Margaret said. "This isn't meant to be happening."

Shocked, Ben said, "What? What are you talking about?"

"I'll go and talk to someone. This isn't what we agreed," Margaret said calmly, backing out of the door.

Becca and Ben watched Margaret leave, just as another nurse rushed in, walking straight through Margaret's body as if she wasn't there.

"Right, what's happening?" the new nurse asked, calm but firmly. She ran around the chair and wheelchair. "Please move out of the way. Let me see."

Ben and Becca stared at each other, then Lilah, still unsure what they had just witnessed. Then he saw a range of emotions drift over Becca's face.

"She'll be fine," he reassured.

"Is she going to die?" Becca asked the nurse.

"You both need to wait outside," the nurse barked. "You shouldn't even be in this room, sir." The nurse pressed an alarm on the monitor and within a few seconds more medical staff burst through the room.

"But it can't end like this," she cried. "Tell me what's going on."

"Please leave the room and let us work."

Ben steered his wheelchair towards the door and gestured for Becca to follow. "We should wait outside, let them work."

"I can't leave. What if she…? I can't take another death, Ben. I can't organise another funeral. I just…I just can't do it."

"It's going to be okay," he said. "She's going to be fine."

Ben ushered her out of the room, allowing the door to close behind them. In the corridor, there was no sound but for the muffled voices and machinery noises behind the door. They looked at each other like two naughty pupils awaiting the Head to punish them for being where they oughtn't.

Slowly, Becca composed herself. "Did you see that? Did you see Margaret…"

Ben shook his head. "I don't know what I saw to be honest. It was…"

"She vanished. That other nurse walked straight through her like Margaret wasn't even there."

"Yeah," he nodded. "That sounds like what I saw too."

"What does that even mean?"

"I don't have the first clue," he said. "But I have a funny feeling it answers some questions."

Chapter Thirty-Six

Catie was overwhelmed with emotion. The chill that began when she got the call had now transformed into numbness and taken up residence in her stomach. It felt like it might be permanent. And now there was a new emotion: shame

Doctor Carla Sullivan comforted her. "It's okay."

"How can it be okay?" Catie gasped. "I-I don't know what to say. Saying sorry doesn't even begin to cover it. How do I apologise for doing such a thing? I mean, tell me because I just…"

"Catie," Drew tried to calm her. "When did you know, Doctor?"

She looked at Catie. "I saw your name on David's information sheet, but I didn't put two and two together until I saw you at the door. I was in two minds whether to tell you but when you asked… I couldn't avoid it. Don't beat yourself up, Catie. I mean it. I knew what Jack was capable of. I've known for a long time."

"Are you still together?" Drew asked.

"Actually, we broke up that night at the diner. For good this time."

"Gotta say, I think you did yourself a favor," he said.

"You're right. And to be honest, it was never going to work. There's a lot you don't know, but between my shifts and Jack's extra marital interests, it was a disaster waiting to happen. We can talk about that later though. Right now, you need to see your father."

Inside David's room, the bedside table lamp dimly lit his bed. The rest of the illumination came from the corridor now the door was open. He lay there, a pale shadow of a man. Tubes snaked in and out of him while an oxygen mask covered his nose and mouth.

Drew watched from the doorway as Catie stepped closer. Carla set up a chair close enough for her to hold David's hand. Her young flesh combined with David's liver-spotted translucent-skinned hand was a stark contrast. There was nothing to show he knew she was present. David was motionless aside from the shallow breath forcing his chest to rise and fall. His gaunt face, his sunken eyes. He looked older than he was. Drew wished he could have met the man years ago. His heart sank to see Catie go through this.

"Daddy? Can you hear me?" Catie said. "Daddy, it's me. It's your Catie-girl."

Drew stood behind stroking her hair. It was breaking his heart. The longer he remained, the longer he felt like he was encroaching upon a private moment.

"I'm gonna give you some time alone."

She turned to face him. "Don't go."

"I'll get you a cup of coffee. I'll be right back."

Outside the room, Carla and Drew talked.

"Thanks for what you've done for him. I know she appreciates it. And I know she's racked with guilt over Jack. Strange situation, huh?"

"Married to Jack, I've experienced stranger."

"I don't doubt it. I'm sorry it was such a mess though. It's not the greatest way to spend Christmas Day and you seem like a good person. You don't deserve to be treated like that." He smirked, "Or being kicked out of a diner for that matter. I'm real sorry about that. It wasn't the most dignified thing I've ever done. But he put her through hell, and I just couldn't let it continue."

"I get it. And it's fine. It was never an easy ride with him. From start to finish there were issues. Probably why I was happy to work away from home most of the week. Catie's lucky to have you. She probably did me a favor in truth. In three years of marriage, she was his third affair."

"I noticed in your office you said *extra marital interests*. Plural. I have to ask, why did you put up with it?"

"Hope? I don't know. He promised it was a one-time thing the first time. The second time, I suppose I chose to ignore it. I was more involved with my job by then and I didn't want to go through the pain again," she shrugged. "Then a couple months ago, I had an inkling something was going on. Similar behaviour as before. Then I found some dinner receipts in his wallet, bided my time and a week later I confronted him. I hadn't realised it'd been going on as long as it had. The thing is, he has this wonderful knack of making a woman feel so incredibly special. I don't blame her at all. I fell for it, why wouldn't she? I remember our wedding day, he said exactly the right things at exactly the right time and made the entire day just about as perfect as I could have ever hoped."

"Sounds amazing."

"My father was his boss and gave him an ultimatum: settle down or lose the job. Looking back, it wasn't a fair decision to put on him. It forced him into being someone he's not. But Jack loves his job, and he loves money more. More than he loved me.

He loves to splash it around, show everyone how important he thinks he is. Money is probably his first love. Apparently, his father was the same as him: women and money. Maybe he grew up believing that kind of behaviour was completely okay." She peered through the window of David's room, keeping an eye them both. "She gave me the kick I needed to file for divorce. Once that's over, he's out of my life forever."

"And you can move on."

"Yeah. It's a good thing we didn't start a family. Someday I want one but it was a blessing Jack wasn't hard-wired that way. He wanted all the attention and I couldn't give that to him because my job would always come first. I've worked hard to get where I am. The shifts just made it possible for him to live this double life he did so well."

"I hope you find someone."

"So do I. Life's short." She glanced at David. "I hope it happens sooner rather than later. Time waits for no-one. Anyway, that's probably quite enough of my life story. Can I get someone to find you something to drink?"

"I was actually on my way to do that."

"The front desk will help you out. I'll be back in fifteen minutes to check on him."

Once Drew returned, he placed the coffee cups on the shelf next to the bed. Catie stood and hugged him.

"What a way to spend Christmas. I don't know if he can hear me but someone came in to say if I speak to him, he might be able to. It makes sense. I hope he can, but…what am I gonna do without him, Drew?"

He wiped her cheeks. "You're going to be fine."

"Because I have you?"

"And I'm not going anywhere."

"I know it would make Dad happy to know I was settled."

"It makes me happy to hear you say that too."

It was one minute to midnight when Doctor Carla Sullivan returned. Christmas Day was almost a memory. And it looked like it was going to take David Cambridge with it. She checked his pulse and gestured to Catie to be with her father.

Catie took his hand. "Daddy, I'm right here. It's Catie-girl. I love you."

What little warmth there was in the room vanished as David's chest stopped rising.

"Daddy?" Catie sobbed.

Carla slowly shook her head. "I'm so sorry. He's gone."

Chapter Thirty-Seven

Ben sighed. Thirty minutes of nurses rushing in and out of the room felt like an eternity as they remained in the corridor. It was fast becoming the worst end to a tough day for everyone.

Becca placed her palms and forehead against the wall as if she could feel her sister's energy. Ben watched, powerless to do anything but be by her side.

"Lilah, can you see Mum and Dad where you are?" she whispered, "Are they with you? Can they help you? Can they send you back? No," she corrected herself. "You're not with them, are you? I think you're with your hero. You're at your most comfortable when you're with them. I hope he's lovely. I hope you've created someone who makes your heart pound. Whatever struggle they have, they get through it, Lilah. You always make it a happy ending. We really need one here right now. Please come back to us. I want to spend Christmas with you and Ben, all of us together."

Ben's heart broke into a million pieces watching her do the same. He reached out and took one of her hands and held it to his lips.

***

Lilah was in a dark space.

A moment ago she was someone different, living a life filled with love, sadness, and joy all mixed together. There were other people, friendly people, children, and a man. She remembered his face but couldn't recall his name. She remembered looking up at him with their height difference. He had dark hair and a smile that made her feel wobbly inside. She recalled his hands caressing her as they held each other.

And she remembered the sadness of losing someone close, someone old but she didn't know who it was. She was in America, wasn't she? Or London? And there was a book to write. Another to read.

Confusion clouded her mind, and while it did, all around her was darkness. She couldn't feel a floor, so she wasn't standing, and she couldn't sense walls. Somehow she was hovering. But where, she didn't know nor could she identify. The more she focused on where she was, the more she couldn't. And panic began, though there seemed no lungs to breath heavily from, and no body to absorb touch, taste, or smell. She could hear a rushing sound, like air, as if something was approaching.

Then light appeared, slowly at first. Gradually. It reminded her of a memory of looking up to space, the stars. She had done that with another person. A child, younger than her by just a couple of years. The thought filled her with cherished memories. They watched the stars shooting across the sky every summer. Some leaving trails of blue, others of purple, and others of the brightest, lightest white. Then the light they created was nearer and somewhere in the distance, she heard a voice but couldn't identify the owner.

"Lilah? I'm Margaret. I've come to take you back."

"Back where?"

"Just focus on my voice. Can you come closer?"

"I can't see anything. It's dark. Where am I?"

"You're in hospital."

"Hospital? Why?"

"It was an accident. You've been quite ill but you're so much better now."

"Am I going to be okay?"

"Yes. Can you follow my voice?"

Lilah moved as if she were blindfolded with her arms outstretched. She walked forwards, then left, then right. "I don't know where you are. I can't hear you."

"I'm here," Margaret reassured her.

Lilah heard the voice behind her. She began to feel desperate. "I can't see you."

"Here, my lovely."

"Where?"

Margaret reached out her hands. "Reach for my fingers."

Lilah extended her reach as far as she could, "Yes! I can feel something. Help me, please?"

"That's all we've all been doing, my lovely. You've got good people waiting for you. Come back to us. Hold on to my hands."

Finally, Lilah felt something solid, warm. "Is that you?" Electric sparks flew out of her hands into Lilah's. Then, as if someone switched on a light, more of Margaret appeared.

"There we are. I've got you. Now, jump!"

Obediently, Lilah jumped into Margaret's arms. Smooth limbs like fired clay, or porcelain held her. She reached around

Margaret's waist holding on tightly. Lilah's fingertips explored something else, something soft and warm, like feathers. Then, the light became so extreme. Her eyelids were heavy and the light forced them closed but she persevered. Blinking diffused the discomfort. She could hardly focus but managed to make out two vast feathery limbs as they outstretched either side of Margaret's figure.

"You're in between planes," Margaret said. "Just stay exactly where you are, I've got you. Just don't move a muscle."

Lilah wanted to do exactly what she was told, but there was an unexpected pull in the opposite direction.

"Lilah! Don't let go!"

Without any control, a loud whoosh filled her ears as she seemed to fly through space. As Lilah's hands were ripped from Margaret's body, the darkness surrounding them both felt catastrophic.

***

The nurse who had reprimanded Ben before opened the door surprising them both.

"Is she alive?" Becca gasped.

"Perhaps you'd like to come back in. Doctor would like a word with you." The nurse stepped to one side as the medical staff left.

Becca pushed Ben's wheelchair towards Lilah's bed. Lilah still looked peaceful. It was as if nothing had happened.

"Well, that was quite the event," Doctor Griffin said. "She's comfortable. We're cautiously optimistic for a recovery but what happened back there was unusual. Sometimes patients come out of their comas all by themselves. Other times they try a few times before they fully return. I think that's what's happening here."

"She's back in it?" Becca asked, weary from exhaustion.

He nodded. "I've sedated her. If she tries again, she'll come back to us more settled. I think it was a little too rapid for her body to cope. She may well try again today, or she may take longer. I'm afraid it's all a guessing game and I don't believe she is in any pain whatsoever."

"I can't believe it," Ben whispered. "It looked like she was coming back."

"She may well have been. Do you remember when I first spoke to you about her coma?" Doctor Griffin said to Becca. "That it could be considered a…"

"Dream state? Yes, I remember."

"Keep hold of that. Only when she is absolutely ready to, will she return."

Ben took Becca's hand. "Maybe reading helped?"

"Reading?" the doctor asked.

Ben gave a quick glance to Becca as if seeking approval for what he was going to say. She nodded discretely. "I've been reading one of her novels to her, hoping she connects with the story. Could she have tried to come back because of that?"

"It can't hurt. She might be able to hear everything we're saying. I can let you have ten minutes with her right now but then visiting time is over for today." As he left the room, he let the door close behind him.

"So…what now?" Becca said, bereft of energy. "We carry on like before?"

"I suppose so." Ben let out a deep sigh, "Except that I won't be here."

Chapter Thirty-Eight

Becca pushed Ben back to his ward in silence. There were too many questions and not nearly enough answers, and the atmosphere was heavy with confusion and sadness. Neither had seen Margaret since her literal vanishing act an hour before.

Ben shuffled into his bed as Becca folded up the wheelchair and left it next to an unattended nurses' station. As the medicine trolley worked its way around the ward, it was only a matter of time until the nurse stopped at Ben's bed. Having a visitor outside of visiting hours would almost certainly get him a telling off. Margaret's opposite number was more than he could manage this evening.

A quick smile, an all-too-brief hug, and Becca stood at the side of the bed. She stared at him, wondering what had happened this evening, and when she would see him next. She studied his face, his hair, his eyes, and his smile and committed them to her mind. In return, he gave her a smile that meant the world. But something else was behind those eyes. Sadness? Loss? Grief? Relief? Unspoken words were exchanged which were just a step away from torture. She broke their stare, threw her coat over her arm, and gave him a subtle wave before leaving the ward.

As she approached her car, she could only think about what stopped her from speaking. It was ridiculous Britishness being the bane and awkwardness of new relationships. But words were never going to be enough, not when he was going to be leaving in the morning. She would miss those eyes though, and that smile. She would miss his witty clowning around too.

Between thoughts of Ben Christopher and Lilah trying to return, exhaustion filled her bones. She checked her phone for updates. There were two messages: Paul and Emma. She opened Paul's message first.

Hope everything is okay? Not heard from you. School concert at 8pm. I'd love it if you could make it. Paul.

She had forgotten everything about the concert. She messaged back that everything was fine. She didn't go into finer details of what a massive lie that was or where she would find the energy to socialise, but she would see him there.

Next was Emma's message. *Finally, some good news! Need to talk to you soon. Emma x*

Rather than messaging back, Becca clicked on her number and phoned.

"Hi Becca," Emma said, using her first name at last. Becca could hear the light notes in her voice and the smile on her face.

"You sound better. What's the news?"

"I met up with Gordon. He's got a job at another agency."

"Ah, that's nice," she said, not sure how she could relay positivity when her own life seemed shambolic, but she was glad at least someone was having a better time of it lately.

"He said they know what Ruth's like and were hoping something like this would happen so they could get him. There's more. He told them about me and they want to interview me. They need someone to assist their social media manager. I've got an interview in three days."

"Good stuff, Emma! Christmas Eve too. What a day for an interview."

"It better go well," Emma said. "Be a rotten Christmas if it doesn't."

"You've loads to offer the right employer. Anyone worth their salt can see it."

"I hope so. We should celebrate the interview. Are you free tonight for a drink? Oh, sorry, I was so caught up in my own stuff I didn't ask about Lilah. How did it go at the hospital?"

"Much the same," she lied. "Nothing to report. Instead of going out for a drink, how do you fancy being my plus one? It's the school's Christmas concert tonight and Paul's expecting me. It'd be nice for you to see him again. Fancy it? I can pick you up at seven-thirty."

"Lovely. See you then."

Driving home, Becca's mind was forced into two parts: Lilah's potential recovery, and Ben Christopher. If Lilah had gone back into her coma, this way of life, this driving back and forth to hospital would become life. She'd have to incorporate working full-time into the equation. She couldn't simply stay on compassionate leave indefinitely. Bills needed to be paid, and Lilah's too.

And then there was Ben. Sweet, charming Ben Christopher. The man who had stolen her heart in just hours. He called it a whirlwind …what? Was it a romance? What was 'it'? Had she looked too deeply into the intensity of their time together? Was that what his mystical expression was before she left? Had she willingly become caught up in a go-nowhere romantic episode? Had there been something between them or were heightened emotions just too much for her to endure alone? Had Ben simply been in the right place at the right time? She didn't know, but one thing was abundantly clear, her natural practical-mindedness was being replaced. The newly acquired emotional mind felt fine when Ben was close but away from him, it was alien. Practical was her safe space and her happy place, the part of her mind that was comforted by all things factual, but it was also a no-Ben-allowed area.

Ben was everything she wasn't: funny, charming, mischievous, playful. Being with him had enabled those qualities to rub off during the most emotionally charged moments lately. Without him, she was just Miss McCallister the English Teacher, not the loved-up-teenager she had been for the past three days. It was amazing being with him, but was it sustainable? Was it practical for Becca to fall for someone after just hours together? Was it possible to just click with someone like that?

Her father would have found every reason under the sun for it not to be realistic. Love at first sight was something for Lilah's creative writing, not for real people who held down proper jobs and paid their mortgages and their car insurance. Conversely, she had absolutely no doubt her mother would have encouraged her to see Ben again. Even Lilah would be enthusiastic about it. Romance was for that side of the family. Romance was for other people.

Finally home, she saw the stale sandwich with two bites taken and was tempted to down it in one. What did it matter if it was now hard and unappetising? But instead of filling her hunger, she threw herself on the sofa and, still inside her coat and scarf, she let the tears fall.

It was only then that she realised, in their joint confusion, that neither she nor Ben had exchanged details anyway.

Chapter Thirty-Nine

Two days after Christmas, Drew distributed muffins, hot chocolate, and coffee to Catie, Sheryl, and the two children as the aroma of paint hung in the air. Each set down their brushes, a day later than originally planned, now the diner was redecorated in cream and white. It looked fresh, neat and well on the way to welcoming new customers.

Framed photographs of Drew's food - sexy close ups and abstracts courtesy of Catie's photographic hand - leaned against the newer tables. Along with certificates, they were ready to be hung. A new menu included all the favourites plus a couple of extra dishes and was completed in agreement of both owner and business partner. Drew and Sheryl had signed the legal paperwork and it was ready to be sent off.

Drew lifted his index finger and thumb an inch apart. "I'd say we were this close to a new beginning and I couldn't have done it without any of you guys. Thanks so much."

"Backatcha, buddy." Sheryl placed an arm around the shoulders of each of her kids. "We've had a great time. The regulars are gonna fall in love with this place."

He toasted them all and the diner. He winked at Catie then caught Sheryl watching him. "Hey, make the most of it. There's gonna be a whole load of love in this place from now on." Drew gestured to his notes on the table. "Catie's got her work cut out, you're going to take the place by storm, and we've got four waiting roles to fill and already a string of people emailing for interviews. We're gonna hit the ground running next week. I hope you're ready."

"Born ready, buddy," she said, thrilled at the challenge.

"Then," he looked at Catie, "in your new role of Events Manager, you're looking at pretty much any kind of community group for evening opening. Book groups, discussion groups, business networking groups, and maybe parent and toddlers in the morning?" He ticked each one off his list as he read. "We're looking at people with disposable income who would be thrilled to spend it in here. And we'll be only too happy to relieve them of it. Scroll through the net and look local, okay?"

"Got it." Catie was ready to get her teeth into the new role. It was what she needed. With the funeral just days away, it was a welcome distraction. "It's all so exciting, isn't it?"

"That's what we're going for. The more people who know about the diner, the better. It's been hard work getting to this stage, but I have a feeling it's all gonna work our way from now on."

The kids hugged him as Sheryl caught Catie. "I'm sorry about your dad. It's good he was there with you," she said, nodding at Drew. "He's the kind of guy you want in your corner. I'm glad you two finally got it together. It means I don't have to kick his ass anymore." She winked. "You're gonna be okay with him. He's one of the best."

"He's been amazing."

"He treats my kids better than their own father did. Go figure! He's gonna make a great dad one day." She gave a quick flick of her eyebrows.

Later, after Sheryl and her family left, Catie took a moment to hug Drew.

"What was that for?"

"You deserved it. Your vision is brilliant. I can't wait to begin."

"Well, the diner's stable. I can focus on developing it now rather than starting from scratch."

He took her hands in his content in the knowledge that the work he had put in over the years was paying off. Creating a sturdy foundation meant he could now focus on building the rest of his life upon it. It also meant he had something tangible to offer.

"You once said you needed a reason to stay in town." Hope and happiness filled his eyes. "You've got a new role in a new diner with a new guy who wants to give you the world if you'll let him. While Sheryl takes care of the business, it'll free up some time for me to focus on building a life outside of the diner and I'd be honored to do that with you, Catie Cambridge."

Her smile grew and lit up the room.

"In time," he continued, "I want to be the husband who gives you the babies you want so bad. And we can raise our little family together. That's if you'll have me, Catie."

She could barely speak but managed to utter the only word inside her head. "Yes!"

Chapter Forty

"Yeah," she lied. "My sister's going to be fine." Becca added a polite smile between juggling sips of lemonade from a plastic cup and nibbling at a mince pie inside a foil tray.

It wasn't a total lie, nor was it the truth, but almost every colleague, and some of the parents, had approached her after the school concert expecting answers. The press coverage alone was enough to get tongues wagging so teasing them with some slightly fabricated good news provided a suitable conflict to the barrage of bad news courtesy of Ruth Trent. Becca had never endured so much attention in all her time as a teacher. They meant well, she knew that, but it was tough keeping up.

"It'll take a bit of time, but they reckon she's going to be back to her old self."

She noticed how they studied her when they approached, as if checking to see if she really was okay or if it was all smoke and mirrors. She hoped they didn't look too closely; cracks had begun to appear days ago. Maybe they were looking for signs of self-neglect like the press had reported. *'Teacher isn't Coping'* and *'Coma Author's Sister Depressed!'* were just two of the headlines she'd seen.

She spoke to each of the parents, thanking them for their patience at her absence. She assured them that while she was going through this unexpected break, her students – their children – wouldn't suffer. Paul had assigned the best available teachers so they wouldn't lose out. Most parents were gracious but the odd one or two gave tasteless responses suggesting she needed a better time of year to nurse a dying sibling.

Breaking away from the crowd under the pretence of refilling her cup, she saw Paul and Emma laughing over a drink. It was good to see them together. She listened in to their conversation.

"And Becca said that I've got loads to offer the right employer and that anyone worth their salt could see it," she grinned, proudly.

It reminded Becca that every word she imparted could make or break a young person's mindset and how important teaching was to her. She missed her job, even if the majority of students were a bigger challenge than she originally expected. She missed the children too. She missed seeing the pride in their eyes when the penny dropped and hearing them yelp when they got a higher mark than expected. She missed driving in each day, parking her car, and grabbing a coffee in the staff room before class began. Such small, mundane practices made a big difference when you didn't do them anymore. Now, the routine had been replaced with driving to the hospital or the police station or Lilah's house to pick up mail, and the never-ending torture of dealing with the poison Ruth Trent spilled out all too easily.

"And the interview is on Christmas Eve?" Paul went on, proud of the bright young woman Emma had become. "I'm not sure I've ever heard of one then. Maybe it'll bring you extra good luck? I think we could all do with a Christmas miracle."

It was heart-warming to be in familiar surroundings and see so many people wearing smiles. Thankful for the support, she said her goodbyes and waited for Emma to do the same while she waited with Paul.

"Everything will work out," he said. Ten years from retirement, he reminded her of her father, but with feelings and compassion. "If this woman doesn't let up, I'd advise a trip to the police to report her."

"I've already done that," Becca said. "And I'm going to find a solicitor. I think it's going to get nasty."

Paul shook his head slowly. "She sounds like the bullies of old when I was at school."

"I feel so guilty with Emma's situation. It's all such a mess, Paul."

"Listen to me, young lady." He took her hand from wiping her eye and held it in his. "The Rebecca McCallister I know is a tough one. She's strong and she's ready for anything."

"I think I might be a different Rebecca McCallister now though."

"But you're still all those things. Nothing has changed." He smiled reassuringly lowering his voice even more so only they could hear his words. "Listen. Emma's just as strong as you because you taught her. She'll find her place in this world, so don't you worry about that. You're one of the strongest women I know…"

"Paul, don't," she said, almost losing it.

"…and you're great at teaching because…"

"Paul, really. I mean it…"

"…you're resilient. And the kids can see that, so they learn how to be resilient too. They learn by example."

She knew that already, that's why she died a death when she cried in front of them days ago. And now tears were falling down her cheeks again. This time she reacted. As they reached her chin, she wiped them away efficiently using the tissue from the mince pies.

"And for what it's worth," he continued. "Tears are a sign of strength. Did you know that? Without them, we become something unenviable. What you're doing right now is exactly what you should be doing. If you were keeping a stiff upper lip with everything you're going through, there would be something extraordinarily wrong with you. It's okay to cry, Rebecca." He pulled her close and held her gently. It was like being held by her dad, except he had never done that when she cried, only when he congratulated her. "I'm incredibly proud of you, you know. I know I shouldn't have favourites, but you really are one of them." He released her and watched her dab her eyes until they were dry, and she was smiling. "It's been lovely seeing you tonight, but I don't want to see you again until next year."

"Are you sure?"

"And, if I may be so bold, young lady. You know what you need, don't you?"

Becca shook her head.

A glint grew in his eye. "You need to get yourself a young man. Someone to distract you. My wife is always asking if you've got anyone."

The idea that Paul was thinking about her love life made her giggle like a schoolgirl. "It's odd you should say that…"

"You've got one?" he asked, his voice a lot louder than before. "Someone here? I'm going to need all the details now. Jean won't stop asking once I tell her."

"Nobody here. We've only just met. It's still very new. He's an artist."

"Excellent," he half yelped half roared with excitement. "And a creative young man is the perfect other half to your practical-mindedness. Ooh, this sounds like a good move, young lady. A very good move."

As Emma approached, the two quickly changed the subject.

"Thanks again for a lovely evening," Becca hugged him. "I really enjoyed seeing everyone again."

"Right, before you go, my wife would never forgive me if I didn't invite you both over for Christmas dinner. We've got our two plus their families so one or two extra at the table won't be any trouble at all." He focused on Becca adding, "If you find yourself alone, I'll be cross if you don't call. Some people are just too important to overlook."

"Thank you but, as festive as that sounds, I'm not really in the mood and I can't leave Lilah alone on Christmas Day."

"Understandable." He tapped the side of his nose as if sharing a secret with her. "And I look forward to more details, or at least Jean will. Right now, off with you both."

As they drove away, Becca couldn't help thinking about Christmas and how, just a few days ago, it was going to take quite a different shape. She dropped off Emma and picked up a take away. Eating dinner straight out of the containers on her bed in her pyjamas wasn't the most elegant way to dine, but she was past caring.

When the light came through the curtain the next morning, she looked through the diary and continued her notes. Misery may have surrounded the situation, but there was nothing to say she couldn't jot down a few words of how Ben Christopher had been reading Hobby Husband every day. Lilah would get a kick out of that.

Later, a missed call brought a voice mail from PC Hutton advising her to avoid Ruth – which she gladly took on board – agreeing that consulting the advice of a solicitor was a step in the right direction. She was relieved they felt the same way.

Before visiting Lilah, she snuck into Jacoby Ward hopeful of a brief meeting with Ben before he was discharged. Instead, an elderly man was sleeping in Ben's bed so she left as quickly as she arrived. In Lilah's room, Margaret's absence was noticed. Lilah's red hair had been smoothed down either side of her head, as if staff had given it a brush when washing her.

"There's so much happening, Lilah, and yet nothing's happening. Margaret's missing, Ben's been discharged. I just wish you were here. Please wake up. I need my big sister so much. It's just me and you now. I can't stop thinking of him though and clever clogs here forgot to even give him my number. I ought to take notes from your novels. They never forget. Though, I wonder if he was just being polite. Maybe he was just a superfan who wanted to see you up close. I don't know. It's all a bit of a blur."

An hour later she found herself taking that same detour again as if she was a lost sheep, looking for her daily routine to be put back in place. The regular one had been replaced by a new one and now that had stopped.

She pulled up in Ben's studio car park and peeked through the window. She hoped to catch sight of him painting or creating some kind of artwork. She knocked on the door but there was no response. She told herself he was asleep. Or out. On crutches though, he wouldn't get very far, but the man was entitled to his privacy. Then she realised behaving like a love-sick teen wasn't giving him that privacy, so she drove home.

For two more days, she visited Lilah and returned home. There was nothing else in between. On Christmas Eve Emma messaged that she had got the job. Embarrassed that Becca had forgotten to wish her good luck, and delight that Emma had been successful, filled her mind. She sent congratulations with a multitude of smiles, heart emojis and kisses. At least someone's life was going in the right direction.

Christmas morning came with a loud alarm she forgot she had even set. Through the window the weather was bright and crisp as if offering her a glimmer of positivity. She wasn't falling for that old trick though. She had been fooled once too often. Plodding around in her pyjamas until midday, Becca finally showered, dried her hair leaving in the natural curls, and put on jeans and a winter jumper.

It might have been any day of the year instead of Christmas Day, she hadn't even bothered with a tree this year. It seemed a pointless endeavour dressing up in festive clothing when she didn't feel the slightest bit bright or cheerful. She didn't bother with make up or earrings when she headed to the hospital, after all, she asked herself, who'd see them?

Few people were in the streets, aside from pub-goers with tinsel around their necks and others dressed as elves on their way to Christmas lunches. Festive merriment went on around her and life continued. The only major plus point was the absence of reporters.

She recalled Paul's words. He was a godsend and a mentor. Despite being raised to supress emotions, being in touch with them felt right, especially now. Her dad wouldn't have approved, but Becca would make peace with that. She had to think for herself and Lilah now.

She walked through the foyer towards the lift noticing how many people still needed a hospital at Christmas. Upon one of the chairs near the lift, a man sat. He was wearing a Santa hat. Aside from the tree at the entrance, he was the only festive thing inside the hospital. Beside him was a pair of crutches and, before Becca's brain registered anything, her heart pounded in realisation.

It was Ben Christopher.

Chapter Forty-One

Ben pulled himself to his full height. A huge smile that screamed excitement covered his lips. "Hello."

"Hello," Becca said in an unexpectedly small voice. Ben wore two corded bands around his neck, each with a wooden pendant, Bohemian style, and his cotton shirt was unbuttoned to just below the dip in his neck. A few-days old beard and moustache framed his smile. "You're taller than I remember."

"Ah yeah, you've only seen me sitting down, haven't you? I'm six two. Merry Christmas, by the way. You look amazing. How are you?"

Becca silently absorbed his high-energy presence. It was as though he had saved all his questions to deliver in one go. She grinned like the proverbial child on Christmas Day seeing her gift beneath the tree. "How come you're here?"

"I was hoping to catch you."

"How long have you been waiting? I might not have shown up until tonight."

"So, I'd have waited all day," he shrugged. "And it would've been worth it. Like the hat?"

"Very festive."

He shook his head enabling the bell at the end to jingle. "Have you been a good girl? Ho, ho, ho."

"Oh, let's not go there," she laughed. "Has Santa's meds been upped?"

"Actually, the pain's not that bad. And on these, I can get around a bit more. How's Lilah?"

"No change."

"Have you seen Margaret?"

She shook her head. "You?"

"Fell off the planet, I reckon. I'm glad I caught you though. Because I'm so incredibly good at this flirting lark, it didn't even occur to me to take your number. To be fair it was a bit of a shock to be discharged so quickly – they practically launch you through the door to get their hands on that bed. Anyway, I got home and sat there for ages twiddling my thumbs wondering how I could get in touch." He held out one finger at a time counting. "I didn't have your number, I don't know your address, you're not on social media. You do exist, don't you? You're not another Margaret?"

"I'm definitely real," she laughed. "I have to keep a low profile on there. You can't be a teacher *and* have opinions. Parents don't like it."

"He handed her a business card. "This is me. If I don't hear from you, I'll understand. And when I say I'll understand, I mean I really won't."

She put it into her pocket. There was no way she would allow it to get lost. "For what it's worth, I did drive to your studio. I looked through the window and I knocked. You must have seen me and hidden."

"Trust me, if I'd seen you, nothing on earth would have made me hide."

"It crossed my mind that all of this might've just been politeness."

He leaned in, as though to whisper. "Why on earth would you think that? Can't you tell I'm crazy about you? I'd have sat here all day if I had to. Have pity on me, I'm a man on crutches for heaven's sake. What's a guy got to do to prove it?" He rolled his eyes then, as if the penny dropped, he said, "Oh, of course. I know."

"What?" She worried what the answer might be.

"Right. Here it is. Cards on the table. I can't let you get away again so, Becca McCallister, would you be my girlfriend?" His eyebrows rose pleading his case. "I know a guy with amazing eyes who needs an answer. And I'm not above begging either. So, will you?"

Giggling, she nodded. "You're really not letting that eye thing go, are you? I'd love to."

He punched the air with excitement. "You just made my Christmas. Am I too much? Sorry. I'm just so excited to see you again."

"I picked up on that. You'll wear yourself out."

"May I, you know…" He stared into her eyes, waiting for the answer.

"May you what? I'm lost."

"May I… kiss you?"

She stood frozen to the spot, awkwardness filling her entire being. "Oh…um…yeah, okay."

He leaned in and pecked her cheek. His breath on her face and the softness of his lips was strangely exhilarating. "Was that okay? I mean, I can probably do better, but…"

She giggled nervously, cringing inside. "It was fine. Thank you." She heard herself and cringed even more.

"It was awful, wasn't it? I was trying to be spontaneous. I thought it might seem incredibly masculine or something. I wasn't really prepared. I mean, you might have said no. I hadn't thought further than asking the question."

"Ben," she interrupted him and focused on his eyes. It was tough not to lose herself completely inside them. They were going to be her downfall, she knew that. "I wonder if we're overthinking this. We're being very British about it. Too polite, and all that. Maybe we ought to just…I don't know. Relax?"

"The next time it happens, it'll be a proper one. I promise. And I'm too excited to see you to relax. It's tricky on these things." He shuffled on his feet, fiddling with one of the crutches. "Still a bit of a sorry state, aren't I?"

"Oh, I don't know. I think you're…"

"Pathetic?"

"Incredible."

"Really?"

"Of course," she nodded. "This is all a bit new. Maybe we ought to get used to the idea first. See how we go."

"Is that what you tell your class?"

"No, but it's the kind of thing Lilah's books say. If I offered dating advice to a class of thirteen-year-olds, I'd be sacked before I could finish my sentence."

"Also a good point. Talking of books, I finished it." He fished it out of his bag and held it in the air as if it were a prize. "Reading it alone wasn't nearly as fun as it was with you, but you were right, I thoroughly love Eden and I want Philip to be my best mate. On the other hand, Chaz can do one."

"I told you, didn't I? You did well though. A lot of guys wouldn't have given it the time of day unless there were three explosions and a dead body per page."

"I thought we'd covered this. I'm not 'a lot of guys'. You'll learn that about me though and when you do, I hope you still like me."

"It's going to be tough not to like you, Ben. You're an absolute breath of fresh air."

"And you're utter perfection. Aww, there's that British embarrassment again when we get a compliment. We're going to have to work on that, the pair of us. Anyway, I brought the novel with me because, aside from hoping I'd see you, I thought Margaret might be around."

"We're presuming she's real then?"

"With the absence of answers, I'm going to say yes."

It sounded like a question rather than a statement. "Even after what we both saw?"

"Maybe the emotion of the situation got to us? We had a lot of good conversations. I can't have been hallucinating every time. She even repeatedly kidnapped me, I couldn't have pulled that off myself, could I? And ghosts don't kidnap people, do they? And you saw her too. She admitted to setting us up, remember?"

Becca noticed how easily he believed, how open and childlike he was. Everything didn't have to be so serious all the time. It was a contrast to her mindset. She could see how his innocence would benefit her.

"Maybe she's related to your sculpture?" She meant it as a joke, but the words resonated with her. She stunned herself into silence as if everything clicked into place and the stars aligned.

Ben stared; his eyes wide. The smile he wore now lost.

"What is it?" she asked. "You look like you've just seen a ghost."

"Not a ghost, no."

"What then?"

"An angel."

"What?"

"I've just remembered something. Right after the accident, I woke up inside the ambulance. This is going to sound weird, but I saw something, someone next to me. I might be going nuts, but I'm pretty sure it was her."

"How do you mean?"

"I don't know. I can't really describe the feeling. Just that in the car she was a sculpture of an angel and in the ambulance she was somehow...her."

"Like the sculpture had manifested into an angel?" Becca listened to herself. This was something from one of her student's supernatural stories and went against everything she had ever been taught about logic. But she had witnessed Margaret for herself, felt the warmth and compassion from her. And here was Ben. A week ago she didn't know he existed and now was almost certainly in love with him. Anything could happen, so why not angels manifesting too?

"If that's even possible, yeah. Maybe that's why she was here, to get us together."

"If that's true, she tried hard enough. I almost didn't meet you."

"Why?"

She shrugged. "I thought you'd be angry. I didn't want to deal with that on top of coping with Lilah."

He stared, crestfallen. "The idea of not meeting you is...I can't think of a word horrible enough. Why would I be angry? I was frustrated I couldn't do anything for her, but not angry."

"You were so compassionate, I was astounded."

"And then you saw my eyes and the rest is history," he grinned. "Actually, come to think of it, since I crafted her, wouldn't that make me some kind of god?"

"Steady on, Ben. That's a heck of a leap." Becca laughed hard. "You've gone from artist to a godlike status in two seconds."

"It fits, don't you think? I could pull it off, couldn't I?"

"If she's still around, I'll ask her outright. Then, at least we could put that ego of yours to bed. Maybe she's up in Lilah's room right now. What do you think?"

He threw his bag over his body and shoved a crutch under each armpit. "I'm getting pretty good on these things. I'll bet I can beat you there. Want to see?"

"Or maybe we'll could just take it slowly," Becca held his arm. "You know, so we don't end up back in hospital again?"

"Oh, you're good at this. I'm going to learn a lot from you."

As they left the lift and walked down the corridor, a medical team rushed out of ICU and into Lilah's room. Alarms screamed out as the door flew open. Before it closed, Becca grabbed it. From the doorway, she and Ben watched in horror as the team surrounded her sister's bed.

Chapter Forty-Two

"Lilah?" Margaret called out into the darkness. "Lilah, can you hear me?"

"You came back?"

"Yes! It's my job to come back for you. And this time I'm not leaving without you."

"I saw you before. You have wings." Her disembodied voice asked in the blackness.

"It's complicated, my lovely. I need you to head towards my voice."

"Where are we going?" She asked. "Where are you taking me?"

"Where you're meant to be."

"Did I die? Are you taking me...there?"

"No, you've got lots to do yet." she chuckled. "You've had quite the adventure."

"Can you hear that?" Lilah said. "Alarms. So much noise. Can you hear them?"

"Don't pay attention. Just focus on me, Lilah."

"They're deafening. What's happening? People are shouting. What's going on?"

"It's for you. We're pulling you back," her voice grew louder to compensate. "Take my hands. That's it! I've got you. I can feel you."

They grasped hands and light shone into Lilah's face. She winced at the suddenness of it, but the warmth of Margaret's connection was electric.

"You're safe. Hold on."

Lilah sensed a pull upwards from her solar plexus. She remembered the darkness that filled her body after she crashed her car. This time there was no pain inside her head, no colours filling her mind. As she rose, darkness merged into a bright light. It was like nothing she had ever felt before. It hurt her eyes as if the sun was shining into her face. Pain began to return. A whooshing sound filled her ears, fast and loud, as the volume increased too rapidly for her senses It sounded like an aeroplane was taking off next to her. Then, in an instant, it ceased but its memory reverberated in her mind.

"Lilah!" Margaret called. "Can you still hear me?"

"Yes."

"Don't get distracted. Keep hold of me, we're pulling you through. Don't let go, Lilah. We're too close for you to leave now."

Margaret suddenly released enormous amounts of energy from her heart which bathed Lilah in energy.

"Yes! We did it," Margaret's celebratory tone filled Lilah with reassurance. "Hold tight, Lilah. This will bump."

Lilah seemed to hover and then her entire body jolted as thought she had been dropped from a great height. She felt winded. Slowly shadows took shape and stretched in length. They moved independently from each other. Confusion and fascination filled her mind. And then the feeling of surprise and extreme positivity filled the room. Now, she was in a hospital room with concerned-looking people surrounding the bed. They all wore white coats except two: a woman with red-hair and a tall, slim man with curly brown hair who stood next to her. In different way, she recognised them both. They held hands, fingers interlinked, like they were never ever going to separate.

The sound of machinery beeping filled her ears. There was no rushing sound, and no Margaret. Lilah blinked. She took a massive breath and let it out like she was gasping. Panicked, she called out.

"Margaret? Where are you?"

But Margaret was gone.

"She's back!" A man in a white coat announced. "She's back. Wow, Delilah, you do like an entrance." He shone something bright into her eyes reminding her of the bright light she had just endured. He grinned wildly. "Can you hear me?"

Lilah nodded, confused. "Yes."

"You're going to be disoriented for a while. Do you understand?"

She nodded again.

"There's someone here who'd like to see you." Then he turned to the someone and spoke to them. Lilah saw it was the red-head. "I can let you have a few minutes with her, Miss McCallister, but she'll need to rest after that."

"Lilah," she sobbed. "It's me. Do you know who I am?"

"Bec," Lilah said weakly.

"I've been so worried."

"I'm back."

"Yes, you are. Where did you go?"

The weakest laugh strayed from her throat. "I was in Boston."

"I knew it." She gently took Lilah's hand and held it to her heart. "Oh god, I'm so glad you're back. This is Ben. He's been with me while you've been away."

"We met briefly," he said. "I'm so glad you're okay."

"I remember you." Then she saw his crutches. "I did that, didn't I? I was angry with Ruth. It happened so quickly."

"It was both of us. I wasn't paying attention," he confessed. "I'm so sorry."

Then the doctor interrupted. "She needs to rest now. You can see her again tomorrow."

Becca released her hand and Lilah closed her eyes once more, but this time it was for a peaceful and innocent sleep.

Chapter Forty-Three

The freezing temperature outside brought Becca and Ben to their senses. Plumes of breath left their mouths as they walked along the street towards the car park. Becca both held his arm and provided support as he hobbled with his crutches. A thin covering of ice on the pavement slowed them down. It looked as if someone had sprinkled icing sugar on the ground.

Processing the events of the evening, neither one spoke. The only sound was their joint exhalations, crutches, and boots on concrete.

"Not wishing to highlight the elephant in the room," Ben said, breaking their silence. "But did you noticed what she said when she woke up?"

"Hard not to, wasn't it?"

"So, let me try to get my head around this. She was with Lilah as well?"

"Maybe?"

"So all three of us got the Margaret treatment?"

Becca shrugged, a beaming smile covering her lips. "Maybe we got our Christmas miracle. It sounds like we were three people in the universe pulled together by a single event," she said, remembering his comment the first time she saw him.

Ben lifted up his palm, and grinned. "Is that snow? Seriously? We're getting a white Christmas too?"

"I'd be happy to drive you home," she offered. "It'd be tough getting a cab tonight anyway."

"I don't want to put you out."

"You're not." She gave a fragile smile. "I'd quite like the company to be honest. I'm only going home to an empty house anyway, and it's not like I don't know where you live."

"Just so you know, I was just going to walk you to your car. I wasn't expecting a lift."

"Well, you did spend all that time waiting for me to show up. The least I can do it take you back. And don't think I haven't noticed, Ben. You've been amazing."

"I've only done what any boyfriend would do. And, just think, all it took was a near-fatal road accident to make it happen."

"And an angel." She helped him into the car, putting his crutches on the back seat. With the engine running and the heater humming, the pair sat in silence while the interior grew warmer.

"We finally got our Christmas Day together."

She tried not to well up, but it was hard not to let it happen. "It's all been a bit overwhelming to be honest. And now I'm emotional again. And I don't do emotions."

Ben leaned forwards, taking her into his arms and stroking her hair. "Hate to break it to you, but you do, you know." He kissed the top of her head, breathing her in. "It's okay, everything's going to be fine. Lilah's back, it's Christmas, and it's even snowing."

She looked into his eyes. They were home, safety, and protection. Ben cupped her face as he leaned in to claim her lips.

Emotion and logic intertwined, it was warm, soft, and beautiful; the most perfect kiss she had ever experienced. But too soon it was over.

"If we're not careful, we'll steam it up in here. I can't believe I was lucky enough to ever meet you."

"I suppose we have my sister to thank for that. Anyway, let's get you back." She drove cautiously in the snow, keeping her wits about her until, finally, she pulled up in a bay outside his studio.

"Home sweet home," he said. "You can finally meet...Oh, I didn't tell you, did I?"

"Now would not be a great time to tell me you've got a wife."

He laughed. "No. Nothing like that. I got the sculpture back from the police the other day. You can finally see it. My client insisted I keep this version because they're convinced it was meant to live with me. I'm to make another for them in the new year. I'm glad it worked out that way to be honest, I was pretty attached to it. Like Lilah with her characters. Creatives, huh? Crazy people."

Inside the studio, she took in all that it was: the artistry, the paintings, the clay, and the angel. Everything welcomed her inside.

"Wow, this is quite the place."

"Sorry about the mess. I can't work any other way though. This is actually quite tidy."

She approached the sculpture. "Are you going to name it?"

"No brainer, really," Ben grinned. "I'm calling her Margaret."

"She's really rather sweet. It's like she was created to live here. Does she look like you thought she would?"

Becca ran her index finger over the angel's face, feeling the smooth features beneath her touch. "This is incredible. This is such a skill. My class are going to love you."

"Well, carry on like that and you're in the running to getting the best girlfriend ever award."

"It's true. I'm not just saying it."

"Stop, you'll make me blush." He walked over to his desk and picked up a sketch pad. "How about I make you blush instead? Wanna see this? I started it the other night."

Becca edged across the studio and looked over his shoulder. Even though it was still in its foundations, it was clear the picture was a sketch of her, Lilah, and Margaret. "This is all from memory?"

He nodded. "Do you like it? I thought I'd get some drawing in. Being laid up in hospital made me really miss it."

"I knew you'd be good, but I had no idea exactly how good."

"Thank you. Things are getting back to normal now. Well, a new normal anyway."

He pulled her to him, and she willingly submitted. "A 'new normal' sounds perfect. I can't tell you how much I'm looking forward to it."

Chapter Forty-Four

In Becca's house on New Year's Eve, classical music played in the background. The aroma of a roast with all the trimmings circled its way throughout the whole house. Fairy lights sparkled on the Christmas tree, and a multitude of festive, get well soon, and welcome home cards adorned the window ledges and mantle now Lilah was staying with her.

A newly acquired charcoal montage in a black wooden frame lay against the wall ready to be hung. It was an accurate and easily recognisable image drawn from memory of Becca, Lilah, and Margaret's faces with the words 'Dream State' by Ben Christopher written beneath. It was an embellished version of the one she saw in his studio. It was his Christmas gift to Becca.

Lilah sipped warmed mulled wine while Becca finished off in the kitchen.

"He should be here in a moment," she called out as she flew from the kitchen, past the living room, and down the hallway.

"I think he's just arrived," Lilah said. "Tall guy with crutches and a Santa hat? Look of besotted love all over his face? Yup, he's here."

"Stop it."

"I wouldn't be embarrassed. He's gorgeous."

"I'm not embarrassed about him. I just feel like one of my kids. Ooh, you're just making up for lost time being awkward."

"I've got a big sister job to do. I might as well do it properly."

From the living room, Lilah heard the door open and her sister say, "Hello, Mr Christopher."

"Happy Merry New Year's Eve, Miss McCallister."

They both giggled. It was a sound that Lilah had missed. Hearing her sister sound so happy was just the best feeling.

"How are you?" Ben lowered his voice. The silence told her they were kissing.

"Better now you're here. My sister's being mischievous, and I could do with an ally."

Lilah grinned at the words. As they both walked in, she lifted her glass as if toasting him. "It's the other lousy driver! How are you?"

Becca took the crutches as Ben sat down. "I'm fine, thanks. Another month and these'll be history. Can't say I'll be sorry to see them go. You?"

"I'm being very good," she giggled. "I've not so much as lifted a finger around here, and I get to have all the mulled wine I want."

"Unlimited mulled wine? I should've got here sooner."

Becca furnished him with a glass of his own. "I'll leave you two while I finish dinner. It'll be in fifteen minutes. I hope you're hungry." She got to the doorway and looked back at them. "Be nice to each other."

"Of course." Ben grinned. "Okay, so how are you really?"

"She's treating me like I'm made of glass."

"I'm not surprised. It was pretty hairy."

"Yeah, I read the diary. Did the police talk to you yet?"

Ben nodded. "I got a fine and points on my licence. Not paying due care and attention."

"Same. Considering what could have happened, I suppose we both got off lightly."

"Have you heard from your agent?"

"It's all a bit awkward. Bottom line is we're parting ways. She breached our author-agent contract, but the publisher still wants the book so they've extended the deadline. All the bad publicity surrounding Ruth meant they didn't want to be associated with her. All the slander was a bit much. The police said something about coercion and blackmail too. With all the evidence, she couldn't really defend herself. Oh, and I'm suing her. You can't really work with someone after all that, can you?"

"Good. I'm glad it's over. What happens to the book you were working on?"

"I've got another agent. It's the one Gordon, my Copy Editor, went to. I'm going to write the novel properly, how it was meant to be. I'm meeting them in January, so it's all worked out favourably, plus they're interested in an idea I've got for a new book."

"Wouldn't have anything to do with a certain hero you spent time with recently, would it?"

"Funny you should say that. I've thought of nothing else since I woke up. It's a slightly different take on love, but I think it'll be exciting."

Ben craned his head through to the kitchen. "Love, huh? There's a lot of that going around."

"Plus a mutual friend of ours will make an appearance," Lilah said. "You might say she'll be making her literary debut."

"Oh I have a feeling she's going to enjoy that."

Chapter Forty-Five

"And without further ado, here's the lady you've all come to see. Lilah McCallister."

An applause broke out through the fifty strong audience. It was an intimate crowd and that suited Lilah perfectly being her first official outing since the accident.

"Thank you so much for coming tonight. It's been quite a year both professionally and personally." She saw Becca and Ben staring back, holding hands. Emma and Gordon stood next to Becca. "I'd like to thank Audrey and her team for representing me with this book. It's been a great year getting to know everyone here and working on this story. It's the result of a very strange incident that happened at the end of last year which most of you already know about. Suffice to say, I feel like I know these characters personally. It's like I went to work with them, and then fell in love with them. And that's my hope for you all too. So, let's raise our glasses and welcome to the world my newest novel, Dream State."

And, as the crowd applauded again, a figure stood in the back row with a proud, beaming smile.